Teitlebaum's Window

by the same author

TO AN EARLY GRAVE

Teitlebaum's Window

WALLACE MARKFIELD

Hathi Twst checked
4/18 No entry this ed.

Jonathan Cape Thirty Bedford Square London

FIRST PUBLISHED IN GREAT BRITAIN 1971

© 1970 BY WALLACE MARKFIELD

JONATHAN CAPE LTD, 30 BEDFORD SQUARE, LONDON WCI

ISBN 0 224 61985 3

020208

PRINTED IN GREAT BRITAIN
BY LOWE AND BRYDONE (PRINTERS) LTD, LONDON
BOUND BY JAMES BURN AND CO. LTD, ESHER, SURREY

for Andrea

Teitlebaum's Window

1

Then in June, 1932, on the second Saturday, a year exactly till Teitlebaum would start in with his signs ("President Roosevelt had a hundred days but you got only till this Monday to enjoy such savings on our Farm Girl pot cheese"), not long after the Workmen's Circle took out space in the *Coney Island Bulletin* urging total membership to stay away from French wines and perfumes until Léon Blum was restored to his parliament; also the same week Luna Park finished off a lousy season with a nice fire; a day after Ringelman, the Dentist, got his glasses broken by Mrs. Weigholtz for proposing certain advanced oral-hygiene treatments; around the time Harry the Fish Man's daughter, Fat Rosalie, gave away her father's beautiful little Schaeffer pen for a Suchard, the semisweet; not too long after Margoshes of the *Forvitz* ran this little item at the foot of his column: "Which hotsy-totsy Mexican actress should be called Amhoretz Del Rio for denying her Jewish blood?"; around the time Mrs. Faygelees kept calling and calling the *News* to find out when Elinor Ames would be using her question ("Should the son of a sick mother whose husband was put on a piecework basis have to pay for the Gravesend Avenue

A*

line transfer of a girl not from his faith?"); nine days since Block and Sully and Belle Baker were on the Rudy Vallee show; this also happening to be the day Gromajinski the Super, in a fit of drunken Polish rage, snipped every radio aerial on the roof of 2094 Brighton Beach Avenue; while Mrs. Aranow's Stanley was still telling the story of how he had been hailed at Grand Central Station by this fellow in a racoon coat and a straw skimmer; how this fellow finished off a whole hip flask during the thirty-five cent ride; how he put three dimes and five pennies into Stanley's palm; how Stanley had extended his arm, saying "Mister, we work for tips" or "Mister, we depend on tips"; how talking and talking of the cabbie's plight he kept this arm extended; how this fellow had smashed at the arm with a cruel-looking cane and said through his fat nose, "Godfrey Daniel, if there's one thing I can't stand it's a one-armed cabdriver!"; while Mary Mixup still had her share, and more than her share, from Bicep the Wrestler; even as Benny still could not get himself to drown his kittens; right after Smitty tried out for a job with Mr. Bailey;

Simon Sloan, all rosy and redolent of matzo and milk, waited till his father, whiffing and chuffing and grumbling away in some old argument, fell into a fuddled snooze. Then with both hands busy Simon came rolling over on top of his mother, going "Lemme lemme!"

"In case Cousin Phillie comes over tonight"—his mother took love-bites at his behind—"that's just in case, and he wants you should kiss him, remember you mustn't, you dassn't dassn't say to him, 'Go way vomithead!'"

"What he is," said Simon as he cupped and clutched.

"You should do a shake-hands with him, a 'How are you' and a 'What's new, Cousin Phillie,'" his mother droned drowsily, "and then you can say to him in a nice way, a not fresh way, 'The reason why I didn't kiss you, Cousin Phillie, is on account of I'm only only eight years old and they're not teaching yet in my 3B1 to be a two-face and you shouldn't expect it from me as I know the whole whole tragic story of what you and yours did to my Mommy, Malvena the Orphan,

4

how you gave her a misleading, you begged and begged her she should come and work for you in Hartford, Connecticut, she wouldn't never never know again from a bad minute, sure she wouldn't know, how was she going to know, the first thing you did you took away from her her watch . . .' "

Simon crooned, softly crooned,

> *A my name is Aaron*
> *And my wife's name is Anna*
> *We come from Alabama*
> *And we sell . . . ALPS!*

"Without opening a big mouth you'll tell him also how he repaid your mommy . . ."

"*Pogrom,*" Simon's father mumbled from his deepest sleep.

"That when she got so so sick and they wanted her to come and bring with her a urination specimen in a bottle you docked her three cents for the bottle."

"Heh heh," went Simon. He pointed and poked. "When they jiggle you know what they look like, Mommy? Heh? Heh, Mommy?"

"In a pleasant way you can mention he's still still throwing up how when your Mommy got married he took care of the liquor."

"Just just just like Betty Boop's eyes!" Simon exclaimed wonderingly.

"You can tell him, 'Cousin Phillie, I heard already how you took care of the liquor, you and yours by themselves took care of half a case nearly.' "

And in her man's undershirt—Reis, extra large, the elastic scissored under her arms and around her belly so it should not bind or chafe—she rocked and rollicked him till the bed creaked on its casters.

A *"Yiden"* was heard from his father. Then agonized snoring.

Over which Simon's mother sang in a piercing and buoyant voice,

Why are you still mitchin'
Workin' in the kitchen?
Why keep the family waiting?
When we can do the grating?

"*M' schlagt yiden,*" his father croaked out.
"Bright eyes, little beauty," his mother muttered at him.
To Simon she sang,

Horlick's Malted Milk
Is good for growing children.

At "children" she wet him with kisses and tears.

Following this they spent a short, sweet time giggling as Simon's father bubbled and burbled, "America" . . . "Green-horn" . . . "Piecework."

He was doing a *Kaddish* with the force of two cantors when they both together rose, trotted to the window, and stuck out their heads like gargoyles. Over the stupendous clutter of the fire escape—seltzer-bottle valves, day-old rolls wetted down for the birds, a snip of Octagon Soap on an oyster shell, a beach-ball bladder, a *yahrzeit* glass, a curtain rod, a clothes-pin bag overflowing with pollyseed husks, a lima-bean plant dying in a Diamond Kosher Salt box—they took in the immense heavens over Brighton Beach.

"God's country," his mother chirped.

Immediately Simon was doing, "Bah-bah-bah-*baum-baum-baum*-bah . . . bah . . . bah . . . bah . . ."

And his mother boosted him on her knee, cried, "Eyes and ears of the world!" and they simultaneously cranked their right arms.

And from their fifth-floor plus stoop, under the good first sun, they panned and picked out Gelfman drawing for himself the first soda of the day; Dopey Duhvee leaning over his tricycle to drool down big, rich spit bombs that burst over his mother's shoes; Mrs. Chepper slipping the leash off her old Pekinese, blaring, "Beauty, don't be in a big hurry, don't

6

force!"; the cripple Fastenberg, who sang on subways, salting his cup with change; the cats of Schactman's Market pawing, delicate as diviners, at the pails of chicken parts; Yenta Gersh, in a cut-down Homburg, blue-satin cocktail dress, and black sneakers dragging her baby buggy up and down and back and forth on the Bay 4 sands, contending with gulls over news-sheets, bottle tops, wooden ice-cream spoons, bathing caps, umbrella handles, kite tails, atomizers, her short-handled one-toothed rake skimming, sifting, sorting, striking like a snake.

"Fill up on it, Shimmy," his mother instructed. "Shimmy Shimmy, take in sweeter and greener memories than your mother has."

Once more she drifted into song.

> It's the pot cheese with a *ta'am*
> It comes right from the farm
> Sweet Maid, Sweet Maid . . .

With tremulous breaths, with a hot and twisted face, she was after a time able to say, "Don't worry, cute tush boy, the ripe time is coming, the whole world is going to get the story of Malvena the Orphan's youthful years . . ."

"Black Hundred," his father announced.

"And all those who shit on her head will hear her finally finally open a mouth."

"Read, Mommy." Simon snapped the waist band of her bloomers. "Mommy read me read me! Journal journal!"

"Even though it's in the drafty stage?"

"Even even though!"

"Remember," his mother begged gently, "that to protect the innocent I made it my business to change certain certain names."

". . . remember."

"Like you could hear the name Darling Soap and it's really . . ."

She winked impishly.

"Sweetheart Soap!"

They had a good laugh on this. Till his father wheezed, "Steerage."

"Dumb old fotz face!" Simon snapped at the bed.

"*Shah, shtill,*" his mother chided, dealing out soft blows and love-bites. "Nobody nobody can help how he looks."

To the tune of *We Want Cantor* Simon went

> Read read Read read
> Read read Read read . . .

So on all fours they labored to the foot of the bed. Which Simon's mother raised up and up by a scrolled beast paw while he crawled under and fetched out the *New York Times Illustrated History of the Great War.*

"Okay, outstanding student? Okay A-A-A-Except-in-Gym-Kid?"

"Okay, Mommy."

"Dispensary," his father caroled as his mother, dipping slightly, using only forearm and wrist, softly and soundlessly let down the bed.

"Talk English," his father directed.

"He's a dopey dirty *shmutz,*" went Simon.

"Shame shame," his mother honed on her fingers. "On a Daddy you dassn't say 'he.' "

But in a second she and Simon were riffling the brownish folio-size pages, and she was saying, "Zeppelins, zeppelins, again zeppelins, go back to the Kaiser, I'm going back, I see the Kaiser, I see Rasputin, I see the Czar, crosses, crosses, crosses-crosses-crosses, soldiers, soldiers *with* guns and soldiers *without* guns, notice you don't see one Jewish face, now the Czar is already dead, they're having their revolution, let me try again zeppelins, the *goyim* and their zeppelins, he tried yesterday to fool the Mommy, he flushes the toilet she should think he made his big business . . ."

"Brownsville," his father whimpered.

.   .   .

8

"*The Truth of My Life,* by Malvena Sloan."

His mother swiftly spread newssheets over the kitchen table, then spread her raft of soft-covered notebooks over the newssheets.

She ceremoniously sniffled, dried both nostrils and one eye with her undershirt.

"What has gone before I don't don't have to tell you."

As though setting himself to hear The Singing Lady Simon shut his eyes slowly and emitted a soft sighing sound.

"When she was left off the Mommy was dealing with her outstanding success achievements in the field of passementerie and telling how with youthful folly, alone in the world at the death of her sweeet sweet mother, she threw away a wonderful little position with Tarshis and Meltzer where she did only only French knots to work for her Cousin Phillie though she knew, and how and how she knew, his *momzer* character and terrible ways covered already in Book Three, *Cousin Phillie: His Momzer Character and Terrible Ways* . . ."

She chewed on a palm; Simon squeezed his eyes into a crimson blindness.

"You're listening, Shimmy? Listen and you won't need any more Stella Dallas."

She raked her cheeks; he bit a knuckle.

"Here—here goes."

She folded back a notebook and jumped to her feet.

" 'Went to Hartford, Connecticut, worked for Cousin Phillie, left same.' "

She plopped down.

"First papers!" his father blared.

"Every every day," his mother cheerily returned, "should be his *yahrzeit.*"

And then she took a stiff shot of breath, saying, "Book Ten. Here is where the Mommy is making many many new friends and keeping company with Victor Mintzer, then business manager for the Yiddish Art Theater but already studying by night toward a future chiropodist profession. She later on comes across him in a chiropodist capacity, where he does a

9

botch job on an ingrown toenail and she goes to Dr. Witkewitz, a big big foot man, to take off your shoe in his office cost those years four dollars. He sends the Mommy on an emergency basis to Dr. Levine, a professor of professors, for a first visit he charged eleven dollars, you asked the doorman, 'Where is Dr. Levine's office?' that was already your first visit. Here we learn how Dr. Levine took one one look at the Mommy's foot and started in about hospitals, X rays, immediate surgery, whirlpool treatments, tests, and how the Mommy cried and kissed his hands and told him, 'Dr. Levine, honey, what are you starting in with hospitals and what are you starting in with whirlpool treatments, realize you're talking to a recent orphan.' Still the Mommy hears from him three hundred for surgery, eight dollars a day special medicine, a needle series twenty-three dollars plus another twenty-three dollars to make sure it's the right needle. And we find out how the Mommy kisses his hands a little more and how she says, 'Professor, dear, my father I never knew, he died in Bolshvetz from complications.' 'Bolshvetz?' 'Bolshvetz.' 'Your father was named Wolf Adler Mendelstern?' 'The same.' 'Go go, *maideleh,* and when you get home put on a little little black salve.' Meanwhile— meanwhile American times are changing and setting the Mommy up for her tragic destiny: There's a big big milk war, they're coming out with vegetable cream cheese, matzo meal is in bags, then it's in boxes, the world is going wild, wild and crazy for the large-curd pot cheese. Here we start seeing, under the section *Cousin Phillie: How He Tried to Hire Me Out to Schvartzers . . .*"

"Lay-off," they heard.

"Tape measure," they also heard.

And the bedroom bloomed with commotion.

"Mommy . . . ?"

"Not yet time."

"G'vald Momma!"

"Heh heh," went Simon, and "Now . . . ?"

"Still not time."

At "BISODOL!" she let Simon enter; while he bounced and

jiggled on the bed she was bantering, "Mr. Personality plus" and "Ricardo Cortez number two."

Whereupon his father, a small man with a face of horsey length and a melancholy, popeyed, lopsided look, trembled his hands and feet like a roach trembling its wands and made his rough awakening.

He said, "Ho-boy."

Then, sitting forward in the bed and chuckling with sad merriment, he went on to say, "Rah-bah-boy, listen to a sweet dream. Starts off that I hear—I hear from Kalish and Klein. Shmuel, come back, we'll be open again, we got—ho-boy—a big rush rush order. Nine thousand caps . . ."

"He has six hairs," his mother was telling Simon, "and they all all six have to fall off on the pillow case . . ."

"Nine thousand caps!" cried his father, bitterly moved.

". . . then first he finishes up and he gives a drool on the six hairs."

"Let's say—say they got the order," his father mused. "An order like that and that kind of an order . . ."

A damp pillowcase suddenly engaged his nose.

". . . they could never get the linings," he finished up.

"Next time," Simon's mother said easily, "and you shouldn't live to have a next time, you should float away altogether."

"If I shouldn't live to have a next time," his father answered remotely, "you should live to be a widow."

As she stretched out lazily on the bed Simon's mother replied, "If I should live to be a widow you should first first drop dead."

"If I should drop dead you should get like a floor and once —wuh-hunce a year they should have to come and scrape you."

To which his mother made amiable reply, "If I should get like a floor you should get like an enema bag and they should hang you only only behind doors."

His father, grumbling out some gas, said, "If I should get like an enema bag you should get like an empty store and gypsies should move into you."

"If I should get like an empty store . . ." Simon's mother clapped hands lightly, "Nu, nu, Shmuel, you'll be late!"

Right away he rose, threw on a red and black flannelette bathrobe, a *yarmalka* of the same cloth, slung a truss over his shoulder like a bandolier, and padded taut-legged and barefoot to the bathroom.

"Rockaway," he was heard blaring.

He followed this with cries of "Manhattan Beach" and "Niagara Falls" till he worked up his tinkle to a splash.

And twirling the tassel of his bathrobe he emerged, blew a happy kiss at the *mezuzah,* and gave his attention to Simon.

"Barf!" he commanded. "Do for the Daddy a barf and a weep."

"Gong!" went Simon, immediately fisty.

"This," said his father, pulling him till they stood belly to belly, "thi-his is by me a best pal."

"Heh heh," answered Simon.

"He is *my* best pal and I am *his* best pal and both together we'll do—ho-boy!—he-man things. Right?"

"Daddy, wowee Daddy . . ."

"Say better—Pop." He now had Simon by the short neck hairs. "The—Pop."

"Hurts. That that . . ."

"You'll call me the Pop and I'll do like in the Jackie Cooper pictures where the father, the Pop, when he's a best pal by Jackie Cooper he does this, this is what he does, this— thi-his he does to the Jackie Cooper hair, they call it, what they call it . . ."

"Woooo . . ."

"A tousle. A tousle or—a tousling," he rumbled, working with both hands, "and for his tousle a Jackie Cooper boy goes crazy, he even brings home black eyes that the Pop should tousle with him . . ."

"A blood poison!" Simon cried.

"That—ho-boy!—that's when he learns from the Pop how to make with the hands, to barf and weep and throw the jib-

12

jabs. In all the Jackie Cooper pictures you have to have the part where he barfs and weeps and throws the jib-jabs . . ."

He had Simon against the sink, his short arms slamming away, his head butting.

"Shmuel . . ."

Simon's mother flicked a finger at the old nickel of the alarm clock.

His father flung Simon away, saying, "Malvena, I try and I try and still I don't get close to him."

"Dumb dopey moron," his mother answered mildly from the icebox. "What you have to do you don't do. You should make with him what the *goyim* call . . ."

She set before him in single file a lox wing, a whitefish tail, the heel of a farmer cheese, the skin from a sable.

". . . a friendship."

She rolled a Greek olive in a snip of matjes herring and popped it playfully into his mouth.

"You have to go places and you have to do things."

"Why not?" Simon's father answered yearningly. "Rah-boy-oh-boy, let him show me only palship and buddyness and I would meet him half-way, I would be like in the jokes, the fun-loving Pop."

He started a laugh which flew off suddenly into open space.

"What wouldn't I do for him?" he demanded, banging the lox wing against the whitefish tail. "I used to have dreams that on *Yom Kippur* we'd go down to Williamsburg, the Pop and the pal, we'd walk over by the river, we'd have a good cry, and I'd show him how you're supposed to throw your sins in the water . . ."

"The way your Daddy throws sins in the water," his mother told Simon, "nobody can throw sins in the water."

"I have to pay Pinya Friedman a condolence call, I even had in mind"—he doffed his *yarmalka*—"to take him along for the ride. And that's a ride," he added, "wuh-hunce in a lifetime."

"Remember, Gold-Seal-Honor-Card-Kid?" Simon's mother

put her hands between Simon's hands. "You were only only four, you wouldn't remember, we took you to the cemetery and you had to had to throw up from the trip." She swayed their hands. "This is even a bigger trip."

She spooned sour cream over half a matzo and pushed it in sections between his father's jaws.

Who made himself heard even over the great strife of his gumming as he said, "I was making plans for regular-guy things that the fun-loving Pop and his American boy pal should be buddy-buddy. One day, maybe, we'd go by Rabbi Leibish, Rabbi Leibish would show him how you take a *trafe* knife and get it kosher again. I'd work in a little side trip. Why not? How many sons I got?" Blinking, squinting, his father momentarily searched the kitchen. "We'd walk over, it's on the way, he could come in with me to the dispensary to renew my clinic card . . ."

"You want him to get a kick out of Leibish?" demanded Simon's mother. "Forget about knives, forget about kosher; you have Leibish do one thing and only only one thing—his pooh-pooh on the evil eye!"

". . . surprise presents. One week—ho-boy!—a Shapiro Wine *Haggadah,* another week a nice white-on-white Sporty Morty type *yarmalka* . . ."

He was out of his chair, dancing around Simon.

"The *Haggadah,*" he cried murderously, "he wouldn't look at. To spite me! The *yarmalka,* rah-bah-boy-oh-boy, that's another story. Right? Right, Jackie Cooper face? He'll save it, the Skippy kid, he should have something to wear to the cemetery . . ." With a whole matzo he slashed at Simon. "He should look good when he stands over my grave. Then"—the matzo circled Simon's throat—"he'll have himself, ho-boy, a lovely little ride in the limousine car, a free ride, he'll come home and the first thing . . ."

He feinted for a headlock; Simon, as usual, butted nicely to the crotch.

". . . to read *Toots and Caspar.*"

Simon, weeping cagily, sneaked in a "Schmucky mutt!"

"That's the first thing," said his father with a prideful chuckle, with clubbing motions, "theh-hen, after he eats up all the candy from the basket —three-seventy-nine, it'll come with our society card. Jackie Cooper *momzer*—he'll run see the Tailspin Tommy chapter . . ."

"Were you six? He wasn't even even six," Simon's mother protested softly, "he used to read to the Mommy *Toots and Caspar*."

And with the heel of her hand she drove Simon's father like a nail into his chair.

To Simon she said, "Who is going to make up with the Daddy and who is going to put him in a happy mood?"

Simon sobbed out *The Pledge of Allegiance*.

"Get killed for Jackie Cooper!" his father told him.

Simon, planting an elbow on the table, made believe he was doing Palmer penmanship, throwing in also the closing hours of the library and the number of books he was allowed on a children's card.

"Get killed with Jackie Cooper."

Simon recited the holiday prices at the Lyric, the day for the changing of bills at the Miramar and the Surf.

"Get killed by Jackie Cooper."

Still he made only the mildest protest when Simon's mother gave them both sour cream from one spoon, and he was already returning her snappy salute as she sprang and capered and chanted

> *Eins, tzvei, drei,*
> You'll be eating *chozerei.*
> They'll shave the beard right off your chin
> So you can chase the Kaiser to Berlin;
> Never mind if you're a Jew-ooh-ooh
> Uncle Sam needs—
> Uncle Sam calls—
> Uncle Sam wants you-ooh-ooh.

His father breasted the table, moving his head one way, his eyes another. A soft, sucking sound escaped his clenched teeth and he said, "Shmuel the Cap Maker. Shmuel the Soldier. Hah-honly yesterday . . ."

"A movie, a movie," went Simon. "*Only Yesterday* is John Boles, it was at the Miramar. . . !"

"In New York I was a nothing. But in the army"—his father tried to snap his fingers—"all of a sudden, like the . . . scholar big shot of the company."

". . . they had it with *Guns of the Pecos* at the Miramar. But when it came down from the Miramar you know what they had it with? Heh? Heh!" piped Simon.

"I had to be the ha-whole Jewish history expert. How come the Jews started the war, how the Jews got all the money in the world, what kind of blood we use when we make matzo . . ."

"*The World Moves On,*" Simon announced. "That was Paul Muni, that was Aline McMahon . . ."

"Where I got the biggest kick . . ."

His father charged off the chair.

"To hear how they talk. It's worth teh-hen armies to hear how they talk."

He had his *yarmalka* over his brows, his head bowed, his arms dangling.

"Shee-yut!" he cried.

And as Simon and his mother whinnied and swelled with mirth he gave them a "Fah-hark you!"

"I have to hold myself back," said his mother, panting and turning away. "Otherwise it gets me right in my dropped stomach."

Laughing also, his father burbled, "Has to come back . . . if I can remember."

"With your ear," declared Simon's mother, "I'm not not worried."

"In my company alone I must have had—I had—ho-boy! —three, four kinds *goyim*."

Hugging herself, then hugging his father, Simon's mother

16

said, "Shmuel, Shmuel, ten good days I probably never had from you, two weeks definitely not. From the minute I met you you had heartburn. When you don't get a diarrhea you're plugged up solid. For an intermission—nosebleeds. You never had nothing to give and if you had something you wouldn't give it anyway. In every every way you come out a failure, a lacking, personality, a strict nix, and in general I would be better off if before I met you I went down with the *Titanic* together. But one thing you have and one thing you got . . ."

She pinched his belly.

". . . a natural natural ear."

"We're hearing first and first we'll hear . . ."

Bending under the sink, Simon's father flipped open the bread box.

". . . a soldier from the South."

He came up with a clothespin on his nose.

"What the *goyim* call—a Southerner."

"It isn't only a natural ear," his mother was explaining to Simon, "it's his knack."

"Knack is a *K*-word," Simon winningly whined. "You know, Mommy?"

And his father twanged, "Dixie, farton-rarton-darton-on-a-carton, Dixie!"

"Picture if that had training," his mother brooded.

"Theh-hen he meets a buddy from the West—the . . . West. They go, the buddies, to what the *goyim* call . . ." his father stamped a foot at Simon. "One word, Jackie Cooper killer. One word—a little word—a *goyish* word."

"By *goyim* the most important word," his mother cued.

"In the cowboy pictures they have it," said Simon, smiling away. "A"—he waited for his mother's kiss—"bar."

"They go-ho into their—BAR and the Western buddy goes, how he goes is . . ."

Simon's father tore away the clothespin.

"Range, beer-and-cantaloupe, range!"

Then he bobbed his head, accepting the applause and two spoonfuls more of sour cream.

And after a spell of silence he had this to say:

"From the army I found out a thing about the *goyim* and that thing I carry on me all my life. *Goyim* are veh-hery handy."

"That's why you have to have them," asserted Simon's mother.

"I don't say the *schvartzers* aren't handy. If they want to be—naturally they don't always want to be—they can be handier than the *goyim.*"

"When you have a jar and the jar is stuck your best bet is a *schvartzer*," said Simon's mother. "They know, they have it in them, and their one little twist is the right twist."

"Ho-boy, when it comes to jars—forget it! Forget it, because you can't do better than a *schvartzer*," his father conceded. "But if you need him where he has to be handy on the animals . . ."

He filled the kitchen with a Bronx cheer.

"You go to the movies, you see already how the *goyim* are with horses. They're good with horses—ho-boy are they good!—but they're better with cows."

"They're by the cows," his mother explained to Simon, "the way *schvartzers* are by the jars."

"But—buh-hut, when it comes to chickens I'll take a Jew any time. *Any* time. A Jew goes over by a chicken, the chicken likes him—fine. The chicken doesn't like him? That's too bad because a Jew wants to be liked by a chicken. He would rather be liked, but if he's not liked—also fine. He don't lose sleep over it, he don't—cater. With the *goyim,* they go near a chicken and right away they start catering."

"Remember, Teacher's-Blackboard-Cleaner-Kid, you had it once in a song"—his mother made Simon clap hands—"a *goy,* a farm, a *goyisher* farmer, how he catered to the chickens, chick-chick *du,* chick-chick *dort, du* a chick, *dort* a chick . . ."

"You see a Jew doing that?" demanded his father. "*Balt!* He'll take care of a chicken, he'll feed a chicken—believe me, he'll feed it better then the *goy*—but he won't take shit from a chicken. And the *goyim* realize it, don't think they don't. They're dumb, but they're not blind."

Bitter, rueful, Simon's mother said, "Maybe if we handled chickens with more *finekeit* they wouldn't have it in for us the way they have it in for us."

"Ho-boy, don't kid yourself," his father answered judiciously. "With them to us it's a case of—you know what?—jealousy. They're jealous of us with our chickens the way we're jealous of them with their cows. And we got—believe me we got what to be jealous. Because you go out of New York, you first see what rich milk is."

To herself, Simon's mother said, "Malvena Malvena, you'd be be better off if it wasn't so rich."

To Simon, she said, "It's in my Book Four, Part Two: *Cousin Phillie and How He Gets Malvena the Orphan to Go to Hartford, Connecticut, by Telling Her That When She Gets Out of New York She'll First See What Rich Milk Is.*"

While she wept Simon pulled at her undershirt and cupped her ear, and they passionately whispered together.

". . . with real real expression," he said aloud, kissing both pinkies.

"Remember," he was warned, "this is a holy holy swear and you're swearing on the Mommy's dropped stomach."

"*Yisgadol, vyiskadash,* booboooo, how I'll do it . . ."

Whereupon his mother pushed Simon against his father, saying, "Shmuel, listen to something cute. The Good-Note-From-His-Teacher-Kid has a bargain that if you do for him your special specialty he'll do over you a *Kaddish* with his wonderful expression . . ."

". . . have to be up to it first," Simon protested. "We don't do it in Hebrew till way way later."

"I heard *Kaddish,*" cried his father. "*Shiva* I didn't hear."

His mother, nodding and nodding with all her might, said simultaneously to Simon, "*Shiva* is where you don't have to do a thing, *Shiva* is where you just just sit and take it easy."

"Blech," went Simon, and "Yuch."

"For seven days!" his father howled. "You could say, like —a week!"

"And for those seven days you dassn't dassn't read the jokes," his mother reminded. But as Simon put his underlip forward and puffed out his cheeks she added hastily, "He can never never take a tease, he doesn't know the Mommy is doing a tease, doesn't he know the Mommy would put the jokes away for him, the Mommy wouldn't touch them and the Mommy would save them . . ."

"It's what the *goyim* call—a mourning," his father pointed out heartily.

"That that's an antonym word," Simon yelled at his mother, "that's A, N, T, O . . ."

"WODDER!"

His father, suddenly in character, clumped around the kitchen, tamped down an imaginary pipe at the side of his mouth.

"Cohen flakes," he cried.

"I notice something now," his mother told Simon. "It's not just his ear."

"Carfee!"

"It's his ear and it's more than his ear," his mother reasoned.

"The *goyim* are in their TOWN, they decide they are GOIN to town, you'll drop dead before you hear a G from a *goy* . . ."

"He lives on *Ex-Lax* and *Feenamint,* but give him give him only rich foods. From the day he was born he looked like he needed a rest. If he was a building he would have been by now condemned. But he has what Moishe Lufthandler had when Moishe Lufthandler was in his prime: The timing!"

"One—wuh-hun *goy* walks down by his Main Street and he meets the other *goy,* the both *goyim* are going to their"— his father winked and twitched at Simon—"from before. The one word—the little word . . ."

"Bar," went Simon.

" 'Heh-lo there . . . Jim.' 'Heh-lo there . . . Roy.' "

"Just just to remember those names," murmured Simon's mother.

" 'Tell me . . . Jim . . . Jim, what is doing and what is new by your wife MARY?' 'My wife, MARY, is much better, she is straightening up in the . . . church. But how is your bi-hig dog Killer?' 'My big dog Killer is fine, and what do you think whether it will . . . rain?' 'Well, it mi-hight rain, also it mi-hight *not* rain.' 'Let's hope and let's pray it should only rain for the rain is good on . . . the grass.' "

He started tittering, soon broke up completely.

"Give them—ho-boy!—give them a bar and give them— THE GRASS!"

"You'll go out of New York," his mother said to Simon, "you'll see them with their grass."

"Grass—grassgrassgrass," barked his father. And in great good humor he fed Simon farmer cheese and sable skin from off his fingers, calling him "Kiddo" and "Little Doughboy" and snapping out tricky questions.

He said, "My manager did it on me, I'll do it on you. Let me—leh-het's hear which one weighs more—the pound of feathers or the pound of coal."

"Feathers—coal. That's a *pound* of feathers and a *pound* of coal, the *feathers* are a pound and the *coal* is a pound . . ."

". . . have to use common sense."

"A pound, each one is a pound, the feathers *and* the coal . . ."

"H-only the common sense."

". . . the samesameexactthing!" Simon cried gloriously.

"For that he has to come close and he has to stand right by the Pop," his father said softly, "and he has to get his Jackie Cooper tousle."

"Heh heh," Simon went.

"Rah-bah-boy-oh-boy," replied his father, stepping back and sighting along his hand, "this is a tall kid, he's going with the Pop soon in the tall-kid department, ho-boy this is going to be what you got to call a TALL KID."

And he right away started springing and slapping, slapping

21

and pinching, with pain in his voice saying, "*Oy,* he'll be taller than me. . . ."

In two seconds Simon's mother had him in hand, shaking him like a can of scouring powder over the sink.

"Latey-latey, Shmuel," she gaily sang.

At once his father popped up from the chair and clomped to the bedroom, on his way undressing ; he was, before shutting the door in their faces, down to *yarmalka* and truss.

"What the Daddy had to go through . . ."

"Crazy cockee nut," went Simon.

". . . you should never never have to know from Second-Highest-In-Achievement-Test-Kid."

His father rapped on the bedroom door, crying, "He should so!"

"When this was with Kalish and Klein this was altogether a different person. This had a one-in-a-million cap face. This used to model for buyers . . ."

"With the flah-haps *on* the face and the flaps *away* from the face," came from his father.

"Then first at his age to start learning the usher trade, don't don't think it's so easy, you have to know where the loge is and you have to know where the orchestra is . . ."

"And what about the searchlights?" his father trumpeted tearily. "Go figure they need two—two batteries."

"Even if now and then once in a while he gets a little little" —Simon's mother warped her face, waggled her tongue, and smacked herself alongside her head—"nervous, you should never forget that this is a forgotten vet."

"Let him sometimes ask me"—His father stuck his face out the door—"What—wah-haht price glory?"

"The Mommy is a little little mixed up about what happened, when he got taken by the army," his mother began, "and I can't tell you exactly if two days before his sister got knocked down by a Sparkling Seltzer truck or a Vitality Seltzer truck."

Amid spells of weeping his mother made them matzo and sour-cream sandwiches and gave him to understand "how the army had fixed and *futzed* his father. How *erev Slichus,* on his grandmother's *yahrzeit,* fourteen-and-a-half years after his parents had been moved by the Wishneff Van Corporation (three broken-down pushcarts, two healthy Polacks) from 199 Eldridge Street to 40B Eldridge Street, three blocks from what was then the Langman Surgical Supply Store, now the Langman Surgical Supply Outlet, right across the street from the stoop where Moey Amsterdam, secretary-treasurer of the Knickers Makers Union, Local 18, would soon have his face scarred by gangster acid, he having been mistaken for Sam Pomerantz, a nothing in the Markers and Pullers Joint Board, the army had sent his father to either North Carolina or South Carolina. How he had been assigned there to egg candling. How on the second day of *Tisha B'Av* disturbed by a piece of bad news from home (Lilyveld, the Painter, had chipped his mother's cut-glass bowl), and further unsettled by sight of a blood spot in one brown jumbo, he had suffered a fit, a conniption, a prostration, an itchiness in the scalp. How doctors by the bunch had given him million-dollar examinations. How they had brought down one specialist for a tsuttzing. ('What what do you say, Doctor?' 'Tsuttz, tsuttz, tsuttz . . .') How he had fallen finally into the best of hands. (A Jewish doctor.) How this top-notch surgeon had come in smiling after the second exploratory. ('We'll take a few few more X rays to be absolutely positive, but the way I see it, my friend, it's definitely a *dybbuk.*') How he had been sent back to his eggs. How on November 11, 1918, the twenty-second anniversary of his Uncle Chaim Yitschak's departure from Pilkaboldrovnyiecz to Strobleki by way of Nova-Hanakye, a road close to Biriprog, where her own mother had been born, his nerves shot to pieces by his sister's last postcard (Lilyveld had stinted on a second coat of pot-cheese white in the closets), he had sent down the candling chute a few too many eggs. How they had burst around him and upon him. How this had shocked his system. How the army, in consequence, had been forced to declare him . . ."

". . . a shell-shock case."

23

And his mother squatted down before the bread box like a Chinaman, telling Simon in a tear-crippled voice, "I'll show you, Advanced-Reading-And-Spelling-Kid, how he got a beautiful beautiful write-up in the *Yeshivah Ram Bam News*, look look at the bag Teitlebaum gives you for nine cans of King Oscar sardines, can he spare it, I'm going down later and I'll throw it in his face, remind me to ask him for an extra key . . ."

There was a stern knocking, then a "Don't—do-hon't look everybody!"

Head lowered, eyes raised, blaring "Puh-lenty standing room only!" Simon's father shambled over and presented arms with a fat flashlight. He had on a black shako, a washed-out looking serge tunic with blue and gold piping and button-down pockets, white duck shorts and white Keds cut open at the toes; a pair of pink elastic bandages braced him in the ankles.

"I have to have one kiss from it," cried Simon's mother, swooping in, getting one kiss and giving back five.

His father, all excited and shining the flashlight, announced, "Now playing the fir-hirst time second run"—he peeped into a pocket—"*Storm over the Bengal.*"

"Mommy, you know what a Bengal is? Heh, Mommy?" went Simon. "Bomba Katz told it, a joke . . ."

"Short wait for immediate seating."

"A Bengal is a LITTLE BANG!"

"Take—tah-hake only one program."

Opening her arms, his mother scooped in Simon and his father, whispering, "It's my my little family unit and nobody else's."

She was answered by a "Heh heh" and a "Ho-boy!"

Then she made Simon link and lock fingers with his father, and she led them in a little dance on the blue squares and on the white squares of the linoleum, saying, "You'll tell me Malvena Malvena keep quiet and bite your tongue, but I feel on my dropped stomach that for this family unit good times are just just around the corner."

24

She was answered by a "Heh heh" and a "Rah-bah-boy, I'm willing to walk a block."

And she made them dance to her right and dance to her left while she said further, "Where I look I see the Depression is getting to be a lost cause. You'll say to me, 'Malvena Malvena, you're such an optimist, how come the marshals moved out Mrs. Shefsel with all her furniture?' and I'll tell you, 'How come her couch had brand-new slip covers?' "

She was answered by a "Heh heh" and a "That's—tha-hat's why Daddy Warbucks lost millions!"

And she moved them clockwise, then counterclockwise, saying, "Then first I get a dream about my sweet sweet Momma, she's calling me from the street, she has a message for me from Uncle Chaim Getzel in heaven that it's good-bye and good luck Mister Hard Times and that I should spend on myself a little, I should get wax paper in the big rolls. And while I'm running to the window she starts in singing, 'Potatoes are cheaper, tomatoes are cheaper . . .' "

She was answered by a "Heh heh" and a "I wouldn't mind already vegetables and sour cream."

And she had them swing their arms in and swing their arms out, saying, "I begged her, 'Sweet sweet Momma darling, could you give me a prosperity sign?' And right right there I saw on the fire escape two beautiful little jars, you couldn't get them two for a nickel, and in each jar there were Octagon coupons."

She got back a "Fartzy Daddy Fotz!" and a "Choke on a charlotte russe, Jackie Cooper killer!"

Crying copiously and warning about her dropped stomach, she waded in and very soon had Simon's father gentled.

"You'll walk with him, Shmuel, you'll love it and you'll enjoy it, the kid walks with the Daddy to work, you'll build up our little family unit and you'll make the whole whole world jealous."

To Simon, his mother said, "Who has a Mommy that when

he comes back from his Daddy and kid walk is going to give him a beautiful beautiful rubberband for his rubberband gun?"

"Ho-sure," his father grumped. "I walk with the Jackie Cooper face, I meet my cap-trade buddies, that's all I need."

"What he does when he walks—you know what he does, Mommy?" Simon's eyes were hooded. "He—like this—he bunks me . . ."

"They see him," his father said triumphantly, "I'm out—I'm finished in the union. And I wouldn't blame them. Because the day Jackie Cooper went in with a naked head to get a hair tousle—that day murdered off the cap trade."

His mother had each of them by an arm, lamenting as she moved them to the door, "Bear in mind how I'm not a well woman . . ."

"Even in *Skippy*," his father mused, "in *Skippy* where he wears himself a cap he makes sure—only a brimless."

". . . I don't tell you everything, how I had to call Mrs. Harlib into Teitlebaum yesterday, she should please please squeeze the rolls for me."

His mother's groans kept them company all the way to the second floor. Where Simon's father beat against Mrs. Shura's peep hole and sought to know if it had been her Lillian who last week popped bubble gum three times in his general direction.

On the ground floor he stopped Mrs. Landes to give her a first fair warning about steaming up the super against him.

By the Brighton Beach El he paused while a train lumbered and slammed into the station, then gave strict instructions that the motorman should take it easy, that he had Jewish lives in his hands.

In silence he passed Magid's Shoe Outlet, Nagelsteen's Imperial Yarn, Madame Schnall's Electrolysis Parlor, and the Apron Emporium. By the window of Schneider's Royal Yarn he braked, then in speedy slow motion doffed his shako, opened two buttons on his tunic, beat upon Simon's head with both fists, hung all his weight on Simon's neck, and sneezed a light sneeze.

Waiting as long as he could, Simon said, "*Leyben.*"

His father built up another sneeze.

"*Leyben,* pull an ear," said Simon.

His father, following a short rest, managed to sniffle.

". . . both ears."

"Ho-boy!"—his father cracked him in the face—"I'm getting a cold."

While Simon wailed softly his father begged him to finish off the job now or in the next few days, before the burial society mailed postcards for the next quarter's dues. "Killer," he said kindly, "murder type. Save yourself a little expense, keep more for Jackie Cooper pictures. You'll live nice, you'll have it—ho-boy!—you'll have it good. You'll go out, you'll buy the *Sunday News,* you'll get *goyish* cup cakes by Dugan's . . ."

"Waha! I'll get? Who'll get?"

"*Who'll get,*" his father mimicked. "Jackie Cooper will get."

He hustled Simon along, notifying him that he had been all this time keeping a little blue notebook with red lines, and in this notebook he was putting down with an Eagle pencil Simon's fresh-mouth snot-nose record, that this record would stay a black and blue mark against Simon's life which, with *Raboynoy-shel-oylom*'s help, would be anyway a short one.

In this fashion and without further incident they covered the more than half-a-block to the Lyric. Yahrblum the Manager, a large-lipped caracul-headed man with rolls of healthy fat under his sleeveless golfer's sweater, was already bouncing his barker's cane on the sidewalk and shouting sonorously at the El, "Four stars in the *Daily News,* four, so help me, Kate Cameron says, 'A superb history drama,' Mandel of the *Forvitz* writes 'You'll enjoy,' the Magid of Vilna puts it this way, 'Harm it can't do,' a dime until five, better than doctors, hello there Shmuel Sloan and son, *Badland Bullets* is the second

B

feature, somewhere else it would be a main feature, very glad you could make it, Shmuel, ten cents, the Coming Attractions alone should cost more, how is my best-looking head usher?"

He winked at Simon, then said, "Hey, Shmuel, you're still such a hoo-ha hotsy-totsy Roosevelt man?"

Simon's father drew himself up to a slouch.

"I'll explain why I ask . . ."

Yahrblum gave Simon a powerful goose.

"I ask because I heard today some shocking, shocking news. I was told by this party, his name is out—in fact, I shouldn't tell you, but if a manager dassn't tell his best-looking head usher it's no America—I was told reliably that . . ."

His smile spread wider.

"I heard . . ."

He cuffed at Simon's crotch.

"Shmuel, I'll ask again, not as your manager, as a friend. A good friend who doesn't want to see you hurt. Did you think it over, did you reconsider, or are you still *ay-ay-ay* for Roosevelt?"

"For Roosevelt—for Roosevelt pluh-hus his missus," Simon's father cried hotly.

"Then your manager is the bearer of bad news. Because I was informed"—Yahrblum drew Simon and his father behind the ticket booth—"the reliable source told me"—he swished his cane operatically—"Roosevelt . . . that Mr. Roosevelt . . . sucks."

"Roosevelt sucks?"

"Believe it, Shmuel."

"Couldn't be a mistake. Couldn't be—ho-boy!—you heard he sucks, you didn't hear on *what* he sucks?"

"He doesn't believe his manager," Yahrblum told Simon bitterly, gently. Then, "Your manager tells you, Shmuel, believe your manager. Roosevelt . . . sucks!"

"Roosevelt sucks?"

"Roosevelt sucks!"

"I feel"—in sorrowful acknowledgement Simon's father shook his head—"for the missus."

"And the kids?"

Simon's father went into hiccups.

"Your manager himself didn't want to believe. Your manager had to first get the"—Yahrblum flashed a small white card—"documentary evidence."

Using his flashlight, Simon's father read, *"The Yellow Stream*, by I. P. Daley."

"Turn over, Shmuel."

"Even so, this is labor's beh-hest friend."

"Your manager gave you an order, Shmuel. Shmuel, turn over!"

"I'm turning, I'm reading, ho-boy, I see already—in green print!"

Then his father showed his teeth to Simon, saying, "Don't tell the Mommy, we don't need to hurt her."

"Nah."

"You're a *momzer* murderer, you hated his guts from the beginning, but even you didn't wish it!"

"Nah, nah Daddy."

He pushed Simon off the curb, saying, "Go, ho-boy, go, Tom Mix and his Tony are calling you!"

And as Simon started to cross his father came after, crying, "Killer-type, you walk away, you don't kiss a Daddy bye-bye?"

Though they held up traffic, though Kushey Kravitz and his older brother, Pinnie, had just then come by and stood looking and laughing, Simon kissed and was kissed. And lingered till his father limped off into the *Lyric* behind Yahrblum.

2

THE JOURNAL*DIARY OF SIMON SLOAN 1653 Brighton Five Street, Brooklyn New York, Apartment 5G, 5AV, PS 84, Home Room 323, Miss Matucci, Class President Herbert Fabricant

My Favorite Actor Is	George O Brien
My Other Favorite Actor Is	Wallace Beery
My Only Favorite Actress Is	Sylvia Sidney
My Favorite Author Is	Joseph P Altsheler
My Favorite Comedy Star Is	Patsy Kelly and Thelma Todd
My Other Favorite Comedy Star Is	No other
My Favorite Magazine Is	Operator 5 Magazine
My Other Favorite Magazine Is	the Spider Magazine
My Most Outstanding Sport Is	Boxball
My Other Most Outstanding Sport Is	None or Chinese Handball
My Ambition For Life Is	A Microbe Hunter

My Other Ambition For Life	
Is	Distant Place and Unknown Exploring
My Best Subject Is	Oral Composition

THE JOURNAL*DIARY OF SIMON SLOAN IS GIVEN DEDICATION BY THE AUTHOR TO MALVENA SLOAN IN SAME ADDRESS AS ABOVE

I want to write how the authors MOMMY MALVENA SLOAN is made very very very happy over such a sweet honor from her son, she's writing here a few words, please please please excuse any grammar mistakes as there are tears in her eyes, she can't help it, that happens to be her nature and don't blame her if the least little thing gets her started. Malvena the Orphan went through more than enough already in her young life, right after her Momma died she went to live by her Aunt Gittel, this was some Gittel, when I took a bath she soaked her housedress in my tub to not waste the hot water, a neighbor said once Gittel you know you should put her in a cheder, how will she know she's Jewish, and Aunt Gittel gave me *azoi* a smack and she said now she knows.

In this spirit I want to wish my son very very very good luck in his present under taking also in all his endeavers, and what I want for him is what he wants and what will give him happiness, my hopes are unselfish hopes, only that he should have a happy mother with him at his side for a hundred and 20 years and that she should only only be in the best of health and that with the help of the ALMIGHTY she should have much better then she had.

Please please excuse the highly abrupt ending as tears are once again straining her sick eyes.

Oct. 12, 1933

Boomie told a good joke.

The JOKE

WHAT IS IT? Every woman has one, everyday a man puts something into it and water comes from the bottom.

WHAT IT IS. An icebox.

This was in school yard.

Also in school yard during the lunch time of same day that was out standing.

I MADE IN A ROW THREE HANDBALL KILLERS.

Also in school yard that was interesting and out standing.

JULIE GOODHEART MADE UP SONG.

Song WHEN A BODY MEETS A BODY COMING THROUGH THE FLY

Oct. 14, 1933

Thinking of a trade   To trade THE OUTLAW OF TORN for a RALPH HENRY BARBOUR

Saw PUBLIC ENEMY and LOVE IS A WONDER   Boomie laid a fotz   In newsreel

Oct. 15, 1933

Miss Matucci has taken a prejudice on me

Oct. 16, 1933

Did not put down how I liked PUBLIC ENEMY   Soso

My main thing against PUBLIC ENEMY   Not sure or He did not have to die at the end, James Cagney

Oct. 18, 1933

I am keeping OUTLAW OF TORN, it has a breast part

HER BREAST HEAVED OUT OF HER BODICE

There is breast part also in THE U. P. TRAIL, I can't find the part today

Oct. 20, 1933

Miss Matucci still has a prejudice on me. She saw me picking nose. She said send me a postcard when you get there   Boomie laid a fotz in HEBREW

Oct. 21, 1933

I was called over by Miss Matucci to have with her a

talk. It made me late for Hebrew. I didn't want to say about Hebrew to her.

She told me how I belong to THE BRIGHT ONES but I was giving her trouble.

She told me that while it was not of great importance I should anyway not use newspaper for the covering of books. Only the brown paper.

She told me the brown paper I could get at STATIONERY stores and I had to spell her this STATIONERY

I spelled it and I threw in it was a honynym word

She told me that as I had done certain things the whole week the HIGHEST mark on my term grade would be only a 74.

I said this was a little highly unfair.

She told me it is hard for her to be fair with a person who only today she caught dreaming and paying no attention in Assignment Time.

I said to her that what happened was I did not hear.

She asked me if I now wanted the assignment, she gave me her own pencil even to write it.

The assignment was SIR WALTER SCOTT.

I knew already and I couldn't hold it back and I right away started in laughing.

She said what is SO funny about the Lay of the last Minstrel.

It ended up that she put down for this month's conduct a red zero and for tomorrow's assignment a blue zero.

Oct. 24, 1933

A new kid next block. 881 Brighton 5 Street, the ground floor.

Marshall Herberg

In general we altogether do not like him.

Miss Matucci went to blackboard today. Miss Matucci drew free hand a perfect circle. This is VERY hard to do. Class applauded. Miss Matucci didn't mind.

Why we don't like Marshall Herberg

1   He is fat and has big tits

2 He smells from salmon

3 He smells from salmon and hard boiled eggs

4 He won't fight HYMIE THE HITTER

5 He is goosey

6 He says dirty words when you grab between his legs, the whole street hears

7 He stands right on top when he makes a urination

He wants to get into the BATTLE ACES S.A.C. We don't want him. Boomie is going to tell him the NO

Oct. 27, 1933

Marshall still still wants to get in BATTLE ACES S.A.C. Very bad

Marshall gave BATTLE ACES S.A.C. four big little books

Marshall put a quarter to treasury

Marshall loaned us Atlas EXERCISER, he is working on it to lose weight on his tits

Marshall donated Orphan Annie Ovaltine Mixer

Marshall stole milky way for us from SUNSET He didn't eat even one bite.

Marshall made up to save seats for us at PARKWAY

BATTLE ACES S.A.C. took vote—BATTLE ACES S.A.C. sent Marshall out for vote. Marshall then got called in. Marshall was told decision

Decision Marshall was told.

He has to prove himself.

Nov. 3, 1933

Fun in Hebrew

Boomie laid SOME fotz

I went and drew swasika on black board

I did rabbi Neuberger how he walks

He was in SOME SOME mood

He wished on me different things

1 I should get killed when I'm shooting on somebody a rubberband, the rubberband should jump in my nose and zip out all the brains

2   I should be fooling around on myself and I should
not be able to stop it until I hear a shofar in the street that
the Mesheach is coming

3   I should be tossing my gum tickets and I should keep
tossing them even when he comes in and a certain certain
angel should start tossing me with the tickets

He started us on CHUMISH

Nov. 8, 1933

Miss Matucci wants a composition
What Miss Matucci wants
The composition should be on a WHAT IF
Like   WHAT IF I owned an airplane
I had an idea, naturaly 1 am not going to do the idea
My idea
WHAT IF all the number two duties you ever made in
your life came up on you in your toilet
When they come up youre ON the toilet

Nov. 10, 1933

Miss Matucci had us have a debate
We could make up the debate question
My question was   IF KING KONG COULD BEAT UP FRANK-
ENSTEIN IN A FAIR FIGHT
Howard Busch took the NO
I took the YES
What I said   Bell rang before my turn

Nov. 12, 1933

A funny thing happened.
It happened on Sunday
What the funny thing was
I took a bath. I made the bath hot. I dryed. When I dryed
I felt very funny feelings.
What the funny feelings were
Mainly that I got sad when I dryed on and around my
B*

nipples. Like when Eddie Cantor finishes up his program and he sings I LOVE TO SPEND EACH SUNDAY WITH YOU AS FRIEND TO FRIEND IM SORRY ITS THROUGH

Also when you come out of the movies and its light outside you get always a headache. That kind of headache I had.

I asked Mommy why

She said its a Daddy department

He said the whole thing has to do with human parts and for between the legs, the goyish name for it is ORGANS

He said I should never say for my human part that its a shlong, only petzel

I asked him if for ladys legs I should say bush

He said he remembers from the army there was another word, the word was like a state

We looked and looked in my geography book, he didn't see it.

He'll ask the Manager tomorrow

Nov. 13, 1933

Boomie told 2 jokes today

He told them in cheder

Joke 1   What is it that dogs make in the back yard that a person doesnt want to step in

The answer   HOLES

Joke 2   What is it thats big and green and people make urinations in it

The answer   THE ATLANTIC OCEAN

Nov. 13, 1933   MORE

Before I forget

Daddy told me the word from the Manager

What the word is   A Montana

Nov. 15, 1933

Nothing new and very very boring

The Surf had it on their program the bill would change today. They were supposed to have George O Brien in the

36

Golden West and The Lost Patrol   This was even in coming attractions

What they had   Joan Crawford in Dancing Lady and a Constance Bennet picture What Price Hollywood

I instead went with Mommy shopping

We went to Teitlebaum

She asked him did his Allie get taken in medical school

He said Allie got taken

Mommy right away winked I should watch him on the scale

Today also a very boring day

We wanted to go to the movies but we saw EVERYTHING

I and Boomie called for Hymie the Hitter

We all three went on Sheepshead Bay to do our plan

What our plan was

We would see an Irish kid, we would say to him Cock on Pat O Brien, Hymie then would fight him

We only saw ginzos

After we only saw ginzos we did Information

How you do Information

You put a nickel in. You say Operator I want Information. You say Information I want the number for Tillie Fuckfaster or I want the number for Seymour Tush, you have to make up also an address.

After we did Information we pestered

We went on Neptune Avenue to the new house. We went into the back. We yelled up Mrs. Cohen Mrs. Cohen yoohoo Mrs. Cohen Mrs. Cohen come to the window.

Two ladies opened the window

We started to laugh and we couldnt say what we wanted to say

What we wanted to say

Mrs. Cohen have you got a boy? Because your boy got kidnaped

Then we went to a candystore where they didn't know us

I said to the man Mrs. COHEN told us to tell you to save
a Forvitz for her everyday

Then we went to a shoemaker

Hymie said to the man Mrs. COHEN says when should she
expect her shoes ready

Boomie made a VERY big fotz

He stank up the store

Then we ran

Then we went by another apartment house

We called up YOOHOO Mrs. LEVY

THREE ladies opened windows

They told us Mrs. LEVY got a Dis Posess and she moved
in with a son

Nov. 19, 1933

We had a RUNOVER today

Right near the house

What happened   A blue car went over Mrs. Rubins
shoes

Nothing happened to Mrs. Rubin   But her folding chair
got busted

A lot of ladies came

Who came out

Mrs. Selber Mrs. Greenfeld Mrs. Harlib Mrs. Mesnikoff
Mrs. Plaut Mrs. Abrams Mrs. Berman Mrs. Povill Mrs. Alter
Mrs. Pollock Mrs. Fromin Mrs. Sonnabend

It was funny

Why it was funny

Anyway to me

Because Mrs. Mesnikoff is on the outs the longest time
with Mrs. Plaut and Mrs. Abrams   But they all coop-
perated together

What they did was Mrs. Mesnikoff and Mrs. Plaut busted
the car windows on the right side   Mrs. Abrams did the
windows on the left side   and even so she finished first
Her husband used to have a car, thats how she knows how
to bust in the windows

38

Tomorrow they change the bill at the SURF

Today they changed the bill at the SURF

They had LAST OUTPOST with Cary Grant and GOLDEN GUNS with Ken Maynard and the Tailspin Tommy chapter Number 11, one more yet till the last one

It was VERY crowded, the line was to Teitlebaum   only for BROADWAY BILL it was that long

I and Boomie and Hymie anyway got good seats

How we got good seats   Marshall saved us

How he saved us   He took along three hats from his father to put on the seats

Marshall brought along to eat yellow raisins for all and Loft sour balls and some Pechter maccaroons and chicken-feed and bubblegum, the long, and pollyseeds

We made him go get Mason black dots Mister Goodbar and Nonprays

We made him go when it was THE CHAPTER

Also we made him boo and hiss on PRESIDENT ROOSEVELT

A lady turned around, she wished him a Jewish thing in his throat

We made him answer her back

We made him say FondolaMatzoFilleeGoo

We made him light three matches to look under the seat

We made him say hes looking for his mother, she's a very short lady

We made him open the exit door to give a draft on people

We made him not to stand up when a lady wanted to get by

We made him also put his knee up, it got her between the legs in the ass

We made him lean over and ask Sharon Shrier to please please do him a favor

What the favor was   Sharon Shrier should rub on his petzel and tell him what happens

We made him on the way out pinch her tit also
He wants to know when he gets in the club
We told him walk away while we vote
He walked away and we all went buzzabuzzapuhpuhpuh
When he came back we said Boomie would speak for us
How Boomie spoke for us   He laid a fotz

Nov. 21, 1933

Bobby Benson was good today, it was how they got the Rocky River Gang

In Myrt and Marge theyre looking for Tom Drew the Reporter

On Just Plain Bill you can get Kolynos samples, Mommy is sending away

I figured out the Orphan Annie Special Message without a code ring   Boomie told me how

The Orphan Annie Special Message   DADDY WARBUCKS WILL BE HEARD FROM SOON LISTEN WHEN SANDY BARKS THREE TIMES

Chandu the Magician I didnt hear

Why I didnt hear   Mommy sent me down just just when it was Chandu time for a sour tomato, only Mrs. Teitlebaum should wait on me

I stood a minute by Waxmans, they were pasting signs on the door, they also put a BIG lock on it, in the subway on the change booth doors you see such locks

Everything from the store was in a pile outside

Waxman went into the gutter and he yelled TEITLEBAUM

Teitlebaum didnt come out

Mrs. Waxman went also in the gutter, also she yelled TEITLEBAUM

She said its all right, were all finished, you don't need to sell King Oscar sardines no more for a quarter

I snitched from them a farmer cheese box

Nov. 22, 1933

I am working on my China REPORT

On the cover I use loose leaf reinforcers that I paste on to spell CHINA and with India ink I go over the letters they should look Chinese.

On the next page I am copying some of the cover from FU MAN CHU, just faces

On the page after I am pasting in real tea and real rice for PRINCIPLE PRODUCTS

On the left-hand side of that page I am pasting in a big picture of NILS ASTHER from the Bitter Tea Of General Yen

On the right-hand side of the next page I will paste in a big picture of EDWARD G. ROBINSON from Hatchet Man

I asked Miss Matucci if I can do that, if its fair to paste in something if its from a picture you never saw

She said its all right, that I showed by asking her an INTEGRITY, she wrote the word on the blackboard

The rest I am going to copy from the WONDERS of the WORLD Encyclopedia, naturaly I am changing around the beginning and the end

Nov. 23, 1933

Boomie has a gripp, Hymie went to Brownsvile, he is buying knickers

I met Marshall, he asked to play boxball, I told him he has to give me something

What he gave me   A VERY GOOD soap eraser, the EBER-HARD kind

Nov. 24, 1933

I had to go with Mommy shopping as she couldnt carry alone

We had to go by Ocean Parkway, LUCKY is there going out of business

They had a sale on Octagon Soap, two only to a customer

We were supposed to get four but we got six

How we got the six   Mommy showed the man a letter from Mrs. Abrams

41

On the way back Mommy got something in her eye

We went to the druggist he should take it out

The druggist said if she went to an EYEMAN with it it would have to cost her four dollars at least

Mommy kissed his hands and she cried

When she cried it washed out what was in the eye

The druggist anyway gave her burro solution she should bathe the eye   Also cotton on a stick

Mommy said I want to do something for you, I am ashamed you see me only only either to take something out of an eye or to buy a few postals

She told him about the Octagon sale

Nov. 25, 1933

I worked on my CHINA REPORT some more

I colored the front and the back yellow

I changed the FU MAN CHU picture to a WARNER OLAND in CHARLIE CHANS DESPARATE CASE

Otherwise nothing or very very little

Nov. 27, 1933

Daddy got today a letter, the mailman rang our downstairs bell

Then he sent up Mrs. Plaut

She rang our upstairs bell

Mrs. Plaut said Malvena dont get scared, the mailman sent me up with a little bad news

Mommy anyway got scared

She got so so scared she didnt even notice I sat down in a livingroom chair

Mrs. Plaut said Malvena the mailman has a special-delivery letter with two cents in postal dues

We all three went down

Mommy gave the mailman a deposit bottle

He said that he wouldnt take it

Mommy went upstairs to get him another bottle

It didnt have a chip on top

The letter was from GERMANY

It was in Jewish and English

The English I could read only HELP

Mommy had to think and think who wrote it, she wasnt sure

She said a very very distant relative to **Daddy**, a first cousin

She wrote back on a postal if they could send her maybe another picture, this one got a little rip

We had also a fight

Why we had the fight She sent me to the druggist to buy the postal just when it was the middle of BOBBY BENSON, she always does that

Nov. 28, 1933

I got 96 on my CHINA REPORT

There were three people only that got higher, Judy Sorkin Herbert Fabricant and Irving Pfeffer

Miss Matucci put down V GOOD on the cover

She took off the four points because in two places the paste marks showed

These were in the PRINCIPLE PRODUCTS place and the National Geographic map

Miss Matucci said to the class that what you learned in doing this is MUCH MUCH more important then what you learned about CHINA

She said what you learned is a rule for life

She said how this rule for life is in two words, but they are two of THE most important words we would ever put on OUR GOLDEN WORDS PAGE

She printed what the words were on the black board

What the words were   NEATNESS COUNTS

Nov. 29, 1933

Mrs. Plaut came in the house

It was when I was hearing Myrt and Marge

It was a whole business, what should she do about her

43

Phyllis, her Phyllis is going with a boy from Manhattan Beach

Mommy said what kind of a boy

Mrs. Plaut said he is some boy

Mommy said what kind of a family

Mrs. Plaut said theyre some family

Mommy asked are they in business

Mrs. Plaut said they were in some business

Mommy wanted to know how she was so far handling it

Mrs. Plaut told her she tied on Phyllisses bloomers red ribbon, also she hung up on the wall a fish picture and when Phylliss leaves the house with the boy she makes a poopoo

Mommy fell on her, she said a person of her intelligent common sense should be ashamed to believe in such booby minesirs and strictly ignorant stuff

Mommy said what are you a greenhorn with the red ribbon and the fish pictures and poopoo

Mrs. Plaut claimed she went to a certain party on Neptune Avenue, they gave her strict instructions about red ribbon and fish pictures and poopoo

Mommy said she wanted to find out if she was smart, she asked Mrs. Plaut if she got the instruction from a dirty gypsy who has the profesionel name Queen Anderius

Mrs. Plaut couldn't get over how Mommy was right, she said she would never handle there again with her

Mommy said absolutely not and from now on she should go in and ask only only for the sister

I found the sunday MIRROR jokes by the dumb waiter

Nov. 30, 1933

Mommy and Daddy had a good mood today

I was listening to CHANDU THE MAGICIAN so I wasnt supposed to see

What I saw   Mommy was by the stove, Daddy got behind her, he put his right hand between her legs, he put his left hand on her titsy and he kissed her on the hair

Mommy said More on dejenerit Dope and dirty nut

where did you get such rotten stuff from what bums you peculiar person who taught you to go in for FRENCH things, on me dont experiment walk into a public toilet first next time youre going to kiss a womans hair

Daddy said I was carried away by how nice you looked the way you can wear clothes it shows you should dress yourself up that way some more

Mommy said What then and Sure Thats all you want, Ill listen to you Why Not, I got nothing else to do, For my everyday work and to go shopping Ill wear for you sleeveless undershirts

Daddy said whats for supper

Mommy told him What do you feel for and Thats what I got

Daddy said What you got is what I feel for

Mommy said thank GOD I got I got a little pot cheese and sour cream I got a little vegetables and sour cream I got a little hardboiled eggs and sour cream

Daddy said I feel for a little plain sour cream

Mommy said the way you were then that's the way you are now, You never had consideration, I always had to make you special meals

I went finally down by Mrs. Harlib to listen to Bobby Benson, thats how they were having a fight

Dec. 1, 1933

I made a quarter today

How I made a quarter   I walked Dopey Duhvee around for three hours until my movie opened   I was his companion

Boy he is STRONG

I didnt realise

He gets a grip on you you cant move   In just plain wrestling he could easy beat up Hymie the Hitter

He is the strongest one in the ungraded class, and there they got STRONG ONES

He has a very small head   He likes you to hit it and

45

when you hit it you feel it hurts up to your elbow

What he likes to do is he blows his nose   His mother showed me when we started out how good he blows

What he also likes to do is go around like hes a car

We went to the boardwalk   On the way I saw Selma Yagodnik

I said Duhvee See See the grage, Go in to the grage

He got her right in the titsys

We then went on the boardwalk   I told him to Sit in the sun

He listened to me   Thats one thing, he listens

There were wooden matches on the bench   He lit them It made him feel like a urination   We went under the boardwalk for him to do it

He has a real big one   He starts taking it out and he takes and he takes and he keeps on taking

Then we walked almost to STEEPLECHASE   Duhvee had a string his mother gave him, he made knots in it

He had left a match   He pulled a hair out and set fire to it   He likes the smell

Then I felt like making him cry

I said Duhvee your mother moved away   She moved far far away

He heard that and thats all he needed, he ran up and down the boardwalk to look for his mother

What I noticed is he doesnt cry   He goes Grahgrahgrah

Then I said Duhvee your mother moved back   She was only fooling

Things like that he understands   Youd be surprised how he got happy   He did his car again

After he did the car he sang Duhvee barmitzva presents presents barmitzva barmitzva

I said Duhvee you cant get a barmitzva

He made believe he was in shool, he did how they spit on their fingers to turn pages

I said Duhvee you cant get barmitzvad youre fifteen and if youre fifteen you dassnt get one

Fifteen he didnt understand, cant he did   He ran away

46

He went by the ocean   He got himself wet   The shoes the socks everything

He did his grahgrahgrah into the ocean, they heard him in Rockaway

I had SOME time getting him back   On account of him I had to be on line twenty minutes

I saw UP THE RIVER WITH SPENCER TRACY and DOWN WYOMING WAY WITH TOM TYLER   In UP THE RIVER Warren Hymer stole the whole picture

Dec. 2, 1933

We had a pretty good SUNDAY

Mommy was listening to W E V D

All of a sudden she heard her name on it

Her postal got picked out in the lucky drawing   They will send her a coupon she can take it in to get a Tuxedo brand farmer cheese

Right away everybody on our floor came in

Mrs. Abrams called from the window a mazel tuff   She said Malvena dont forget your old friends

The super rang the bell   He said tomorrow hes coming to fix under the icebox

Mrs. Plaut came in   She kissed Mommy she said life should hold out for us similer joyfull occasions

A little after Mrs. Harlib came in   She said we should like wise know only from simkars

Mommy started to cry

She said Why Im crying is Im reminded of my Momma who was a very very wise and a highly highly learned woman, she used to have an expression she would use from the old-country

Mommy again started to cry, she couldnt control

She said it was an expression her Momma would say in Hebrew, in Hebrew its beautiful, especially the way her Momma said it, but she could say it only in English

Mrs. Harlib put down Mommys head between the knees, It helped a little

47

Mommy said the expression had a richness to it, it had her Mommas wisdom and high learning

Then she couldnt talk more, she made like signs to write it down and Mrs. Harlib brought in a snip of bag

What Mommy wrote   Everybody loves a winner

Dec. 4, 1933

Doris Reitzer vomited in school today

We had the CITYWIDE music teacher   Miss Frayn

We had a fire drill

It came rightright before lunch so we didnt have to go back in class

After lunch we were in the yard   Boomie called over me and Hymie and Melvin Haas and Jesse Cosoff

He said Who wants dirty jokes

Everybody went yahyah, I kept quiet, the only one

He then took out the SUNDAY NEWS JOKES   They were dirty from his lunch

We got our composition homework

We have to do a page and a half composition on a true story, the story has to make or have in it an important point

Mommy gave me help

She told me the story how she was by Teitlebaum, she was buying 3 things he had on special The three things were American cheese, Swiss Knight cheese and Horowitz Margareten matzo meal, it was three for twenty   Firemen came They said Mr. we dont see no fire   Who called about a fire Mrs. Teitlebaum said If you dont mind wait a few minutes, my husband got only two hands

I couldnt figure it out, I asked Mommy give me the point

She said the point is you should buy in Teitlebaum only when he has specials

Dec. 5, 1933

We had today a very interesting OPEN DISCUSSION period

What we discussed was

Why You Should Give To The Red Cross

48

Why Silence Is Important In Fire Drill

Who should get The School Award For Outstanding Public Service

Miss Matucci had a good mood so I took a chance, I nominated Joe Penner. She said she wouldnt give me a demerit if I gave her a good reason for Joe Penner

I said because he has the line Wanna Buy a Duck, and this is good for our forests

Miss Matucci said why is it good for our forests

I said because it makes everybody think about POLE TREE

Miss Matucci said you really should get a demerit but that was WITTY

Lila Edelstein said I think I read it in junior Scholastic

Boomie went DEE DEE DA DA DEE junior Scholastic

Manny Hochman raised then an interesting problem for OPEN DISCUSSION

The problem he had was a fairness problem

He was playing Actors And Actresses with a friend. The friend gave him one, R T, an actor

That one he couldnt get   He gave up   His friend said then, RT an actor thats Rin Tin Tin

Manny said it was a fairness problem because his friend was not fair. His friend should have said the middle letter

On this there was open discussion   The points raised were

One side said if his friend gave him the middle letter this would make it very easy

Another side said his friend should have given him the middle letter because the full and whole name is RIN TIN TIN not RIN TIN

I raised my hand   I said if you said only E R for Edward G Robinson and E O for Edna May Oliver they wouldnt count because you wouldnt be giving the full and whole name   So why should it count if you say only R T for Rin Tin Tin

Lila Edelstein said Rin Tin Tin isnt an actor OR an actress

49

Boomie went Rin Tin Tin Dee Dee DEE dee dee dee

Lila Edelstein said same to you

We had a vote by hands and it came out 27 to 9 that Manny was right

Also we had a movie for the afternoon, The Great Mount Everest

Also we had a short Hebrew

We sat and sat in chedar and then Rabbi Neubergers wife came out

She said the Rabbi found out bad news in Europe

Boomie did the way she makes with her mouth

I got home in time for part of Bobby Benson

Dec. 6, 1933

Miss Matucci gave us area and square feet today

The School Nurse had a surprise Inspection

She did something that made me happy, I was overjoyed

She said Lila Edelstein was a nailbiter

Miss Matucci passed an announcement to join the Shop Club

I and Boomie signed up

Mr. Karlin is the Shop Club adviser, Bomba Katz had him once

Bomba told us Mr. Karlin is very tough, he throws chalk and he grabs your ear and he once said to a kid Go and open the windows   When the kid took a long time and kept dropping the window pole Mr. Karlin said whats the matter

The kid said I cant find the window hole

Mr. Karlin said I bet you would know how to find it if it had hair around it

After school I and Boomie made up a poem for Lila Edelstein

We recited it to her from across the street

LILA EDELSTEIN WHO LIKES FRANCHOT TONE
BITES ALL HER NAILS TO THE BONE

Today also we had a short Hebrew

Rabbi Neuberger had us only sing Ayn Kellohaynew and do five minutes chumish

When we finished he said GO GO PLAY

When we ran out he called after it should be in heavy traffic only

Dec. 8, 1933

I had a funny dream

Daddy was in the dream

In the dream while I was dreaming it I knew he was Daddy but he made believe he wasnt

I think he was the one in LITTLE CAESAR the gang leader in the beginning I forget his name, he was also in another Edward G. Robinson picture

In the dream he goes around stealing Ferndale deposit bottles

I am myself in the dream but part of me is Richard Arlen and I have to fight Daddy

Then after Mommy is putting him in the electric chair

What I remember exactly, she says I could go for a Hebrew National frank but I have to wait for his Last Mile

Then I remember exactly also I say to her you walk with me Mommy to get the frank

When I told it Mommy cried a little bit She said Im very very pleased and for the rest of my life and even when Im a big big boy I should keep wanting to walk with a Mommy

Dec. 9, 1933

Marshall came around to find out when can he prove himself

I and Boomie and Hymie the Hitter figured out today he should pester Gelfman

So he read all the papers and blocked the stand

He took up a whole table for a penny pollyseeds

He said to Gelfman he has to go to the toilet

51

He said I cant get in and Gelfman had to move away the papers from yesterday, three big bundles, and a whole whole soda case

He bought a long pretzel   He said Take off the salt from it

He said Give me half a frozen twist and Gelfman had to first take out ice and move around the fudgsicles and milky ways

He said cut it for me with your knife

He said how about a napkin

He said can I have with it some water, let the water run a while

He said write me down Miskys number I want him to deliver my mother a carton of cigarettes and a case and a half mixed soda

When we got thrown out Marshall said How about now Did I prove myself

We made believe we had a secret discussion

We said Now we have to teach you the BATTLE ACES S A C special grip

I put my hand between his legs from the front

Hymie put his hands in from the back

We rode him that way to nearly Brighton 6

Dec. 10, 1933

Today was an interesting experience

Nothing HAPPENED but it was anyway interesting

I by myself went to the SURF, Boomie had to go with his family in east New York, they are maybe buying top coats, and Hymie the Hitter is going to see a cousin in the hospital, she has a cancer

They had THE LOST PATROL with Victor Mclaglen and PECOS TRAIL with Johnny Mack Brown

Daddy already spoiled the Lost Patrol. He told me the end. Where Mclaglen is the only one alive and kills with a machine gun   Also he said it was in the Forvitz Mclaglen doesnt like Jews

They got a matron now I had to sit in the childrens section on the side where I hate

The cartoon I liked better then the pictures. It was a Merrie Melodies all under water

They had a whole bunch of baby fish and an octopus was rocking them to sleep all at the same time in one cradle with the name on it THE CRADLE OF THE DEEP

Also they had a fish walking around that he looked Jewish with a sign on him WE SELL SEA SHELLS BY THE SEA SHORE

When I got out there was a slush snow

I had a sort of headache with also a funny feeling and the sadness I get when I dry on my nipples

I was positive Mommy was dead

Then I met her by the house We went into Teitlebaum

She said to him good shabis Master criminal

She cried and cried but Teitlebaum said it wasnt his bottles

So we crossed over to Frankel, Mommy bought there a shopping bag

What she did I knew she would do from her wink She said Frankel you dont have to wrap, I have the exact 2¢ Im leaving it near the rolls

We ran all the way home

Frankels wife got us anyway on the second floor, she made us take back the Canadien penny

Dec. 13, 1933

We had DICTATION today

It was about when Benjamin Franklin came to Philedelphia He had rolls in his hand and the girl he would later on marry saw him with the rolls and she laughed

Miss Matucci then wrote the exact correct dictation on the blackboard and we changed papers

All the papers had to be face down

I got Herbie Fabricants paper

He had just one spelling mistake, Inne instead of Inn

Myron Rich got my paper

I got a 100

I showed it to Mommy

She couldnt get over this was how he first met his wife with rolls in his hand

We had almost an argument and I opened a mouth, I said she should come on and she should stop it, its in history

She said thats something and thats something and what got her is how even in those years if they could get away with it they would try not to give you a bag

Dec. 14, 1933

Tonight Mommy said I should take a nice walk with Daddy

He didnt want

Mommy told him he has to for closeness and companionship, its a Holy thing a Daddy and his boy should be the best friends and she could use a Swiss Knight from SACRAMENTO.

I and Daddy went on the boardwalk

We met there Hershey Madlicks grandfather

Daddy said to him sholim ahlaychum Red Menace

They got into a Roosevelt fight

Hershey Madlicks grandfather didnt like Roosevelt and his yankee smile for selling the workers out

Daddy said to him definitely and positively

The grandfather said Roosevelt is serving the fruits of labor on other peoples tables

Daddy said yeah yeah

The grandfather said whats wrong is we dont produce in such a way that the goods go where the goods are needed

Daddy said you should cock so

The grandfather said Daddy should get wise to himself and learn with all the workers what the workers are starting in to find out

Daddy said blow it out your ass

54

On the way home Daddy had a good mood, he wanted to know how I liked the way he handled himself

I had to remind him we should get the Swiss knight

I got home from Hebrew there was a note from Mommy that if I dont see her I shouldnt get scared and I should come down right away by Mrs. Abrams

I went down, the whole house was there almost. They were all dressed up

They wouldnt let me go inside

Mrs. Abrams said to people I knew it was coming and it had to come any day but even so its hard to take in and realise

Mommy I saw in the kitchen. She was crying, she said thats how I am, these things get to me, its going to take me a long time to get used to it

Mrs. Feldner said does Mr. Abrams know, itll be some shock to him and maybe somebody should meet him downstairs first

Two big goyish men came out then they went inside again

Mrs. Berman said put it on top the icebox at least there it wouldnt scratch

Mrs. Feldner said not on top of the icebox because Mr. Abrams would see it there the first thing

The two goyish men went outside, Mommy went after

She started talking to them that it was so unexpected

One goyish man said thats how it is lady, we never can tell when, its out of our hands

Mrs. Feldner went to get sponge cake. She told the goyish men they should have some also because on such ocassions in the Jewish religion you have something sweet

Mrs. Plaut got seltzer and strawberry syrup, we all drank from paper cups

We all then went in the kitchen to look

Mommy said she couldnt get over it was so small, she never expected it would look so small and so black

Mrs. Plaut wanted us to not crowd up the house because there was going to be soon a lot of family

Then it rang and we all got scared   It was only one of the goyish men testing if it was in right

They let me call up for the exact time, its a free call

Dec. 16, 1933

Eugene Marcus had to go to the school nurse

He picked and picked his nose, it started in bleeding

Miss Matucci read us some of the CHRISTMAS CAROL

I almost got in trouble for laughing, Boomie also

It was when she got to the part that Scrooge sends some kid for a goose

In Hebrew I made a dime

What happened was I had to give Neuberger the 50¢ for the week   I put down only 4 dimes, he took it away not counting

I and Boomie went by my house after   We played box-ball

What we did was just just volley   Boomie hit to my left hand mostly I should develop it better

Then we didnt exactly see how it started, only that there was barking

Mrs. Chepper was in the middle of the gutter, her Beauty got runover

The car went away

Beauty had no blood and wasnt squashed

Mrs. Chepper sat right in the gutter, her dress was up by the bloomers

She said I know you dont I know you how you like to fool the Momma

She said You know what Beauty You know Momma doesnt like you Oh no no no Momma absolutely doesnt like you, Momma LOVES YOU

Beauty moved her tail   Just just just a little move, it wasnt even a wag

Mrs. Chepper said You see Beauty cutee when you dont listen to Momma you get in trouble   You see this morning you were a lazy Beauty cutee you didnt want to go down to make your movement you held it in so long you did what you never do you got such cramps you ran right out in the gutter

Then Beauty opened her mouth   Something came out, a red vomit

Mrs. Chepper said you know what Beauty cutee can have for supper   How about some chuk I made them grind it twice theres no fat and Ill frenchfry a potato, you love that the best thing

A little truck then came

It had in it two men   They had police man uniforms but without badges and no guns

They put Beauty in   First they put her in a bag like they have mail in   It has a cord on top, to close it you have to give a pull

Mrs. Chepper was talking to them in a nice way, that they come from Bensonhurst and where in Bensonhurst and she has a brother in Bensonhurst and that its some terrible trip except if you go by car and if you go by car its no trip almost

She wanted to know if what they do is for the city and if you have to take a test like for civil service, and the whole street said civil service is the best thing

When they got ready to drive she told them if they got La guardia for a boss they got a good boss

When they started she said to tell him with Fay Chepper hes got himself a real booster

She then ran after the truck

I and Boomie were surprised how fast she could run and that she had the breath

But after she got around the corner she came back, she lost a slipper

I and Boomie found it way over near Brighton 7

Boomie had a good joke

What is it a Jewish Boy has to get that a Rabbi does it to him and a goyish boy never gets

What it is   A barmitzva

Otherwise not too much

We decided to do pestering   I and Boomie and Hymie the Hitter went on the boardwalk till where the Polar Bear Club goes in the water

We stood by the railing till they came out, there was one lady

We yelled BLUE BLUE OH ARE THEY BLUE

Then we pointed all together to her titsys

She said to me dont you worry more on boy, I know your mother Ill see her Ill tell her what a more on boy she has

I said to her You know my mother you dumb bich my mothers dead

After Boomie said to me WHAT YOU SAID

I said it slipped out

Hymie the Hitter said it should never slip out what you said

When I got home I rang the downstairs bell

I was very glad when Mommy ticked back her special tick

I went upstairs and while I went I covered my head with a handkerchief and I did Baruk Attoor and I promised GOD I would never say about a mother that shes dead

Daddy dont feel good today

Mommy gave me the nickel, I went by Mrs. Abrams and I called Dr. Schein by myself, he should come to the house

Dr. Schein came   He took the tempriture and he listened to Daddys heart

Mommy said so what do you think dr. and what has he got

Dr. Schein said it looks to me hes got what he always gets

Mommy asked how long hell be so weak

Dr. Schein said at least till he gets back his strength

Mommy said in case he wants to eat should she give him to eat

Dr. Schein asked what were the strict instructions last time

Mommy said it was that she has to use her common sense

Dr. Schein said He would stick by that

Mrs. Plaut came in later She was surprised Mommy uses Schein, in the whole neighborhood no one has a good word for him

Mommy agreed with her, she claimed she also isnt crazy about him, he sucks you dry and hes interested only in the money and from the minute he steps in a house his hand is out, but the reason she sticks with him is at least hes someone you can talk to

Dec. 20, 1933

Cousin Lottie Cousin Phillie Cousin Hettie with her two girls Minnie and Gertie and also Cousin Tillie came to see Daddy They heard in the society he didnt feel good

Cousin Lottie brought a jar of Lofts sour balls, the small

Mommy right away put it in the medicine chest

Cousin Phillie wanted to know how come she puts a jar of Lofts sour balls in the medicine chest

Mommy said it keeps better that way, in the medicine chest it helps loosen up the top when she has to open the jar on her dropped stomach

Cousin Phillie said let me have it Ill open it for you I got strong fingers

Mommy started in to cry

She said tell me how come I went back to your house after your sister goldies unveiling and you had just gone bankrupt in the drug supply line wherever I looked you had bankrupt drug line supplys and you didnt once say Malvena after what you did for me in Hartford Connecticut take home a nickel fine comb

c

Cousin Lottie said I dont stick up for him because hes my husband Malvena but that gets me sore From our house you never went emptyhanded

Mommy said whats true is true I never went emptyhanded from your house, you always gave me the garbage to take down

Cousin Hettie said You know in this family Im the Swisserland Im strictly newtral I like to butt out but you yourself complained to me Phillie gave you once a fine comb and you used it and the next week you noticed a bleeding in your gums

Cousin Phillie said Why dont she mention how her Shimmy was over the house he went to where my pencils are he broke the points

Cousin Tillie said You have to go by what the song says Look Away Look Away

Cousin Lottie said Thats your philosophy Look Away Look Away

Cousin Tillie said Look Away Look Away is my philosophy

Cousin Lottie said Now first I understand why when I dragged in from the Bronx 23 years ago to your Barneys pinyun a ben and I said mazeltough you looked away

Mommy said That was the affair you didnt invite me to but who blames you, what did you need Malvena the Orphan

Cousin Tillie said It was an absolutely last minute idea, we figured we didnt want a big affair only like a little get together for the nearest and dearest

Mommy said Believe me Im not insulted I understand and anyway thats what I heard from Irving the Seltzer Man, he said my wife didnt feel like going but I told her how can you not go its for the nearest and dearest

Cousin Phillie said Youre talking about seltzer youre getting me thirsty Malvena how about a little seltzer

Mommy said How is it you never had any use for my Momma, When you were selling bing cherries on Rivington Street that time and my Momma the Widow went to you she said Phillie maybe you can use me once in a while on the push cart you answered her Im sorry honey I got no use for you

Cousin Minnie said I have such a terrible taste I wouldnt mind if I had a Lofts sour ball to suck on

Mommy said Im still waiting for your sister Beckies house warming present Im in my house only 17 years

Cousin Phillie said hey people what do you say its time to make by-by

Cousin Minnie said right now we better go otherwise Lofts is closed we wont get any sour balls

I and Mommy went down, we walked them to the trolley

Mommy said next time dont wait for a sickness to visit, after all who have we got, we got only each other, we're a small family and a small family should stick together, it was some some pleasant surprise and a good time was had by all

Dec. 21, 1933

Daddy felt a little bit better

He got hungry, Mommy told him he should eat light after a fever

She made him a farmer cheese and hard egg sandwihich on matzo, I had too

Daddy got in a good mood

He said Malvena youre some swell wife to me

He put his hand on Mommys tush and Mommy didnt even hit him so hard

Mommy said she even even has a big surprise for him, she gave him nearly the whole forvitz from last sunday

I stayed up stairs on account it was pouring

Mommy said what's so terrible, leave it to the Mommy, youll see well have fun in the house

Daddy read in the forvitz who died. He knew three of the people, Mommy knew one

Mommy then did the sink and the stove. She sang a song in Jewish

It was catchy, Mommy explained what it was about

What it was about   An old lady is in the street, shes poor. Theres snow and shes saying Dark Is My World Dark Is My Life because shes so sick and also because a daughter threw her out of the house and a son shut the door in her face

After Mommy did the sink and the stove she did around the molding, I helped

She started to sing another Jewish song and Daddy sang it also

It was about an old lady who goes to the doctor He tells her she has a cancer   She wants to tell her daughter she got a cancer but the daughter isnt interested, she has to go to the beauty parlor   She wants to tell the daughter inlaw about it and the daughter inlaw doesnt have time, she has to buy a persian lamb coat   How it ends is the old lady lays down on her husbands grave, she tells him

After Mommy did the molding she did the windowsills and she turned on W E V D

They had on a play about how they want to make a rabbi eat ham in Russia and he kills himself

Daddy then had an idea that while he has time he should write up postals for the society, they have an unveiling in two weeks

Mommy said I should help with the postals we should get a closeness

While I helped Daddy they had on Jennie Goldstein, she did a poem about how Hitler throws out an old lady and the rich daughter has no room for her in America

Mommy came over, she gave me a kiss

She said see what was so terrible, you stay home with a Mommy and a Daddy once in a while, you can have have plenty plenty fun with them in the house

We all three counted Octagon cupons, I ended up with Daddy in a fight, I forget for what

Dec. 22, 1933

I and Boomie went over to Hymie the Hitter   We had

made up to go to McGinnis for a roast beef and then go see the George O Brien picture

There was some business in his house

His bubbee was moving in on them, they threw her out where she was a border

Hymie told us it was mostly for laying fotzes   He says she lays them better then Boomie even

For that reason we stayed around, but all she did was a sneeze and blow out the snot with her fingers

Hymie had to watch her she shouldnt go in a closet, thats where she likes to make her urinations

Hymie asked us do we want to see something. He went over, he said hey bubbee WANG WANG

Three times he did it, and nothing. He claims if he gets it just just right she spits

A little bit she played with her mustach hairs, also she took out from her sweater a snip of rye bread and she ate only the seed

Hymies mother came in to the bubbee, she helped take out the seeds and she told her Ma everything is going to be good for you again and Ma youll have it good and will you have it good Ma

The bubbee went GOOD

Hymies mother said Ma it wont be only good its going to be for you better than good and Ma itll be wonderful

The bubbee went WONDERFUL WONDERFUL

Hymies mother said Ma youll have its so good and so wonderful and youll put yourself in my hands and theyll be good hands and Ill take some swell care of you and youll see how its going to be in my hands here and here you wont need anything Ma because youre in my hands Ma so Ma let me have the diamonds

The bubbee went GEVALT

Hymie then held the bubbees leg and his mother rolled down the stocking

The bubbee had a handkerchief with cotton tied on her

63

knee, thats where she had the rings. The rings Hymies mother wouldnt let us see

Hymie thought she would then do a fotz, he saw it in her face. We waited and waited and still she didnt

It ended up Hymie couldnt go with us as his mother wanted him to help look for the bubbees bankbooks

We saw the picture, Hymie didnt miss anything

Dec. 23, 1933

In the afternoon we had the Christmas Party

Miss Matucci collected in the morning a nickel from everybody   Only Arnie Gutwillig and Zeena Segal forgot to bring

We had small pretzels Hershey kisses nonprays potato chips and chocolate-covered graham crackers with orange sprinkles   Some of the crackers had a Christmas tree and some of the crackers had a Santa Claus shape

Then we had the class entertainment   Rhoda Perl sang Theres Something About A Soldier and tapdanced a little Everybody wanted her to do more but she didnt have on her good taps

Diane Koplik played the accordion   She asked the class What should I play Boomie yelled Play Far far away   So Miss Matucci had him good, she said Well perhaps our class wit would like to go up and do something for us, let us all share in his wit

Marty Pfeffer and Ira Freedler pulled on Boomie so he had to stand up

Boomie then took Arnie Gutwilligs lumberjacket from the closet and he put it on backwards and he put his knickers over his socks and stuck a ruler all the way down behind his neck

Then he did the way Frankenstein walks from the windows to the door and to where Diane Mandels seat is   She got very scared when he touched her, thats how good he did it

Then he did Joe Penner and he did Lew Lahr the way

64

Lew Lahr does about monkies and he did King Kong when King Kong is going to fall down the Empire state building, the way he goes back and forth and back and forth and then he told us This one you have to guess

It was so so good practically the whole class knew

He did Mr. Gladstone when hes trying to get us quiet for the Flag Salute

Boomie got the most claps Miss Matucci said well I guess you have redeemed yourself

She wrote on the blackboard REDEEMED for an assignment to look up

Then she said Well in three minutes the bell will ring and Vacation will start and I bet the class is sorry Is the class sorry

The whole class did a fake groan, I dont think it was so fake

Then Miss Matucci made us stand up and cross our arms and take the hands of our neighbors

My neighbor was Lila Edelstein

We then together sang the New Years Eve Song

Lila Edelstein had a funny look

She was holding on my hand tighter then I was holding on her hand

I told Boomie, he said she was afraid you would tickle her palm

Dec. 25, 1933

Merry Xmas

We had Hebrew today anyway

When Rabbi Neuberger went to the toilet we sang SILENT NIGHT We did the CHRIST in Christ our saver is born very very loud

Morty Shafer picked his nose and put the snot on his ruler

Then he bent the ruler all the way back and he made believe he shot the snot on Boomie

Boomie made believe he caught it in his hand

Then he dribbled it on the bench and just just when Rabbi Neuberger got back he said oh what a beautiful snot hunk

Rabbi Neuberger came over with the big sidder, Boomie flinched

Rabbi Neuberger said By you its the jesus season and on the jesus season youre not supposed to hit so I dont hit

He said Ill show you Im in the jesus season spirit Ill give you each and every one the bunch a special jesus season spirit blessing

He did it very very fast in Jewish

I got only something with Hitler and us and that he was willing

Gelfmans indian nut machine is broken and when you want nuts all you have to do is tilt it left and give a bang on the handle

Teitlebaum is having a Christmas special on american cheese but Mommy said its only the ends

I and Boomie and Hymie the Hitter walked to the Half Moon Hotel and back

Hymie had matches We took garbage can paper and we lit it under the boardwalk and we all three made urinations to put out the fire

As it started to get very very cold we all went home

On the way back by nutsy Irving we met Marshall Herberg He wanted to know if there was any BATTLE ACES S.A.C. meeting

Boomie said I cant help it can you help it Hymie

Hymie said I cant help it can you help it Shimmy

I said I cant help it

We gave him all three right on the head

When I went up Mommy and Daddy were talking about the unveiling from the society

Mommy said Mrs. Plaut worked it out that they could go with only one fare

Daddy said they could even walk over from where the unveiling is to where her Mommas grave is

Mommy said for that that matter once theyre there its no trip at all and they can go over say hello to Daddys Cousin Shlomo in the hospital, she dont forget so easy how he used to save her his shirt cardboards for under the sink

Daddy said if were at the hospital already then it means were practically passing by Label Steiner, we could say hello how are you I understand he cant last much longer

Mommy said on the way home from him how do you like this for an idea well go into Oslers Surgical Supply well get you a new elastic bandage you can save plenty by Osler because what he can sell for nobody can sell for

Daddy then kissed Mommy and Mommy let him

After that she cried a little

She said how we should all of us live and be well and be together as a family unit and know only good good things and for the next 120 years we should only only be making happy plans

Dec. 27, 1933

I and Daddy had a fight

For a change

Mommy said that whats wrong with Daddy is he was in the house too long and he should be aired out a little

She made me go walk with him

We met Marilyn Benders father on the way, he worked once with Daddy

Mr. Bender embarassed me in a nice way

He said Marilyn likes me and comes home to tell how I am the smartest one in the class

We all went into Lubin, Mr. Bender bought me a lemon-lime

Lubin came over and he wanted to know why Mr. Bender gets from him only the Forvitz now

Mr. Bender told him he loved all the papers and when

c*

they had normal conditions he was the best customer for papers

Lubin said that with a Hitler you dassnt talk normal conditions and that that is definitely not a normal man

I showed off a little for Mr. Bender, I said that Hitlers real name is Shicklegruber

Lubin and Mr. Bender couldnt get over I knew, Daddy said from baseball I know shit

Lubin said how were better off here with a Deppresion then with a Hitler

Daddy said in these things he likes to listen to his Manager, his Manager told him Hitler has it in for the Jews

Mr. Bender said what got him and he got sick over it was that the Jews had to wash down Hitlers streets

Daddy said he saw it in the movietone

Lubin said what got him was that while the Jews washed down the streets the German soldiers were laughing and laughing

Daddy said he noticed in the movietone all the soldiers had on the number-three line cap

Mr. Bender said that for all the dictaters its the favorite line, when their people put on caps they put on only the number-three line

Daddy said they know whats good and it was always a classy line

More on Dec. 27, 1933

Two things I forgot to put down for yesterday

The two are

1 Marilyn Bender came in looking for her father and he then bought the both of us lemonlimes

2 I read practically a whole OPERATOR 5 for nothing Lubin didnt like it but he couldnt say anything if Daddy was there

3

Then in late September, 1935, after a *Yom Kippur* of such unseasonable heat that Cantor Myron Pogensky keeled over while blowing the *shofar* and Gelfman, for the first time since he was in business, sold out completely his loose ice cream; around the time Mrs. Berman's Seymour broke off with the bakery lady's daughter, causing his mother in the pleasure of the moment to finally pass a medium-sized kidney stone; when small signs bloomed all over Teitlebaum's window (GAS AND ELECTRIC BILLS CAN BE PAID HERE; OFFICIAL CATERERS TO B. CHARNEY VLADECK BRANCH WORKMEN'S CIRCLE; TO SERVE YOU BETTER THERE WILL BE A 3¢ CHARGE FOR ALL SHOPPING BAGS ON ORDERS UNDER $1.10); when Ringelman the Dentist was said to be laying hands on young wives and talking to them of married love; when Mrs. Holzberg, turned wild and a little crazy from change of life, threw her husband, then her bedding out of the house; when the Sacramento announced it would carry a full kosher meat line under the supervision of Rabbi Leo Eisenman; when Hymie's *bubbee* suffered her first small stroke and began crooning "Suckyfucky" from the window; a few days after the *Mirror* ran a photo of Liba Shefner dancing with Senator Wagner during the Skirt Workers General Assembly in Atlantic City; near the time Rita Pomerantz rid herself of her labial S and became a permanent substitute in the junior high-school system; while the Knishe Queen still had not decided about putting in tables; the day Willy, the super for 1895 and 1897 Brighton 3rd, was caught exposing himself near the back of the Corsetorium; when sixty-three pigeons were poisoned outside the Pokerino on Bay 7; during the week Chic Sale died and Lupe Velez was a surprise guest on the Joe Penner show and Mrs. Leibson claimed to have seen Belle Baker snoozing in a deck chair before the Half-Moon Hotel; Simon, Boomie, Hymie the Hitter, and Marshall Herberg, having disposed of all outstanding Battle Aces business (Resolved: to eat Chinks, to write away for Hit Parade tickets, to walk to Kings Highway and back or at least halfway back, to buy a set of throwing knives or a Benjamin air pistol, to save up for the airplane ride at Floyd Bennett Field, to work together on the Famous Faces Contest in the *News,* to hold out till the *King Kong* and the *Son of Kong* bill came down to the Neptune, to accidentally-on-purpose drop a lipsticked Kotex near Lila Edelstein), plopped themselves on the Oriental rug in Marshall's living room, and, by the flickering yellowish light of his mother's two *yahrzeit* lamps, very slowly opened their flies.

Marshall spoke first, saying, "Do it in handkerchiefs."

Boomie went, *"Oy,* godder do in hangchiffs."

"Right, that's *right,"* Marshall came back. "It's my *house* and it's my *rug* and I don't feel like when my mother walks in, she'll walk in, and she should—"

"Hi-ho, hooh-hah, hello, hello boy-iss"—Boomie jacked himself up by an elbow—"votcha doing, yuh playink nice? Mine goodness, giff hah looky-looky how mine Marshel*eh* got such hensome frentz, they got such byuhdiful big fat red *putzes,* yummy yummy, shlurp shlurp, lemme giff hah lickey on the dickey . . ."

70

"She'll walk in," Marshall persisted, "she'll right away see scum in the rug."

"*Oy*, I'm dyink, I'm right now killink myself, they got scum in mine ruk. . . !"

"You know you know how to take out scum in the rug? Heh?" said Simon.

"I give hah walk-in, I dun take off even mine cawset, I ride away see scum in mine ruk . . ."

"You rub SHIT on it!" Simon yelled.

"Listen. You know what? Just"—Marshall sniffed in—"cut it out and shut your ass with my mother."

"Now I lost my hardon," Hymie muttered, kicking his heels like a swimming frog.

"Think think think of your *bubbee*," Boomie intoned. "You are thinking of your *bubbee* . . ."

"Buhletch!"

". . . only of your *buhbee*. She is taking off the bloomers, the *buhbee* is taking off the dirty, the filthy, the *fahcokter* bloomers, and while she is taking off the dirty, the filthy, the *fahcokter* bloomers she's going 'Uhtz . . . uhtz . . . uhtz' and she lets off a long, a smelly, a dribbly, a gurgly, a disgusting . . ."

"I don't do your mother," said Marshall. "I don't do how your mother calls you from the window!"

"You wanna hear what *he* does with his mother? What he does with his mother is"—Boomie kissed a pinkie—"I swear to God . . ."

"This—this is your mother, and like this she calls you: 'Boom*eleh*, gaw by dah bakery, tell them they should pud avay fah me hah tvist.' "

". . . he listens when she gets laid."

Hymie smacked the side of his head.

Simon made a hard, cold, mean, little face.

And both together emitted a great gloating whinny.

" 'Should be hah tvist,' " Marshall went on doggedly, " 'mid-out seeds.' "

"And what he does—you'll hear what he does . . ."

"Waddah waddah fucking bastard, wowee you are a real fucking bastard, a *fuck*in bastard," Marshall droned, fighting down a swift squirty smile.

". . . she gets laid, his mother, and this guy pulls off."

"You see? See how you're a fuckinbastid? A fuckinbastid *and* a lousy rat *and* a snitchartist! Ooh, are you a snitch-artist!" Monkeylike, Marshall flapped his arms.

"Waddahya mean 'she gets laid'?" asked Hymie, blinking and frowning with great concentration.

"Fucked," Simon chirped cheerfully, helpfully. "Banged."

"Vod id iss," said Boomie in his Lew Lahr voice, "iss dot der man shtupps inside der tvat mid der pecker und mid der pecker all der vay in he . . ."

"I didn't mean for a definition, I meant," Hymie considered for a moment, "hahdaya know—no kidding, I'm not kidding around—like if she's really *doing* it—hahdaya *know?*"

"*Hahdaya know!*" Marshall mimicked. "How I know is I know, that's how I . . ."

"Because like with my mother," said Hymie, "when my mother does it I never even . . ."

"She tells him," Simon said.

"Marshell*eh*," Boomie piped, "hoo-hah, Marshell*eh*, om suh heppy, om suh gled, your fodduh is givink me tonight suh-huch hah ni-hice fuck . . ."

"Didn't I tell you?" Marshall snapped. "I told you! Shut . . . your . . . assonmymother!"

"No, without the shit"—Hymie worked something out of his throat—"and no kidding around. How come you *knew. . . ?*"

"Hehhehheh," went Simon. "The Shadow-ow-ow knows."

". . . on account of there's *supposed* to be a special smell."

All present laughed him down.

"If she didn't have a smell, there was no smell or nothing, so what happened? Tell what happened!"

"What happened, I hafta tell him what happened," Marshall muttered as though in heavy grief.

"What happened?" Boomie bowed his head and swayed slowly sideways. "What happened is—she got fucked!"

Marshall, after his share of laughing, said, "I am getting sore, and why I am getting sore, I am getting sore *really,* is that in the whole bunch I hafta be the dirty one, I hafta tell about my mother a thing like that, *that's* what I am supposed to do, and you, you guys—you never, you wouldn't, you absolutely dassn't. I, if I go up Hymie's *house* and his aunt *comes* and I say that his aunt has a nice pair of knockers . . ."

"Titties, you said!"

". . . fuck *you,* because I remember *knockers.* And what kinda shit is that anyway? If I said *titties* or if I said *knockers* or if I said *boobies.* So you know what he does? I'll *tell* you what he does! He . . . gives me . . . a rap . . . a shot. . . . In the arm, right on the bone, with all his might. *Sure.* That was for an aunt, and an aunt is far from a mother."

"I—*like* my Aunt Hennie," Hymie said shakily. "On my *bar-mitzvah* she baked everything herself. She hadda take two taxis, that's how much she baked. She brings me model airplanes, the dollar kind."

"The thing, the problem is," Boomie said cagily, "*as* I see it, is if he has *a* lot of aunts how do we know which aunt is his Aunt Hennie?"

"Wa-ah, ooh-ootz"—Marshall was rubbing and blowing at his arm—"where he gave me that shot, yaknow it hurts like anything and it still didn't go way?"

"I *think* I know which aunt his Aunt Hennie must be," said Boomie in a small voice.

"I bet I bet," said Simon with great wonder, "she must be and his Aunt Hennie must be . . ."

And both together chanted: "THE ONE WITH THE BIG-IG TITS!"

"With all his might," Marshall lamented.

"You know what?" Hymie was suddenly philosophical and detached. "You wanna deal? You tell a little bit about what happened—a little bit and not even the whole thing—I lecher gimme a free boff back. A deal?"

"*Not* a deal," announced Marshall.

"*Two* boffs free, they can be both on the same arm."

"Not a deal, no deal, lemme alone, and you got a big—fat—fuckingnerve."

"Two boffs free and I gotta fuckingnerve!"

"The biggest fuckingnerve I ever saw!" And Boomie, with both hands, measured off a good eleven inches of air.

"Know why ya got a fuckingnerve?" Marshall roughed up his voice. "*Why* ya got a fuckingnerve and also you're a wise guy is that I am supposed to, for two boffs free . . ."

". . . the same arm, what I said."

". . . I should tell on my mother something like that, so I should be the dirty one, *sure,* I, myself, and me."

"That's dirty?" Simon enlarged his eyes and batted his lashes. "Just just just to tell how your mother gets laid, what's so dirty?"

"Ya know the one, you know it, the hillbilly brother is laying the hillbilly sister and he says to her, 'Duh, Sis, you're a better, duh, lay then Ma.' And she says, 'Duh, yeah, that's what' "—Boomie sputtered with glee—" 'Duh, yeah, that's what PAW tells me!' "

Marshall went, "Duh, yeah, duh, yeah."

"Marshie does it *too* good," Simon observed.

"If *he* had a sister—" Boomie made a moron face and long slow pumping motions.

"If *he* had a sister!" Marshall cried. "So? So if I had a sister. So? What about if *you* had a sister? That's what I mean. *Sure.* I'm the jerkfiend, I'm the dirty guy, my mother is the only one who does it, but your mothers"—his voice began a rise and a tremble—"they're the biggest angels in the world."

"Ma, duh, Ma!" Boomie was still pumping away. "How come, duh, you're the only one, duh, does it, duh?"

74

"Hey, *schmuck,* cut it out!" Hymie blared with refined indignation. To Marshall he said, "I'll makeya another deal, how's this for a deal . . ."

"Vy hom dee huhnly vun, Marshall*eh,* iz dot dee udder mommehs . . ."

Hymie croaked a "*Schmuck!*" at Boomie, saying, "I asked you in a nice way, you know you're sometimes a *schmuck, schmuck* waddaya read?"

"Dee-udder-mommehs-dun-know-vats-good," Boomie rattled off.

"Finished?" said Hymie.

"Finished," said Boomie.

And both together cried, "WIPE YOURSELF!"

"Let's go and how about it." Simon started a tentative fingering. "Let's do—I say we should do—let's do Anne Shirley. Anne Shirley in the one where she's just just gonna take a bath and she's futzing around and she pulls up the dress and you see near the ass . . ."

"Anne Shirley." Boomie's eyes and hands swished skyward. "Anne Shirley and Anne Shirley and Anne Shirley and Anne Shirley, him with his . . ."

"You didn't say—nah nah, not much," went Simon, "oh not much—you said to me exactly, 'Gee, I'd like to . . . fuck . . . that!' "

"Right, right, I'd like to fuck her, what I said," Boomie affirmed. "Sure, I wouldn't mind *fucking* her and fucking her I wouldn't mind. But I don't feel like jerking off on her."

"Fuck Anne Shirley!" Hymie cried.

"Lufto . . ." Simon began.

"Where . . . ?" Boomie began at the same instant.

Hymie first cuffed them like handballs, then in a voice pitched for an auditorium said, "I propose hereby that—this is what I propose for a deal—Marshie should tell the thing with his mother, but he should tell it *after*—that we hafta tell a thing with our mothers, first *we* hafta."

"Hasta be," Marshall faltered, "put in with the proposal 'a *dirty* thing.'"

"Right, and no shit, a dirty thing. I propose *and* make hereby the motion how it hasta be a dirty thing."

By voice vote the motion was carried.

Then Hymie let this be known: That he had one day searched all drawers for loose change; that near a jockstrap and a batch of old union books his hand had struck against something hard; that he had fished out a Louis Sherry Continental Mixture box; that while rummaging around the crochet needles, fountain-pen bladders, cigarette-lighter cases, barrettes, and snips of tailor's chalk he had for no good reason begun to breathe through his mouth and to fill up with criminal joy; that he likened this feeling to the feeling he had once under the bakery lady's daughter's window, when he knew without knowing he knew that she would soon undress; that he had shaken out from a Camp Mohavet dinner menu ribbon, a tissue, and three snapshots; that these three snapshots were blotchy and without borders and faded to the color of vanilla syrup; that he had spotted his mother easily despite the playful aviator's goggles that swam on her; that she had been otherwise naked; that she had been posed between two big mirrors in such a way as to show off his father's young face and her own black bush; that he had been struck with great force by this bush; that it had reminded him of Mutt's moustache and Captain Katzenjammer's beard.

Then Simon let it be known that he too had beheld his mother's black bush, and in this fashion: That on a certain Saturday morning his father had cramps; that all through the day he lay about groaning and in great pain; that his mother considered a call to Levinger, the Society doctor; that she spoke of how she lacked confidence in him, of how long years ago she had tried reaching him and had lost two nickels on the call; that she had anyway taken one more chance on him; that when he came she had kissed him and

knuckled his neck and pleaded for old movie magazines; that
when he had written out his prescription she stuck her face
into her hands; that shaken by tearless sobbing she told him
of what had recently befallen her; that after doing the floors
and the windows and taking the bedding down from the roof
she had suffered hot flushes on one cheek; that she had been
his mother's best customer for pearl barley; that for the fun
of it and to ease an orphan's mind he should take her pressure; that she would make it quick and easy for him; that
with one hand she had pulled him into the bedroom and
with the other shucked off house dress, undershirt, and
bloomers; that her black bush did not remind him of Mutt's
moustache or Captain Katzenjammer's beard; that with a
hat and a cigarette holder it could be Charlie Chan.

Then Boomie let it be known that he had never exactly
seen his mother's black bush; that such joys he could still
spare himself; that a sneaky peek once at her knockers was
good or bad enough; that they had lapped over her fat front
like a pair of *latkes,* that they came down a good three inches
below her navel; that with the least little stooping she could
use them for shoehorns; that the nipples reminded him of
cat shit or of what was on the bottom of enema bags; that
he wondered how his father ever laid eyes or anything else
on her twat; that she most likely had to first piss and give
him a clue; that along with her other delights she was an
open prober of nose and navel; that her belches could keep
a zeppelin aloft; that she was in general and in every particular a slob; that if they did her in the movies she would be
played by Wallace Beery; that the moment his father started
shaving was the moment she spread herself on the toilet seat;
that she smelled of wet mops and old vaseline; that she
seemed to have the rag on every Monday and Thursday; that
when and where she walked she picked at her skirt, front
and back; that she was continually rubbing zinc ointment
into her chapped and blotchy thighs; that after this rubbing
she would sniff her fingers, then her armpits, then her bloom-

ers; that when he considered these odors, singly or in amalgam, he cleansed himself by thoughts of gargling with shit.

". . . with loose shit," Boomie finished up.

"Loose shit," Simon said languorously. "Yummy, yummy, yummy, yum."

"Loose . . . green . . . dribbly shit-t-t." Boomie let out his tongue and sucked in saliva. "Plippy, ploppy, plyuchy shit from Hymie's *bubbee*'s asshole, guhshy, wuhshy shit with hair on it."

Marshall, to show he was of their humor, leered awfully and did a "Vomit. Slishy, glishy, pishy, snotty, and with . . . scumonit!"

Whereupon Boomie looked at Simon, saying, "Hey, right ball!"

And Simon looked at Boomie, answering, "Hey, left ball!"

And both together looked at Marshall, and in the same sociable, good-natured tone recited, "WHO'S THAT PRICK IN THE MIDDLE!"

And both together moved suddenly and grabbed and squeezed.

And Marshall fought them off with soft, girlish slaps, and he called them fucks and fairies and fairy-fucks.

And while he was cupping his crotch Hymie tweaked his nipples and growled, "So?"

Marshall gave back the same "So?"

"So? So. So so so."

Marshall made a dumb show of threading and stitching.

"Your turn," said Hymie, and "You go."

Marshall was snipping thread.

"We went, now you go," Hymie said righteously. "Your turn, you hafter . . ."

"I hafta? Wakiner hafta? I doan hafta and wherezit *written* I hafta."

Hymie slouched forward and banged his brows, going "Wowee!" and "Zaddafuck, waddafuck!"

And Boomie fluttered fingers at Marshall. "You wanna

78

know—he wantsa know—wherezit written."

". . . wanna know."

"In our constitution is wherezit written."

"Yeah, oh yeah, sure. *Sure.*" Marshall nodded and drummed on his lips. "Suresuresuresure, in the constitution is wherezit written, itzin the constitution I hafta tell you how my mother gets laid."

"Is your dick big enough to touch your ass?" Boomie was honestly curious.

"Doan hafta worry," Marshall told the *yahrzeit* lamps. "You *hafta* worry, you *wanna* worry, worry about *your* dick, you got *more* to worry . . ."

"That's not a fair question? Thatza fair question, so answer. Answer!" Boomie said. "Zit big enough to touch your ass?"

"Big enough," Marshall told the potted plants.

"So go fuck yourself."

"Know anything about hockey?" Marshall returned.

"Yeah, yeah, puck you," Boomie finished. "And you're a real fucking baby. Because. Because one of the first things— the first thing in the constitution is there's a motion and there's a majority on the motion, that's it. That's *it!* Otherwise the person gets under the"—Boomie did his Shadow laugh—"penalty clause."

"The puh-puh-puh-puh-penalty clause . . ." Simon pitched forward to the rug, clutching his throat.

"*Yisgadal, vyiskadash,*" cried Hymie, covering his head with a doily. "Have I got a penalty and have I got a penalty."

"Waddaya doing *Kaddish?*" Marshall said dully. "*Kaddish* he has to do. Ya fuck around with *Kaddish,* that's doing a sin."

"Buy condrums!" Hymie screamed. "In the Silver Rod and when it's jammed."

"Jammed!" Simon screamed also. "And to wait on him there's only only a lady!"

"I . . . got . . . a . . . better penalty." And Boomie snarled, "Showusyourdick!"

"The only one who never never did," said Simon.

"No, nah, never." Marshall blinked and squinted as though dealing with smoke in his eyes.

"Name me one time," said Simon.

"One time, I hafta name you one time, okay, *sure* I'll name you one time." Marshall made a pass in the air. "From now on your name is—ONE TIME!"

"Name me one one one time for a nickel."

"A nickel a *shtickel!*" yipped Hymie.

"A nickel a dickel!" yipped Boomie.

"The one time I did it, I'll *tell* you the one time I did it . . ."

"Mine liddle Marshall*eh*," Boomie simpered, "he got zuch hah big dickel, you wahna hear how its's big?"

"In the Surf I did it, when they had *Viva Villa*."

". . . venn he vantsa take id out I godda helff him mid it!"

"You know how big it is?" Hymie brought his pinkie slowly, slowly out of his fly and stopped at the first joint.

"On the part where Wallace Beery's gonna do it to Fay Wray . . ."

"Oohoohoohooh, I'd . . . like . . . to . . . fuck THAT!" Hymie reflected. "That already I would like to fuck."

"Only one time that was . . ."

"Is he fulla shit!" cried Simon with a face of despair. "You are so so so fulla shit, wowee, it's coming outta your ears!"

"I'm fulla shit? *Sure.* If I'm fulla shit what are you?"

"You know what about Fay Wray?" Hymie reflected darkly. "They put her in parts where they always wanna do it to her. Like in *King Kong*."

Boomie murmured, "*Oy oy oy,* mine Marshall*eh* god hah *shlong* like King Kong."

"He took it out!" Simon wailed. "Know how he took it out? For oneoneone second. For not even a second."

"I'll do it for an hour!" Marshall burst out. Then feigning mildness and affability, he said softly, *"Sure, that's right, sure.* Absolutely and why *not.* Ya *wan* me to do it for an hour, I'll *do* it an hour, who says no, I'll do it *more* then an hour, *sure,* I'll do it till when they put on the lights, when they do Lucky Number, that's *right,* I'll call my Cousin Lillie to turn around, 'Cousin Lillie, hey Cousin Lillie, turn around, ya wanna see something Cousin Lillie, see, see Cousin Lillie, lemme stand on the seat ya should see better,' absolutely, definitely and positively, why not. *Sure . . ."*

There was silence for quite a while.

Then Boomie rose and winked at Simon; and Simon rose and made signs to Hymie; and Hymie rose and patted his chest and got busy picking a scab off an elbow; and Simon moved in on Marshall's left side; and Hymie moved in on Marshall's right side; and Boomie moved first against Marshall's right side and then against his left side and when Marshall was out of position Boomie dipped between his legs; and Simon and Hymie tickled and pinched under his armpits and around his nipples; and though Marshall cried "Fuck off!" and "Not ticklish!" his hands were driven up and away from his fly; and Boomie shouted "Hutz-hutz, show us the *putz!*"; and Simon shouted "Ding-dong, take out the *shlong!*"; and Hymie shouted "Tick-tock, we want the cock!"; and Marshall, giggly and in a baby voice said, "Eheheheheh" and "Meheheheh," and shut his eyes and squeezed and quivered as though straining on a potty and whimpered "Mah-hommy"; and Marshall followed this with a "Mommy-Mommy"; and then Marshall's voice went off in six directions; and very soon he said in his own voice and with strange regularity, "Ma . . . Ma . . . Ma . . . Ma"; and he seemed no longer to feel the tickling and pinching; and Boomie and Simon and Hymie let up on him; and they laughed, largely from astonishment; and Marshall caught his breath and locked it against his palate and pretended that he had all along sought to deceive them; and Boomie and Simon and Hymie whooped with laughter to show that they had not been at all deceived but that in seeking to practice such deceit Marshall had violated a trust and merited from them much more meanness; and that Marshall had willed this meanness in something like the same way that Laurel willed Hardy's smacks and smashes; and when Marshall sought to raise himself from the rug they pushed him down; and Marshall pushed back, but carefully and with less force; and Marshall clamped his thighs together and grabbed his groin and called, "Mommy, come to the window," and "Mommy, they're starting up with me"; and Boomie answered him with a "Marshell*eh,* dun bodder deh mommy ven she's gedding herself some nice fuxing"; and Marshall laughed inordinately at this; and Boomie sucked in air and opened his mouth as though for a belch but farted instead; and Simon and Hymie ran right away and opened the windows and while at the windows sang *Lulu Had a Baby* into the air shaft; and Boomie started Marshall laughing again with his "Marshell*eh*"; and Hymie dug into Marshall's thigh and twisted the fatty part; and Simon gave him a two-fingered slice right under his testicles; and all three talked over his head.

SIMON: Let's let's pull out his cock hair.

HYMIE: Three atta time.

BOOMIE: He got only three.

HYMIE: How about the ball hairs. The teensy-weensy-weensy-weensy-weensy-weensy—

BOOMIE: He got no balls.

MARSHALL: Balls cried the queen, if I hadem I'd be king, and the king laughed because he had to.

SIMON: How about he hasta suck himself off.

MARSHALL: Yummy yummy yummy, gobble gobble gobble.

BOOMIE: Take it in the mouth for a trip down South!

SIMON: Take it in the ear for a bottle of beer!

MARSHALL: Glub glub, gobble gobble, shlurp shlurp, yum yum.

SIMON: Take it in the belly for Patsy Kelly!

BOOMIE: Take it in the throat for a Quaker Oat!

82

MARSHALL: Ma . . .

BOOMIE: Take it in the chin for Rin Tin Tin!

MARSHALL: Mah-hah . . .

SIMON: Take it in the snatch for a Diamond match!

BOOMIE: Take it in the tits for Zazu Pitts!

HYMIE: Take it in the soup for Alley Oop!

SIMON: Soup is no good . . .

BOOMIE: Body, hastabe . . .

HYMIE: Hastabe?

BOOMIE:
SIMON: Hastabe!

MARSHALL: Mah-hah-hah-hah!

HYMIE: Boopcoopdoop . . . kloop shloop ploop . . . poop, in
the *poop,* poop is body, poop is ass . . .

BOOMIE: Poop is ass!

SIMON: Shit, whakiner shit!

HYMIE: In the poop for Alley Oop!

MARSHALL (*palming his ears*): Ma, tellem stop, Mommy!

SIMON (*shouting into* Marshall's *left ear*): Take it in the
shlong for Anna May Wong!

MARSHALL (*rolling on the rug*): Nuh, nah, not that!

BOOMIE (*shouting into* Marshall's *left ear*): Take it in the tit
for a can of Flit!

MARSHALL (*pretending to faint, revive, faint again*): Ahr, I'll
talk, I'll tell! The murd . . . ruh . . . is . . . AHR . . .

HYMIE (*shouting into* Marshall's *face*): Take it in the sun for
Irene Dunne!

BOOMIE: Body!

SIMON: Sun isn't . . .

MARSHALL: No, no, not that, anything but that, ooh, aah,
I'll talk, I'll tell, I'll sing how my mother got laid!

HYMIE: Seriously?

MARSHALL: Sure. That's right. *Sure.*

BOOMIE: Vod hah doidy boy tuh tell on how his mommy gets
fuxed!

HYMIE: Nah, seriously. Seriously?

MARSHALL: Seriously, I'm being serious, I said "seriously," I was serious, sure, that's right, I seriously said I would sing how my mother gets laid so now I'll sing how my mother gets laid: How, dah-deeh-dah, my mother, doo-do-dah, gets . . .

HYMIE: Okay, never mind, you're not being serious.

MARSHALL: *How . . . My . . . Mother . . . Gets . . . Laid.* By Marshall Herberg. *A* composition. Ahem, ahem. Topic sentence: My mother gets laid.

SIMON: He doesn't even even do a good topic sentence.

HYMIE: I don't like it when I'm serious to a guy and the guy isn't serious back.

MARSHALL: Want me to be serious?

HYMIE (*to* Simon *and* Boomie): In gym, you know what? He goes and undresses in the toilet.

MARSHALL: Four . . . free . . . boffs. For four free boffs I'll be serious.

HYMIE: Fuck you on four, fuck yourself, I gave you two only.

MARSHALL: That's *right.* You gave me two, *sure* you gave me two. *Sure.* Only your two are like my four. And fuck you, too.

BOOMIE (*suddenly jumps up and stiffens and quavers*): Mrs. H-h-herberg, hello, hello, Mrs. Herberg.

All present are startled, then all present pretend to be showing off their open flies. Marshall goes over to Hymie and stands around flexing his fingers, massaging his right fist, and stroking Hymie's arm, saying, "Boff!" Hymie mouths a "Two" and holds up two fingers. Marshall mouths a "Fuck you" and holds up four fingers. Boomie argues against four boffs on the same arm and in the same spot. Simon suggests two boffs on each arm and in the same spot, and Boomie suggests four boffs on the same arm but in different spots. Marshall rolls up a sleeve and shows all present the green and yellow marks he bears yet from Hymie's boffs. Hymie manfully cries "Fuck you, do four, do the four where ya want!" Marshall dusts off Hymie's arm, blows on it, studies it from a crouch and from tiptoe, wipes each of his fingers and between his fingers. He cackles cruelly at Hymie's "So?", he licks his lips, he measures off six, seven, eight steps, he tamps down with his heel a snip of rug, he backs up three more steps, he shouts "TARDAH!", he bounds forward, and going "Boffee, boffee, boffee, boom," he gives Hymie four high, soft, open-handed swats. Boomie and Simon laugh and laugh at the way Hymie gapes mutely. Simon sings "Two, four, six, eight, who do we appreciate?" All present yell out the "Marshall!"

"He's starting again his shit," Hymie grumbled.

"*Schmuck, putzo*, givim a chance!" commanded Boomie, striking Hymie lightly on the head with both fists. "He opens his mouth ya don't givim a chance, right away it's shit." And to Marshall: "Waddaya starting the shit again?"

"He was just just just reading to her?" said Simon.

"That's right. *Sure*," Marshall muttered. "All he's doing, he's reading to her a hot book. To you a hot book is just only reading. That's right. *Sure*."

"Was he reading or was he fucking?" Hymie upped his voice.

"He was reading *and* he was fucking!" And Marshall also upped his voice.

"Your father," Boomie hastily came in, "must be some fuckin reader."

Marshall made his back completely straight and still, locked fingers, centered his hands on an imaginary desk, and with maddening slowness once again began. "He put on the little night light, what they use only for *Shabos*, that's what maybe woke me up, I say 'maybe' because—because I can sleep usually if they got every light burning in the house. So maybe I was in, like, a light sleep, that's right, sure. *Sure*, I was in a light sleep, like, you know when you're in a light sleep and ya get one of those dreams, sort of you walk in the dream, not *sort* of, because in the dream ya really do walk, and while ya walk ya make a bad step, like, and that bad step, it wakes ya up and when ya wake up the leg is going like ya *really* made a bad step. Right? That's how my leg is going, and it wakes me up, and I hear my father. I hear him before I even notice the *Shabos* light is on, and I think the first thing I thought of on account of the *way* he was talking was he talking about how somebody died. He talked in the exact same way when he heard my *zaideh* died, like he's—in *shul* and he's *dovinning* and ya do it in a singsong: 'Geh-peh-meh, Poppa's dead, it's a dream and they're kidding me, shmeh-beh-deh, waddaya talking about he's dead, it's a *kibbitz*, they're giving me a *kibbitz*, geh-peh-shmeh-beh-deh, what then, I know him, how I know him, reh-peh-peh-peh-peh, Poppa Poppa, you'll surprise me, I betcha I betcha that's what it is, zeh-zeh-zeh-deh-deh, I'll go inside the *shvitz*, I'm telling you because I know him, he'll be taking it easy on the daybed. Oh boy, he'll be *fressing* an egg and onion sandwich, ha-beh-beh-beh, and he'll gimme the crust, the hard part, what then, he knows, you know how I love the crust, Poppa Poppa, keh-keh . . .' "

". . . leh-leh," sang Boomie, "how about hot-tot parts?"

". . . shmeh-shmeh," Simon picked up, "the hot hot hot parts!"

To which Marshall made reply, "You *want* hot parts? Youkin *get* hot parts. *Sure.* Why *not*? Ab-solutely. *Sure.* Ya know what to do? I'll *tell* ya what to do. What ya should do is—take your prick, go to the gas range, put it on topper the gas range and—ya *got* a hot part. Right? That's *right*."

Simon went "Heh-heh-heh-heh." Boomie made his head hang and his tongue protrude, and Hymie, straining forward between them, begged for one, only one *zetss*.

Marshall did a spiteful "Ha-zeh-zeh-zeh," then said, "I'm getting to the hot part, gimme a chance, ya don't gimme a chance, give a person a chance . . ."

Hymie, after looking high and low and back and forth, declared that he would always and anytime give a person a chance. A *person* . . .

Marshall said, "Zatso?"

Hymie said, "Zatso."

Marshall rose, raised his fists, and instructed Hymie to do the same.

"I got one word for you," said Marshall.

Hymie, his back like a cat's, begged for the word.

"Ya want the word? I'll *give* ya the word. Sure. Why *not?*"

And Marshall opened his mouth slowly and as high and wide as it would go and brought up an agonized constricted "Ma!"

All present whooped and whinnied, and they stamped and pounded the floor. Till the airshaft rumbled with a "Hey hey, Coxey's Army!" and "Y'understand English? Sharrup *dort!*"

Simon and Boomie and Hymie scooted to the window, and though Marshall pulled them by their belts and gave them slices and gooses, they nevertheless bloomed into song:

> In the shade of the old apple tree.
> It was there that she showed it to me.
> It looked like a dot,
> She called it her twat
> In the shade of the old apple tree!

"Okay. That's it. I'm finished. No more. Good-bye. Good luck. That's it." Marshall buttoned his fly and pointed to the door.

"No no no guy has a fourteen-inch cock," said Simon.

"What he *read* to her, what I *heard,*" said Marshall.

"That big," announced Hymie, "is too big. That big is —yaknow how big?—it's like a ruler, a regular, ordinary ruler *plus* two inches."

Patiently, Marshall said, "The fourteen-inch part is the part I got exactly. Ya want me to swear I got everything exact? Okay, sure, I'll swear. That's *right!* Why *not!* Ya *want* bull shit—I'll *give* ya bull shit." Through his hands, Marshall called out, "Hey, Daddy, hey read a little louder before ya fuck, I can't hear! Sure . . ."

"Do, kinya do that part again?" Hymie asked. " 'I rammed my prick—her wet frothy cunt . . .' "

"I put lox in her box," Boomie mused. "I put a match in her snatch."

" 'Rammed' I'm not *sure*," Marshall said to Hymie. "I don't want to be a bull-shit artist, I shouldn't say positively it was rammed because—because maybe it was *crammed* or *jammed*. Right?"

Boomie answered, "That's *right!*"

Simon said, "*Sure . . .*"

"Like this, this is how it, like, went." Marshall tapped his brows, shut his eyes, and chewed on his tongue. " 'Have you ever been fucked?' I softly asked or I asked softly. 'No, I am cherry,' I was told, 'for I am something something something and something about my pussy, I have a small pussy and would something something get it hurt by a long, thick dick or a long, thick *prick*.' I said, while I took off my pants slowly, 'Dear, don't you know that a big prick will not hurt you, not at all, something something, your pussy *wants* a big prick, a big prick is *good* for a small pussy.' 'But I something something afraid.' With my pants off I turned and—this is absolutely exact—and put my fourteen, it was fourteen, my *fourteen* inches *of* prick, before I said fourteen-inch prick but it was fourteen inches *of* prick, between her parted or parting thighs and with the power-ful head tickled her wet frothy cunt . . ."

"That part I love," piped Hymie.

"Fourteen inches!" Simon cried. "That that that would go, fourteen inches . . ."

"I really love that part."

." 'Do you something something possible for your long, thick dick or long, thick prick to fit into my small pussy? Oh . . . oh . . . oh if it is only . . .' "

". . . your knees," Simon said, "and even even to your knees it wouldn't be fourteen inches, not with a hardon."

"Fourteen inches. So? So what's so wonderful and what's so hot about fourteen inches?" Boomie demanded.

"Yask me why I love that part"—Hymie chuckled—"I couldn't tell why I love it."

"Ya don't *wanna* hear"—Marshall folded his arms—"ya don't *have* to hear. Sure . . ."

"Fourteen inches," Boomie mumbled, "that's nothing, that's shit, and I bet, I bet ya between Marshie and me we got fourteen inches."

"*Sure. That's right!*"

"Easy, an easy fourteen inches. Ya know how? Ya take"— Boomie was filling with laughter—"my twelve and Marshie's two."

"That's . . . *it.*" Marshall folded his arms.

"How about my . . . " Simon waited and waited, then dove in under the laughter. "My seven, your six, and Marshey's ONE!"

"For-*get* it. It's finished. Fuck *you*," said Marshall.

Simon went, "Heh heh."

Boomie pinched his nose and furiously fanned air.

Hymie blared, "Waddaya putting the stink on me?"

"Hoddaya know"—Simon considered a moment—"how how how do you know your *mother* laid the fart?"

"Hey-ah, watsa the mat wit choo!" Boomie cried in his Henry Armetta voice. "Who elsa mudder gonna lay-uh! A mudder, she lays-uh only da fart . . . !"

"In the middle of fucking she farts!" Hymie did something delicate with his mouth.

"How I know is she's my mother. She's my mother and I know how my mother farts."

"His-a mudder's fart!" exclaimed Boomie.

"Betcha betcha he put it in the wrong hole." And Hymie cackled a C. Henry Gordon cackle.

"I-uh know-uh his-uh mudder's fart, his-uh mudder's fart, thassa his-uh *grand*-uh-fart!"

"Also how I know is my father laughed . . ."

"*Sure* he laughed. *Sure*," said Boomie. "After all, they were farting around."

"Were they fucking when she farted?" Hymie asked.

"I think," Marshall told him, "I'm not *sure*, I think he was sucking on her tit."

"Which one?" Hymie demanded.

"Which one?" Marshall answered in Hymie's tone.

"Which one?" Hymie insisted in Marshall's tone.

"Which one? All *right*, ya wanna know which one, I'll *tell* ya which one. Sure. The *middle* one."

"Why I ask—know why I ask?"

"*Sure* I know. Why you ask is—you're a *schmuck*."

"The left one you're supposed to do it on," Hymie explained.

". . . *supposed* to do it on the left one so he was *doing* it on the left one," Marshall conceded. "Why . . . *not*."

"*Sure*," said Simon.

"That's *right*," said Boomie.

"When ya do it on the left one," Hymie said with determination, "it works on them, it's supposed to work on them a certain way, it gets them hot in the box."

"He's worried, don't worry," Marshall assured him. "Ya don't hafta worry about if my mother was hot in the box. She was *plenty* hot in the box. Oh *boy* was she hot in the box! Ya wanna hear how she was hot in the box, listen to how she was hot. . . !"

"It got got on fire," Simon speculated.

"On fire, it got on fire," Boomie kept going, "and your father hadda piss out the flames."

"That's *right!*" declared Marshall. And he settled into punitive silence.

"Teasing," said Boomie.

"Just just just kidding," said Simon.

"That-ss teasing?" Marshall gazed at them sadly. "*Okay*, it's teasing. To you, it's teasing. To me . . ."

"Marshey, hey, Marshey," pleaded Hymie, "one more

time, c'mon, again, I love it! 'Her wet frothy . . .' "

"Definitely it's teasing. Absolutely it's teasing. Sure it's teasing. My mother's pussy—ho ho, hah hah—is on fire, I'm supposed to laugh. Positively. Why . . . *not!*"

Marshall went "Zinga. Zinga. Zingazinga. Zingazinga-zingazingazinga. Zinga . . . Zinga . . . Zinga . . ."

"I didn't didn't get that," Simon said.

"So long he took?" Hymie moaned. "How long did he take?"

"Long," answered Marshall.

"That long," Hymie mused. "I figured . . ."

"He got lost," Simon butted in.

"He fell in," Boomie added.

". . . no, seriously! Seriously. I figured . . . ya puddid in . . . ya geddid in . . . tzin . . . and bimbamboom."

"Bimbamboom." Marshall made a pass with his hand. "*Sure.* That's *right.*"

"Why it took so long, know why?" Simon said. "He was just just looking for his wristwatch."

"Ya wanna know how long he fucked?" Marshall was asking. "I'll *tell* ya how long. He fucked for such a long time, for so long, he kept fucking and fucking and in and out and in and out . . ."

"Whakiner *out!*" demanded Boomie.

"He hadda hadda cool it off!" screamed Simon.

"He hadda fill it like a fountain pen!" Boomie screamed back.

Firmly, deliberately, Marshall chanted, "*In* and out, in and out, *and* in and out. And my mother says, '*Oy.*' And my father says, 'Clara, I'm hurting ya, something something,' in Jewish. And my mother says, "Lester, something something in Jewish, not hurting me, I felt a rip in the sheet, the Chink oughtta drop dead.' And my father says, '*Nu.*' And my mother says, 'All he knows is to starch, givim starch he's a happy Chink.' And my father says, 'Wow, ooh, ooh, get ready, aah,

D

aah, hehooh, hehooh, hehooh.' And my mother says, 'On shirts he can do beautiful work.' And my father says, 'Heh-hehhootzootzohehheh, get ready, wow, you're getting ready, Clara, wow, get set, in a second, a second, one second, ready, set, I'm gonna make myself happy, sweetheart, something something in Jewish, any second, huh, huh, huh, ooh, you also make a happy, ahahahuffahffaff, *oy, oy, oy,* I . . . made . . . happy-y-y-y.' And my mother says, 'From now uhuhuhuh on, only, hah, hah, shah, shah-shirts.' And that's—the—end."

"Know what?" Boomie jabbed both index fingers at Marshall and started to giggle.

"Don't don't see," said Simon.

"*Schmuck,* ya looking right at it. Right—at—it. *Putzo!*"

And Simon at last went, "Heh heh."

And Hymie yelled, "Makeim room!"

And Simon yelled, "Lift the ceiling!"

And capering and clapping hands all together yelled, "Marshey's godda hardon, Marshey's godda hard-on!"

Marshall gave back a "*Sure.* Why—not? Absol*utely.*"

Though Marshall had called his "Chickee!" in plenty of time they were still wet and wheezing when his parents marched in.

"Never again," said Mrs. Herberg.

"This is it," said Mr. Herberg.

"No more," said Mrs. Herberg.

"Good-bye and good luck," said Mr. Herberg.

"Fifteen cents for their orange drink," said Mrs. Herberg.

"Sugar water," said Mr. Herberg.

"It first made me thirsty," said Mrs. Herberg.

"They wonder why the Jewish stage is dying," said Mr. Herberg.

"Marshell*eh,* it's late," said Mrs. Herberg.

"I'll say at least for the *goyim,* when they put on a show they give you a show," said Mr. Herberg.

"Marshell*eh,* make night," said Mrs. Herberg.

"We hafta hafta hafta go," said Simon.

"Anyway I hafta go," said Boomie.

"Their music is music, their dancing is dancing and their acting is acting," said Mr. Herberg.

"Say good night to your boy friends, ask them if they want some sponge cake before they go, tell them tomorrow morning is another day," said Mrs. Herberg.

"I godda go because I godda get up early, I godda do something for my mother," said Boomie.

"The *goyish* shows don't make a fool out of the public," said Mr. Herberg.

"I hafta bring a whole buncha shirts to the Chink," said Boomie.

"A whole whole whole bunch," said Simon.

"She likes how he does shirts, right Shimmy?" said Boomie.

"She says on shirts he does some some beautiful work," said Simon.

"Sheets she don't give him, sheets he kills, she says on sheets all he knows is to starch," said Boomie.

"I don't say the *goyim* don't give you *dreck,* but their *dreck* has at least a *finesse,*" said Mr. Herberg.

"Your boy friends don't mind, Marshell*eh,* they're not insulted, they also got working people for parents," said Mrs. Herberg.

"*Sure,*" said Simon.

"That's *right,*" said Boomie.

On the way home they went by the Neptune and hung around to watch the ushers setting up the billboards for *King Kong.*

Hymie said that in some parts he looked big and in some parts he looked small.

Simon wondered how it was that they show you King Kong naked but they never show on him a cock.

Boomie told them he had seen the picture three times

already and all three times he was disappointed that when Kong gets loose in the city he does it hardly any damage, only one train he wrecks a little.

Hymie claimed he was bothered always by something else, not that it was so important, but he would have liked them to show where exactly King Kong lives on his island, they never show you where he lives exactly.

Simon recalled that in the part where he takes Fay Wray the first first time he takes her up a cliff and by a cave, so it must be you're supposed to realize he lives in caves.

Boomie gave them to understand that if he got a nickel, only a nickel for every time he had pulled off on Fay Wray's tits in that part the Depression would be over.

Hymie also used Fay Wray in that part, but only to start himself off because he liked to go usually from her tits to Ruby Keeler's legs and finish on the part in *Tarzan Finds His Mate* where Johnny Weismuller saves Maureen O'Sullivan from crocodiles and when they come out the water he's holding her by the ass.

Simon speculated how someday the Battle Aces might end up all together in Hollywood and in Hollywood they might go to a party and at this party there would be a bunch a bunch of actresses and Fay Wray and Maureen O'Sullivan would be in this bunch for Boomie and Hymie and there would be Anne Shirley for him and these actresses would have to shake their hands.

This made them so crazy with laughter that they lurched all over the sidewalk and bumped into Nutsy Irving's newsstand and he came after them with his iron bar saying, "Dogs should have to come and throw cold water on you!"

94

4

Then on the early afternoon of Wednesday, February 15, 1936, the week Teitlebaum ran this sign: "Forget about bringing back the N.R.A. but don't forget to start bringing back the Sheffield empties"; not so long after Mrs. Raphael, meaning to put some luck money in the new pocketbook of Shirley, her middle daughter, fished out a crucifix and a mimeographed postcard confirming an appointment with a Father O'Herlihy; when the neighborhood was still talking and talking about how the Hi-Ho Casino had announced the star of *Hell's Angels* and then brought out not Jean Harlow but Ben Lyon to tell a few jokes and sing a lousy *Eli, Eli!*; and about how Dopey Duhvee had for no reason turned on his mother and scarred her probably for life with a fountain-pen point; when Mrs. Lampel claimed that Dr. Ringelman, after a cleaning, had kissed her on the mouth and told her he was from now on specializing in women's cavities; the day after Hymie's *bubbee* started throwing dimes and quarters out the window and promising plenty more to any Jewish heart who would get word to President Roosevelt that her daughter gave her no sugar cubes to suck; the same general time certain dark forces sought to take the secret of Eonite from Daddy Warbucks and Pop Jenks was in danger of losing the Sugar Bowl and Madam Zenda had Bim Gump out of his mind from drugs and terrible beatings; when Mrs. Aranow told how her Stanley had picked up in his taxi a pleasant little woman near Ohrbach's and taken her all the way to the Bronx; how he kept telling her she looked familiar, how she laughed and laughed and at the end of the ride let him know she was Milton Berle's mother; when Mrs. Vogel definitely spotted the brother she had not seen these nineteen years lighting a cigarette for Bette Davis in *Front Page Woman;* when Mister George the Beautician sold out to the electrolysis parlor upstairs and went back to work for others; after Mrs. Menashim found out, never mind how, that by *shtupping* Gelfman's brother-in-law a ten-dollar bill her Howie could be fixed up in the post office for the summer months; after Yenta Gersh was tossed out of the Isaac Gellis because she had once too often pestered customers for used tea bags; after the new landlord at 1894 Brighton 3rd notified all tenants by registered letter that starting with the first of next month absolutely nothing could be stored in the basement; right when a seltzer bottle exploded in Mrs. Holtzberg's bathroom; a week or so since Mrs. Jacobey sent her letter to the "Voice of the People" in the *Daily News*

This is to conductor number A1004 or A1009, I didn't have my glasses, who played dumb when I rang the bell for my stop next and lets say even it wasnt my stop there was a red light he went right through and though the whole car yelled on him getting off getting off conductor number A1004 or A1009 played dumb and not only he didnt stop on Brighton 5 where believe me I was far from the only person getting off, here's what he did, he went very fast to Neptune Ave, that's four short blocks and three AVENUE blocks from Brighton 5, and then first conductor number A1004 or A1009 made a stop it was a wonder I didnt re-break my hip—no wonder we still got the Depression when right near Judge Leibowitz's house in Manhattan Beach an eagle or a very large sea gull was seen; Simon's mother and Mrs. Plaut and Mrs. Harlib were on their stoop catching the last sun and passing around a *Photoplay* and half-a-*Modern Screen*.

"Since I heard he came out against Roosevelt," Simon's mother was saying, "I have very very very little use for Adolph Menjou."

Mrs. Harlib studied the remark for a bit, then said, "I'm surprised, that surprises me. He's supposed to be Jewish."

"Nah, who says," cried Mrs. Plaut.

"Adolph Menjou?" muttered Simon's mother.

"Adolph—Kravitz," Mrs. Harlib whispered. "Kravitz or Kavitz."

"John Boles also is supposed to be definitely a Jewish fella," said Mrs. Plaut.

"John Boles?" Simon's mother shuddered a little.

"JULES!" Mrs. Harlib lowered her voice, "Jules Ziprin."

"You know who John Boles has for a best friend?" Mrs. Plaut asked.

"Ricardo Cortez," answered Simon's mother.

"Irving—Shifcart," Mrs. Harlib hissed.

"He and Ricardo Cortez are supposed to be so one and inseparable"—Mrs. Plaut moved herself onto Mrs. Harlib's newspaper—"they made a *seder* together. They invited Richard *Dix* and his wife and they invited Warren *William* and his wife and they invited George Brent—he came *without* the wife—and they invited George *Bancroft* and his wife and they invited Harry Davenport, he came with H. B. Warner . . ."

"God God should forgive," Simon's mother said grimly, "but when it comes to H. B. Warner I got one one one criticism: stinky-stink."

"What is wrong with him isn't exactly he's stinky-stink," Mrs. Harlib insisted. "What's wrong with is he's like Walter Connolly, he goes in for *fumfing*."

"I don't mind it when Walter Connolly *fumfehs*," said

Simon's mother. "His *fumfing* I can take. Only when H. B. Warner *fumfehs* he don't just just just *fumfeh*. He *fumfehs* the way Lewis Stone *fumfehs*: He *boorchahs*!"

"Yeah, but when a Lewis Stone *boorchahs*, I'll tell you why he *boorchahs*"—Mrs. Harlib fluttered fingers—"he's playing *boorching* type parts."

"When it comes to *boorching*"—Simon's mother grabbed Mrs. Harlib's hand—"you got to got to got to know where and when. And you know who knows where and when? Only only a Jean Hersholt."

"You want to hear *boorching*, I'll send you to the right actor," said Mrs. Harlib. "Edward Ellis."

They had finished up a discussion about Herbert Marshall's gimpy leg and were just getting into Arlene Judge's weak hair when Mrs. Leichter from the third floor sounded her first "*Gevalt!*"

Simon's mother twisted around to blow kisses at her, saying, "Look look look who's there! How are you, true-blue type, good neighbor, Mrs. Clean House?"

"Hiya, hello stranger," Mrs. Harlib called up through the megaphone of her hands. "Since you moved from the back nobody sees you."

"That's the way it is," said Mrs. Harlib. "They get fancy, they forget their old pals, they want—to be—ah-lone."

"Hoo hoo!" cried Simon's mother. "You can look high and low and you'll still still still find out there's only one one Greta Garbo."

"Greta—*Kriesberg*," Mrs. Harlib hissed.

But Mrs. Leichter let go another "*G'vald!*" and out of different windows the "*Gottenyus!*" came in bunches and people were in front of stores and walking fast and running from the boardwalk and from Brighton Beach Avenue and standing on bridge chairs and milk boxes right in the gutter, and Dopey Duhvee was going among them on his tricycle and crooning a "See see see," and squinting through the wrong end of his little telescope. At the fire escape four floors above Gelfman where a small but fattish man in T-shirt and black felt slippers scaled the railing, worked a foot and half his behind into the fretwork, and stared stupidly down.

He at last yelled, "Hello, hello, hello!," waving an arm and flapping a slipper. "Sol Merz, M, E, R, Z, rhymes with *schmerz*, AM I TALKING LOUD ENOUGH?"

From the elevated a few "Fines!" were returned.

"Where, where's Liba?" Merz next demanded. He gazed up and down, then blared, "Hey, Widow Merz!"

A woman in a rose wrapper leaned over the roof and screeched.

"I never"—Merz bowed his head and strummed his lips while a train flashed by—"now all right?"

Mrs. Chepper, standing on a chair, yowled, "Good enough!"

He spoke again. "Was going to—wanted to say, to say —and I forgot."

"*Never,*" Mrs. Chepper cued. "How you never . . ."

"Ah, sure," said Merz. He made a motion as though to salute Mrs. Chepper but somehow botched it. A second later Dopey Duhvee had caught one of his slippers.

"I can't can't can't watch." Simon's mother put her face into Mrs. Harlib's muffler. "The funny thing, the interesting thing is—you want to hear something?—I can do my own windows and I can sit outside and I can lean all all the way out. But if my Shmuel goes on the bathtub, he has to change a bulb, I feel it right right away"—she squeezed her throat —"and it hits me in my dropped stomach."

"Me too, the same way," Mrs. Plaut admitted. "In my house also they stand on the bathtub and they stand on the sink and they stand on the toilet and they kill my enamel."

"The best thing," Mrs. Harlib advised, "is a little Bon Ami with ammonia."

"I wanted to bring out," Merz was saying, "that from my wife I never—here's where the 'never' came in—I never had a good day."

". . . you first use the ammonia in a slightly damp newspaper."

D*

"Listen to a true story that's not to be believed," said Merz, going strong now. "We're married, it's going to be thirty-one years, you hear me, thirty-one, that's thirty-one years"—Merz opened and closed a hand six times in the air, then paused, then flicked up his middle finger—"and in those thirty-one years I'm an operator on boy's knickers at the Twin Kays for twenty-two-and-a-half years . . ."

"Where, where?" someone cried from the boardwalk.

"Twin. TWIN KAYS!" Mrs. Chepper replied.

And again from the boardwalk: "Originally the THREE Kays?"

"Till Old Man Katz died," Merz said.

Another voice came in with, "They turn out a beautiful little garment, the best of the best."

Slowly, slowly, Merz removed his one slipper and rapped on the railing. "Do I get your attention?" he inquired. "Because too much longer"—the slipper sailed out of his hand—"you won't be detained."

"People!" His wife showed herself. "Call up for a cop."

And a babushka popped up alongside. "Don't worry, I'll be good for the nickel. Mrs. Gotshal, 2A."

"Again I started, again I forgot my point." Merz shook a fist at the roof.

"Whoever calls," his wife was instructing, "they shouldn't give no names. No names!"

"Did I mention—I mentioned already—how I never had a good day from her."

"Listen what to say," his wife came in hastily. " 'I'm new in the neighborhood, I just moved in, officer, I can't give no names.' No names . . ."

"Thirty-one years married, Twin Kays, twenty-two-and-a-half years at Twin Kays," Merz rumbled, "here it comes, shah!"

" '. . . Don't worry officer, you'll be taken care of nicely.' Or you can say it another way, you can say, 'You'll be taken good care of.' "

"Twenty-two-and-a-half years, hear, you hear? Hey, people, hey, neighbors, hey, *chaverim!*" Merz, in high glee, banged his temple on the railing. "I'm setting up for you a picture, I want to give you, I'm giving you—like in the movies, they say about the truth—when they say it's the truth but it's more then the truth . . ."

"Whole truth, nothing but truth, so help me drahdrahdrah." And Mrs. Chepper shyly raised her right hand.

Merz tipped an imaginary hat as he said, "Bear with me. I'll repeat it one time and the last time. Twenty-two-and-a-half years, an operator on Knickers, Twin Kays, and—here it comes!—if you killed her, my wife, my bride, if you cut her in little pieces she couldn't tell, she—could—not—tell—you—the address where I work." He flapped a hand at the roof. "She not only—forgot about the *exact* address, the building number. Their street, what *street* it's on she don't even know!"

"No, sure not!" his wife spat out. "Can you live from him?"

And from the boardwalk: "They moved where Dressy Dress was."

"From Levine and Smith," put in his wife, "they're like a stone's throw."

"Remind me"—Merz gave a two-fingered whistle—"the creamed-spinach story, that's . . ."

"Hold *it!*" Mrs. Chepper warned. "Not now, not yet, three trolleys coming."

Simon's mother was saying, "Let me ask a foolish question. You'll say, 'Malvena, you're asking a foolish question.' Supposing—if if if, make believe, that this was like something in a picture . . ."

"A picture," affirmed Mrs. Harlib.

". . . it's naturally not exactly exactly what was in that picture, but it could remind you of the picture—so what what what's the picture?"

"What you're expecting me to answer," Mrs. Harlib said

with a pleased smile, "I'm not going to answer."

Mrs. Plaut winked. "I got a feeling, see if the feeling is the right feeling, we saw it all together."

"CREAMED SPINACH," bawled Merz.

"Not coming over!" Mrs. Chepper touched her ears.

"Don't don't say *Street Scene*," Simon's mother warned. "Forget about *Street Scene*. The only reason I mention *Street Scene* is that it's a little little little bit like *Street Scene* because *Street Scene* also has a person on a fire escape and he's also like in the clothing line and she's also in it, she plays some beautiful part, with the Chinkee eyes, Sylvia Sidney."

"Sylvia—Dietz. *Or* Dietzer," Mrs. Harlib hissed.

"Is it me or is it Sylvia Sidney?" asked Mrs. Plaut. "I *used* to like her, I *used* to have with Teitlebaum the biggest arguments because he would say she has a certain little habit he couldn't stand, a little something she does with her *pisk*."

"That's a *pisk?*" Mrs. Harlib said fiercely. "That's not a *pisk*."

"That that that's a *piskeleh*," said Simon's mother.

"Testing testing," Merz began. "*Baruch shaym k'vood,* the music goes round and round."

"Bah-bah-bah *mitzvah*," went Dopey Duhvee, spitting at his mother's breasts.

"*Shm'ah Yisroel,* again testing, wanna buy a duck," Merz sang.

"Coming over, creamed spinach, you said to remind you," Mrs. Chepper sang back.

"Every two Mondays," said Merz, "our local holds what we çall—a procedure meeting . . ."

"Solly," his wife croaked, "you'll get a police record."

From the babushka: "Follows you all your life."

". . . during a procedure meeting we discuss, like—procedures."

"Tell him if I'm a liar," his wife appealed to the crowd, "tell him if they're not very strict when they see somebody, he's blocking a fire escape."

"First thing—a summons!" the babushka affirmed.

"On account of the meeting is after work and it can be sometimes a two-, three-hour proposition and we get hungry, our local has a custom started by our manager . . ."

From the boardwalk: "Abe Elkin, right!"

"Right!" Merz answered.

From the boardwalk: "A prince!"

"*Also* right!" Merz answered.

"Tell him how he'll be in real trouble," his wife implored, "how you dassn't have on the fire escape even a galosh."

"You want a government job, it'll go against you," the babushka warned.

"On this particular Monday," Merz picked up, "we had a really nice, an exceptional meeting. We took into the union three of the temporaries, they chipped in together for *shnapps* and cookies, and we voted a three-dollar assessment to help out toward when a member in good standing has like a situation that after an illness of no less then twenty-one days in the hospital, he has to be hospitalized, and upon the written advisement from the doctor that a recuperating rest is demanded and called for by the state of his health, the member in good standing should get up to—here up to means the . . . most—twelve-fifty a week for the first three weeks he's away . . ."

A storm of applause broke from the boardwalk.

Merz waved, swayed, caught himself, and over the concussion of a train said something about progressive trade unionism and good leadership.

"What I got against Sylvia Sidney," Simon's mother was bringing out, "is the same same thing I got against George Arliss: They both take parts where they play up too too much to the *goyim*."

"A message from the missus!" the babushka yelled. "Hold one second!"

"You never never see her in a picture without a cross,"

said Simon's mother. "Without the cross she can't move."

Now Mrs. Merz appeared, saying, "To call the police it's a free call."

"Rest assured," said Simon's mother, "you wouldn't see a Nancy Carroll or a Sally Eilers or a Patricia Ellis with a *Mogen Dovid*. They hold by their religion and that's why, they should drop dead, I give them the highest highest highest credit and I respect them and I admire them."

The babushka, snapping fingers, cried, "Another few words from the missus!"

And Mrs. Merz announced, "The operator gives back the nickel. Something goes wrong, God forbid, they mail stamps."

"Stamps you can always use," the babushka added.

"In the movies," said Mrs. Harlib, "I love how they're always using the phone. The least little nothing and it's long distance."

"Hey, hey, you're listening there?" Merz wanted to know.

"Don't you worry," Mrs. Chepper answered him. "*I'm* listening. *I'm* interested."

"I don't need to do this and nobody has to do me no favors. Because I can go right away inside and take a little gas."

Merz stuck out his tongue and took short, gasping breaths.

"Tell him don't start up with the gas company!" his wife instructed. "Tell him you get into their hands and you're finished!"

"They can hound you, oh can they hound you!" the babushka warned. "To your dying day."

"You want my advice," Mrs. Chepper remarked. "You'll stay where you are."

"If I don't jump—*if,*" Merz told her, "you're going to have to make it your business to come up the house."

Mrs. Chepper beamed. "Anytime."

"Today is no good," Mrs. Merz called harshly.

"Could you use number-nine trimmings? Whether you can use it or not you'll help yourself to number-nine trimmings." And Merz added passionately, "You know what kind of trimmings number-nine trimmings are?"

"The best of the best!" was heard from the boardwalk.

"Tell them"—Mrs. Merz beckoned to the babushka—"why today is out."

"The missus didn't shop yet," the babushka piped promptly. "She got an empty icebox."

"I feel for her," said Simon's mother. "I'm also also the type that has to has to shop every day."

"Later, *if* there's a later," Merz said happily, "I'll tell you what kind a hostess I got, that when my brother came in from Jersey for a visit, I'm talking about from *way* out in Jersey, and he said to her, 'Okay, Sweetheart, what's in the icebox?' she answered him 'Ice.'"

"I meant harm," wailed his wife.

"Harm she didn't mean," the babushka said grimly.

"Right away it's my fault, you notice I'm the bad one, give it to me, good, good, I deserve it," lamented Mrs. Merz. "Because his brother has sugar blood and I didn't want to open the icebox, he should see there Hershey's Kisses."

"Bring out," snapped the babushka, "how by you nothing ever came easy."

"By me, nothing ever came easy"—Mrs. Merz momentarily faltered—"except, excuse me, *Reader's Digest,* they got my name two years ago . . ."

But Merz was whistling, whistling and waving. "Hey, lady lady, not you, next to you, with the two seltzer bottles. . . ."

"That's Mrs. Ratzkin," said Mrs. Chepper.

". . . hands off, stay away from the fire alarm, and don't monkey with my nerves!"

"Bella," Mrs. Chepper called over, "you got time with alarms. Let him finish first about the creamed spinach."

"Wahwahwahzah," went Dopey Duhvee, cranking his arms and ringing and ringing his little tricycle bell.

"He's doing how a fire engine goes," his mother explained. "Give him fire engines and you're his best friend."

"Bah-bah-*mitzvah*," went Dopey Duhvee, riding over her shoes.

"Fire engines"—she kissed his wobbly head—"plus *bar-mitzvahs*."

"Ebbing is the word, ebbing, ebbing," crooned Merz, "the strength is ebbing, Gelfman move your stand a little, you don't need my blood on your papers . . ."

"If you get a chance, that's if if you get a chance," Simon's mother said to Mrs. Plaut, "you'll save me the *Mirror*."

> *The people's flag is deepest red,*
> *It's shrouded oft their martyred dead.*

Merz sang in a sobbing voice.

And from the boardwalk:

> *When their blood grows thick and cold,*
> *The rest I don't remem-ber-ber . . .*

> *Workers, workers,*
> *Don't be shirkers!*

Merz belted out nicely. Then he shook a fist and said, "Make it short and sweet, give me a simple little ceremony, maybe the Pantsworker wants to put in a few words . . ."

And from the boardwalk: "For this week forget it!"

". . . could say that the industry and the trade mourns and regrets the passing and the loss of a brother and a fellow worker, a staunch and a loyal trade-union man, a fighter and a militant, an old Socialist and . . ."

"Socialist you don't have to put in," cried Mrs. Chepper. "Also, you're not so old."

"They can say—hold on—it's written down—that in 1922 the bosses cracked my head—I made a few reference notes—don't get restless—" Merz dug into his watch pocket. "Brother and fellow worker you had—fighter and militant you had—" Merz pinched out a piece of envelope. "Never had a good day from her is covered—where I work she don't know is also covered—how she once begrudged me mineral oil let pass . . ."

"Two things I believe in," Mrs. Chepper announced. "God and mineral oil."

". . . creamed spinach I have down, creamed spinach I was . . ."

Merz gestured at Mrs. Chepper ". . . where?"

"What are you worried?" she answered. "With your mouthpiece let Boake Carter worry."

"Did I cover, let's see if I covered"—Merz brought his head down and his envelope up—"assessment, that it was unanimously passed and approved, that it relieves and eases the sick and the needy?"

From the boardwalk: "In my local you don't see that!"

"Did I make clear and explain that it takes care of up to five eye-doctor visits? An eye doctor," he emphasized, "is not an optometrist. An eye doctor you can go to when you *want* glasses and also when you *don't* want glasses."

And again from the boardwalk: "In my local they won't even make a Free Tom Mooney resolution!"

"Is it me or is it everybody?" mused Mrs. Plaut. "But if somebody says Tom Mooney, I hear Paul Muni."

"Muni—Weisenfreund," Mrs. Harlib hissed.

"My Shmuel has one one one complaint with Paul Muni," said Simon's mother. "You'll say to him 'Paul Muni' and he'll answer you, 'Paul Muni, he *chakehs.*' "

"Only when he's with Ann Dvorak," Mrs. Harlib declared. "With an Ann Dvorak you have to *chakeh.*"

"You'll notice, I don't know if you noticed"—Mrs. Plaut squeezed each of them on an elbow—"how Muni never played together with Pat O'Brien. Not even in the same Coming Attractions."

"Move in, get close," were Merz's next words. "Hold on and stay patient because I promise, you'll see that on account of Sol Merz nobody—nobody will miss Myrt and Marge."

"Grah grah grah!" warned Dopey Duhvee.

"You shouldn't say anything against Myrt and Marge," his mother advised. "He lives for Myrt and Marge."

"Excuse me, overlook it," Merz said amicably. "I'll make it—how about Just Plain Bill?"

"You got an hour-and-a-half yet," Mrs. Chepper boomed out. "A *good* hour-and-a-half."

"Assessments, finished." Merz tore off a snip of his paper. "Good and welfare, to hell with it." Merz tossed away the rest of his paper. "Anyway, without no more—without— what Eddie Cantor says when he wants to introduce Rubin- off."

"Without *further* ado," Mrs. Chepper prompted. "Used to be *now* without further ado."

"For things like that," Merz told her, "I had an iron head. You'd say to me—you'd say 'Rudy Vallee' and I'd say 'Rudy Vallee, my time is your time.' "

"Grah grah grah," went Dopey Duhvee.

"You know what?" his mother said. "You ought to say something nice about Myrt and Marge. He's still a little angry on you."

"Hey hey, what's doing with Marge's Ed?" Mrs. Harlib demanded.

Simon's mother whimpered and bit a knuckle.

"It looked so good," Mrs. Harlib mused. "He was nearly finished in the hospital, he was getting his memory again . . ."

"A lost cause," Simon's mother said bitterly. "The one the one who used to be Just Plain Bill's Nancy pushed her- self in."

". . . the doctor was so pleased with him, he was putting him on broth."

"Marge is going now with a boy, he's got a name"— Simon's mother swallowed her lips—"Listen listen listen to this for a name, you'll break your teeth on it, the way the *goyim* have names, you have to have to listen to a name: Tom—Fenwick!"

> *So let's have another cup of coffee*
> *And lets have another piece of pie,*

Merz half-sang, half-sobbed. For a second or two he hummed, keeping time with nervous hands, then said, "That's what he was singing, our manager, and that's the swell mood he was in from the meeting. We got such a kick out of him with his mood we started to carry on, we gave him, like—a razzing. I wouldn't say a razzing, I'll say a little *kibbitz*. Maxie Schiller made believe he was playing the violin and I myself, I said to him, 'Listen, Mister Manager, by union leaders you're a union leader, but I'm going to tell you that by *chazins*— by *chazins* you're no *chazin*.' He says, 'Boys, I want to put over a point.' He even stands up, to show he's going to put over a point. 'In the labor history story we're a pip-squeak and they don't know from us. You go over to a John L. Lewis to ask him about the Pants and Knickers Makers, Local 9, he'll answer, 'They're pip-squeak and I don't know from them.' To which I hurl back into his teeth this message, these burning words, 'So what? I hurl back these burning words because tonight we have done here a definitely noble purpose in that quietly, quietly and without no fanfare, we took affirming action to put on the history-book record what the late Daniel De Leon—I don't have to tell you who he is and how he stands with me—if he had only lived on a little bit longer—' "

And from the boardwalk: "*That* was a loss. That was—a *loss!*"

" 'This labor statesman, this giant, this silver tongue used to have a certain expression, and his expression was—A Noble Act.' "

And again from the boardwalk: "A noble act or a noble piece of action!"

" 'So how about it, what do you say we celebrate, let's make it a little *simchah*.' Bingo bango, the motion was carried, we went downstairs and without"—Merz paused, caught

Mrs. Chepper's eye and smiled—"without further ado we went downstairs and our manager took us over in three taxis to the Paramount Cafeteria and he treated his boys to what Merz happens to love, it's called protose steak . . ."

"He didn't let the missus know!" yelped the babushka.

"I waited for him a little under two hours and ten minutes where the express has a middle exit by the broken scale," Mrs. Merz cried gloriously.

"Three times she fainted," the babushka filled in. "A motorman had to pinch her under the neck."

Merz whistled, waited. "The protose steak," he said at last, "entitled you to two vegetables. One could be a *raw* vegetable, one could be a *not* raw vegetable. Vegetable one was no problem, vegetable one for Merz has to be a cucumber. That's how I am, all my life a meal is no meal without a cucumber."

"Hey hey, you're a *Galitzianer!*" Mrs. Chepper chuckled. "Right?"

Merz locked fingers and waved like a happy prizefighter.

"Touch a *Galitzianer* and you're holding a cucumber," Mrs. Chepper told the crowd. "It's an old saying."

"Scratch a *Litvak* and you're peeling radishes," Merz countered happily. "It's a Sol Merz saying." He allowed a little laughter but cut off the "Hooray for our side!" "Vegetable number two," he said soberly, "was a—different story. To save my life, if they came to me with a hundred-dollar offer to pick that second vegetable I—could—not—do it! And meanwhile I'm holding up the line. And meanwhile all the boys are sitting down already. And meanwhile my protose steak is getting ice cold. Then, by coincidence, if it happened in the movies you'd say, 'Yeah, sure, it happens in the movies,' that second they wheel out from the kitchen a wagon and the wagon has on it one tray and one vegetable. And without further ado"—he blew a kiss at Mrs. Chepper—"I say to the vegetable lady, 'To hell with it, give me that vegetable for my second vegetable!' That vegetable was—I don't need to tell you—CREAMED SPINACH!"

"Grah grah grah," went Dopey Duhvee, and he made a muscle.

"Is this a kid or is this a kid!" cried his mother. "He hears a spinach, right away he has to sing the Popeye song."

"Usually—usually spinach is for me"—Merz pinched his lower belly—"it has an effect—bingobango, immediately . . ."

"Also, me too, also! Except"—Mrs. Chepper snapped a thumb at her throat—"me it gives heartburn."

Merz, after prescribing weak tea and a few bites of old roll, twice tried to speak and could not. "Bear with"—he sniffled back the start of tears, sucked air—"Merz's life—on the radio—you'd get static . . ."

"Grah grah grah!" went Dopey Duhvee.

"You know why he's angry," his mother let the crowd know. "When he sings the Popeye song he loves you should sing with him."

Now Merz's voice rang as he said, "I fell on that creamed spinach—oh, oh, did I fall on it! Even my manager noticed, what doesn't he notice, and he himself without saying a word, he went back—this is a guy who dassn't move too much, moving is for him poison—and he bought me a plate of only creamed spinach . . ."

From the boardwalk: "My *paskudnyak* manager would also do that!"

". . . that plate I finished óff—oh, oh, oh, did I finish it off! In fact, my manager wanted to bring me some more, he started to get up already and I told him, 'What are you doing, don't you dare, your boys need you, the labor movement needs you, sit where you are!' I had to hold him down, that's the nature of the man, except this is not a man, this is an absolute prince!"

From the boardwalk again: "My manager we call Mister Coffee Nerves!"

"I got home and the first thing I said, here's the exact words or I shouldn't live to jump off this fire escape, open the quotes: 'Liba, I want you to once a week make me the cooked vegetable I ate tonight in the Paramount Cafeteria, it's called—' "

"He walks in without a 'Hello,' " commented the babushka.

" '—creamed spinach,' close the quotes."

"You cook for him," the babushka said glumly, "you can *plotz.*"

"If I give him hard-boiled egg," lamented Mrs. Merz, "it has to be with the heavy salt."

"After I close that quote she picks up the butter dish, she hands it to me, and she says, open the quotes, 'Stab me,' close the quotes, and I never heard from her again for nine days by the calendar."

"He doesn't tell you he *took* the butter dish," the babushka pointed out. "It shows what was in his heart."

"I'm not even counting that same night, if I counted that same night it would come to almost ten days."

"It don't interest him that maybe the missus had other things on her mind." And the babushka withdrew.

"I had on my mind other things," Mrs. Merz came in. "I had *erev Pesach* to worry about, that's when I take out all the dishes from my closet and I clean it around and I put in brand new oilcloth."

"*Vei,* I feel for the woman." Simon's mother cupped both her breasts. "Just just just to undertake the oilcloth is a terrible proposition."

Mrs. Harlib said, "I would do her oilcloth if she would do my camphorizing."

"The oilcloth I don't mind, the camphorizing I don't mind," Mrs. Plaut reflected. "It's when I have to go through my wire hangers. If I have an enemy I would wish on my enemy she should be healthy, she should have it very good, she should know from good luck and good luck only, and once a week she should have to go through my wire hangers."

Now Merz wept openly and with all his might. A "Three" sprang out of him as if it had been sneezed out, and he pulled at his hairs and he nodded and nodded.

"Go ahead, good for you!" his wife grumbled. "Get a cold!"

"He don't get colds," the babushka spat out. "He gets *chest* colds!"

"My three biggest, small pleasures," Merz sighed, "she murdered. Pleasure number one is right after supper and right after I hear Lowell Thomas Brings You the News, I enjoy taking to the—please overlook the expression as it's due to my circumstances—bathroom something to read. Can be *Men Who Lead Labor,* can be *A Marine Tells it to You,* can be *Liberty. Liberty* I go in for that they have little stories, and if you want to time yourself they put on top it should take you two minutes and fifteen seconds or two minutes and thirty-*five* seconds . . ."

"Go know you like *Liberty.* I'll give you a pile"—Mrs. Chepper brought her hand up and up and up—"like this a pile."

"Don't do the missus no favors," said the babushka.

"I'll give *you* a pile," said Mrs. Merz.

"While it's on my mind," Merz was telling Mrs. Chepper, "you ought to get a pencil and write down—peanut cracker." His mouth and then his whole face began working. "Peanut crackers—by some candy stores they're peanut thins. Anyway, peanut crackers or peanut thins was my small pleasure number two."

Mrs. Chepper tapped her head. "Rely on yours truly. Yours truly don't need no pencils."

Merz mumbled, "In good hands—not worried." And while tears spilled, he started again. "Was reading *Coal is King* or *King Coal* and I took in also *Whither the Needle Trades.* I wanted to finish up *Whither the Needle Trades* because it was first of all more along my lines of interest and the library had it stamped a one-week book."

From the boardwalk: "What do you say, should I read it?"

"Skim through it," answered Merz. "I brought it in with me that night mostly because I was curious, I was highly interested what it would have about Sidney Hillman. *And* I

113

walk into the bathroom. *And* I grab hold the string. *And* I give a pull. *And* bingo bango, the light goes on." He strained toward the roof. "The bulb you put in for me—those fifteen watts—they should have to use it to wash down your body."

"She didn't mean harm!" the babushka howled.

"In a small bathroom what do you need seventy-five watts!" Mrs. Merz insisted.

"Peanut crackers"—Mrs. Chepper clapped hands—"*or* peanut thins!"

"Peanut crackers," mused Merz, "we're on peanut crackers or peanut thins, yeah yeah, Merz, dark is your world, you should have paid the twenty-five dollars—in those years they charged only twenty-five dollars—that before you stood under the *chupeh* with her the gangsters should've broken on you—it didn't have to be a leg—a nice little ankle bone . . ."

"I got in my house a bigger bathroom"—the babushka swelled with anger—"and what I do, I do on ten watts."

"He don't realize that in a small bathroom you dry out from seventy-five watts," Mrs. Merz said resolutely.

"Seventy-five watts," the babushka repeated. "This is a moron for electricity. This is a type that every morning wants the exact time from the radio and every morning he turns on"—she clutched Mrs. Merz—"tell what he turns on!"

"A Stromberg-Carlson, twenty-two tubes, they made it you have to burn the whole twenty-two tubes. Till it warms up—" And all at once Mrs. Merz began to jump and jibber, "Utt utt utt . . . officer . . . *azoi azoi* . . . Mister Policeman."

"Look where he's going!" the babushka shrieked. "Where you going, hey? Hey, glump, *tochiss, goyisher kopp!*"

"He smells his Christmas, he's looking already for his few cents," Mrs. Merz told people.

"You know what to give him? Give him your *tzures!*" instructed the babushka.

"That's our Jewish word for trouble," Mrs. Chepper shouted to the policeman. "Trouble or—sorrow."

"For a second, one second"—Dopey Duhvee's mother

shoved a finger into the policeman's face—"You say to him 'Duhvee, in the morning big boys have to make a sissee!' To you he'll listen."

Zagt der arbeiter: Ich benk ah bissel broyt!
Zagt der balabuss: Ich vell dir machen toyt!

and Merz pulled off his T-shirt, and he removed also his wedding band and his pinkie ring and a piece of bridgework, and he pulled from one pocket a package of Chiclets which he held and shook against his ear, and half-a-watchband and a nail clipper, and he pulled from the other pocket three or four midget playing cards and a Haldeman-Julius Blue Book and an eyeglass case and a social-security card and a silver thimble; and all these things he set down with great ceremony on the fire escape, and he said to the policeman, "You'll do yourself a favor, you'll do Merz a favor, you'll turn around and walk away. If you want, go in by Gelfman, smoke a cigarette, tell Gelfman to give you a gratis pack, Merz's pleasure . . ."

"Gelfman don't need the business!" the babushka screamed.

"Listen"—Mrs. Merz was half off the roof—"he sells also loose!"

". . . You'll mean well, you'll try to do the right thing, you'll say, 'Sol'—you see Merz is smart, he knows you'll use a first name—'Solly, don't make me a hard day, I got my own troubles, I don't want this on my civil-service record, help me do my job, you'll come down and after you get to yourself a little we'll be friends, Solly Solly, realize I'm also a working man, I put in today a long day and a hard day, don't make me climb up, one slip and I'm finished, you want that Solly? Solly you don't want that. So what if I'm from a slightly different faith, it's more important that we should live and learn together under the working-class brotherhood banner.' " And Merz peeked over and down. "No? Right? What do you say, my friend?"

The policeman pounded his nightstick on the pavement and said, "Inside."

And Merz climbed immediately down from the fretwork, paused to pop in his bridge, then sank to his knees before his window. Where he heaved and strained and pressed and threw around his weight and pummeled with a fist and with the flat of his hand, saying "Once it's closed—I begged her—tip the fifteen cents—call in the . . .

". . . Super," he got out a second or so before he took himself a beautiful skid for one, two, three flights and finished up twitching and bleeding from both ears on Mrs. Furman's bread box.

"That that that's a face," Simon's mother said, gazing after the ambulance, "that's a face you see only in the movies."

"The other intern," said Mrs. Harlib, "was also good-looking. Only he didn't have such a build on him."

"He talked—you know how he talked?" said Mrs. Plaut. "He talked the way Warner Baxter sometimes talks."

"From the nose," said Mrs. Harlib. "He—*rahtchehs.*"

"If Warner Baxter *rahtchehs*," said Mrs. Plaut, "what about a Donald Cook?"

"You know when Donald Cook *rahtchehs?*" said Simon's mother. "Only only only when he's on the radio."

In the course of time the sun left the stoop, and so did they.

5

Then late in the morning of Saturday, December 28, 1936, when the Knishe Queen announced the coming of three new flavors (apple-cherry, sour lemon, nutty onion); after Jerky Jacob the Old Clothes Man sent out postcards to his best customers ("I am right now in a good position to make *VERY* terrific deals on gamps and vestovers"); two months after Mrs. Merz finished up her mourning and moved into the junior two rooms at 1864 Brighton 7th Street; a few days only since Dr. Ringelman pleaded with Mrs. Lichter to ease off her girdle so he might check her for pyorrhea; the week that Mrs. Flicka's middle girl, Tova, was interviewed outside S. Klein's by the "Inquiring Photographer" ("Yes, if we had a strong love bond I would certainly marry an unemployed fellow. Because this is a depression, which can keep a fellow unemployed, even if he has initiative. Say, I happen to have very fine assistant-bookkeeper experience if a prospective employer sees this"); also the week Hymie's *bubbee* was observed packing her bloomers with peanut brittle in the S. S. Kresge near Ocean Parkway; one or two days after Teitlebaum filled his window with the news that labor unrest in the copper and raw-iron industries had compelled an upward revision in the price of egg bagels; somewhere around the time Gelfman started stocking a few *Civil Service Leaders* and discontinued hot chocolates; this being the week when Yenta Gersh, announcing something about a Palestine Paper Drive, pulled her baby buggy into the Brighton Savings Bank and filled it with deposit slips and blotters; when Mrs. Aranow's Stanley related that he had gone into an Automat for the baked beans; that he had seated himself at a window table; that a man with a soft, high, faltering voice had begged profuse pardons and sought to know if he still needed or was going to need the mustard jar; that Stanley had absently answered either "Go ahead, take" or "Take take take"; that in passing the jar a drop, a pinch, a smidgen of mustard had fallen on Stanley's fingernail; that Stanley had licked off the fingernail and laughed down the apologies, saying, "For mustard I'm not going to hit" or "I wouldn't hit for mustard"; that his fingernail had anyway been wiped and buffed with a wetted napkin; that after the wiping and the buffing he had sent away the borrower with a hard love-tap or a soft knuckling; that he had done very nicely by the baked beans plus a piece of cocoanut ring; that he was, in fact, starting up his cab when a buddy gave him to understand he had just had dealings with Barney Ross; shortly after Schoenbaum, the Druggist, hired Bomba Katz to help him empty his shelves and wrote with soap on a mirror that all prescriptions were now on file with Silver Rod; this being the time Ken Maynard, refusing to use a stuntman in *Strawberry Roan,* missed his leap from a boulder to a stagecoach; and Jimmy Fiedler kept mentioning troubles between Thelma Todd and Patsy Kelly; after Bobby Breen was brought back to the Eddie Cantor Show for the third time; when Janet Gaynor and Charles Farrell were reunited and did a so-so *Ramona* on the Lux Radio Theater; Simon, Boomie, Hymie the Hitter, and Marshall, with four franks and one order of french fries, the large, made themselves at home around the best self-service table in the Hebrew National and set forth ways and means of killing a good two hours till the Surf opened its doors:

Steal searchlight batteries from Strauss Auto Supply.
Mail a dirty condom to Lila Edelstein.
Go by the public toilets near Sea Gate and bang on the lady's room.
Squeeze tits on Ocean Parkway.
Steal searchlight batteries from Strauss Auto Supply, take them to Sheepshead Bay, and sell them to ginzos half-price.
Go in the library and reserve *The End is Near* by B. M. Cocking.
Squeeze tits on Ocean Parkway and throw burning paper down the Shoreline Arms incinerator.
Knock on Manhattan Beach doors and make believe they were collecting for the Jewish National Fund.
Go to the library and reserve, in Lila Edelstein's name, *The Happy Pussy,* by A. Wetcock.
Go to the public toilets near Sea Gate and bang on the lady's room and yell, 'I'm busting.'

Soon Steinbrink, the weekend waiter, knocked the table with his broom, accidentally-on-purpose dribbled sawdust over their shoes, and rode himself into the conversation. He first wished them his own happy boyhood in a Lublin bedding factory and free choice between a beautiful baby sister eaten by Polish pigs or a mild case of typhus with lasting liver damage, then proposed that they pass their time profitably and pleasantly and do God, man, and devil the biggest of favors by:

Finding out if the Eagle Pencil Company needed someone to take the eagle for a leak.
Eating a few boxes of Feen-a-Mint to see if everything came out all right.
Following behind the horses in Prospect Park to get themselves a good hot meal.

Whereupon Boomie flogged himself with his hands and from high up in his nose caroled, "*Sh'mah Rabu,* the *putz* is *du;*" and Simon recited in simple sing-song, "*Kish mir in luch/ Ah ganzer vuch*"; and Hymie half-sang, half-said, "*Bei mir bist du shayn/ You give my nuts a pain*"; and Marshall muttered, "*A pain, go fall under a train,*" then swished around a palm as though erasing a blackboard, then rattled off, "*Bei mir bist du shayn/ You give my nuts a pain/ Get flushed down the drain.*"

But Zwerkel, the owner, shut off his electric knife and sought to shame them, saying, "Nuts, *putz,* that's how you talk?"

"How we talk," said Boomie.

"All all all the time," said Simon.

"*Sure,*" said Marshall.

"Fuck you fuck you fuck curiosity," said Hymie.

"I would like to know"—Zwerkel wiped around the blade and between each of the spikes—"if that's how you talk in your own house and if you happen to hear that from your parents, from your mothers and your dads, if you hear nuts and if you hear *putz.*"

"That's *right,*" said Marshall.

Simon peeped into Boomie's face and said, "Duh, Boomie, I hear from my parents, from my mother and my dad, wowee, just just just yesterday they were saying nuts and *putz* and *putz* and nuts!"

Boomie peeped into Simon's face and said, "Duh, Shimmy, you heard from your parents, from your mother and dad, duh, from them you heard nuts and *putz* and *putz* and nuts?"

"Duh, my mother was picking her nose," said Simon weepily.

"Duh, your mother was picking her nose," said Boomie, with a gentle glow in his eyes.

"Duh, she was picking her nose"—Simon slowly wiped the tip and nail of his index finger on Marshall's muffler—"and my dad said, 'I don't mind if she picks her nose . . .'"

"Duh, your dad said, 'I don't mind if she picks her nose . . .' " Boomie dipped both his index fingers into Marshall's water glass and slowly stirred.

" 'Duh, I don't mind if she picks her nose' "—Simon added his fingers to Boomie's fingers—" 'only I don't like when she *Putz* it on my NUTS!' "

"Today's kids." Steinbrink flapped a rag at them.

"The kids of today." Zwerkel lobbed a snip of fat toward their table.

"Who talks the dirtiest?" Steinbrink mused. "Mainly the Jewish kids."

"Jewish kids mainly." Zwerkel nibbled on fat.

"You listen to them dirty talk." Steinbrink ate the last french fry on the plate, then took away the plate. "Only listen and pay a little attention to the Jewish kids of today . . ."

"Today's Jewish kids," Zwerkel confirmed. "The Jewish kids of today are the worst Hitlers."

"They could use, what they could use"—Steinbrink twisted and twisted his rag—"is a Hitler."

"One Hitler!" Zwerkel proclaimed.

"One taste, one little taste of Hitler!" Steinbrink flicked out a tongue.

"A . . . *leck!*" Zwerkel said through tight teeth.

"Then, then first you'd see!" cried Steinbrink.

"First then you'd see!" snorted Zwerkel.

"Oh yes, oh yes," Steinbrink said miserably, "they wouldn't have time then for what they have time now."

"The Jewish kids of today have too much time," Zwerkel observed.

"He would see to it, oh, yes, he would make it his business, oh, yes, oh, yes, he'd take *good* care that they should have on their minds"—Steinbrink beat their heads lightly with a menu—"a few other little things besides—smut and *shmutz.*"

"That's all we got on our minds?" said Boomie.

"*Sure,*" said Marshall.

"Just just just smut and *shmutz* and *shmutz* and smut?"
said Simon.

"That's *right*," said Marshall.

"You know what else we got on our minds?" said Boomie.

"He wansa know? All *right*. *Tell*—him," said Marshall.

"Fucking," said Boomie.

"Today's kids," Steinbrink cried hoarsely.

"The kids of today," answered Zwerkel.

So Zwerkel gave notice that one, one more dirty word
would get them the bum's rush; that they would be bounced
O, U, T on their behinds; that they would be mutilated and
mishandled by a particular party who had been once upon
a time called Zwerkel the *Shtarkeh;* that he would hit them
with small salamies to make them bleed on the inside; that
they would soon start looking for their teeth the way Pete
the Tramp looked for cigar butts; and that by him and his
they could cash no more empties.

Then Simon instructed Boomie and Hymie and Marshall
to kiss pinkies and to swear what he swore: That nothing
dirty would be heard from them, though their mouths were
filled with S, H, I, T; and that from now on they must use
only the cleanest cleanest cleanest of words.

And Simon had just started them off with a *Rinso,* when
a dreadful draft tore off Steinbrink's *yarmalka* and fluttered
the pilot light in Zwerkel's grill.

"Merry *Kratz mir* and *gut shabos.*"

At the doorway stood a hefty, orange-headed woman in
a colorless beret and a sheepskin coat with burn holes and
bald spots. Maybe an inch of cigarette stuck out like a tusk
over her fuzzy chin and a set of matched shopping bags
knocked against the blunt iron tips of her orthopedic boots.

"*Flanken?*" she whispered, drawing deeply, dreamily on
her cigarette.

"The *flanken,* Madam Ducoff . . ."

Zwerkel came from behind his counter and dragged in
her shopping bags. He gazed slowly up and down and across
the street, then shut the door noiselessly, then gave the

street a last long look, then tapped his lips and shook his head.

"... is not for you."

"I'll say to you what God said to the Wir-gin Mary," said Madam Ducoff. "When she told him she wanted a girl. *'Nisht bahshert.'* "

She clumped to a booth, on the way over using three ash trays; in a fourth she killed her butt.

"It's not for you not because you're a good customer. It's not for you," Zwerkel told her, "because—you're a friend of mine!"

Simon wonderingly exclaimed, "She she she's a friend of yours!"

"That's *right*," said Marshall.

"Duh, Madam, duh, Ducoff is a friend of his, duh?" inquired Boomie.

"Duh, yeah," answered Simon. "And you know, you, duh, know what? She's duh, a friend of MINE!"

And Simon sang: "Madam Booboo is a friend of mine."

And Boomie sang: "For a nickel OR a dime"

And Marshall sang: "She will do it ANYtime!"

And Hymie sang: "Fifteen cents for OVERtime!"

"*Schmu-hu-huck,*" warbled Boomie.

"Twenty. Twenty twenty *twenty* cents!" Simon cried.

And Zwerkel started for their table, snapping his fingers and clapping his hands. "That's how you talk with an older person? How—are you—*talk*ing!"

"*Cockers,*" Madam Ducoff called over. "Don't look for no *tzures.*"

"Ooh, ooh what you said!" Simon mocked.

"Don't look for ANY *tzures,*" Boomie said sweetly.

"I had from the last few nights"—Madam Ducoff drew a deep, trembly breath—"enough."

"I noticed on you," said Steinbrink, "something, something . . ."

"What's the matter?" asked Zwerkel, "you look so, so . . ."

Madam Ducoff laughed mirthlessly. "I'll say to you like

E

the Mad Russian says to Eddie Cantor: 'Shell I tell him?' "

She removed her coat, two sleeveless sweaters, opened the mismated buttons of a cardigan, and peeled off her chest some folded newssheets.

"You maybe have what I sometimes have," said Steinbrink.

"And when that grabs you that can grab you!" said Zwerkel.

Madam Ducoff made her small eyes smaller, answering, "What it is is what you once in a while get in my line. When you start in *hondling* with the dark powers, the *finsternish,* the mystery from mysteries, the number from numbers—a whole business."

"Talking from numbers . . ." Steinbrink squinted and wet his lips as if threading a needle.

"What what comes after seventy-five?" Simon shot at Marshall.

"*Speaking* from numbers . . ."

"*What* comes after seventy-five? I'll *tell*ya what comes after seventy-five. Seventy-*six!*"

"That that that's the spirit!"

At which Zwerkel gave fair warning: "Buy or bye-bye."

And Madam Ducoff said to them, "I'll tell you what the angel told Jacob. When they did wrestling. 'In my time I handled tougher.' "

"You mentioned numbers," said Steinbrink airily. "So how about a number? For a *kopsin* that's without one little hit, it's already, it's already—I'll tell you how long—seventeen weeks!"

"Say better—four months," declared Zwerkel.

"I'll repeat to you," Madam Ducoff slyly answered, "what the rabbi said. When they told him, 'Hey, Rabbi, you're walking around by the ladies baths.' 'I got on my mind more important things.' "

"She don' wanna givim a number," Simon was telling Boomie.

"We'll givim a number!" Boomie shouted.

124

"Doesn't have to be an exact number," Steinbrink was wheedling. "Approximate is also good."

"With approximate," said Zwerkel, "you can be better off then with exact."

"That's a *very* good number," Simon could be heard saying. "That that that's a hot number!"

"A word. One word, maybe," Steinbrink coaxed.

"An approximate word," muttered Zwerkel.

"The best best number is—" Simon began.

And all four blared: "Sixty-nine!"

"Beautiful. Gorgeous. Keep up, keep up." Madam Ducoff swayed in her seat. "And I'll tell you what Pharaoh told Moses. When Moses begged him, 'Let my people go!' 'You got me in a very bad mood.'"

Then to Steinbrink she murmured hoarsely, "To give a number . . ."

"In you and Roosevelt—one confidence," Steinbrink whispered.

". . . I need get from you a dream."

"To save my life . . ." Steinbrink shrugged with one shoulder.

"You dreamed, I'll tell you what you dreamed, here's what you dreamed"—Madam Ducoff raised her arms, then touched Steinbrink over the heart—"you dreamed—a flying dream."

Steinbrink moaned, Zwerkel went, "Pooh-pooh."

"You flew"—Madam Ducoff dragged at the air—"should I say?"

"Is this something or is this something?" said Steinbrink.

"I want to tell you," said Zwerkel. "She is—something."

"You flew in your flying dream, I'll say—what I'll say is not exactly naked, I'll say—you had on—let's say you wasn't —*too* dressed up."

"This is," Steinbrink marveled, "without question . . ."

"No question about it," said Zwerkel.

Madam Ducoff with a soft "Shah" dipped into both shopping bags and swished around her hands. She next made two, three passes over the handles, quivered her jaw, and looked long into the far distance.

"Sixteen," she ultimately said. An instant later she added, "In combinations."

Simon nickered.

Boomie said, "I hadda dream . . ."

Hymie brayed.

Marshall brayed and bit a palm.

"Combinations," Steinbrink reflected. "I like nine—and seven . . ."

"Gives you a choice," cried Zwerkel. "Say you don't like nine and seven, you make it—twelve and four!"

"Duh, you know what, duh, Boomie?" Simon was blaring. "When I, duh, dream, there's only one one one trouble!"

"Duh, you got, duh, one, duh, trouble . . ."

"My trouble is, duh, when I wake up, duh, it's very very HARD!"

"The kids of today," said Steinbrink.

"Today's kids," said Zwerkel.

"I'll say to you"—from behind an ear Madam Ducoff fetched a cigarette—"I'll say to you what the elephant said to the mouse." She shook out of her hair a fat wooden match. "When the mouse was making love on him: 'You know, you're working on my nerves.'"

She struck the match, and in her rage broke off the head.

"Hey, Marshey," cried Boomie, "she needs a match."

"Giver a match," ordered Hymie.

"I hafta," Marshall grumbled.

And without much interest he mumbled, "Ya *wanna* match? I'll *give* ya a match. My ass and your face."

"The way they are," said Steinbrink, "is the way everything is."

"And the way everything is," said Steinbrink, "is no good."

The door opened and pretty soon Zwerkel was dealing with the draft and a nice few customers. For a while the boys studied him silently, though once in a while calling, "Who got the next?" and "Mustard, puddin more mustard!" Then, after Zwerkel enlisted Steinbrink and both had their hands full, Simon yelled for a cream soda; and Boomie yelled for four glasses and eight straws; and Hymie yelled for one frank, very well done and with sauerkraut; and Marshall yelled for the frank to be cut in half, exactly in half, and for mustard to be on one, only one of the halves.

The big-faced lady parked herself in Madam Ducoff's booth and murmured, "Could you fit me today?"

Though she kept bleary, bitter eyes on her assorted cold cuts, Madam Ducoff said amiably, "Mrs. Udell, I'll put it to you the way God put it to the Jews. When he was warning how they dassn't have no other gods: 'Look, I need the business.'"

"Before I forget"—Mrs. Udell clinked down two, three, four quarters—"I owe for a house call."

Madam Ducoff swished the coins into a shopping bag. "Was a *night* call," she said, with a shy and stricken smile.

"You were anyway in my building," Mrs. Udell contended.

Madam Ducoff gazed at her sadly. "I'll say to you what Moses said. When he came down Mount Sinai: 'Look where I had to *shlep* up.'"

Out of a knotted handkerchief Mrs. Udell extracted another coin.

Handkerchief and coin vanished somewhere on Madam Ducoff's person.

"From a half-dollar," said Mrs. Udell throatily, "I don't get change?"

Madam Ducoff returned the handkerchief.

Mrs. Udell blotted her eyes with it and began, "I'm all set to call it quits on my life and to close up the book."

"Ah ah, Lady"—cream soda sloshed out of Boomie's mouth—"don't call it *qvitz!*"

"I'll tell you," said Madam Ducoff, "what the *rebbitsin*

told the Cossacks when they were dragging her from the bed: 'Don't make me get up to you.' " To Mrs. Udell she muttered, "The book, closing it up, you were making a very interesting point."

"Started in my sorrows," Mrs. Udell reflected, "twenty-three-and-a-half weeks ago . . ."

Madam Ducoff said quietly, "I'm off by that half-a-week."

". . . my Ira got from his boss a ticket to the Clothing Cutters Ball, the cheapest ticket is three dollars and they give you only headline entertainment. He met there a girl that I'll name her by what she is: *bummikeh*. On account of only a *bummikeh* makes a boy go into Schrafft's for coffee, just to sit down is a quarter each person. Then he first took her home, and where she lives you need three trolleys. Later I find out"—Mrs. Udell momentarily gagged—"to travel from trolley number two to trolley number three you can travel only by taxi."

"This," Madam Ducoff sighed, "I already knew." She added, after a second, "The Schrafft's I wasn't—hundred percent."

"I'll skip over," Mrs. Udell went on, "to when he brought her to the house. She walks in, the first thing—immediately she kisses me. I say to her, 'Miss Feldman, I don't know how you do and what you do in your religion, but kuhtzenyoo-muhtzenyoo stuff is not for Jewish people.' She says to me, 'May I call you Mom?' I say to her, 'To play it absolutely safe I would have to first ask a rabbi, Miss Feldman. A rabbi is like what a priest is in your religion.' The *bummikeh* has next the brazen gall to say, 'Could I help you on the dinner?' I say, 'Only God can help me now.' "

"Your dinner—for dinner you had . . ." Madam Ducoff shut her eyes and frowned with fearful concentration. "Eggs and onions. Chicken soup. *Puppick. Helzel. Deckel.*" She pressed on her brows, her lids. "The *deckel*—was on the slightly dry side."

Mrs. Udell cried out and stuck her face into her hands.

"Deckel," croaked Boomie.

He whispered into Simon's ear; and Simon whispered into Hymie's ear; and Hymie, holding his nose, whispered into Marshall's ear.

"Also happened"—Madam Ducoff peered into a shopping bag—"with the guest—a accident."

Mrs. Udell seized and pinched Madam Ducoff's hands.

Boomie started, "Why is *deckel*—" then broke up.

"You spilled on her—wait, wait!" Madam Ducoff was breathing badly. "Maybe seltzer, maybe soup."

"Seltzer *and* soup," Mrs. Udell wheezed.

"Why is *deckel* like when"—Boomie's index finger slashed the air diagonally—"you're getting cir-cumcised?"

Marshall said, "All *right!* Why *is deckel?*"

"Why why why is *deckel* like when you're getting circumcised?" Simon tilted back in his chair and pointed his face at Madam Ducoff.

Boomie stamped his feet and beat on the table. "Because . . . it's . . . a . . . JEWISH CUT!"

"I'll say, I'll say," Madam Ducoff rumbled, "what the Queen of Sheba said. When they were telling her about King Solomon: 'I don't like wise guys.' "

She seemed on the verge of more, but Mrs. Udell was now weeping vigorously, and it took wetted napkins and scalp massage to restore her. After two tries she burped and came to herself a little, saying, "For the right girl I would be a second mother. For the right girl I would turn over my two rooms. For the right girl I would leave behind the three-way bulb in the kitchen. For the right girl I would stock her up with what a little bride dreams in her heart: A *hocking* knife, sour salt, my certain polish to shine cut glass, rubber-bands galore, two toaster covers, a sponge with a grip on it that you can never get your hands wet, a soap dish, rubber coasters, they'll fit underneath any bed and the bed never slips, a brick from when Luna Park burned down, it's the perfect right size to put underneath an ironing board. Who would care and who would count; from an open heart an open hand."

She reared back, gripped her throat, and hiccuped softly.

"Oh yeah, oh yeah," she said tonelessly to herself. "You're fixing me good already, *bummikeh. Bummikeh, bummikeh,* you're finishing up what the Depression started." She averted her face, at the same time popping something into her mouth. "This is what keeps me going," she told Madam Ducoff. "Tums. Every half-hour on the half-hour I need to suck a Tums."

"Ah tah tah tah tah tah," went Boomie.

Hymie sniffled and moaned.

"She hasta hasta hasta suck on Tums," Simon cued Marshall.

"She—*hasta!* Waddaya *mean* she—*hasta?*" Marshall, working both lips without showing teeth, looked into his lap. "I'll giver something *better* to suck on."

Flushing thickly, pushing her clodhoppers one at a time out of the booth, Madam Ducoff rose. "I'll tell you"—She resumed her seat—"I am telling you what the cow told the bull. When the bull was getting on the tenth time: 'I'm getting now really sore.'"

"Twat?" Simon cupped an ear. "Twat twat did she say?"

"I *cunt* hear," answered Boomie.

"What Jewish kids talk today," said Steinbrink, "you can *plotz.*"

"You want to *plotz?*" said Zwerkel. "Listen to today's Jewish kids."

At this, the boys ordered one knishe with four forks, half a half-sour tomato, one Mason Mint wrapped and in a double bag, and toothpicks from a fresh box.

On separate checks.

To her next client Madam Ducoff said, "Behind this world is another. By the end of that world is already world without end."

The woman, fiftyish but with Shirley Temple ringlets, shook in her shawl and murmured, "Right, right."

"You can have darkness and you can have the light that's darker then darkness."

"That's the whole trouble."

"Sometimes—only sometimes—you start in with the material and you're pretty soon dealing with the immaterial. You get into form and the next minute you got the formless."

"The way it is so I wish it wasn't so."

"You think that's bad, wait," said Madam Ducoff. "What about when you look into one thing and it turns out—how many, many times it turns out!—that in this one thing is the beginning of all things and in the beginning of all things is where there's no beginning."

"Tell me what I don't know."

"I hear stuff, I can get cases"—Madam Ducoff indicated her shopping bags—"tears your heart out. Comes to me, not so long ago, a little woman, a real *rachmones*. Her husband was having some trouble with one of the demons, I forget exactly who, whether it was Asherludtz or Pirpick, I would have to look up."

"They had that a lot in Sea Gate."

"Before I even walked in the house the first thing I did— this was the first thing!—I tried to make the husband comfortable, he shouldn't have such a sore spirit. You can say I'm old-fashioned, you can say I should be more up-to-date, I ought to do like plenty of them do in my line, right away the pentagrams and anagrams."

"You fall into their hands, you're *farfallen*."

"I did what I always do for a sore spirit. I played it safe, I didn't hurry-hurry, I . . . took . . . my time. I got through to the vital powers—that's how I do things—I raised up Sharetanik and Hodretzoh, I heard what *they* had to say."

"With them you never go wrong."

"I didn't need pentagrams. I didn't need anagrams." Madam Ducoff narrowed her face cunningly. "I fixed up a

E*

nice little charm, I put in it the Seal of Solomon, I waited till it was Saturday and I said what you're supposed to say, 'Norporetz, Testardoff, Maragamid.' "

"You used your common sense."

"Then I made the house visit, I did a couple tests, I raised up Sharetanik and Hodretzoh again and even so—even so I wasn't a hundred percent satisfied."

"That's your nature and that's how you are."

"I checked three times his horoscope. I looked up in the zodiac, and to show you how I take a case serious—on account of I'm one of the few people in the line who seldom uses them—I even dealt out a couple hands of Tarot cards."

"What could hurt?"

"But once I made up my mind I got right away on the job and I fixed up a regular on-the-dot course of treatment. Nothing fancy, nothing hocus-pocus. Plain, simple, the way they handled sore spirits before me, the way they'll handle sore spirits after me. I used the double three instead of the single six . . ."

"The best thing."

". . . and I right away put myself in a harmony with the fish of the fire, the goats of the earth, and the snakes of the water. Then I first fasted a little, I put myself in a coma, and I got through—*yoish*, till you get through—to the five orders of imps."

"Them you have to catch in the right mood."

"From Beramalud and Gozreh I had my hands full. In fact, they absolutely wouldn't come until I made a special fast and a special coma and even so I had to plead with Tabak."

"He saw you were good natured, he took advantage."

"It's all in there," Madam Ducoff lighted a cigarette and bounced massive smoke rings against her shopping bags. "How I had to find the secret of secrets, the principle of principles, the key to the lock of locks, the key for the key of keys, the answer to the six questions, the lowest in the highest, the highest in the lowest, the page without the book, the word on the page, the letter in the word, the name of the nameless, the time of the nine beginnings, the seventh purpose for the first purpose, the eleven laws for the one law, the all in the nothing, the nothing out of the all, the difference between the reason that has no reason and the accident that's no accident."

"That's already"—her client snuffled—"some little difference."

"But your case is another case," Madame Ducoff said cheerily. "Your case I'm positive—all right, let me not say . . . positive, because with the angel Sussekranz you can't be and you dassn't say positive. He's what you call a negative type."

"He's worse than Shtymbar. From Shtymbar at least you could get once in a while a favor."

"Your case, I could say, it's a question of working through the undermind a little bit. We work through the undermind and from the undermind we can get to the sphere of spheres and once we *hondle* with the sphere of spheres—"

"That's if Sussekranz is in the right mood. He gets on his high horse, forget about the sphere of spheres."

"*I'll* take care of Sussekranz. *I'll* worry about Sussekranz," Madam Ducoff avowed. "Happens he likes the circle of circles with a candle in the middle. So I'll give him the circle of circles and I'll put in *two* candles. In fact"—Madam Ducoff clapped, then clasped her hands—"how's this for a suggestion? I'll say to him three times three what you're supposed to say to only the highest of the highest angel order —'Shtelbintel, Shtakrossvel, Shefkaporitz.' "

"Now you're talking!" her client exulted.

"I want also to take care of the universal law. Make up your mind from now on you'll be in universal law and you'll attach your forces to miracle and life."

"That's all along my trouble."

"Once you do that, you're on easy street. Because from

miracle and life you'll get soul harmony, you'll get the measurement from all things, you'll get the higher wisdom, you'll get the saving health, you'll get the unity of spirit, and you'll have it good." Madam Ducoff coughed casually. "Meanwhile, let's be on the safe side. Starting tonight—tonight the latest!—take step one to the bond of peace."

"In other words . . ."

"Put yourself on the highest height."

"I should forget Lakewood, I should try Monticello."

"Bring out the now in the here and the here in the now."

"In Monticello they get a younger crowd . . ."

"Pay strict attention to the snake and the bull and the lion."

"If I meet a professional fine. If not, also fine . . ."

"Realize that from the all in all has to be the nothing with nothing."

"He's with a few years younger? Who counts!"

"Keep in mind and don't forget the four corners of the world. Number one corner . . ."

Madam Ducoff stopped, sniffed, sniffed again, and slowly turned toward the boys.

Simon pinched his nose and covered his mouth.

Hymie went "Bleh-heh" and "Yuch" and fanned the air in all directions.

Marshall covered his face with two napkins, then covered the napkins with a menu.

And Boomie, his behind still pointed at Madam Ducoff's booth, said, "Farts hah medder wid yoo?"

Madam Ducoff's first reply was to raise her arms and pass them back and forth, back and forth over the shopping bags while she moved her lips silently. Then she let her arms fall, blinked her red, dry eyes and said shakily, "I'll tell to you what the *Riboynoy-shel-oylom* said to Job. When Job is *krechtzing*, 'You killed my family, You made me a pauper and a bum, and You gave me boils; so what are You keeping me alive?' 'Be very grateful I got a Jewish heart.' "

. . .

134

The horsy fat-backed woman for the third time droned, "What's going to be and what's going to be?"

Madam Ducoff, spooning water over the smoking coal of a cigarette, said dryly, "I'll say to you what the he dog said to the she dog when he got stuck in her, 'Things work themselves out.'"

"What you told me I did exactly. I put the powder in her farina half-strength, I watched out she shouldn't get too dopey, I buried on Bay Four what she cut from the nails . . ."

"The powders," Madam Ducoff said thoughtfully, "we'll maybe discontinue."

"I put under her mattress raisins and nuts."

"Next time, bridge mix," Madam Ducoff instructed. "The dark chocolate."

"I waited until she was fast asleep, I looked if the moon was by Luna Park."

"By Luna Park or"—Madam Ducoff peeked into a shopping bag—"by Feltman's."

"And even so, a nix," her client reported. "My Rhoda wants a boy, the boy don't walk the earth yet. She wants a boy"—the woman shut her eyes tightly and haughtily and thinned out her underlip—"loo-loo-loo, that he should know from the tea-yater and he should have only deep thoughts and he should wonder all the time about what's in the soul . . ."

"For that I could give drops."

". . . and he should know from current events and he shouldn't listen too much to the radio, only to the Town Meeting of the Air, and he should go in for Cooper Union courses."

"Although the drops I don't like. The drops you dassn't keep around too long."

"If I was the type mother that pushed," declared her client, "all right, I'd understand. But I talk to her with kid gloves. 'Rhoda, listen to your best friend, look in the mirror, you'll see you're not Toots Matzoknaydel that . . .'"

"Lady," Simon croaked, "we we we got a boy for her."

"That's *right!*" said Marshall.

Hymie said, "He gotta big, ooh, such a big . . ."

"COCKtail gingerale, five cents a glass," sang Boomie.

Whereupon Madam Ducoff, white in the face and breathing through her mouth, labored out of the booth and crossed to their table. In a second Steinbrink, growling and with a rolled-up menu, was at her side, but she held him back. And wavering in her tracks she laid hands upon the boys.

Upon Simon first, saying, "You got in Krasnowicz an uncle with two boys, and the younger one will pretty soon go to Moldonya and he'll wear a cross. It won't help, it won't help."

Boomie's brow and breast she touched, saying, "In Zitomar you got one cousin, Sura Beryl, that she's already starting to run and she'll keep running. It won't help, it won't help."

Hymie's brow and breast she also touched, saying, "By Polkotrovitz there's a certain Amram Goldug, by your momma a nephew, that he's a drinker and a fighter and four men together can't throw him down. It won't help, it won't help."

Marshall's both hands she gripped, saying, "In Vlotcheniki your Aunt Tzeena the Baker is going to make it her business to everyday bake a special little baking and give away free to the priests. It won't help, it won't help."

"Waha!" went Boomie.

". . . teasing," muttered Hymie.

"Just just just teasing," Simon wheedled.

"*Sure,*" said Marshall.

"She can't take a tease," Boomie announced loftily.

Then Steinbrink walked them to the door, saying, "Scrammayvoo."

And Zwerkel said, "Goom-bye."

Then Steinbrink said, "This is what it is with today's Jewish kids."

And Zwerkel said, "The Jewish kids of today are all this way."

But Madam Ducoff called back the boys and handed Simon and Boomie each a quarter, saying, *"Kinde, kinde,* you know what I'll tell you? I'll tell you how the widower told his son right after the funeral. When his son sees he's in bed with the maid: 'In my grief do I know what I'm doing?'"

All the way to the Surf the boys went, "It won't help, it won't help." On the line, a long one, going almost to the Knishe Queen, they encountered Lila Edelstein. And for fifteen, twenty minutes, till she called over the matron, they made her life miserable.

6

March 9, 1938

Last night Dad got in a philosophy mood. He was reading
Gasoline Alley and they had in it what they have every year
when its Skeezix's birthday. They go all the way back to
when he was put on Uncle Walt's doorstep and they give the
old cartoons how he started to get big. Dad then said how
fast the time goes.

Mom said Believe me, you look around and its all over
and a person is a big big dope if she puts off her youthful
dreams and thats why if GOD spares us, we should live and
be well and she should feel better than she's been feeling
on her dropped stomach we're all three going before Pesach
to see Ohrbachs.

I right away remembered its a long time since I went
near my Journal*Diary, and here I am. Plenty has happened,
so I naturally will give only the Highlights. Some of the
Highlights are——

I go to James Russell Lowell. Lowell the Hole! High
School. The third term. I skipped.

I belong still to the Battle Aces S.A.C. We are thinking

of changing the name to the Last Mohicans or the Stars of David.

Boomie and Hymie go also to James Russell Lowell. We are in the same Home Room and are all three taking a General Course.

Marshall goes to Brooklyn Tech. He did very well on the admission test, one of the highest, because they give you mostly math and math he happens to be good in. Now all of a sudden he wants to be an aeronautical engineer.

I smoke now.

I get wet dreams. Theyre much much better then jerking off, except that you can jerk off as much as you want and wet dreams you never know when you get.

I have decided to be in love. The girl's initials are C.D. Why I fell in love with her is that she reminds me of the one who played Dale Arden in the Flash Gordon chapter and she has a Jean Parker voice. The reason I say LOVE is she doesn't even have big tits.

I have pretty good teachers. They are——

For Home Room Mrs. Jacobey. I have her also for Elementary Biology 2. She is interesting, she has a good sense of humor. Once she asked Give me another word for conjugation. Somebody giggled and she right away said Not THAT word.

For French Mr. Wexler. He is pretty good, he makes you have to pay attention. Everybody said Watch for a certain habit, they were right. He always walks around and stands in a certain way with one foot on the radiator like he wants to show off he has big balls.

For Geometry Mr. Zeldach. He was voted most popular teacher in Lowell. His wife is Mrs. Zeldach, she teaches Commercial Law. He is faculty advisor on the Photography Squad. Bomba Katz belongs and he told me how he was once invited to his house and he saw about six big pictures of Mrs. Zeldach where you don't exactly see her naked but you know she has to be naked.

For English   Miss Hochman. She is interesting and she tries and attempts to do different things. When we had to read "A Tale Of Two Cities" she made us write up our reports as if what happened in the book was just just yesterday and we were newspaper reporters. She liked my headline, Sidney Carten Loses Head Over Lucy Manet. If I could jerk off on a teacher she's who I'd use. Because I happen to sit third row first seat she plops herself right on top my desk. I have to naturally pay attention and look up and when I look up I look up like right under her armpit. She wears only sleeveless, you can see where the tit starts.

For Gym   Mr. Stock. They call him Stock the Jock because he's always worrying if you wear a jock strap. He's always saying You'll be grateful later for the protection you give your testicles now. Everybody who has him knows how you get out of doing gym work with him. He'll say Today is Horse Practice, or Today is Tumbling. So all you have to do is raise your hand and say You read or You heard that in Turkey there's a lot of Syphillis. He will say That particular item I have not read or heard but I am not surprised boys as Syphillis has killed more persons then the wars all put together and is very highly prevelent today even. That is why we have to get into and establish strong cleanliness and protective habits and make it our regular and daily business to take good care of things like our testicles.

March 11, 1938

Hymie's bubbee got another stroke and one leg is paralyzed on her.

I went up yesterday with Boomie to do my Bio and she was sitting around grinning and grinning. Hymie's mom was yelling on her in Jewish, Laugh go ahead laugh. Believe me, I'd also laugh good if I know its four weeks before Pesach and I don't have to move a finger.

In Hymie's building they got a new super. Hohner. He likes us. His ambition is he wants to fuck one kind of girl from every country. He says he fucked ninety-three different girls from forty-seven countries and he found out one thing. That how you know when a girl wants to fuck is she lets you lick her bushkee. Hymie says he can't fix shit.

Yesterday in Gelfman he had to go and call Mrs. Chepper to the phone. He left my malted on the machine so I went behind the counter, I threw in three melorols.

March 15, 1938

I forgot yesterday to put in that I saw Miss Matucci.

I say I forgot but I don't know if I forgot or I didn't want to.

What happened was I went to get Dads Forvitz and I saw Miss Matucci across the street go in the bakery. I got very excited as I hadn't seen her in a long time, I think only once after I got out of public school. She had said to me on the last day I was one of the smart ones and she wanted me definitely to come see her and that she would follow my carreer with great interest. It was the first time anybody said to me CARREER.

In fact she even signed my album TO SIMON SLOAN BRIGHT AND BRASH, IN HIS FUTURE CARREER HE WILL BE A SMASH, WITH FOND HOPES AND BEST WISHES TERESA MATUCCI.

I crossed over and I went also in the bakery. I stood not too close to her, like by the coffee ring section. She was by their aclair and napoleon section.

I then made believe I was really all along looking for the aclair and napoleon section. I even said to the bakery lady, Do you have today aclairs and napoleons? She showed me where and I looked just at her and I moved where she was moving.

I then made believe as though I had not seen Miss Matucci before but that now she was familiar to me.

I turned around the forvitz to the back where they have only the English print and I said, Excuse me, Hello Miss Matucci.

I was then without realizing it sort of raising my hand.

Miss Matucci said Well hello there.

Then it was her next and she told the bakery lady she wanted to pick up what was put away in the morning for Matucci. I said I remember you from P.S. 84. She said Oh I believe I remember you too.

I swear to GOD it just came out that I said Well we remember each other. In a sort of snotty way.

I then just went outside. Actually I didnt JUST go outside but I said like to myself I want to see whats in the window.

Where she could see me through the window I stood. I made believe I was looking at the aclairs and napoleons. I smoked a cigarette I had left over.

Why I smoked a cigarette.

For 2 important reasons.

One is a baby reason. That I wanted to show her I was now a big boy.

Two was to show her not only and not so much I was a big boy but that she got older.

On this no more and that's it.

March 18, 1938

Today it rained and nobody went out so the school cafeteria was jammed.

C.D. sat right by my table. She was walking and walking and I kept wishing her over. SIT BY MY TABLE SIT BY MY TABLE SIT BY MY TABLE.

As I was the only one she knew and she was the only one I knew we talked a little. It was so noisy she couldn't hear. I was talking inside my head and without moving my mouth. This is what I do sometimes on the subway, I can go AHAHAHAH. With the vibrations. In that way I talked, I looked right at her and I said I LOVE YOU I LOVE YOU I LOVE YOU.

An interesting thought occurred. That supposing everybody in the cafeteria and everybody everywhere in the world is doing the same exact thing but has in them a different vibration. Like I'm doing I LOVE YOU I LOVE YOU I LOVE YOU and somebody from the next table is going FUCK YOU FUCK YOU FUCK YOU. Never mind.

A continuation on March 18, 1938

What I forgot is when C.D. sat by my table I hadn't eaten as yet my lunch. It was right on the table in a double bag. A chala and sardine sandwich, one piece of chala alone was two inches. The whole thing I threw away. Mom was sore I didn't save the bags. Dad said What did you expect from him you dumb dope you. I don't blame him he walks all over you and he takes advantage. Why not and I would do the same thing if I had a mother a good natured lemon, when she nursed me she ate Suchard to make her milk rich.

March 19, 1938

We were doing journalism in Miss Hochman's class and Boomie gave the whole class such a laugh that Mr. Gladstone sent in somebody from next door to find out what happened.

Miss Hochman wanted us to write a headline that would tell and reveal a whole news event. She asked for blackboard volunteers. Boomie volunteered.

He wrote this headline.

FOWL PLAY IN CHICKEN MARKET.

Before I forget I'm putting down that I am feeling a little bad about the sandwich from yesterday. It must have had in it a whole King Oscar can. My action shows in a way lack of character. I admit. Zachie Schaefer will wear a yarmalka right in cafeteria when he eats and I should in the same way not be ashamed if I have thick sandwiches. What if I went to school with only goyim, I then would have to starve?

March 20, 1938

Something interesting.
I can't jerk off on C.D.
Not in the bathroom.

In bed I can do it only if I use somebody elses body and then at the end just her face.

March 22, 1938

Hohner told another way you can tell if a girl wants to get laid. She takes your cock and she starts rubbing it inside her twatzer.

More on March 22, 1938

We had assembly and Dr. Perlig announced we would from now on have to sing the first AND the second stanza of "The Star Spankled Banner." Also the boys could not wear sweaters in halls and classes and any sweater offense will be treated the same way as a lack of tie offense.

MYRT AND MARGE went off the radio, this afternoon was their last time. At the end of the fifteen minutes the ones who play them said goodbye but they couldn't talk. They cried. Mom couldn't get over shikses could cry like that.

March 28, 1938

A Battle Aces S.A.C. meeting was held today.

We had no real business. From last time there was a tabled resolution, whether we should consider uniting and unifying with Bomba Katz and the Spartan S.A.C. We again tabled it because while the Spartan S.A.C. has ping pong and weight lifting they are mostly highly orthodox. So on Friday night and all day Saturday we would have to do hardly a thing which is not for us.

We kidded around. Marshey had with him old guns, the Hoot Gibson set, they used to be definitely the best, and we tried for who was the fastest draw.

I beat everybody.

The way you do it is you tie the gun right over your knee. Thats where your hand exactly goes, it doesn't have to move up or down and you save that little bit of time.

We next did what we didn't do in a long time. Its in the Constitution. Everyone has to regularly tell a personel secret.

We stopped doing it from I forget when.

Hymie told that till he was between ten and eleven he thought when you went to the movies you had real actors and actresses and they were behind the screen.

Marshey told that when he was about seven and they lived in Boro Park they had a neighbor Mr. Shatz and he thought Mr. Shatz was God.

Boomie told that he had a cousin Cele and when they visited her he used to go into her bathroom because he was crazy about the smell of her shit.

I for a second thought I would tell about C.D. but instead I told that when I was about ten I was positive I was Richard Dix's son.

We afterwards went near Ocean Parkway and Neck Road to squeeze tits. No girls were around. There was just a lady, she had a pair down to her belly. We all bounced them but we couldn't squeeze as her coat was too heavy. On the way back she was still around. She wanted to know if we were Jewish. Boomie made believe he was dovening. The lady said Its not nice for Jewish boys to walk around in a Jewish neighborhood on *Shabos* and they should smoke.

March 26, 1938

Hohner told us the best best lays he ever had live in the middle of Australia. He said there the girls have a lot of hair around their twatzers, that's why they call it the bush country.

Mrs. Abrams Sheldon passed high on the post office test. She invited in the whole floor for delicatessen. Mom got angry at Sheldon. She asked him if where he would work he could do something for her on postals, she uses them a lot. He didn't answer.

The downstairs bell rang, Mom got very nervous. She ticked back. It turned out it was Cousin Phillie. She said Hello stranger how are you, this is a very very pleasant surprise, and what brings you here. Cousin Phillie said he was in the neighborhood and he wanted to use the bathroom.

It was a really beautiful day later so Mom and Dad and I went on the boardwalk. Mom told Dad in Jewish he should walk with me to talk and make better friends. Dad said I don't know what to say. Mom said What whats the difference, just have like a little discussion. Dad said A discussion, how about we should have a discussion sonny. What do you like better, you like better a sour pickle or a half sour pickle? I told him I used to like the half sour pickles better but I think now I like them both the same. Dad went back to Mom and he said, What do you want from me, What can I do, From the day he was born this boy is my enemy.

March 27, 1938

I wanted to put in something. Its philosophy but its not exactly philosophy.

Never mind.

March 28, 1938

We had gym today.

We were supposed to run around the indoor track ten times at least. Mr. Stock gave the announcement last week yet.

I didn't feel like it as did nobody else in the class. We made up what to do.

We went to gym and we lined up. After Mr. Stock took the attendance he read notices. We made believe we didn't understand them. One guy would say which exit do we have to use for a fire drill and another guy would say How can it be that exit, that exit they keep closed. Mr. Stock had to explain, this took ten minutes.

Then Mr. Stock said Lets get on the track. Right away Shecky Meltzer said Mr. Stock, a venereal disease question. I have a friend and I was talking with this friend and he told me about gonerea. My friend says you can have the gonerea and sometimes you don't know and you can't tell.

Mr. Stock said It is not hard to know and there are certain laymen ways to tell about gonerea. The best layman way is that you get a burning and annoying pain inside your male organ. This is like the pain you can get sometimes and occasionally when you are soaping around the male organ and soap gets inside. Mr. Stock said You should watch there for the condition of your testicles, if you make it your business to keep your testicles in good health everything else will take care of itself.

This took fifteen minutes.

Juley Sher then got him with another question. What if you come to the gym and you forget your jock? Should you borrow somebody elses jock?

Mr. Stock got more excited even than with the gonerea question and he said Absolutely the worst thing you could do to the health of your testicles is to wear another persons jock. He said He himself owns many different jocks that he keeps washed and clean and he never wears the same one more then a couple of days running.

When he said running this reminded him about our track and he made us get going. The bell rang before we went around even twice.

More on March 27, 1938

It will be remembered that I here wrote NEVER MIND recently.

This was for thoughts I had on Sunday Night.

These thoughts started first with a thought of Chic Sale, that he's dead.

I then went to another thought about when I met Miss Matucci. This gave me cramps.

My next thought was how Chic Sale played once Lincoln and that Lincoln also was dead. I figured out that Lincoln was dead and Chic Sale was dead and I also would be dead. This wasn't just imagining. I can IMAGINE myself a lot of times dead, but I'm dead the way you're dead in the movies. In other words you're dead but you're not really dead because you know you have to play in another movie. I all of a sudden knew what dead was. And what it was was such a lousey rotten thing I started in to go AHAHAHAH and I squeezed and squeezed my throat. With both hands.

The next thought I went to was this could be the best secret weapon in the world. In the SPIDER once they had a secret weapon. It was a certain sound. A machine made that sound and could kill all the people anywhere who heard it. This would be just as good. This would be BETTER. If you somehow could get control of this thought and if you could put this thought into the minds of people and if you could regulate it and make this thought stronger and stronger and stronger nobody could stand it. They would be killed by a busting of the brain.

That's how it was bad, that's why for that night I put down NEVER MIND.

March 30, 1938

Where Mister George the beauty parlor was a store is supposed to open up. They have a sign HYMANS HONEYPOT a new line of health foods.

Dad has a chance for a promotion. Old Man Eislin is going to move with a daughter to Lakewood and Dad said the manager dropped him hints if he wants to be the ticket tearer. Mom cried. She said Shmuel you can say you got a smart wife. I knew I knew I knew something good would happen, I had in a dream that my momma met C. Aubrey Smith and he gave her for me a beautiful bunch of undershirts, I didn't even have to pick up the hem. Dad said I hope you washed them good, not that C. Aubrey Smith isn't a clean type but you can't tell who he got them from.

March 31, 1938

I looked in the girls toilet for a second today. This was because as I was passing a girl opened the door. Boomie said he thinks they have machines there where the girls buy napkins two for a nickel.

We were talking about when a girl gets periods with Hohner. He said if you look at their snatchers from certain angles you wonder how something that looks so terrible could feel so good.

He told sort of a good one.

How do bananas fuck? In bunches.

April 3, 1938

I am probably even more in love with C.D.

Today in French there were absences and I was moved up three seats from my regular seat. This put me in the next row and one seat in front of C.D.

As Mr. Wexler was giving us number drill he filled up the blackboard in front and so he went to use the side blackboard.

I turned around to see him and in doing so I looked up C.D.s dress. This was not even my fault, she had her legs crossed.

I saw definitely up to her pants. I think I saw twat hair but Im not definite.

C.D. saw that I had seen. This is definite.

What she then did was not to move her legs for a few minutes. If I wanted I could have kept looking up her dress but I naturally didnt.

After a few minutes she moved her legs and crossed them a different way. She did something with her shoe as if she was telling me Im moving my legs in a different way ONLY because I have to do something with my shoe not because I want to embarass you for your accidental looking.

Never mind.

April 4, 1938

A letter came from school today that I have an over 91 average. Next term if I want I can take 5 majors.

Captain Blood is coming down to the Surf. We missed it, I forget why. I and Boomie and Hymie and Marshey will all go together.

Rabbi Neuberger died.

For my fifth major it will be either History or Spanish.

Most likely History as I'm afraid to get mixed up with Spanish and French.

I got back an EXCELLENT! from Miss Hochman today.

This was from the assignment last week to write at least a page and a half on a very ordinary saying. What we wrote was not supposed to be ordinary. She gave us like A STITCH IN TIME SAVES NINE and DON'T CROSS YOUR BRIDGES TILL YOU COME TO THEM.

I took WHAT YOU DON'T KNOW WON'T HURT YOU.

What I wrote I wrote in not even a half-hour, then another fifteen minutes to re-write on good paper and with the headings.

For my concrete example I put in something you see all the time in cartoons. This is when like in a Terrytoons the animal is chased up a tree. He keeps climbing the tree and he will always go up and up to where there is no more tree. But he doesn't realize, he climbs and he climbs the thin and empty air. Then he will always at a certain part take a look into this thin and empty air, he will all of a sudden realize what he is doing has to be impossible and he will then fall and crash down.

I showed it to Mom and Dad. Mom cried, Dad said I got my own troubles.

No teacher did too much today as it was the last day before the Easter Week Vacation.

We got a big letter from one of Dad's relatives in Europe. She is a girl who wants to go to America, if we could help. Mom said this is from a part of dad's family that when I was born didn't send even a mazeltoff.

Fun today with Hymie's bubbee.

She was sitting around talking to herself in Jewish. Some

hing like the whole world should give one one little move
and turn upside down.

Hymies mom told us You're smart boys, maybe you can
do me a little favor.

What she wanted was we should figure out a way that
he bubbee would sign a certain thing from the Williamsburg Saving Bank. I WANT THE BEARER TO DO ME A FAVOR
AND TAKE OUT FROM MY ACCOUNT ONLY THE INTEREST FOR
THE LAST FIVE MONTHS.

At my idea we all tried signature practice.

We said that the bubbee should hear Let's have a contest
to see who has the nicest signature. I wrote on the back of
the bank thing my signature, also Hymie and Hymie's mom
wrote their signature. We then turned it over and Hymie
said Hey bubbee show us how you do your signature, you
know everybody that my bubbee she has the best signature.

The bubbee took her both hands and she showed us her
ass.

At Boomie's idea we then all went to the window and we
made believe we were waving. Hymie's mom even went out
on the fire escape.

She said very loud What is it President Roosevelt, I
don't hear you too good.

Boomie said You too President Roosevelt, you too have a
happy Pesach.

I said The bubbee can't come to the window President
Roosevelt, she's also a cripple.

Hymie's mom said You want her to sign what, I can't
hear you President Roosevelt, what should she sign?

Boomie said Gee and no kidding President Roosevelt,
you tried to call the bubbee by Gelfman only the line was
busy, gee.

I said, What you should do President Roosevelt, you
know what, when you go on the radio again say MY FRANZ
AND THE BUBBEE TOO.

Hymie's mom said In other words President Roosevelt,
let me understand how you put it, you put it this way and

this is the way you would put it. The bubbee should sign, the bubbee has to sign, the bubbee better sign or she can't get no more pollyseeds.

We then closed the window and we all went looking in the bubbee's draw for pollyseeds and we took away the bag. Hymie's mom thought she had one probably in the bloomers but she would get it later.

The bubbee said in Jewish she would sign they should take out the interest. Not for five months interest, for three months.

Hymie's mom said It's a deal, let it be three months, it's erev Pesach, Pesach is a happy holiday, I will be the good one.

When we went down Hymie showed that he snitched a dime from the bubbee's draw. He treated to egg creams at Gelfman, the small.

April 9, 1938

We saw today Captain Blood with Errol Flynn and Frame Up with Dick Foran.

Captain Blood I liked VERY much. It was a long double bill, they gave four cartoons and the March of Time. We all wanted to see Captain Blood over and we couldn't, it would make us late to the seder.

In Captain Blood they had the best duel scenes I ever saw. When it was over I had to go to the toilet which was very crowded. Everybody kidded around, they shoved and they shpritzed water. I felt very tough and wanted to have a fight. That feeling I remember I got when I saw G Man, in the part where James Cagney throws a guy all over the room. Also from the Prizefighter and the Lady, when Max Baer starts in to win Primo Carnera.

Then what happened is we went out in the street and the first thing is that by the Knishe Queen they're putting the chairs on top of the tables to close early for the seder. I right away and immediately didn't feel tough and I didn't want to have a fight or anything. I had the feeling like there was a squeeze of my balls.

Enough on this.

No more and never mind.

The seder was all right. Dad did it in fifteen, twenty minutes less than last year, he didn't feel like bothering with all the plagues.

Mom cried. She said she just just just remembered how when she was in Hartford Connecticut Cousin Phillie promised when she got married he would take care of the liquor, sure he took care of the liquor, he and his came, and all by themselves they took care of nearly a whole whole case.

Dad was talking how when I was a little boy I got my biggest kick on the seder playing with his yarmalka.

He showed me how I used to grab the yarmalka and I used to swing it around and I used to then put it in my mouth.

He said Look what you did to it momzer murderer and Look at the mark you made on an all-silk yarmalka, even the stitching is silk.

He started zetzing me with it, he wasn't kidding around. Mom had to hold him under the sink water and sing him Jewish songs after.

April 10, 1938

I by myself walked on the boardwalk all the way to Sea Gate. Boomie and Hymie were away with family for the seders and Marshey I didn't feel like seeing. That's all about him. Never mind and forget it.

I smoked 2 cigarettes and in the new place I bought a waffle and ice cream. This is definitely a chumitz.

Then something happened to give me a sad feeling.

What happened——

There was a husband and a wife on a bench. I swear to God and I should drop dead that the man looked like me. Not how I look now exactly, how I could look when Im his age.

The wife I just just couldn't stand. I right away and immediately threw a hate on her. For no exact reason. On account of her mouth was too thin and her lips were too thin I wanted her to go to hell.

My feeling was that this was the REAL TRUTH, the way that time I had the REAL TRUTH about Miss Matucci and Chic Sale and being dead. The wife was the REAL TRUTH about getting laid like that was the REAL TRUTH about being dead. God gives you nothing for nothing, he gives you shit.

I later talked to Hohner about this, but in a kidding way. He showed me with a pencil and paper how you're better off not getting married and that its much much cheaper when you feel like getting laid to go to the whores. Even the most expensive ones.

April 11, 1938

I and Boomie and Hymie went to squeeze tits near Neck Road.

Marshey didn't feel like going and his mother didn't let us even in the house. She said he's in with a new crowd from Brooklyn Tech, they have in common together engineering things, and as you get older you go to different interests.

By mistake we grabbed the tit of a girl we know. This is because who looks at the faces?

She was Marie Esposito, she went to Junior High with us and she took a Commercial Course.

We later went to a movie we were never in before, the Elmont on Neck Road. They had two old pictures that were very good. Captured with Douglas Fairbanks Jr. and Leslie Howard and Paul Lukas and Riff Raff with Spencer Tracy and Jean Harlow. Even so I like it better in a movie I know. Here I didn't want to go to the toilet. It takes me a long time to get used to a movie toilet, the one in the Surf I wasn't used to till I think I was nine or ten.

Dad came home in a good mood and excited. His manager told him he'll have a ticket tearer tryout next week maybe. So before supper we practiced with cardboard. I and Mom would go up to him, we would be the mother and her boy who's more than twelve and she's trying to sneak him in on a half-price. Mom made me write up in ink a little chart for Dad he should have it handy and know what to say in the differing situations.

DON'T TELL ME THIS LUMP IS ONLY 11 LADY OR MRS.

I SHOULD HAVE IN THE BANK $100 BILLS HOW MUCH YOUR GOLEM IS OVER 11.

DEFINITELY HE'S 11 HE'S 11 POSITIVELY YOU KNOW WHERE HE'S 11 IN HIS SHOES HE'S ELEVEN.

LADY OR MRS. GO BACK AND TELL YOUR HUSBAND BUY HIM- SELF A FULL PRICE.

Dad did pretty good. Mom's only criticism is he shouldn't shouldn't shouldn't forget he's in front of the public and when you're in front of the public you have to keep smiling.

April 12, 1938

Nothing I didn't see is in the movies.

When Mom went shopping I shaved off cock hair.

Also I burned up toilet paper.

Boomie and Hymie later called for me. We went down-stairs and kidded around with Hohner. He had a good joke. He asks Why do you call a snatch a snatch? You're supposed to say I'll bite. He answers Me too.

He also told a new Mae West joke. That one I forgot.

Dopey Duhvee's mother called us from the window if we wanted to take him for an airing. We said all right for ten cents each.

We went with him to Bay 11 near where the penny arcade is. We then had an idea.

We made believe the penny arcade man wanted to give him a bar mitzva present.

We told him Go inside Duhvee, he's got some wonder-ful presents for you, wow does he have for Duhvee presents, you'll get presents.

He went inside, they didn't know what he was talking about. This got him sore.

F

Right away he ran on the beach, he put a lot of sand in his stocking hat and also in his pocket and he went back in the arcade. He there threw around the sand everywhere and on everything. Also he banged his head on that glass thing with the mechanical gypsy inside. It cracked the glass a little and part of what makes her hand move fell off.

The penny arcade man and his wife and another lady tried to get him out. We all made believe we just just happened to walk in.

We all three together said, Look who's here, Marshall Herberg, 881 Brighton 5 St., Apt. 1GG.

On the way home Duhvee was pretty good except he threw sand on us. His mother didn't like that there was sand in his hat. She said we didn't take such hot care of him and gave us only a quarter all together.

April 13, 1938

Mrs. Plaut got us up very early.

She wanted Mom should do her a favor. She said Mr. Plaut is sleeping in an unusual way and I don't like how he looks.

We went down and we all looked. He was blue and he had a smell.

Mom started in to cry a lot and then Mrs. Plaut started in to cry a little.

Mom said in Jewish, Rifka Rifka your pearl, your jewel, your diamond is gone. He's gone, good bye and good luck your lover that to him you were the sun the moon and the stars, he wouldn't let you open a door yourself and he wouldn't let you take an extra step and he wouldn't let you lift a heavy bag and he cried if he saw you cleaning out the ice box, he would run upstairs to me and he would cry Malvena I can't can't can't take it and I don't want to be there to see my bride my princess clean out the ice box.

Mom started to cry a little and Mrs. Plaut started to cry a lot.

Mom said I'm not crying now for him because for him

it's all over, he's taken care of and finished off, he got no more worries. Malvena the Orphan is crying for the living widow that she'll be all alone by herself on the earth and in such such a big apartment, what does she need like this three and ½ rooms, you could say four rooms because the foyer by itself is practically a room.

Mom started to pull her hair and Mrs. Plaut started to choke herself.

Mom said For now and in the next weeks I'm not so worried about the living widow. For now and in the next few weeks she'll have coming and going and hustle and bustle and a full house. Its after and its later on I start in thinking and getting shooting cramps on my dropped stomach, when the time comes and she realizes shes Mrs. Nobody and a Teitlebaum who handles her now with kid gloves and opens up for her half a quarter a fresh box of farmer cheese starts in with his big mouth.

Mom started in banging on the wall and Mrs. Plaut started in kicking on the floor.

Mom said What I don't don't don't want to think about is how the living widow is going to start in not eating and she'll figure how for one person it don't pay to prepare and for herself alone a snip of tomato and onion is plenty good enough. That's why not only a Teitlebaum is going to take terrible advantage of her but also a type like Joe the Vegetable Man, he'll figure why not and what does it hurt, I need her very very badly with her tomato and onion business.

Mom made believe she was going to stab herself with a cut glass bowl and Mrs. Plaut made believe she was throwing herself out of the window.

Mom said she's going to have to have to have broad shoulders the living widow Mrs. Nobody, she'll have to realize people won't have no interest in her, she'll be walking in the street, that's when she has the strength to leave the house, she'll see somebody and she'll say hello how are you and what's happening, they'll answer her excuse me if I rush along and hurt your feelings but I'm not interested in you.

Her own own children will behave to her no different, what's the matter don't I remember a certain case you should remember it too, they had it on W E V D, how the living widow comes back from the funeral, her husband's grave is still still fresh, she opens up a closet to change into a little house dress and she looks and looks and she finally asks her boy, whether he was Milton or Myron I don't remember, she says Milton or Myron did you happen to notice a house dress that in my sorrow I wanted to change into and he tells her Lady for the work you'll be doing in the chicken market you don't need no fancy house dresses.

Mom fainted on the floor and Mrs. Plaut fainted on the chester draws.

I then went to get Mrs. Abrams and Mrs. Harlib and they took over so Mom could make breakfast.

We had sour cream and pear and Mom put on a fresh undershirt.

Mom said To hell with it, who cares and never mind, today I'll neglect the house a little, we'll live one one day in a dirty house, I'll run back to the widow a few hours, it'll be a real real real mitzvoor.

Mom sent me down to Mrs. Plaut, I should tell her Please please please take it easy, she's coming right down in a few minutes to cheer her sorrow and ease up her grief.

April 14, 1938

Mom went to the funeral, Dad and I were in the house alone the whole morning.

He had a real good mood.

He made me a scrambled egg in the Special Daddy Way and he let me eat from the pot to get all the fried part.

We had nice discussion.

He told me an Old Country story about why he always loved the emperer FRANZ JOSEPH.

His father was like in the Austrian Army and they were having a special inspection and the emperer Franz Joseph was walking up and down with the generals and all the soldiers had to absolutely not move.

Then a little before they get to the row where his father is his father sneezes. So emperer Franz Joseph with all the generals stop and they look and they look at his father.

Dad got an old hat and he put it on his head in a crazy way to show the way they all looked.

Then the emperer Franz Joseph says to the generals they should bring him later this soldier who sneezed at his emperer for a special punishment.

So a whole bunch of soldiers come and they march march march his father to the emperer.

Dad did around the kitchen how they went march march march.

The soldiers then stand behind the father with the guns and his father gets down on his knees.

Dad even got down on his knees.

The emperer Franz Joseph gives his father a look but he doesn't say anything.

Then he says Are you the soldier who gave a sneeze before?

His father tries to answer only nothing comes out. So all the soldiers kick him and with the guns they hit him.

Then the emperer Franz Joseph asks him again Are you the soldier who gave a sneeze before?

Again his father tries to answer and again he can't talk. So all the soldiers again beat him up.

Then the emperer Franz Joseph says I will ask one more time for the last time are you the soldier that gave a sneeze before?

His father finally answers him how he's the soldier. So the emperer Franz Joseph says Gezundheight.

I then helped Dad straighten up and also he let me put new batteries in his search light. Also he gave me 2 ¢ and I got the NEWS by Gelfman, Dad let me have the jokes first.

Dad talked about when Smitty didn't have Herby and

when Dick Tracy was named Plainclothes Tracy and how Moon Mullins used to look different.

He said Some day we should go only the two of us on the West End Line.

Also he said If the West End Line goes near the Roxy movie and if the Roxy movie happens to have on the stage Jan Peerce we might go to the Roxy. This is because his manager told him how everyone has to see the Roxy before he dies.

I swear to God and let me drop dead that I didn't do anything.

He just just got sore and he nearly broke the search light on me. He said You rotten momzer murderer you know you're going to outlive me.

I went in the toilet and I locked the door until he had to go to work.

Tomorrow is back to school.

April 15, 1938

I got a notice in Home Room to fill out and hand in my fifth major request by ten days.

Mr. Zeldach did something interesting in Geometry. He showed us with geometry how a slide machine works. Its not his fault but I got very annoyed and also depressed. Because it made me think of engineering and from engineering I went to Marshey. I have to put here that this morning when I was going to school he was going upstairs on the Brighton, he was holding a model plane. I will write in here that it was a beauty and I never in my life saw a better model plane, which is something I can't do, I do not have the knack. So although I had planned and figured out for this kind of happening, that we would bump into each other and I would play dumb, natural habit made me right away grin and wave. Definitely he saw how I waved but made believe he didn't. So I am planning my revenge for years from now. He'll be a big shot and with a lot of people and I'll go over,

I'll say Hello shmuk and I'll shake hands with him. While
I'm shaking hands I'll give him an indian burn.

We had songs in French today, Mr. Wexler brought in
a little victrola. THE MARSEILLAISE everybody loved. Mr.
Wexler like conducted us. On the marchons marchons part
C.D. without realizing it held longer to her note then everybody else. She has some voice. She went for a second as high
as Deanna Durbin. I forgot over the vacation how I loved
her. I did in my throat I love you I love you I love you.
Never mind.

This reminds me.

I had a dream I was talking to Hohner. He was definitely
Hohner even though in the dream he was supposed to be a
movie actor, I think Dewey Robinson, the big shlubb, he's
usually a waiter or he owns the bar.

The both of us are standing on line to see Transatlantic
Tunnel. He's either treating me or I gave him the money
for my ticket, I forget why.

In the dream I remember that I'm afraid when we get
inside I won't get a good seat. Like I'll be sitting facing the
wrong way or they'll put me on the outside. I had this in
dreams before where they put me on the outside and I see
the movie only from far away.

I tell this to Hohner in the dream, that he should be
careful when he buys the ticket and to make sure they have
a regular seat for me.

This is how he answers me, he says, his exact exact words,
Look don't worry. Every body gets laid.

Right away or pretty soon I made myself wake up. I forget why but I felt so lousey and I got such cramps I had to
go to the toilet. Usually I don't need to go till after I eat
breakfast.

I didn't really forget why but never mind and no more.

April 16, 1938

For my fifth major I handed in History.

In the Sugar Bowl I saw C.D. She said just to talk I don't know if I should get the lime rickey.

I said They make a good one here. I think she wanted me to buy her one or to say I would buy her one but I didn't have the money.

Like from the dream I did in my throat Some body is going to lay you Some body is going to lay you.

I jerked off on Hohner doing it to her and to Helen Mack and Frances Dee.

April 17, 1938

I notice between my wrists and my elbows I'm getting like a muscle with veins. Hymie has it a year already.

In Biology there was a movie on digestion. Every body was kidding around. Like when it said on the bottom AND NOW THE SMALL INTESTINE IN ACTION Sol Wershba clapped. It was to me definitely sort of disgusting, all the organs going in and out and you see the juices for PERISTALSIS. I sat up front with Boomie to see better. Naturally we started laughing. We laughed so hard the whole row shook. Then just when I was stopping Boomie went PERISTALSIS and I got it worse then before. Mrs. Jacobey didn't notice.

In English we were having a discussion from the NEW YORK TIMES. Miss Hochman said what are the three main points brought out by the editorial? The three main points brought out by the editorial are Implementation of the League of Nations, the Reduction of Armaments and Greater Intercourse between different countries. Boomie passed a note FUCK GERMANY and that finished me. Miss Hochman said We shall wait until the babies come to order.

April 18, 1938

The Battle Aces S.A.C. were supposed to have a meeting today. We made up not to as there was no new business. Anyway we all had homework.

Dad started in today to be the ticket tearer. He had a good mood today and Mom made us do the Happiness

Dance. He showed us a note that came for him in care of his manager. Congratulations and mazel tuff to you and yours on the beginning of a new career, your very good friend President Roosevelt.

April 19, 1938

LaGuardia talked last night in the Lowell auditorium and he went up Brighton Beach Avenue. We saw from the roof.

He was in a big car that you could move back the top and he sat on something high. Mrs. Harlib said He's as big as a minute and Mr. Harlib said That's all right and don't worry, he's plenty big enough and God bless him the little luksh.

Mrs. Plaut said All the lukshin are very strong and if you look careful you can see that for his size he's solid.

Mrs. Harlib said I'd like to see him for two minutes that's all I want, two minutes let him get locked up in one room with Mussolini.

Dad said He could have done a lot more then he did for the cap industry.

A lady across the street yelled Hello little flower hello there my piezon.

He yelled back Hello lonslight.

Mrs. Harlib and Mrs. Plaut said how he speaks a beautiful Jewish.

Mr. Harlin said The Jewish people got in him a good friend.

Mrs. Harlib said In him and in Senator Wagner.

Dad said Senator Wagner could also have done a lot more then he did for the cap industry.

As I had my homework done I went over to Hymie's house. His mom was having fun with the bubbee. The bubbee kept asking in Jewish why there was a commotion. His mom answered her in Jewish, the exact words I couldn't get, that it was Mayor LaGuardia and he came over special to see the bubbee but she wouldn't let him, she told him

F*

163

Mayor LaGuardia I'm very sorry only I got to punish the bubbee and she can't see you as she did a wet on the toilet seat.

April 20, 1938

I didn't feel good and stayed home with a hundred and a half.

I read an old Boy Allies. THE BOY ALLIES AT THE ARGONNE. I still liked it a little. Also I looked through the New York Times Illustrated History Of The Great War. Mom rested in bed with me a while and looked through it with me. She cried from it and said what a terrible time that was and we and the whole whole world should never again know from such a terrible time, people were paying sixty-nine and seventy-nine cents a dozen eggs. What I noticed was that in the pictures the people look very different from how people look today. It wasn't just the clothes, I even covered the clothes with my hand to get only the faces. What it is is on the eyes. On the eyes they have that Real Truth look. Like they know already when people look at the pictures of them they will be dead. Also I had the feeling that if I as I am now was in the picture too with them as they were then and there was something in front of us we definitely would not see the same thing. They would see a house and I would see a house but it wouldn't be the same REAL Truth about a house. This is a worry I have for a long time. Not a long time but definitely a couple of years. It has to do with once I was in the movies, it was Sally Eilers in Small Town Girl and I started all of a sudden to wonder. What if what I am watching in the movies, a certain part, is not the same thing as others are watching? I never asked anybody this, just in case, most likely not, but just in case it would turn out I am watching differently from every body else and I don't want to know.

I listened to Jimmy Fiedler. He had on Charley Ruggles and Mary Boland.

When I was listening to The Earth Turns Boomie and Hymie came over. They brought me the homework. I was lucky as there wasn't much. The whole school had no first period and my first period is Geometry which is the most homework. Instead of a first period they had in all the home rooms a discussion on too much noise and kidding around in the cafeteria and before we go to assembly.

April 21, 1938

I felt all right and I had no temperature, it was even a little bit under normal. So I went to school.

In the cafeteria a commercial course girl fainted. There were two girls near me and one of them I saw write in the other girl's notebook. It took her no time to write so it had to be one or two words. The other one looked in the notebook and she laughed. This was a real dirty laugh, it was much worse then when I and Boomie are laughing dirty. Then the other girl said You HAD to write it in my notebook you slobbina. She tore out the whole page. What was on it I'm positive had to be PERIOD or HER PERIOD. I'm sorry for a girl that she could faint from it but also it makes me very nausous. Never mind and forget it.

The one who fainted was taken away by Mr. Dembo and Mr. Swig. They didn't carry her. What they did was each one got a grip on her under the arm. I definitely saw from where I was that Mr. Dembo was making his elbow rub on her tit. Bernie Schrier came over, he also saw.

The only other thing today to note and mention was before the girl fainted I saw C.D. at a table without friends. She gave me a little wave and I gave her a little wave. I could have definitely sat down to eat with her but decided not to as again I had one of Mom's chala sandwiches. I had on me only a nickel and I was too hungry for just milk or just a Drakes cake.

April 22, 1938

Today I was in Geometry and a kid from the dean's office came in. He had a blue card and he gave it to Mr. Wexler. Mr. Wexler said Go with him Sloan Simon and take your

165

books. I dropped my loose leaf one and half the pages came out.

When we got to the dean's office the kid like pushed me into a chair. I want to here put down honest to God and I should only drop dead that even in front of Dr. Richler or anybody I wouldn't have let him get away with the push. In fact I even so sort of pushed back. But I got the thought, it was like a pop and then a whistle in my ears that I was being called down for only only one thing, for squeezing Marie Esposito's tits that time.

Dr. Richler went out of his office and he right away said to me You sit. You just sit there. I said I'm sitting I'm sitting. He said One sitting, I want only one sitting from you. Also he said No crossing of legs. I did in my throat Drop Dead Fucking Bastard Prick. Then when I opened my loose leaf notebook to fix the pages a little, they were all mixed up and dirty from when I dropped them in Geometry, he told me no studying here and no notebooks here, this is not the study hall and he shut the book on me. He was yelling and I said May I say something Dr. Richler and Dr. Richler I SHOULD like to say something, I am AWARE this is not study hall. Why I used aware was to show him I had a nice vocabulary. He in a way understood and definitely he didn't like that and he told the secretary I want a Character Card for this one, oh this one is to get a Character Card.

Before I forget he had all this time in his office a mother and a father. They sat where I couldn't see exactly. When he went back in he purposely left open the door. The reason I here say Purposely is that two times the father went over to shut it. Both times he worked and worked on the knob so the door should shut without noise and both times Dr. Richler banged it open.

The father then said in a nice way to tell him what the gym ball costs, he'll settle it up right away here with pleasure because if he doesn't go to work before twenty after ten he gets docked in his place the whole half a day.

Dr. Richler said Uhhuh yow yow but I would be more

concerned Mr. and Mrs. is it Shapiro with an e or Shapiro with an i with your boy, your son in that he reveals and demonstrates personality defect.

The mother said to the father in Jewish I don't understand do you understand. She said to the father and to Dr. Richler in English A defect I understand, thats like you buy a garment or a stocking and you see a pull you say that pull is a defect.

The father said Its the same thing but its in the personality.

The mother said So then what it is is not good.

Dr. Richler said Uh huh yow yow well that certainly is not good.

The father said I realize Dr.

Dr. Richler said to the mother I wonder, truly I wonder and indeed I wonder if yow you realize this fact, if you understand fully this situation and GRASP it.

The father said to the mother He wants to know, the Dr. is asking if you have an understanding if you got a GRASP.

The mother said I get the grasp that its important and she started in to cry.

Dr. Richler said Well I don't think do you think becoming emotional and giving way and vent to an outburst will help and aid the trouble your boy is in, his situation.

The mother said I grasp how there's trouble.

Dr. Richler said I would like you to see and view what is down here, down and entered and inscribed upon his record.

The mother said I left my reader glasses in the house, we wanted not to be late for you Dr.

What he did, this is what he did Dr. Richler, he wouldn't pass over the record. He made them have to get up and walk behind and stand near his chair. He didn't even move away the chair they should have room to stand.

I forgot to put down that before that the bell rang to change period and I felt like before I throw up. I did in my throat Marie Esposito Marie Esposito Ginzo Ginzo.

What exactly the mother and the father said I then

missed. Dr. Richler started in telling them the record would go forever with their son, it would show and reveal him a negative character for his disturbances in study hall and being a cafeteria nuisance and indulging in gym ball destruction.

The mother cried. The father said Dr. we'll give it to him, believe me he will get it from us oh he'll get it don't worry about that Dr.

Dr. Richler told them about how he was not worried and not at all was he worried, they should worry that their son's record would count always in the future against him with possible and potential employers by showing personality defect and negative character.

I did in my throat BULL SHIT COW SHIT CHICKEN SHIT CAT SHIT HORSE SHIT BULL SHIT. Probably I did it a little loud and he turned around and told me Fermez la bouche you shut that trap there. I didn't put in he teaches French, he's supposed to be a lousy teacher and every body tries not to get him.

I'll definitely forget so let me put it down here. That I begin now to understand from the movies something. Like from Let Us Live and Fury. I really didn't understand before how in these and similar movies there was a REAL TRUTH. That you could go along nice and fine and you don't know all the time and everywhere there are people who in a minute, in a second from the little nothing you do can get a power and control over you. They leave you alone, they'll just wait but if they get you once in their hands they finish you.

There was then a whole business with records. The mother said she didn't think and she never in her life knew things like that should go on a boy's record.

Dr. Richler said Yow uh huh well you didn't think you should think.

The bell rang for classes to start. I got very dizzy, I had to put my head down on top my books. Definitely I had temperature. On account of that there was a whole thing I couldn't hear. Dr. Richler was yelling OF COURSE.

The mother said Dr. you mean to say.

Dr. Richler said I mean to say. Yes.

The father said What she wants to express Dr. is how we want to pay what the gym ball costs so the gym ball should be taken away from the record.

Dr. Richler like sang in a slow way It Stays On The Record The Record Stays S T A Y S

The father and the mother talked both together and Dr. Richler went again The Record Stays S T A Y S

The mother said Please it shouldn't stay. Dr. Richler wrote down something and he showed them. The mother said Dr. I don't see without my reader glasses and the father told her the Dr. wrote no.

I don't have here down that another kid was brought in. He had dandruff in his eye lashes even, he looked like he jerked off in shit. Dr. Richler went over and pinched his cheek with a twist, then he said not to him but to the whole office This one yow this chappy I am looking forward to, he definitely is an old friend this chappy. And the kid even though you could see tears from the pinch was going heh heh heh, also he was grinning like a real shmuk. I did in my throat fuck you Dr. Richler prick fuckhead you should only cock so I would ever grin like that for you.

What happened finally with the mother and father I don't know exactly, they went and the mother was crying. Because the shmuk kept whispering what did you do and what did you do and what did you do. I answered him Go way will you do me a favor and go way you dumb idiot prick. Also I said to him a good one. You know the Otz brothers? He fell right in, naturally, he said Who are the Otz brothers? I said go Fotz and Plotz and he did his shmuk grin.

I had to go to the toilet, when I go usually is after Geometry. But Dr. Richler then called me in. Right away I found out it wasn't for Marie Esposito. He said to me Sloan Simon where is your dental note? We did back and forth My dental note Your dental note My dental note Your dental note. I told him my dental note was handed in for a long long time already, the beginning of the term. He said Sloan Simon yow you're down for a note. You know what it was? What it was and the note I was down for is Mrs. Jacobey by mistake put me down for an absence note from yesterday, I forgot to bring it. So Dr. Richler went and looked up my whole record, he saw my average that I had a 91. He told the secretary This is one of the superiors, mark this as Mistake Probable. He gave me a pass and he said All right all right go back, return to classes mon vieux, do you know what mon vieux means. I told him its an idiom, like my old friend my buddy.

Then I went to the toilet and during washing my hands I noticed something. Never mind.

All right I'll put it in. That in the mirror I saw how I was grinning that same same exact shmuk grin.

I, myself, and me.

April 23, 1938

This is funny.

In the hall I and Boomie bumped right into Marie Esposito. Boomie had real nerve, he said right away to her Hello Marie, hi ya piezon. She said hello, she even waved. But she didn't know us from shit.

We mentioned to Hohner about it. He said something interesting, he said Don't worry, she knew you but she liked getting her tits squeezed. Also we should remember girls like to get fucked as much as boys.

April 24, 1938

Miss Hochman gave us an interesting and an easy assignment. To take something in a magazine or a newspaper and make it much shorter but to keep in all the principle ideas.

A whole bunch of locks got clipped off in gym today, the plain locks not the combination. Every body says it was done by Mr. Stock because you have to get the combination ones from him and he makes money.

C.D. crossed her legs and I think she looked at me to see was I watching.

An embarrassing moment in English, I forgot.

Miss Hochman still has that habit, she walks to my row and she plops on my desk. So today she didn't know I had my hand there and I didn't know she would sit. Tonight I think is the first first night I ever jerked off on a teacher.

April 26, 1938

I went to the school library to look up and choose a magazine thing for Miss Hochman's assignment. It has to be in Tuesday.

C.D. was there. She told me she was doing honor work on Edgar Allen Poe. A friend was with her, Faye Citrin. I know Faye a little bit from junior high, she was in the two class. We all three talked for a minute. I asked did you see Sequoia, they said they would see it probably. Sequoia I mentioned for Jean Parker, C.D. makes me always think of her.

On the way out I and Faye Citrin walked together because C.D. had to rush. Her class was all the way on the first floor but we had to be right near the library. Before she went C.D. for a second turned around and she like shook hands with Faye Citrin. Immediately I noticed this because girls never or very very seldom shake hands. Faye Citrin then said to me right after Gee she's a very nice person. I said like Marshey, SURE, who said NO?

I then forgot about it till at night when I got cramps. Because first I had a feeling that C.D. must definitely have been talking about me to Faye Citrin and Faye Citrin wanted to know from me how I felt about C.D., that's why they shook hands. For a signal.

I right away figured out C.D. must like me and from that I jumped in my mind to C.D. on a toilet seat and getting the period. Never mind.

We went to McGinnis for a roast beef before Sequoia and a bunch of ginzos started up.

Because probably there were plenty of Jewish people around they didn't gang up. They wanted our best fighter against their best fighter, a fair fight. We picked naturally Hymie, they picked a guy Sal and we went behind the new house on Ocean Avenue.

Hymie and this guy Sal didn't just fight right away, they had first a warmup. Hymie jumped on a fire escape ladder and he chinned himself eight nine times one handed, that's the hardest way to chin. Also he did the flip and the jackknife. Sal only jumped on the ladder and he jumped right off. Definitely he couldn't chin himself good as he had a different type build, the way Hohner is built. You look at Hohner you wouldn't pick him for punchball but boy he can lift.

Then Hymie took off his ring and he put his money in a different pocket and he made his belt looser and he rolled up the sleeves on his sweater all the way. This Sal didn't do a thing, he just spit and he made fun of Hymie. He said You want to fuck around you want to fight.

Hymie said You worried. He's worried.

This Sal said I don't worry I worry for shit shit is what you are I don't worry for you. His gang went Start in Start in so he made believe he was going to hit but he only pushed Hymie with both hands.

Hymie dodged, it was a beauty how he dodged, but he didn't push back. He said I need to be sore to fight, get me sore.

This Sal said You're full of fucking shit.

Hymie said So I'm full of fucking shit, fucking shit don't get me sore.

Sal said I don't have to get you sore, what do I have to get you sore, you got a sore, they gave you a sore already on your cock.

Hymie told him now he was getting a little bit angry but

he still wasn't sore. Sal said it was too fucking bad he wasn't sore and he gave Hymie a rap on the head.

Hymie gave him a nice one in the belly. I and Boomie said That's one for one, Sal's gang went Give him in the kilyoons.

Sal kept rushing Hymie all the time and he would swing with his eyes shut and Hymie would give him nice little shots but only in the belly. He absolutely didn't go for the head, he just boxed him.

Then they like clinched and a lady yelled down they should stop and she threw water, it got us on the shoes. Every body wanted them to fight some other place but Hymie said he still wasn't sore and we went away.

I didn't write that this Sal was so so winded he couldn't hold up his hands and Hymie had plenty of wind. He was breathing from his nose, that's how much wind he had left. Even so Sal wanted to keep up the fight and Hymie didn't.

Boomie asked him How come you only boxed him on the defensive because you're usually the offensive slugger.

Hymie said he wanted to take it a little easy because from the chinning before he strained near his shoulder.

What I said I shouldn't have said. I said You strained your shoulder, you didn't strain your shoulder you strained your ass.

He said Don't get me sore.

I said You get sore at me and at me you can get sore but with him you wouldn't get sore. And Boomie said to him You were plenty sore with him, you got red pimples by your mouth, that's how you were sore.

Hymie went and walked ahead of us.

I and Boomie talked only to each other. We did it loud so Hymie would hear.

Like this we did it BOOMIE DO YOU THINK HE WASN'T SORE AT THIS SAL?

OH NO HE WASN'T SORE, NAH NAH NOT MUCH OH NO.

MAKE A GUESS WHY HE BOXED HIM ONLY ON THE DEFENSIVE AND HE DIDN'T ABSOLUTELY KICK THE SHIT OUT OF HIM.

BECAUSE THIS SAL WASN'T A JEWISH KID A JEWISH KID HE WOULDN'T WORRY BUT WITH A GINZO HE WORRIES.

Hymie stopped walking and he said Did I win it, I won it.

I and Boomie told him he won it but with a Jewish kid he wouldn't just win it he would kick the shit out of the guy also.

Hymie said How about when I had the fight with Vinnie Luginio, I had two fights with Vinnie Luginio both times I kicked the shit out of him, he's a ginzo.

I told him Vinnie lives in a Jewish neighborhood and Boomie told him he hangs around only with Jewish kids, he's like not really a ginzo.

Hymie said What do I have to do I have to go to Italy and kick the shit out of Mussolini.

He walked fast and got way ahead of us. We walked a little faster just to follow but not to catch up. From two blocks away we saw him go by himself into the movies.

When we went in we looked but didn't see him. Then in the Coming Attractions we noticed him move and change his seat to nearer the front. We heard him laugh when we laughed.

Even so it spoiled Sequoia for us. We didn't even feel like seeing it twice so we went out and Hymie went out with us. We then made up.

April 28, 1938

Cousin Phillie came over in his car. As it was very nice out he rode us to Prospect Park.

I was sitting up in the front and I said Cousin Phillie how fast could you go with this car.

Mom said I should leave him alone and when a person is behind the wheel you let him concentrate.

Cousin Phillie said I can answer him a little question AND I can concentrate.

Mom said If I sing in a quiet way would that interfere with your concentration.

Cousin Phillie said Sing go ahead with the greatest pleasure.

Mom said To give you less trouble and more concentration tell me if I should sing If I Had My Life To Live Over I'd Never Do It Again or if I should sing Tears From The Orphans Eyes.

Cousin Phillie said Whatever you sing is good enough and it wouldn't bother my concentration.

Mom said I would sing them both except they remind me too too much how you mishandled me when I worked for you in Hartford Connecticut and the way you sent me to your Cousin Droodel the dentist and he handed me a bill I said to him Cousin Droodel you put down for a filling and a cleaning but where do you get off with a dollar twentynine entertainment and he told me what's the matter Malvena, you forgot I had on the radio.

Cousin Phillie made us get out at Neck Road and we had to walk.

April 29, 1938

In assembly there was a show.

Marion Blechman and Bert Sissler sang some Naughty Marietta songs. When Marion Blechman bowed the top of her tits showed and a whole bunch in the front clapped and clapped so she had to keep bowing. Also Larry Himmelfarb did imitations. His best one is Wallace Beery, he made it like Wallace Beery is rubbing his nose and throwing the snot on the floor.

Mr. Stock wanted us to work out on the bars and do tumbles. We did it for fifteen minutes then we made up to ask him testicle questions. Artie Binswanger said he had a cousin who lifted weights and once when he was doing it he got a pain in his testicles.

Mr. Stock said first of all his cousin should see a doctor for that might mar him for later life and also he would guess the cousin had not taken jock strap precautions.

Artie said How is it horses do all kinds of lifting and

175

straining and pulling and they jump and they don't wear jock straps but they never hurt themselves on the testicles. Mr. Stock gave a good answer, How do you know, did you ever ask a horse.

April 30, 1938

I handed in my digest of an article. When Miss Hochman collected them she just happened to look at mine because it was the top one. She said Oh what I see, shame on Simon. What I did was instead of conceive I wrote concieve.

The article I did the digest of was Men With Wings And Guns by Berne Teague about how airplane gunners get trained. This reminds me that I again saw Marshey who I always think of when I see about airplanes. This was yesterday morning, he turned around his books so I should notice he has a slide rule. I said to him What have you got there, is that your lunch? He said Hi Shimmy hi what do you say and I answered him in the way he talks. What do I say? I'll TELL you what I say, I say SHMUK. I shouldn't have done that as it wasn't nice, right away it gave me sad feelings. In fact I knew it would even before I said it but I wanted to get the power over him. What's now interesting is if I think about it I still have my sad feeling and not so much because I said shmuk to him but because I'm not positive anyway I got the power over him. Never mind.

May 1, 1938

Boomie is maybe trying to get the power over me. Im not sure.

I and he went to buy loosies in the Sweet Shop and C.D. was with Faye Citrin and Rhoda Barsky and a girl I don't know. They were having a malted and I said to C.D. Hows the malted. She said it was too sweet.

Right away then Boomie said to me Faye has a fantastic pair of tits, they were big even in public school. But C.D. has no tits and her both tits together could fit one corner of Faye Citrin's brassiere.

176

I fell in, my voice got chokey. I said She has no tits so So· what do you want from me. And there's more important things with a girl then her tits.

Boomie gave me a look.

So what I did was talk like Boomie talks when he does his Ronald Colman voice. Yes ah yes my friend there are ah there are more ah important things ah with a girl than ah her tits.

He had to do the voice if I did it. It's hard exactly to explain but anyway he had to. What ah what is more ah important with a girl than her ah tits ah.

I answered him Her ah cunt ah.

He wanted to give a real laugh but he went only Ha Ha Ha. I think and I'm naturally not positive it's because he just just missed getting power over me.

Miss Hochman gave back my Men With Wings And Guns digest with a Really Excellent and a star. The star was to read to the class but there was no time.

May 2, 1938

I and C.D. ate together in the cafeteria. What happened is it was very crowded but I was near two seats and I saw she was looking and looking and waiting and I yelled Here here.

Mom's sandwich I kept on the inside of the bag so the whole thickness wouldn't show and I ate it by tearing off only little hunks.

I said to her What you are eating smells good.

She said Have some I'll give you some.

I was nervous I would have to eat from her mouth. But what she did was smart, she took out from the inside of the sandwich and put it on my chala.

There then happened what I would definitely say is the most embarrassing moment of my life.

I said to her This I love, I love greebin.

So she asked me What's greebin, what's that.

I told her I was not probably pronouncing it exactly in the right Jewish, maybe it's not greebin it's groobin.

Groobin or greebin, she didn't know.

I said Groobin or greebin is what you call it when yo
take the pieces of chicken fat and you make them like in
fried way.

She got all red and I think I got all red. She then tol
me, her exact words I forget, I didn't hear as I got a pop an
a whistling in my ears, how what she gave me was baco

I made up something that in my house my mother whe
she makes bacon uses probably another kind and type c
bacon.

She said that in her house it was absolutely not koshe
and I said in my house we're practically not kosher.

I made up also that my parents, I called them MY FOLK
keep their little bit of kosher not because they believe in
really but not to hurt my grandparents and that my granc
father is like a rabbi.

She said it was sort of the same thing with her granc
parents and her folks used to have big fights and argumen
with them on being kosher and going to shul and her granc
parents won't eat in her house. When they come they brin
all their own stuff, their own plates even.

I told her something like as if God cares if you're koshe
and I mentioned how being kosher has nothing to do wit
God, it goes back to when certain animals and certain fis
had diseases thousands and thousands of years ago and th
Jews then made up kosher rulings not to catch the disease

So C.D. said My parents aren't kosher because they don
believe in God.

We then got in a discussion on the difference between a
athiest and an agnostic and I said You're always better o
being an agnostic because an agnostic is almost an athies
but just in case there's a God he wouldn't turn out such
shmoo. For shmoo I nearly said shmuk.

She said My parents are Marxists.

I think I must have gone Ahah, like she said her parent
were blind.

She maybe noticed because she said Well I am sorry i

they are Marxists, that is what they are.

I said I think I will have that next term, next term I am taking History for a fifth major.

She started kidding me What's a Marxist.

I said Those who believe in what Karl Marx said.

She said to me So who was Karl Marx and I kidded her back, I said Who was Karl Marx, I'll TELL you who was Karl Marx. SURE. He was the son of Old Man Marx.

She said You ought to read the book I read on it, it's not really ON it but sort of. Jews Without Money.

What I did was I wrote down the name, but in a scribble, then I said I would look to see if it was on the supplemental reading list Miss Hochman gave us.

When the first bell rang we got pushed together and I had a feel off her ass. Twice I jerked off on it, the first time I made her Anne Shirley the second time Jean Parker.

May 3, 1938

I looked up in the encyclopedia under Marxism, they didn't have too much. It said see Communism, but a guy just beat me to the Cs.

Jews Without Money they didn't have in the school library so I went to the public library. Before I forget I'll put the author down as its funny. Mike Gold.

They had it in the public library only it was under Closed Shelf. Fuck it and never mind.

More on May 3, 1938

Why I wrote never mind is because I didn't feel yesterday like doing what you have to do when they have a book in Closed Shelf. You have to go the librarian yourself to ask her and I didn't want to say Jews.

May 5, 1938

Today I shaved with the door open. Mom and Dad looked.

Mom cried, Dad said a mazel tuff.

Dad gave me a new blade to put in the razor, also he gave me his brush to use and witch hazel and he put down a piece of styptic pencil.

He then went and got me his nail clippers and his fine comb and his Polymol and he put on a towel talcum and he showed me how I should use it after the shave.

He had me shut the door and he took away Mom, he told her a boy that's becoming a man has to be alone on his first big boy shave. He asked me Sonny what else do you want and tell me if you need something.

While I was shaving I thought I heard noise but I wasn't sure as the door was closed and I had the both faucets on.

When I finished I couldn't get the door open and I had to push and push. Dad had put there all his coats and all his suits and his two belts and his bathrobe and he told me I should take what I want, I should even take his life. The only thing is I shouldn't take his life for the next few days as he didn't want to leave the manager short handed.

Mom cried, she noticed on a pair of pants the cleaner didn't clean out under the cuffs.

May 6, 1938

Yesterday and the whole Saturday morning I didn't talk to Dad. Even when he went to shul I wouldn't go with Mom and wave from the window. Also to spite her I ate hardly a breakfast, just half a piece matzo with cream cheese and milk.

Mom wanted to know how come I ate hardly a breakfast just just just half a piece matzo with cream cheese and milk.

On account of him I told her, on account of he's a filthy rat and a dirty louse and a hunk of shit and he should only drop dead.

Mom cried and she opened the window I should say again what I said and the whole whole world should hear how it paid them to have a child, she was under labor with me for three days on her dropped stomach and the Daddy on his hernia had to break up ice for her ice bag.

I couldn't answer, I got very chokey. She said Go go and I said I'm going I'm going and she said I want you to go, go go and I said I'll go I'll go and she said Go go already and I said Don't you worry I'm going I'm going, he doesn't have to worry either that hunk of shit because I'm going and she said Go go and you should only live not to come back and I said The same to you and to him that hunk of shit don't worry I'm going I'm going.

I then went and got all dressed and I took my Bio and my French books.

Mom said So where you going.

I told her either I would get a room or either I would move in by Boomie.

She said a room is a better idea, it's always the best best thing not to move in by the next one, what's the matter I forgot already when she moved in with Cousin Phillie in Hartford Connecticut.

I told her goodby and I had nothing really aginst her but I was just just sick and tired of him, the lousy hunk of shit.

She said Believe me a room isn't a bad idea if the room is where I wouldn't have to walk the five flights, it wouldn't hurt if I got away from him a while with his ways, we could get for the two of us a slightly slightly bigger room with kitchen privilege and I'd go back to my old passementerie line, what's the matter and why not, Puritz and Sachs would take me in a minute.

I waited for her to get dressed and we both looked in three two family houses but we didn't see any rooms she liked. On the way back Sacramento was just putting a sign in the window Bon Ami 4 for 28¢. Teitlebaum saw us with the Sacramento bag, he said Don't ask no more to sharpen your knives on my grinder.

May 7, 1938

I and Boomie and Hymie went on the boardwalk.

As we didn't go yesterday to the movies we had the money and we went to Steeplechase, ten rides a quarter.

181

Most of the rides are shit, just the horses and the sliding pond we liked.

Where we had fun was the barrel. It's not even really a ride, it just turns and shakes you, but they got like a midget clown where you come out and he blows up the girls dresses with an air thing.

One girl had on no bloomers and we yelled PUSSY. I noticed and Boomie too her pussy hair was a darker color then on her head. Hymie said Who looked at the head.

On one other girl we saw a hole in the bloomers, she cried.

We had then like an adventure.

A man came over and told us he likes to buy young fellows frozen custard and talk with them about young fellow problems.

We answered him like Marshey. Sure, why not, SURE. And we then all went out together and he bought us frozen custard, the double.

He said Well who wants to talk first about his young fellow problem and we made him first get us a hot corn each.

He sat on a bench with us and when we ate the hot corn we kidded around by wiping our hands on his jacket. This made him laugh and laugh. He then just like that said Do you know young fellows that masturbation will not drive you crazy.

I said No no shit and Boomie said Oy Oy Thank God.

The guy told us a lot of young fellows have masturbation problems, it's one of the biggest young fellow problems he noticed in his experience. They think it will give them weakness.

Hymie right away made believe he fainted.

The guy said It would be my pleasure to help you out in a discussion of any of your masturbation problems, that kind of thing you can't talk over with your moms and pops.

I said What are you talking about, I and my pop do it together.

Boomie said They do it together and his mom loves to watch.

The guy made himself laugh and laugh, he pumped it up the way Boomie can pump up a belch and he copped feels from us. Mostly he felt Hymie, I was even a little jealous.

He wanted to know if we wanted to go to his room, he had a big big room in the Half-Moon where we could all stretch out and learn from him how to enjoy masturbation more.

We made him first buy us watermelon slices, the large. Then we gave him an argument, Hey where are the napkins, you forgot the napkins, and when he went to get the napkins he put his hat on the bench, it was a panama hat, and we spit out the pits in it.

He told us he had a lot of sweeties in his room and also he would give us fifteen cents apiece to go to the movies.

We told him we wanted to go to the Brooklyn Fox, there it's a quarter on Sunday. He said Well if that will give you pleasure all right, for I get my pleasure when I can give young fellows like you pleasure.

We let him for a little while cop feels off Hymie, then we told him we didn't know and we weren't sure and we were a little bit nervous and we wanted to talk and discuss in private.

He said While you talk about it I will go and buy a lot more sweeties for the room and plan out all the young fellow pleasures.

When he came back he gave us toffee. We ate it all and we told him the toffee made us thirsty, get us soda.

So he got us soda and we told him on account of he was very very nice to us we wanted to reciprocate and we wouldn't charge him a quarter apiece.

I started to say We'll charge you only a dime apiece and I started in to laugh and shpritz out soda, Boomie had to finish.

He said Not even a dime, we'll charge you only a nickel

apiece, for a nickel apiece we'll all piss on you, and we all three ran like anything. We ran practically to Ocean Parkway even though the guy wasn't running after. Boomie figured we were maybe shmuks not to go with the guy, that if we asked him a half a buck he'd give us a half a buck.

We went on Bay 6 a while. As the sun was very strong we took off our shirts and our undershirts. A lot of people even went in the water and we were sorry we didn't have on bathing suits. All of a sudden it jumped in my mind how I am married to C.D. and she is in the water, a big fat yenta with boobies down to her bush. Never mind and no more.

May 8, 1938

I last night had a wet dream. I was in the movies and my seat was like the wrong way, I could see just the wall. A girl then came over and instead of in the movie we were on the trolley but the trolley was more the subway, it said De Kalb Avenue. The girl looked sort of like a girl from a picture Teitlebaum had by his register, the girl is standing with a cow and she's drinking milk from a pail. I sucked on her tits, then when she was letting me push in my cock something happened, she had to go on another trolley or she had to go back to the movies. I shot when I was practically wide awake.

In Home Room we had a discussion on nominations for the Lowell Award. Every time it's the same thing. Somebody says I nominate Hitler and somebody says I nominate Clark Gable or somebody says I propose hereby Mae West or my nomination is Mickey Finn for his fine police work. The most votes in our class were for Senator Wagner.

C.D. was absent today from French. This is maybe when she gets the period. I got the thought that this would be interesting, how we both on the same identical day get emptied out.

May 9, 1938

I had a fight with Dad in the morning.

He got up early with me, he had to say yizker for his mother and we had breakfast together.

He was reading the Forvitz and he read to Mom how there's a story they would like more Jews to go to Palestine.

This got him sore, he said That's all they want and that's all I need, I'll listen to them and I'll leave a manager like my manager and I'll go live with the African shvartzers, they're worse then what you get in Harlem, at least in Harlem they wear snappy stuff, without them the spats industry would be finished years ago.

I said to him Palestine is nowhere nowhere near Africa, Palestine is the Middle East.

He said How come you were a baby and you never let me nowheres near you and until you were four if we took you to the next one's house you looked for where they had up calendars and you ripped the pages.

He threw at me pot cheese and cream and Mom then got a dropped stomach attack.

I went out I didn't even take my lunch. Dad came running after with it and I had to take it from him because Marshey was across the street and I didn't want a whole scene. Dad like wanted to make up, he said What do you need Palestine, you got right here the most beautiful beaches in the world, you get sick of these beaches so what, it's a stone's throw and you go over to Rockaway.

May 10, 1938

Mr. Wexler today was really funny. He told us one story the whole period practically. How he was in France and he wanted to go to a certain street in Paris and he goes around asking and asking how you get to the street, and every body he asks just just looks at him. What happened was he had not done the pronunciation of the street from up in his nose, he had a cold. He said it came out as if here you wanted OCEAN PARKWAY but you said ORGAN PARKWAY, and this got the absolutely biggest laugh. So Mr. Wexler told us I was

185

referring to the INSTRUMENT, this made it worse. Lenny Roseman had to leave the room.

It was announced in English we are going to have a debate. Miss Hochman put a bunch of topics in the wastebasket and one from every row picked. My row got WAS IT RIGHT TO MURDER JULIUS CAESAR. I raised my hand and asked a good question. That if you use the word murder before you even debate you right away are practically losing the debate as murder has to be always wrong. Miss Hochman agreed with me and she changed it to assassinate. We have a week from today to prepare.

C.D. came late to the cafeteria, she had her gym before and the teacher kept them past the bell. The only thing that was good from this is I had time to finish my sandwich.

For a second she scared the shit out of me. She said I said hello to you Sunday on the boardwalk, you didn't notice. I thought OY she saw me with that guy, but it was when we were on the beach. I made her laugh after. She said I guess to make conversation What were you doing on the beach, I answered her We were Jews without money.

May 11, 1938

This week definitely will be dirty week. It used to happen especially in junior high, there would be a whole week where whatever you said or anybody said it would turn into something dirty.

In English therefore today Josh Berzoff went to the blackboard to write his descriptive paragraphs. All the boys had to describe a ball game, all the girls had to be like reporters of a party.

He put on one paragraph with a sentence Carl Hubbell burned his ball in. Miss Hochman said Now this sentence has a color verb but I think I see something wrong with the color verb usage, does anyone see what I notice.

What she meant we had a couple of weeks ago, that you could use a colloquialism but to use it you have to use it right and with grammar even if to you it's only a colloquialism. Like here Josh had burned his ball in, the colloquialism to be used right is burned IN the ball.

So she said again Josh what's wrong with that, do you see, look at it again and tell me if you see.

He got nervous, he like fumfed Carl Hubbell burned the ball, Carl Hubbell had his ball in burning, boobooboo, Carl Hubbell HAD A BURNING BALL.

We would have probably only laughed a little, but Normey Levan yells out That's why he pitched such a lousey game.

Then in Bio Mrs. Jacobey told us at the end of the period I think you should expect a little testy tomorrow, that's what she said exactly. Boomie fixed me up good, he passes me a note A TESTY IS ONE BALL FROM A MIDGET.

Dad's shul had a tora party, I forget what they call it in Jewish. When somebody donates a tora and they celebrate. Mom made me go with Dad to develop closeness, also she had to clean out her shopping bags and it gets her nervous if people are in the house.

For five blocks almost he didn't open his mouth and I didn't open my mouth. Then we were by the Knishe Queen he finally tells me I'm warning you don't step into that shmutz, watch out with your brand new shoes.

I said What watch out, its nowheres nowheres near me, it's in the gutter practically.

He said That's where you're all along headed and that's where you'll end up.

I answered him in a fresh way You should also.

He told me I should drop dead and go to hell and I shouldn't have lived to be born and he said in Jewish it's either a crime or a shame the earth carries me and he would be better off if he had instead shot his load in the kitchen sink.

Old Man Faygeles then came over from across the street, he said NU NU Shmuel. Dad answered him NU NU back and say hello to my kaddishel.

I saw Marshey's father in shul. He said How come you

G

and Marshall aren't no more such good friends, you two used to be such good friends. I answered something about we have different interests or now we don't have exactly the same interests. He said What can you do and that's what it is, in America it's the easiest thing to grow apart, over nothing people can break up. You see two kids the best of friends, then it happens one has to travel the Sea Beach Line and one has to travel the Brighton Line and its fartig and its finished and they won't know from each other.

He started in then to kid around that anyway at our age and stage I and Marshey should have just just one interest. Thank God they started putting out the delicatessen as I was becoming embarassed. How I felt was like once in Boomie's house his father told him You had to wet the toilet seat, what's the matter, your thing is big enough that you can take good aim.

May 12, 1938

Boomie was sick and Hymie had to go to Tumbling practice. I forgot to put down he's on the Tumbling Squad. Anyway it worked out that I went alone to the Sweet Shop for loose cigarettes and C.D. came in after. She looked for her friends and they weren't there. She therefore didn't feel like hanging around for them and we ended up walking together.

C.D. had a bag of pistachio nuts and we shared. We then decided to go on the beach and I said I will show you The Secret Way, and she said Oh I obey oh Master Master.

I took her through the back of the Parkway Baths and from Ocean Parkway to Bay 5 under the boardwalk and I and she made echoes with yelling. When I yelled Heil Hitler she said Don't do that, that you shouldn't do and she wanted me to yell All Power To The Soviets but I instead made it Tyrone Powers Clothes Are Wet. Also we sang a whole bunch of public school songs, Welcome Sweet Springtime and Poor Punchinello The Clown and Ancient Of Days and Holy Holy Holy. I let her all by herself sing Shipmates Stand

Together and from the song I had a very sad feeling. In my imagination I and Boomie and Hymie were on a battleship and the battleship was sinking and we had our arms around each others shoulders. The thing that gave me the sad feeling was my thought of come on stop the shit, what kind of shit with battleships, where do you come to battleships, you know what you are, what you are is just just just a Jewish boy from Brighton, you'll get a job where you have to shit for the bosses look and you'll do like Bomba Katz's brother, when he got married he moved in across the hall from his mother. Not even really across the hall, his mother is in 2J and he's in 2H.

So when she was doing a high note I pushed down my sad feeling by singing in a mockey way I Am A Yankee Doodle Father, I Got A Yankee Doodle Son, He Works Downtown For Three Dollars A Week, He's Honest Like Washington, Last Night He Brought Me Home The Pay Dear, I Saw It Was A Quarter Shy, Hub Ich Der Totten Gayben Aym Kloppin, Ikey's Got a Shikse On The Sly.

C.D. started to get sore. She kicked sand on me and she said You know that's not nice, I don't think that's nice. I imitated her Not Nice Not Nice, Nyeh Nyeh Nyeh. She said You never should say shikser, she hates and detests it when Jews say shikser or shvartzer and they shouldn't do it, they ought to be the last people to do that and how do they like it when they are called sheenie and kike. I made up like a joke, What song do you think of or what song would you sing if a shikse and a shvartzer got married and I sang then Thats How Darkies Are Born. She went Oh really and I went Not Oh really Oh Reilly.

So she kicked more sand on me, it even got in my hair. She said That's your trouble, you know what your main and basic trouble is, you're not SERIOUS.

I couldn't help it and it just came out. SURE I'm not serious, how can I be serious, I'm JEWISH.

She said to me Are you going to be serious. Be SERIOUS and she gave me a little smack on the chest. I made believe

189

we were sort of boxing and I by accident landed a soft one right in the tit. Like with the back or top of fingers. Naturally I couldn't help it that I got a feel for a second, not even a second. What I was scared of was I would get a hardon, I already could could feel a semi and I had to do in my throat Baruch Attuh, keep it down oy pussy booboo peepee periods.

My exact exact words were then That I didn't mean, seriously, I am being serious.

She said Oh sure you're Serious but it doesn't mean you're Sincere. A person can be absolutely serious but who says even if he's serious he's sincere.

I kissed my pinkie and I grabbed her hand and I kissed her pinkie.

Definitely she didn't want me to let go her hand so I held on and we walked practically to Bay 3. As we both had sand in our shoes what we did was take off our shoes and I in one hand carried the both pair of shoes and she in one hand carried our books. A couple of times we almost tripped where the sand got hilly or it had holes but she held on and I held on. I had the feeling like you see in a Tarzan picture. Tarzan is swimming and swimming with his mate, they're teasing with turtles in the water. Where you absolutely don't want to think about how before they went in he fucked her probably.

We sat down by the rocks and even to sit down we kept the grip. In fact we even tickled palms, I didn't remember till now.

I then lit a cigarette, not so much that I wanted to smoke but I wanted to let go her hand already. I asked if she wanted a puff, she said she once or twice tried it but its bad for her sinus.

She got up and I got up and we both wet our feet a little. We both for no reason started to sing the Marsellaise, then she yelled very loud like over the ocean You prisoners of starvation hello, how are you, oh I love you you prisoners of starvation.

I without realizing started in the way Marshey talks, You LOVE the prisoners of starvation, all right SURE, I am starving.

For no reason I went over and I told her make yourself very stiff and put your elbows very very tight by your chest. Right away she did it, it was interesting that she didn't say why should I or what do I have to. With my palms only I did the trick, I lifted her way up and when I put her down I again got her in the tit. Actually I got only brassiere but it gave me really a hardon. What I did was get on my stomach in the sand and grind down. Something struck me funny, that if the earth is round there could be right now a guy exactly opposite me from the other end of the world and he's doing the same thing.

C.D. lay down also on her stomach and she asked me if you could make everything ideal and perfect what would it be for you? In other words what would you want to be able to do that now you can't do.

I did my Ronald Colman, My deehah, I would wahant to behah herehah forevah besidehah youhah.

She said Seriously, again you are not being serious.

I told her naturally I would want to be able to do what every body wants to do, they would want to do things to be happy, they would want a million dollars I would want a million dollars.

She said But ideally how would you be happy, what would be for you the IDEAL happiness.

So I said For me and just just for me, in other words you don't want me to say I want a million dollars.

She said Only what you Simon Sloan the individual dream about ideally, your ideal dream.

I wanted her to tell me first and she wanted me to tell her first so we chose and she lost.

She said What I would want and my ideal dream is for the world to be the kind of world where if a person needs it, lets say we would need it, even if we didn't absolutely need it, we just wanted it because it was nice, then we

191

should be able to go to any house and say for example, this is just an example, my hands are dirty and I would like to if you don't mind wash them in your sink and they shouldn't mind. In other words I wouldn't necessarily do that but it should be the kind and type of a world where if I wanted to I would be ABLE to do it.

All I could think of for my turn had to do with the movies. I would sleep in the movies and I would eat in the movies and the world is fixed up in a way that I never never have to get out of the movies. What I did I made up a bunch of shit. There shouldn't be more wars and this should be a REALLY free country for every body and that something would be done for the ordinary man, for the little people. The little people thing I got from Mr. Deeds Goes To Town.

That she definitely liked. How I know is she took my hand and she dribbled sand on it so I dribbled sand on her blouse. I aimed for her tits and she knew I was aiming for there and probably if it wasn't the beach I could have given her more shit and tried for a finger fuck. Only people already were coming out by Parkway Baths. Also I was thinking, it annoyed me, the real real crappy shit you have to do if you want to get laid.

She then talked chokey we should get started. So we carried our shoes and we put them on on the boardwalk steps. Going back we just kidded around and we talked about school. I bought a charlotte russe and I had the woman cut it in half, I almost then said something she should have the cherry, I didn't. We had sort of a race from the boardwalk to Brighton Beach Avenue, I kept up with her easy. To say good bye we shook hands and we swung them back and forth and we sang Did You Ever See A Lassie.

I now will put down C.D.s name.

Her name is Clare Dushler.

May 13, 1938

Mom and Dad last night started in on me.

192

Mom was giving me supper separate, I wanted hard eggs mashed up and Dad wanted them chopped up.

Dad said to me You know it don't look bad the way you're eating the egg, why not, I would also eat it that way if I had a mother a slaving servant for taking advantage on, after all it's coming to you, first she mashes with a spoon and then she mashes with a fork, that's the way and it's your America.

I went like Please or Jeez.

Mom told me God should only only forgive you the way you talk to a father. Then she said to Dad Bite your tongue and grind down hard, who asked you and who needs you butting in moron dopey person with your peculiar ways, he gets himself an upset stomach he paints his throat with argyrol.

Dad answered her I can't help it, it hurts me he sits there that everything is coming to him, I don't mind you're a crazy mother and you mash down his egg, mash it down, fine, only remember you got a husband and your husband needs you, save me a little strength in coming years, the momzer murderer wants russian type dressing let him mix himself the mayonnaise and the ketchup.

I said like Tzoo or Tzahsh.

Mom said You're listening Shmuel, Shmuel listen how she's working on him, it didn't take her long to turn him already against the parents.

I said She, who she and what she.

Mom said the older girl who poisoned your mind.

Dad said Go mix him up more mayonnaise and ketchup.

Mom said Since he was a kid he was the same way, any any woman could wrap him around, don't I remember, those things you don't don't forget how we went to the beach and with me he wouldn't sit, he ran over to be on Mrs. Scheindlitzer's blanket. What what what she wanted from him she could get, for me he wouldn't carry a shopping bag but for her he'd go kidnap the Lindbergh baby.

I said I used to just just just want to use her big tube.

Dad said Bruno Hauptman also had a Jackie Cooper face.

Mom said I didn't know when I gave birth to you in a dry labor for three days how you'd turn out a moron for the maidluch.

I asked her where maidluch and what maidluch.

Mom said You want the story I'll give you the story from me you'll hear it straight simple sincere. A certain certain party that is to me a true blue friend and feels for my suffering, if I told you the name you'd know in a minute, is very very grateful to me. What I did for her isn't a story for now, how this true blue party had a daughter, a brilliant girl, and the daughter wanted to belong to the library and they asked her in the library if she would give them one one reference signature and everybody turned her down. Her own brother told her I don't sign nothing for nobody, that's his roughneck grammar, he's a multi millionaire from shopping bag handles, so she came to Malvena the Orphan for the signature. And because I did her that favor my true blue friend is since then looking out for my interest. That's why she just just just happened to be looking out from her bathroom window and she saw you near Brighton Beach Avenue with an old looking girl, she even figured it was me and for the second she couldn't recognize me that I got so old looking.

I said A girl from my class, from in my class I know her, a girl.

Dad said Sure and definitely and who's denying, that's how Loeb and Leopold got to know Bobby Franks, he was also in their class.

Mom said I don't blame the woman, a woman gets to a certain age she goes for young kids, they had the same thing in a William Powell picture, the reason I say William Powell is I understand your elderly lady looked like William Powell only her nose was bigger.

Dad said I'll tell you something, Once he goes to the

electric chair good bye and good luck, I'm finished with him.

Mom said Shmuel don't talk that way you're a father give him another chance, he's a young kid and he doesn't doesn't know.

Dad said Right now I'm ready to tear him out of my life, I lost a father I can lose him.

Mom said Just just just give him one one more chance, let him promise he won't see her no more and if she comes over he'll say in a nice way get going lady or lady get going.

Dad said I'm starting my Kaddish on him, get set, Yisgadal Vyiskadash.

Mom said Everything will be fine, he won't see her no more, we'll get some loose ice cream, you'll go down Shimmy you'll get half a pint loose ice cream.

Dad said Shmay Rabuh.

Mom said go go go to Gelfman, it's all over, it's finished, it's forgotten, half a pint, watch how he packs it.

Dad said Oy Yisgadal Yisgadal Vyiskadash Oy make it strawberry Shmah Rabuh only strawberry don't give me heartburn.

I had to go all the way to Teshler, Gelfman had no strawberry.

May 14, 1938

Senator Wagner is getting the Lowell Award, Hank Greenberg was second.

On account of last night I had a bad mood and it lasted into Bio.

Mrs. Jacobey was showing us about one celled life and also the life cycle, how everything that's in nature is used for something and even when any kind of life is dead it goes in the soil or in the air or in the water where it gets used again. She said this is one of the marvels of old mother nature.

Naturally we were all supposed to be putting it down in our notebook. What I did, I closed up my fountain pen, then I put it on the desk with a bang. Mrs. Jacobey right

G*

away noticed and asked me if don't I think that something which will possibly show up on the final is worth writing down or does one of the marvels of nature not engage my interest.

I answered her It engages it engages.

Mrs. Jacobey said I might say Simon I am surprised, I am hurt and somewhat surprised you show lack of respect for me, for the class, and for mother nature.

I then knew I had the power over her. All of a sudden. This is hard to explain and never mind.

I told her I'm sorry, I apologize to you and to the class but I don't apologize to mother nature and I would like to explain my exact feelings about mother nature.

Mrs. Jacobey then asked the class because it was class time Shall we listen to Simon explain about mother nature?

The whole class clapped and went yay, Boomie went My hah franz.

I got up in the front and I faced the class, the feeling I had was anything I'd say I couldn't go wrong.

I said Mrs. Jacobey and fellow class members, we have been learning about and discussing the mysteries and marvels of mother nature. But it seems to me there are definitely plenty of mysteries about mother nature and the biggest mystery is why we should say it is so marvelous. For if we think, if we realize mother nature could have in absolutely any way she wanted and desired set up various and differing kinds of laws, in other words instead of having life die and get used again and again, mother nature had nothing to stop her from taking human beings and working it out or so working out another way or system whereby for example man could be immortal. That is he need not and wouldn't have to die, mother nature could arrange for him more important things and laws then to be a fertilizer. Therefore why should we say MARVELOUS mother nature, what is so marvelous about mother nature, what kind of favors did she do for us such as keeping and preventing us from getting illness. What did she do for us so MARVELOUS that she didn't do for the amoebas?

Mrs. Jacobey clapped and the class also right away clapped. Boomie went Hooray for our side. Mrs. Jacobey said Simon that was very good and very interesting and brought up interesting and significant questions which we will probably be covering in a few weeks. I have only one criticism, look up the plural for amoeba.

After class I went up to see her in the excuse that I wanted to know the plural of amoeba but really to get more praise. She told me why don't you write that up for the Lowell Lantern. I promised her I would try.

The next class was however French and Mr. Wexler there gave me all of a sudden a question in fast French for which I was paying no attention. I later answered three questions nobody else could answer, one he said Formidable Monsieur Sloan. That did not even so cancel out and do away with when I missed.

As I walked to Study Period Clare went to Gym and she mentioned what a nice time she had on the beach but she couldn't eat her supper, it was my fault. I said How was it my fault? She told me I had spoiled her appetite by giving her that charlotte russe. She said I'm only joking, now I'm not being serious, after all who forced me to eat the charlotte russe if I didn't want it and I knew it would spoil my appetite. I told my mother and my mother said I think you did right to eat it even if it spoiled your appetite because you never want to unnecessarily hurt the feelings of a fellow.

I couldn't stand it, the way she made with her mouth and the way she made with her tongue and the way she made with her chin when she said fellow. It came out FELL AH and she looked older then Hymie's bubbee.

In Study Period I started to write up my thing from Bio. My power was gone. I later felt bad at my annoyance with Clare because she came to our cafeteria table with three sandwiches of lettuce and tomato, one of them was for me definitely. We even so had an argument about my Julius Caesar debate, she said, her exact words, Assassination in certain cases and instances can have a very healthy effect. I started naturally to laugh. I said Look what you said and do you know what you said. She said So what, you know what I meant, you only look for something not to be serious about.

May 15, 1938

I and Boomie and Hymie went to the Surf. They brought back Captains Courageous with Magnificent Brute and they had the last chapter of Flash Gordon. Boomie got us almost thrown out with Captains Courageous. This was the part in the end where Spencer Tracy gets killed, he's like trapped in the water and you see him only from the top. Underneath he's supposed to be all bashed in. Boomie went all of a sudden Oy it hurts mine balls, oy do mine balls hurt, oy watch out for mine balls.

After we walked on the boardwalk. The ski ball in the penny arcade was broken and we got each three games on the one nickel. We could have gotten even more but there was a commotion on the boardwalk and we went to see.

What it was is a cop was running after Yenta Gersh on the beach and I swear to God he couldn't catch her, that's how fast she was even with the baby carriage. Why he could get her is only because the carriage got tipped over in the sand and she went back to hit people for grabbing her pollyseeds.

The cop said I know you lady, I seen you from before, you like to make trouble for me, you like to peddle without a license.

Yenta Gersh talked in Jewish to a lady and the lady told the cop in English, Officer she don't understand English, her English ain't too good, from one word of English she don't understand.

Yenta Gersh grabbed the lady and she whispered in her ear something.

The lady said She don't want to be a liar for you officer, maybe a word and one word maybe she'll understand.

Yenta Gersh like stuck up a finger and she said Depretzon.

The cop said I give you summons. Summons I give you, I sorry. License you no got.

He took out his ticket book, the whole beach went boobooboo.

The lady said You think that's nice, I don't think that's too nice officer darling, you shouldn't make her a summons, a person like that, to her English is a foreign language.

Yenta Gersh went on her fingers Juh Lewss hex-lex feenamintz tziklitz.

The lady said She don't even know in English what she done, in English maybe she broke a law, in Yiddish she's altogether an innocent party.

The cop said You run, so why you run.

The lady had to ask Yenta Gersh twice in Jewish, then she said It's in English hard to explain, it's like you would say it's a nervous habit.

Yenta Gersh grabbed the lady and again she whispered in her ear. The lady said in Jewish It could be that in her Jewish way she was only walking fast.

The cop put away his ticket book, he said Now no summons, I no give summons.

The lady told Yenta Gersh and Yenta Gersh told the lady something and the lady told the cop She wants to give you her gratitude in English.

Yenta Gersh tried and tried but she couldn't express it.

The lady said In Yiddish it would be you should get blessed by your god and she wants to call up your bosses to say how fine you acted.

Yenta Gersh went Warden Lawes Warden Lawes.

The cop walked away then every body walked away. Boomie got thirsty so he bought from Yenta Gersh some orange drink. He spit it right out, he claimed there was no ice in the pail and it tastes like shit.

Yenta Gersh turned around, she said You don't like the taste kiss my ass and fuck on you.

Mom didn't feel good, we went to Dr. Felkin.

He examined her fifteen minutes and he said Malvena if I wanted to make from you a few dollars and if I was a sucker I'd say come back again and I'd give you medicine and powders. Only you don't need medicine and you don't need powders, what you need I can write down on my prescription paper, it's one word and one word only.

He wrote down A CHANGE OF PACE.

He said That's all you need, you don't need me, save your money, I don't want to see you any more and I don't want to hear about you, I want you from now on to take it easy, I want you to spend on yourself, enjoy and have good times, for once be selfish, don't be a fool, right now get out of here and change your pace.

Mom said You're right you're right, I'm fed up and I'm disgusted, from now on Malvena the Orphan takes better care of herself, no more step child of the world.

We started to go and Dr. Felkin walked us out, he told Mom Right now pack a little bag and get yourself a place in Fallsburg.

Mom said Who needs to pack, I'm not going to waste time packing, what I need I'll buy there, they have beautiful beautiful beautiful little stores in Fallsburg.

We went down and Mom sang a happiness song in Jewish and she danced us around by the Knishe Queen.

Mom said First first first I go to the beauty parlor and I put myself in the hands of Mister Moey, what it costs it costs, I'll tell him Mister Moey I'm putting myself in your hands and what it costs it costs.

She again danced us around and she sang in Jewish I Begged My Momma Dear To Get Up From The Grave To Make Me Some Tzimmis.

Mom said The first first first train that goes to Fallsburg is the train I take, what I was is in the past and them days are gone forever, I'm putting myself first and first I'll put myself.

Mom sang in Jewish Put The Stone By My Head It Shouldn't Lay Heavy On My Feet.

Mom said I'll think of myself, I'll spend on myself, I'll give in to myself, I'll cater to myself. Get used to it, that's how it'll be and how it'll be is what you'll get used to.

We crossed over to Waxman and Mom called out Waxman, Hey Waxman you got in your window a beach chair, how much is that beach chair for me.

Waxman said You got good taste, have you got good taste, good taste is what you got, let me tell you when you got it you got it and nobody can take it away from you.

Mom said In my life and since I was born I never had a beach chair, now it's high high high time. I had a mother also and if she was with me now she would tell me Malvena fool don't wait no more, wake up and live, forget about Cousin Phillie and what you did for him, 23 years already he's promising you a beach chair, Cousin Phillie where's my beach chair you're promising me 23 years, Malvena hold your horses, I want to wait till they come out already with the new models, how much is that beach chair for me, Waxman for me, give me the right right price Waxman.

Waxman said I can't get over you got such good taste, good taste when you got it is something you're already born with and nobody can take it away from you because taste when its born in you is an inborn thing, for you the right price and the special price is $3.79.

Mom said If that's the price that's the price, no hondling and no bargaining, that's it and that's it, a nickel more or a nickel less won't give me back my momma, I'm not tearing your heart out for a nickel.

Waxman said You know what, I'm taking off the nickel for you and only for you and don't tell anybody, because you know what good is, you got the knack and that's a knack that's born in you, if it's born in you you got it and it's a natural knack.

Waxman then wrapped the chair up in newspaper and he tied it around with string and then he put over some more newspaper.

Mom said Waxman put on a little newspaper.

Waxman put on the whole yesterdays Mirror and a Sunday Journal.

Mom took one end and I took the other end and Waxman took the middle and we that way lugged it across the street and upstairs.

Mom sent back Waxman for a little more newspaper to be on the safe side. Waxman brought up the Forvitz and the American and he helped Mom and me put the chair in the cedar closet on the top underneath her old Hudson seal coat.

Mom after locked up the closet and the key she put in the bread box in a big jar that's very hard to open.

Then we took newspaper and we went downstairs on the stoop. Pretty soon it started to drizzle, right now even it's drizzling.

May 17, 1938

Very very early our bell rang.

A mailman gave Mom a special delivery from The Lovely Lady Program.

Mom said This is it and this is it.

Dad said You want to hear something, you'll see you have a smart husband, listen what I'll tell you, I'm telling you this is it.

Mom first put on the girdle before she opened it and Dad said Hey Malvena the Celebrity.

Mom when she opened the letter cried, it had on so many stamps. Dad said a Jewish face you don't see on their stamps.

The letter was that Mom's postal had gotten read with interest by The Lovely Lady Program and they would like her at the studio between half past ten and eleven to try for the Lovely Lady Grand Prize.

Mom said This this this is it.

Dad said Mark my words that if this isn't it then what is it?

We made up I should go with Mom on the subway and while she got ready the banana and cream cheese sandwiches Dad gave me directions.

Mom said That's one thing your Daddy knows, he'll give you step by step directions.

I told Dad How many times did I make the same exact trip, I made it so so many times already by myself.

Dad said Let me hear your step by step way.

The whole thing I had to do. How I go on the Brighton Beach and how I stand where the last car stops and how I can get off by 34th St. or by 42nd St. because I have to either way get the same local.

Dad said You got it, your step by step way is the best way it's the only way.

He all of a sudden grabbed a hanger, he tried to hit me and he yelled Tell me how come and why it is that from the day you were born I never had in you confidence.

Mom then came out, she had on the dress from my bar mitzva and she was putting the sandwiches in her best shopping bag.

Dad like kissed his hand at her and he said Celebrity twirl a little.

Mom got cute, she sat down and crossed her legs and posed with the shopping bag on her knee.

Dad was very very chokey, he blew out his nose in the sink and he said Thank you for marrying me.

We then got started. Mom picked up first Mrs. Plaut and Mrs. Harlib, they walked us to the station. We stopped by Teitlebaum and Mom yelled in the good news. Teitlebaum said Let me give you a little something for good luck, he gave her a half sour pickle, the midget.

Mrs. Harlib and Mrs. Plaut kissed us good bye and when Mom and I climbed the stairs they sang the Lovely Lady theme song, Lovely Lady I'm Falling Madly In Love With You, Lovely Lady There's No Concealing What Can I Do.

This made Mom cry and and she wished on them that in years to come they should only only only have the strength to do similar nice things for her and hers.

We had a pretty good trip. Mom got into a conversation with a man that he lost his third wife two years ago, she also used to wear undershirts. He told Mom if she came over some night to his room she could see if they fit. Also he would give her a big bunch of old movie magazines. He said When you come over I'll make you a very happy woman. Mom at this cried, she said Believe me you're talking to some body who could use a little happiness. The man got off at Canal St., he has an oilcloth store. Mom wished him out of the window that every day for him should be a Grand Opening.

As we didn't eat really a decent breakfast, we were in such a rush, we ate our sandwiches when we got to 42nd St. on the local side. Mom started talking to the old man who ran the newsstand in Jewish, she told him about her dropped stomach and he let her sit and eat in his booth.

We then went to 47th St. near Broadway, we had no no trouble finding the building. They had inside an arrow pointing to a special elevator for Lovely Lady and when we got off a good looking goyish guy, he was exactly like Buster Crabbe, asked to see her letter. He said Good very good and May I welcome you to The Lovely Lady Show and offer you this to help make a lovely lady lovelier still.

He gave Mom a cellophane bag with a little mirror and a little comb and a little piece of the Lovely Lady Soap, everything had on it Sample Only, retail sale in any form is prohibited by law.

Mom said to him Thank you very very much Mr. Gorgeous Dimples, don't you worry perfect specimen, if I should only only win your grand prize I'll take very good care of you, you like paper plates you'll get paper plates in all colors, just just check me on my feeling, my feeling is that from my postal they'll have for me a few few little questions about Hartford Connecticut, don't don't tell me let me be surprised, you like paper cups for your whiskey, I got them with or without handles but only only in white, also you could ask me anything about the movie stars, my Cousin Phillie grew up with Warren Hymer, so what if they're white, white is the best thing, by the time you finish up with your whiskey you're not going to notice colors.

The guy winked at her and he looked over where he had her down on a list. He said Well fine Malvena, we're all here to have a fine time and a fine time is what we shall have, all of us Malvena, say Malvena is truly a lovely name for a lovely lady.

An usher took us in to where they do the broadcasting, he was also like Buster Crabbe. Mom sat right in the front, she kept whispering and poking and poking and whispering. She said in Jewish to reach over, it's only two rows, what does it hurt, it's like a brand new paper, that's one one thing I have to say for the goyim and for that I love them, they finish up reading a paper they leave it in beautiful beautiful shape.

I looked around, I told Mom they have letters also, the whole bunch of women had the same exact kind of letter.

Mom didn't hear me, she was waving her shopping bag at the master of ceremonies, hello Lanny Shaw, how are you Mr. Sweet Voice.

He sang the Lovely Lady Song, then they flashed a sign Fifteen Minutes To Air Time and he went down with a microphone where we sat. Everyone clapped and yelled Come to me Come to me, Mom yelled louder.

He like did a little dance over and he sang the Lovely Lady Song in Mom's face. Mom cried and he gave her a Lovely Lady face tissue box, the small. Then he said to her Pray tell me Lovely Lady, what is your name.

Mom answered him Malvena Sloan.

He said A lovely name for a Lovely Lady, and where, pray tell, do you live lovely lady.

Mom told him 1896 Brighton 5th St., it's already seventeen years and if I'm a lucky lovely lady today and God should only only spare me that's it and that's it, I have no more strength on my dropped stomach for 3½ rooms, although I'll tell you something Lanny, cross ventilation like I got I'll never get again.

He said Well that's a grand Lovely Lady Malvena, and let's have a great big hand for cross ventilation.

An usher came over and he gave Mom a dollar bill.

Mom said That's all, how come that's all, I answered two questions, since when do you get away with two questions for a dollar.

The usher said We'll make an adjustment outside Lovely Lady.

We went with him and then he did it real fast, he locked the door behind us.

Mom went to the guy by the elevator, she grabbed his tie. I started pulling her, I said Mom don't do that and that she shouldn't do, will you just just just don't do that, and the more I pulled the more she grabbed the tie.

I then, I myself and me started to cry, I swear to God I haven't cried since I first met Hymie and he won me in a wrestle.

Mom told the guy You lost plenty now, I hate to hate to tell you what you and your people lost, you lost me for an audience, you lost my husband's whole society and when I finish believe me you can kiss Brighton Beach good bye.

Finally finally I pulled her off his tie and I pushed her in an elevator. She said to the guy From now on drink your whiskey out of glasses.

Almost to the subway I was crying and when the train came I ran in and I went to the first car where the motorman is. Mom followed me, she tried to do with me the happiness dance, I didn't let. I said to her Mom don't you ever ever ever do that, with goyim don't do that.

I stopped crying and we sort of made up. She said it reminds me when I stand here and I watch how the train goes the way I would feed you when you were a baby, I would say See how the train goes into the tunnel, it goes Chew Chew Chew.

May 18, 1938

On account of I was out yesterday I forgot all about the debate.

Naturally.

Miss Hochman called on me the second one, there was more than half the period yet. What I did was talk back and forth and this way and that way. I kept making a mistake, instead of saying Julius Caesar was killed on the IDES of March I three times said the EYES of March. I got the lowest mark I ever got in English, C+ and Miss Hochman wrote on the comment sheet Not Well Prepared.

I and Boomie had Study Period together, we got into a conversation. Boomie said I wonder when we'll get laid. I answered him with a snap, I said what kind of when WE'LL get laid. I'll get laid when I get laid and you'll get laid when you get laid. He looked a little bit hurt so I tried sort of a joke, I said in other words I'll go fuck myself and you'll go fuck yourself. He said In my feelings or in my imagination I always had it that we're friends and because we're friends we would get laid together.

I said like Marshey You WANT us to get laid together? All RIGHT. Why NOT.

Boomie said We should send him a note that he owes for months and months Battle Aces dues.

I said It's four months. It slipped out that I remembered practically the exact time he stopped being friends.

Boomie said When the term is over and we finish with finals and everything we should make a Battle Aces party.

I said it should be a masquerade party and we should invite Marshey and he should come how he really is, with a condrum on his head to show he's a prick.

In the cafeteria I and Clare had sort of an argument. She

said to me I missed you yesterday in French, I said You missed me in French how come you didn't miss me in English.

We later got into a conversation What does your father do and what does your father do. I said my father was sort of in the movie business. She said My father used to be in wholesale fruit and vegetables, now he's in pocketbooks. So I said, I couldn't help it, Your father is in pocketbooks, wowee he must be a small guy. Clare said I don't mind if you say kidding things about me. But when it comes to my father I have to say something, don't you really think you have some nerve with a man you don't know to make such remarks, this man gave his life practically for working class freedom, when I was a little girl once I'll never forget he was in the hospital two weeks for being beaten up near the mastoid, I wonder if you know how serious that is, anything near the mastoid is a serious thing.

I said in a very very sincere way to really excuse me as I have dumb habits and she made me then promise for atoning I would definitely read it when she brought it for me, Jews Without Money and something The Coming Struggle For Power. I was almost ready to say Does the Coming Struggle For Power have any hot parts but didn't want to start more trouble as she had for me a terrific sandwich, it was a certain kind of goyish baloney.

May 19, 1938

I had a dream. I made myself not even remember it. Something again with being in the movies and sitting where I couldn't see and things under the bed were pulling me down. This has to do with when I don't cover my feet. Anyway never mind and forget it.

I asked Miss Hochman if I could do an extra book report to make up for the debate mark. She was very very nice and made me feel good by saying I will be happy to read anything you wish and care to write but you needn't worry Simon, you are not among the students I worry about.

C.D. brought me the books, I promised her I'd cover them. She said her father wanted to know why she wanted them and she told him they were for a FELLAH and he would take good care of them. Her father said That's not my worry, I'm not worried, I know a boy you lend my books to is going to be responsible, you wouldn't lend them if he wasn't to you a proletarian conscience, I want to know only that he has a proletarian conscience. I said I know what proletarian is but I don't know what he means, what does he mean A Proletarian Conscience. Clare said It's if you think of what is good for workers and what workers go through, like sometimes me when I think about my father I sometimes could cry.

I told her I definitely must have it then, a proletarian conscience and it's the same same thing with me, when I think about my father I also could cry.

May 20, 1938

Hymie told me Hohner quit yesterday.

What happened was he had a fight with Mrs. Chepper and Mrs. Sandberg, he said they're the last ones always to put out the garbage for the dumbwaiter, they said he never empties their pails right, they would always find on the bottom their pits and things. So he went in the basement and turned the steam on full blast, the whole house had to go on the roof to cool off.

In Bio Mrs. Jacobey was drawing on the blackboard some things about leaves and she told us the lines on them are called striations. Someone went Men striations, this got her very very sore and she pulled a short answer test on the whole class. I think I got ten out of ten unless she takes off for the plural of amoeba, I kept putting it down amoebas.

Before I forget I and Boomie saw Lila Edlelstein go into a typing room. Boomie told me her father died, I didn't know, and she's taking now the straight commercial course. That's where you don't get a language and you don't get history and the english is business english. You write letters Dear Mr. Jones We Are Most Pleased At Your Order And

Will Fill It Promptly, I saw once the book they use. That's why I got a sad feeling and I did in my throat to her sorry sorry sorry. Boomie said OOOOH did I hate her guts, you remember how I hated her guts and I couldn't stand her. I said You used to have a good one for her, that everything she is rhymes with itch, a bitch a snitch and a kvitch. Boomie said She was smart, one thing is she was smart but it was smart that you couldn't stand, like if on a test somebody got 96 she would get 98.

Boomie then ran ahead, he had his gym. I for no reason went to the typewriter room and I looked in and I saw Lila. She was sitting in the first row first seat and she was just just starting in to type, she absolutely was doing it faster and with more concentration then anybody else. Also the teacher was talking to her while she typed, definitely he said nice things.

What made me sorry for her is she had sort of a big water pimple by her chin and hair was growing from it. I think that's why I did what I did, I knocked on the door window, and I waved fingers and I jumped up a little she should see me. Naturally and of course when she saw me she right away stuck out her tongue.

This gave me a bad mood and a little bit I took it out on Clare. She asked me So what do you think about Jews Without Money, I answered her I bet it must be hard if they want to go in the subway. She wouldn't make up with me until I wrote in her notebook five times Simon Sloan Hereby Apologizes To The Working Class.

May 21, 1938

I am so tired it's a wonder I can write.

In the middle of the night Dad woke us up to please help him as his end is near.

Mom made him hot water and lemon and I went to the toilet with him he should throw up.

Dad couldn't throw up so Mom made him an enema.

The enema worked, it cleaned him out and he felt better.

When I saw him looking good again I had like a chokey mood and I went over to him and even though he smelled bad and he pushed away I kissed him.

He yelled on me I should go away and get killed with the shmutshy-wutshy, if I want to shmutshy-wutshy I should shmutshy-wutshy with Jackie Cooper.

I said You're my Dad and what's so terrible if I want to give you kisses and I kiss you to feel good.

The real reason I did it I didn't tell him and never mind.

All right.

For two reasons I did it.

Reason number one is I didn't want him to die and I should have to take a commercial course and reason number two is I didn't want to have to ride that trip all the way to the cemetery to visit his grave.

May 22, 1938

I didn't put down I read finally Jews Without Money and I liked it very much. My favorite part was where the kid goes on the roof and he kills all the gangsters pigeons for what the gangster did with his sister. The Coming Struggle For Power I didn't really read, I like skimmed through it to talk about it in a smart way.

So naturally Clare in the cafeteria talked just just about The Coming Struggle For Power. She said I bet it shows you, did it show you how socialism is the only way for mankind.

I said like Marshey SURE, and also how it shows that its a WAY but why necessarily is it the ONLY way.

She said You should tell that, you know to who you should say its not the way, go and say its not the way to the American Millions who are now under the yoke of starvation.

I said UNDER the yoke of starvation is like a mixed metaphor, you made a mixed metaphor neh neh.

She went neh neh back on me and she said So I did a mixed metaphor, I don't care and I do not mind when I mix up a metaphor if I'm doing it for the American Millions who are FEELING the yoke of starvation.

She then opened the sandwiches for me, she told me they were her mother's best specialty, crab meat salad with pepper chopped in.

I started in a tease laugh and my tease laugh turned into a real laugh, it got me so I was kicking my feet and my elbows were weak.

Three times I tried, the fourth time finally I could talk, I said OOOH OOOH OOOH and WAH WAH WAH, The American Millions, OY OY OY The Yoke Of Starvation.

What I meant was it struck me funny that she went right away from starving millions to crab meat sandwiches. She took it only that I was making fun of the starving millions.

That's why she answered me You know what you are, what you are exactly is a class enemy.

I said Why am I a class enemy? I like my class and it's the best class I was ever in.

She said to me If we ever have the time, if the period comes when they say to me here's a list of the FELLAHS who are in the way, they stand in the way of our getting socialism and if I see your name is on the list I will tell them, you know what I will say, I knew him and he was a nice person but he is a class enemy so shoot him.

I was eating then a sandwich and when I looked once in her face I was so help me God afraid to look again.

We then changed the subject to French and what would most likely be on the final. We even made up to study together.

What I should have done was forget and drop the whole subject, I didn't though. So when the bell rang I said to her Hey you really really mean it, they would shoot me and you would say go ahead, you would let them.

She made believe she didn't hear and we lined up. I was right behind her and I again said They would shoot me and you would let them, you mean it really. The thing is it began to get me and sink in, I like saw it the way I SAW it the time I saw myself really dead and under the earth and I wanted her to show me she was kidding. So I gave her a little tickle on the neck, absolutely nothing dirty, I did it the way you tickle a baby.

Listen to what she did.

She kicked back with one foot and got me good in the ankle. It hurt so much for a second I got sick to the stomach.

She right away turned around and said I'm sorry, I didn't mean it, that I didn't mean.

So in the same place I tickled her again and she said I mean I am sorry for kicking you, for kicking you I am sorry, not for letting them shoot you.

When we were walking up I felt like asking her You say you would let them shoot me, THEM. But if you had to would you do it, you yourself and you. I was afraid of the answer.

I instead asked something about if it was all right with her father and if he wouldn't mind for me to keep a little longer The Coming Struggle For Power as there were parts I wanted to read over.

I just now looked where she kicked me, it's purple and I think its getting pus.

May 23, 1938

I and Boomie went to get Hymie but he had to watch the bubbee. She now is almost blind from cataracts in the eyes, they have to sort of get ripe and then you take them out.

The bubbee was a big nudge and wouldn't leave us alone. She every second pulled us by the window we should tell her what's doing outside.

We got an idea.

First Boomie went to the window. He went Mammenyou bubbee, you know what you are missing, what you're missing, Mrs. Abrams is making a peepee in the street.

Hymie then ran to the window, he said Woo Gelfman is running out now, is he sore, he's hitting her in her pussy and she's banging on his cock.

I went also to the window, I said Now they're not fight-

ing, they made up now, and Mrs. Abrams is sucking Gelfman's cock and Gelfman is licking Mrs. Abrams pussy.

The bubbee cried and Hymie's mom walked in from
shopping. She said Shame on you to tease a bubbee and when
I put away my packages you'll get it good.

The bubbee wanted to help her put away, Hymie's mom
wouldn't let. She said in Jewish All your life you worked
hard for me Momma heart, let me work and let me do something for you.

She hummed Jewish songs for the bubbee to enjoy, then
she said You know what Momma shane, you'll never guess
who I met in the Sacramento dairy, I met Mrs. Roosevelt,
she said her boys are crazy about a certain kind of chicken
carp you don't get in her neighborhood. It turns out she
anyway had to come see me, she and the president were talking about you, he's all set to give you some old age money
only he's afraid for the neighbors it wouldn't look good,
how is it going to look if he should give you old age money
and you should have under your name the two family house
in Rockaway, right away the vice president would be jealous.
So his idea, listen to this for an idea, you should right away
put the house in my name.

While they were hitting each other Hymie went to the
bubbee's pocketbook, he snitched fifteen cents and we used
it for candy money in the movies. We saw an old picture in
the Regal, Smiling Through with Norma Shearer and
Frederic March and Leslie Howard. We saw it twice for the
one scene when Frederic March shoots Norma Shearer by
accident, he's aiming really for Leslie Howard. She falls in
a way that you can see half the tits come out.

May 24, 1938
I and Boomie and Hymie went in the water as it was very
very warm.

We all of us swam out past the third rope and the life-
guard whistled us to go back. I was glad, I never like to be
in water over my head. Its the same thing wanting my feet

should be always covered, I'm afraid things could pull me under the bed. What things I never put down exactly and never mind.

After we went out we had fun with a lady. She had with her two kids and we made believe we were crazy about the kids. So she showed off for us how nice they could dig in the sand, she would say to them Bury mommy and then lay down and we looked up between her legs, the bush kept coming out of the bathing suit.

The whole beach then started getting up and moving and yelling, we figured somebody drowned but for a while we had to stay down as we all had fantastic hardons. It turned out there was an airplane flying all around our beach from the News, it was really low and we could see the guy taking pictures.

We got bored and we decided to walk and get frozen custard near Sea Gate, only they have the chocolate chip. Boomie and Hymie took off their bathing suits under a towel, they have the knack so nobody sees. I did the same thing and sand got in my underwear. This made me have a terrible mood and lousy thoughts, I had to absolutely walk away by myself and stand a second in the water. I saw again the woman from the two kids, she smiled at me and she like sat in the water in a way that I thought she was making a urination and she said to me Its such a muhchiyer. Right away I had a disgust. She wasn't any more a nice bush and big tits to me, she was only shit and scumbags and I went in my throat Hitler come over, right now come over, come over kill the whole beach Hitler with me on it.

The lady then talked to me again. Its just right the water, its not too hot and its not too cold, you once in a great while get it when its like this the water, when its not too hot and its not too cold, thats when its a muhchiyer.

I answered her like I was a greenhorn mockey, I said to her the way Boomie used to do Marshey's mom, Dot's ride, snot too hot snot too cold, like dis ven it iz iz bah me halso hah muhchiyer.

She looked away from me and she said Maybe I sound that way, if I sound that way and that's how I sound I'm sorry and it's too bad and what should I do about it because I can't help it. It is nothing I can help and even if I do sound that way, let's say its how I sound, do you think you are doing the right thing. I don't think its nice to make fun, a person doesn't have a choice how she sounds, if they asked how I would want to sound I'd say I want to sound like Helen Mencken. Its the same thing if they asked you here's a choice and how would you want to look you'd want to look like Clark Gable. I don't make fun of you that you don't look like Clark Gable, not everybody in the whole world is going to look like Clark Gable, that's why theres one Clark Gable, you can't help it if you look how you look you mutt-face you.

I walked away, I didn't answer back. The mood I had I had the whole whole day and when I went to sleep it was so bad I took the covers off my feet and I did in my throat Go ahead, you want to take me, take me down. I made myself fall asleep without the covers and I had a dream with Rabbi Neuberger, he was having me write for him in Jewish and I was writing some marvelous and very deep things. In the dream I kept thinking how what I was writing was the greatest thing that was ever written, then when I got up I remembered some stuff from it and it was a bunch of shit. Except I think Hohner got mixed up in it, he was telling me Everybody gets laid, everybody is Hitler.

My feet were freezing and I hope to God I don't catch a cold as thats all I need before finals.

May 25, 1938
Clare today told me her father said I could keep awhile The Coming Struggle For Power and also he sent along another book if I wanted to read it to expand and enlarge my workers horizon, I Went To Pitt College.

Also she told me she liked what I said before in French.

What happened was we were all reading out loud together and Mr. Wexler called on anybody to translate the word BLESSER. I had my hand half way up anyway as I had looked it up, something something told me this word he would call on us for. I said BLESSER is Wound, To Wound, and also I said What is interesting for this word, what makes it to me interesting is it shows how in words there are hidden things. For instance they make it the same thing here that if you are Blessed By God he also is giving you a wound or a hurt, in other words for a blessing you sort of have to get also suffering.

Mr. Wexler went Bien Bien, he put something on my Delaney Card. Some of the kids definitely were jealous. Artie Bier afterward came over, he said God should bless you and he gave me a shot. I naturally couldn't hit back as it was supposed to be a joke.

So Clare was talking about it and she said to me Sometimes I love you and sometimes I hate you. I can kill you sometimes for the way you talk about Socialism. Then you say something like in French, what you said was so smart I felt like giving you a kiss in French.

What I naturally was dying to answer was Oh you felt like giving me a French Kiss only I didn't want to get her started. She was just opening the lunch, I saw she had brownies.

Before I forget Hymie was very sore as for the third time this term he got his lock clipped. He is positive Mr. Stock is doing it to get a commission for Masters locks. I told him Go get a Masters lock already, what's the difference, it costs you already more not to get one. He said Its a definite difference, to me its a difference. I told him every teacher has a craziness, this is Stock's craziness and to me it's not a difference. He said God should only help Stock if he finds out and gets proof he does the clipping. I said Hymie what are you being a shmuk, you know you are a real real shmuk and he told me I'm walking away from you not to hit you.

We are starting to review in Bio and French for the finals.

We had our last Assembly for the term and Dr. Gladstone made a speech how summer is coming and it gives us the opportunity to go and discover again nature. That is what he used to do, he used to go out in his youth every summer and say I hear the birds and how lovely is their song, I see the grass and how green is the grass. Sheicky Liebson afterward told me his mother and Dr. Gladstone's mother were best friends, they both grew up on Rivington St. and the only thing he saw there green was his asshole.

Hymie is steamed up again with his lock. He told me he found out definitely it isn't Mr. Stock who goes around clipping, it's Mr. Foote the custodian. What happened is Hymie went down early for Tumbling Team workout and he saw Foote go around to all the lockers with clippers. Hymie is still not getting a Masters lock, he's putting on another one from the 5 and 10. I think he feels what I feel, he's glad it's a goy doing it.

Clare forgot to take for me an extra sandwich and she says her father wants The Coming Struggle For Power back as he needs it for a cousin.

A good thing and a bad thing.

The good thing is Miss Hochman excused me and two others from the English final, she said from all our records in the term there's nothing we could do to get less than a 95. Boomie passed me a note, it almost finished me. NOW YOU CAN JERK OFF IN CLASS.

The bad thing is Clare came very very late to the cafeteria and she said to me the first thing, Where is The Coming Struggle For Power, did you bring The Coming Struggle For Power. I gave it to her, she right away took off the cover I put on it from the Forvitz, she held it like it was a scumbag.

She then took out the lunch and said to me This is the

last sandwich I am bringing you. Not because of something in particular, as a FELLA I like you, if I think of you as only a FELLA I think of you as a nice FELLA, there are many nice things I would say about you. But I have to listen to my mother and my father, they think also you're a nice FELLA and you can't help it that what you are to what they believe in is a Class Enemy. A person can be a nice FELLA and a Class Enemy. My mother says its not against you personally but I should look more for a FELLA that is from our movement background. Also she's getting tired of making sandwiches.

I didn't even get a chance to answer back as the bell rang. I said Well okay, Good Luck on your French final. We then got on different lines.

In my imagination I had an idea. How years and years from now a guy and a girl would be in the cafeteria and he would say to her all of a sudden Hey look at that, do you see that? She would look and say Look where, I don't see. What it would be is that where Clara and I sat, by our table, a bag would open up without hands and in the middle of the air two sandwiches would get eaten up.

This is not from my original imagination. It's from that picture, the name I don't remember, when William Powell and Kay Francis are at the end both dead and the last scene is their ghostly spirits drink and break the two glasses in the special way they had.

May 28, 1938

After French Clara waved to me and walked over, I went in my throat Love Love Love.

She said You didn't give me back I Went To PITT College.

I answered her Don't worry you'll get it you'll get it.

She said I'm not worried, worried I am not, I wanted to tell you only I want it and I need it.

I didn't mean to only it came out a yell YOU'LL GET IT YOU'LL GET IT.

H

Mr. Wexler noticed, he told me Fermez la bouche.

May 29, 1938

The schedule for finals was announced and I am going to have Geometry right right after Bio. Geometry is going to be 8:30 and French will be 10:40, I'll have ten minutes in between. I told Mrs. Jacobey I think this is highly highly unfair, she said Talk to me again next week and we may perhaps make other arrangements.

Clare again today asked me about I Went To Pitt College, I told her I forgot. This is the truth as I got upset from a fight with Dad in the morning. He said to me How come you never say to me like a normal human child to a father, Hello Pop, how are you Pop, is the prostate bothering you. From there it first started in.

On top of everything Mom is crying and carrying on, she'll never go again to Teitlebaum. I didn't put down last night he came to the house, he wanted to know how come he didn't see her lately. Mom told him next time she's on the way back from Sacramento Dairy she'll knock on his window, that way he can see her. Teitlebaum said This I don't understand I don't understand this from my favorite customer. Mom said I'm the favorite customer, that that's why I ask you for half a quarter pearl barley, you tell me it's a little little bit over, is it okay a little little bit over, your little little bit over was close to a pound. He answered her I'm surprised you don't realize when you're handling pearl barley its hard to get it the exact ounce. In the middle we got company, it was Cousin Phillie and he

7

Then on the evening of February 17, 1939, when Teitlebaum could be seen writing in black crayon all over his
window: "Two long years without you, Jean Harlow! There
will be always in our hearts only one Jean Harlow and there
will be always only one SWEETMAID FARMER CHEESE!
Watch this window tomorrow morning when it goes on
Surprise Special!"; and Mrs. Gleicher, still spitting blood,
marched once and for all from Ringelman's office after he
plunged the three middle fingers of his left hand up her
dress and spoke of intensive gum massage; around the time
Dopey Duhvee got himself a new little habit and started
doing his nyeh-nyehs in Gelfman's phone booths; when the
Workmen's Circle sent out a special mailing calling upon all
Brighton Beach Brothers and Sisters to desist and refrain
from taking passage on the *Hindenburg;* the same week
Harry the Fish Man's daughter, Fat Rosalie, was picked up
finally in the lobby of the Saint George Hotel with a copy
of *Anthony Adverse* and close to three dollars worth of
Mason's Mints; this also happening to be the week Julian P.
Cohen put into the *Forvitz* a commercial notice: "It is with
sad regret I announce to my loyal patrons that health factors

compel a limitation of my activities to between Neptune Avenue and Ocean Parkway. Be confidentially assured that Mr. Louis Gutwillig who starts soon to take over my practice comes to you equipped with many years of trained experience to serve your butter and egg needs"; just around the time Leon Eismuth died in Upper Fallsburg while serving as delegate-at-large to the Ticket and Label Sewers Eleventh National Assembly; not so long after Moishe Oisher hopped off the Brighton Theater stage, pulled Mrs. Teichitz from her seat and waltzed her around the aisle singing, *Ich Hab Dir Tzu Viel Lieb;* maybe a few days after Sheicky Stein was spotted on Seventh Avenue and Thirty-eighth Street offering sharkskin suits for next to nothing from an unmarked truck; a week only since Ira Polsky appeared before a Workmen's Compensation referee to argue that his boss's remark, "I *farf* on you and I *cock* on you," had been a contributing cause and a responsible factor in his strangulated hernia; right after the Knishe Queen put out a sign, "We are now interviewing to fill a few CHOICE openings in our derma department"; while Mrs. Aranow's Stanley swore by his taxi medallion that he had been hailed at Times Square by a peanut of a man; that he had told this little fellow, "You know, you remind me of someone, someone"; that this little fellow cackled and cackled but remained otherwise still; that Stanley had let him off at Rockefeller Center; that after paying his fare plus a beautiful tip the little fellow had boosted himself up on the running board and in a voice as familiar to Stanley as the voice of President Roosevelt had shrilled, "Did you ever . . . Call . . . For . . . Phillip . . . Morris!"; when Mrs. Wachtel accused Mrs. Perlig of telling half the world and the whole street that her Lily had a barren womb and went for electrolysis; right before Bomba Katz's mother wrote to Father Divine in care of Fox Movietone, "If you are the same fellow that you used to light the gas Friday night by my late beloved sister Chanah Elke Bershad when she lived on 119 Roebling Street between South 1 and South 2 Street

I want to wish you a real *mazel tov* from me and mine that you're doing so nice now, also I must tell you when my late beloved sister was packing up to go to the hospital she came across that cut glass bowl"; the day after Harriet Wershba went into Macy's to return a poacher for her office manager and picked up a copy of *Gone With the Wind* for sixty-one cents; when they finally fixed the broken scale near the change booth on the Brighton Beach Station; a couple of weeks already since Jan Peerce came unannounced to the Clothing Cutter's Ball, hugged Sidney Hillman and in his honor sang *Der Urimeh Broyt;* when Mimi Brecher had a terrible fight in the John Reed Theater with her Hershey, calling him "Social Fascist" and "Dummy" because he had not yelled "Strike!" at the end of *Waiting for Lefty;* when Mrs. Schiller stepped up to the Save the Spanish Republican Refugees booth near the Sacramento Dairy and donated three of her Yosele Rosenblatt records; the week Ida, the bakery lady's daughter, was hauled down to the psychological advisor in Brooklyn College for telling her Economics 11.5 professor, "When it comes to the labor theory of value I say you know *bubkes*"; after Charlie the Radio Man did such a botch job for Mrs. Hechshel that she could barely get W E A F; after Luna Park had a fire for a change; Simon, to be on the safe side, pinched out a second Trojan from his three-pack, nested it in his wallet and rang the upstairs bell of a certain certain Maxine Roseman concerning whom he had heard some very good reports.

The peephole leaked light and he caught a musical, "Bimbo, your tootsie is here!"

". . . If Maxine is in?"

A lock was turned, a chain withdrawn.

"She's in. She . . . is . . . IN!"

By inches the door opened. As Simon pushed through, crinkling newspaper underfoot, it was slammed with such force that the foyer lights twittered. In a breathy rush he offered his "Hello and a Good *Shabos*" like a little card.

"Looky looky!"

Big teeth and big gums were bared at him and he smelled *schmaltz* and moonseed and halvah.

"This is a very very very nice building, Mrs. Roseman," Simon said lucidly, politely, while under the guarded blur of his gaze he took in the bathrobe loosely tied with twine, the man's pants, the bare fat-heeled feet.

"Bimbo!" Mrs. Roseman roared over her shoulder, "your tootsie is all dressed up for you!"

From deep inside the apartment she was answered, "Ma, you wanna do me a favor? Do me a favor . . . ?"

"Hi!" sang out Simon. And, "You sound different on the phone . . ."

". . . shut your hole."

"Get killed in there, bimbo," Mrs. Roseman instructed. "Bimbo only get killed and I'll plant a tree for you in Palestine." Grinning, radiant, she said to Simon, "You also talk to your mother that way?"

Simon went, "Well, heh heh . . ."

She turned brusquely and stamped off to the living room, leaving him amid seltzer bottles. At her "*Nu,* come on already," he ambled after, saying, "You know, Mrs. Roseman, what you have here, you have just just exactly what my mother wants. You know? For her, *the* greatest thing, what she wants in an apartment is that *all* the rooms should be—"

"Bimbo!" With both hands Mrs. Roseman slapped the living room wall, "you're studying?"

"—off the foyer."

"I bet, oh, oh, I bet that's what you're doing, hah? Hah, bimbo? Your studying your—biology, you're getting all ready to surprise me with highest marks. Right? Am I right, bimbo? You're going to raise your forty-eight to at least—oh, at least, at *least* a—fifty-one!"

She punished the wall till a crack leaped out and flecks of plaster dotted the sofa. Then came a languid, "Please shut up, go to hell and you should drop dead, old shit pot."

"Biology," Simon whispered wetly, "can be a very very

224

hard subject. You know, Mrs. Roseman? You can be good in English, you can be good in History, you can be good in . . ."

"Let her be good in the grave!" Mrs. Roseman cried gaily.

"Ma?"

"Forty-eight she should have on her thermometer."

"Same to you, Ma, and go and VOMITAH on my THER-MOMITAH!"

"Hey, bimbo, have forty-eight small strokes. You know what a stroke is? A stroke"—Mrs. Roseman waggled her toes exultantly—"is like a hemritch. And after you get hemritches and strokes you should end up like me in lonelied widowhood . . ."

She stopped and stretched out a foot toward Simon, saying, "See if you notice a puffiness."

Crouching, Simon considered. "Puffiness," he told her finally, "I don't don't don't see. It's definitely not *puffy*."

"How about a—redness."

"A redness is there. But only," Simon hastened to say, "if you really look. You have to have to look to see where the redness is."

"An abscess," Mrs. Roseman croaked cheerfully, then turned her face to the wall. "In lonelied widowhood," she picked up, "where your husband's garage business that he had in such a wonderful location right in the middle of Brownsville . . ."

To Simon, she said, "Used to be some neighborhood."

"Ma. Ma, I'M DEDICATING A SONG TO YOU LISTEN TO THE SONG!"

A toilet was flushed.

"In the middle of Brownsville and you should have to sell it bimbo, bimbo, and after you sell it you should hear a song and a dance from an old friend and you should put your lonelied widowhood money with his money into a commission bakery . . ."

"Can I, may I tell you something? Heh, Mrs. Roseman?" Simon moved from a chair to a stool, from the stool to the sofa. "You have in *your* living room what I really really hope

it should be in, within *my* power and *my* means to see sometime, someday for *my* mother." He lowered glazed seraphic
eyes.

"Listen, bimbo. Learn how a child considers a mother."

"Venetian blinds."

"Ma."

"And you know what also would make her jealous? But
really really jealous . . ."

"Ma, do me two favors."

"Have your tootsie do you favors!"

"I'm not going to mention it to her, I don't want to make
her jealous, Mrs. Roseman"—Simon made a sorry-baby's face
—"that you got a built-in clothes drier."

"Favor number one is—by the way-yay, should I call you
Si? I don't know why-yiy, but I like Si . . ."

"Usually and generally I would say no, but"—Simon's
voice turned sonorous and unctious—"the way *you* say it . . ."

"I don't know WHY but I like SI, I'm a poet and I don't
know it."

"I'd fix you a sweeter poem," Mrs. Roseman called, "only
I can't think what rhymes with bimbo, bimbo."

"Ma, think what rhymes with PLOTZ. That's the favor
number one I-yiy wanted. Please go and PLOTZ—RUN and
PLOTZ—cots, pots, lots . . ."

"Let me ask you, Mrs. Roseman"—Simon tracked her
eyes with his eyes—"I have to have to ask you because I'm
going to definitely have to report to my mother . . ."

"Favor number one—Ma, you listening, Ma, I want you
to listen,Ma—go and PLOTZ on top of your POTS!"

"Your Spanish teacher has the right name for you, bimbo."
Mrs. Roseman humped her back and worked her jaws passionately. "You're an IN-dolent."

"Favor number two—Go and get a CRAMP where it tis
DAMP."

"I'll say to my mother"—Simon spread his arms—" 'Gee,
you know I was in a very very nice apartment' and she'll ask

me, 'Tell me what kind of floors,' that's why if you noticed, I don't know if you noticed, Mrs. Roseman, all I do is look at them, your—"

"A bett-ett-er one, Ma. Ma? Go get a DAMP CRAMP that gives you a—CLAMP."

"—floors, Mrs. Roseman. Where I go my mother makes me makes me look at the floors, she gets angry if I tell her I forgot or I didn't notice."

"Ma? Ma, put out the ladyfingers for—Si."

Simon brightly and blandly answered, "Maxine, I don't want her to go to trouble, after all . . ."

"Your tootsie'll have *you*, bimbo, what does he need ladyfingers?"

"That that is what I say, Maxine," said Simon. "I really do not want your mother to PUT OUT ladyfingers."

"Woo woof. Waroof." The wall exploded with a disjointed thumping.

"I honestly, absolutely, positively, and definitely don't want your MOTHER to go to trouble and to PUT OUT."

"Si? For what's in your HEAD you should only drop DEAD!"

Her lips quivering, swelling, Mrs. Roseman blew out a "Bimbo! Hey, IN-dolent! Next time you tell a person—the next time!—'Drop dead,' dip your tongue first in the toilet!"

"Wahoo hoof, it tastes good, Ma. It tis absolutely delicious, it tis a YUMMY in the TUMMY."

"That's one thing," said Mrs. Roseman, a warm lilt in her voice, "I'll train her out of. Because if I say things to you that ain't exactly one hundred percent nice I'm entitled . . ."

"Mrs. Roseman," Simon said sternly, tenderly, "let me tell you something. May I tell you something please. I was honestly honestly too busy looking at your floors to get insulted."

"I'm after all a widow, and in my widowhood I have a right to say such stuff."

"I have to have to tell you, Mrs. Roseman I must tell you

your floors"—Simon shivered—"I am going to tell my mother, 'Mother, I finally finally saw somebody who keeps her floors better then you.' "

"Her trouble and why she has the mouth to say on a boy 'Drop dead' is"—Mrs. Roseman's voice sank to a hoarse whisper—"she's too popular."

"Can't hear what she's shushing Si, Si-yiy you hafta stick up for me."

"Do not worry," Simon overarticulated, "you need not worry, Maxine, for I will certainly certainly STICK UP for you."

"Warhoof," declared Maxine. "You are a rotten rat, you rotten rat you."

"When a girl is too popular," Mrs. Roseman reflected, "it's not good. Too popular makes an IN-dolent. Too popular gives you 48 in Biology."

"I wonder," Simon inquired softly, "if she might let, wish me to help her in Biology. You want me to ask her, Mrs. Roseman? I will ask her! Oh, Max-ee-nne . . ."

"Waddaya wa-ha-hant you rotten rat you?"

" 'Rotten rat,' 'drop dead.' In my time—and I was *also* popular—you'd say that to a boy . . ."

". . . glad to give you a HOT TIP for Biology, we could BONE up!"

Mrs. Roseman, searching her feet, said, "I blame you. If I was a boy and a popular girl—let her be THE most popular girl in the world—said on me 'drop dead' and 'rotten rat' I would answer her, I would give it to her, I would let her have it in a way that she'd start getting flushings before her time. You know how I'd answer her if she said a 'drop dead' and 'rotten rat' on me?"

"Ma? Ma-ha-ha go around-d-d the corner and tell me is it raining-g-g!"

"Kiss your ear," replied Mrs. Roseman, "your bimbo mouth is plenty big enough!" And to Simon, "Against her 'rotten rat' and 'drop dead' you should answer—naturally you can't think of it on the second—'You . . . too!' "

"Si-hi. I forgot to ask you, Si-yiy, do you go in much for sports-iss?"

"Well no, Maxine. I do not go in much, overly for sports. The *only* sport"—Simon primly coughed—"the only sport which I enjoy a *little* is swimming. In swimming I practice my STROKING."

Maxine exploded a malignant giggle.

"I'll tell you something"—Mrs. Roseman's toes stroked Simon's shoes—"she gets away with a mouth on all her boys. And you know what? They . . . they all *love* it, they eat it up!"

"Well, you know what it is, Mrs. Roseman? What *I* think it is, probably probably the reason . . ."

"Si? Si-yiy shut up-ee, you don't say nothing!"

"They love your gremmeh, bimbo," suggested Mrs. Roseman. "Your gremmeh and your biology."

"Gremmehbemmehdemmeh, oof warhoof!"

"Everyone says she has a very very nice personality. And personality is important to a person."

"You know why, Ma? Ma! My personality is nice conner I take after you, you dumb old shlub."

"I decided something, bimbo. Here's what I decided," Mrs. Roseman announced. "I don't want you to get killed. Don't get killed and live a long time. Only while you live I would love you to walk like President Roosevelt, to see good the way Helen Keller sees good, to eat what John D. Rockefeller eats, and to be good-looking like Primo Carnera. Then —then first pieces should be cut off from you everyday, and everyday a different little piece." Her voice dwindled. "All right, the same piece."

"Si. Si-yiy-yiy? I am putting SOMEthing in my HAIR, then I warhoof will be THERE."

Mrs. Roseman whimpered, *"Vei iz mir,* she's wetting her head."

"Glad you could STAY, warhoof on my WAY!"

"Maybe in my widowhood I'll have luck. Maybe she'll go outside with a wet head," Mrs. Roseman exulted.

"The wait-tit-ing is OVER, we'll be warhoof in CLOVER."

". . . high time I had luck."

The lights went off.

"Howdeedoodoo to—"

The lights went on.

"—youhoohoo."

And Simon had his first sight of Maxine as she pirouetted under the clothes drier and between a pair of potted plants: Broad-faced, goggle-eyed; smudged mouth, oily skin; big in the behind, lacking up front; dirndle blouse, dirndle skirt.

"Hi, hello, at long last." Simon rose, putting forth a hand and all his charm.

While he helped her into a short, purple coat Maxine was murmuring "Lang lost, lost lang."

"Make sure you come back late," Mrs. Roseman begged. "In fact, you know when I want you home? When you hear *M'sheech* blow his horn three times."

"Ma. Dry up-pup please and gimme your muff."

"Don't forget. You'll wait for his third blowing, then start home."

Simon and Maxine were halfway down the foyer when the muff hit the door and bounced at their feet.

As they walked on Surf Avenue toward the Miramar, Maxine mumbled through her teeth, "I do not warner doo-doo any sex."

Simon groaned, slapped his thighs, whistled in, stamped his feet, whistled out, swayed on his toes, twisted his head like a startled bird, flattened himself against a building, and in an implacable voice said, "Do you think that was nice? Because I don't think that was at all at all nice. In fact"—he settled into mournful tranquility—"I'm just not going to say more, if I say more I'll maybe, perhaps, say too much and I want to hold my very very fine impression of you."

To the tune of *The Farmer in the Dell* Maxine sang, languorously sang:

Where was I holding what?
Wah-ha-hat was I-yiy holding where?

"Let's see and let's be fair," Simon said. "Let's walk together in exactly exactly the way we were walking . . ."

He banged his hip into her hip and started her off.

"Am I right that this is how we were walking?"

"You are RIGHT, I won't FIGHT."

He dipped and dangled fingers under her coat.

Maxine, in a soft rising wail went, "Warhoof, terrible
boy."

"Just just tell me if I said to you—you are after all making an accusation and if you accuse somebody you should
have to prove it. So . . ."

He lightly fingered and flicked, flicked and fondled.

Maxine, keeping perfect step, muttered, "What you did
with your NAIL you should go only to HAIL."

"Be honest and honestly tell me if when we were walking
like this, because this is how we happened to be walking"—
he complacently cupped—"whether I said to you, 'Maxine,
I want you to—do—sex.' "

Maxine pulled him off finger by finger, then peeped at
him one-sidedly. "A boy-yoy has to beebee inter-ES-ted in me
because I am somebody and not-tot because I am SOME
BODY!"

Simon, with oracular calm, had this to say: "I was not
even *think*ing anywhere near, not even re*motel*y of or
about . . ." Moodily, he broke away, gazed off at Feltman's,
at Luna Park, and he breathed heavily, harshly, holding the
breath so that his lips and cheeks would quiver. "Would you
like to know what I was thinking, what was actually actually,
so help me booboooboo and I swear, the THOUGHTS I was
having?"

"I doodoo nut moynd if a boy is friend-erly," Maxine
reasoned. "But you were nut getting friend-erly, you were
getting personal. And when a boy-yoy gets personal—on my
PERSON . . ."

She bopped his head and shoulders with her muff.

"Nothing can be WORSEN!"

"My REAL thoughts," Simon said solemnly, "were so so different from what you think my thoughts *were*—you'll laugh."

"Warhoof," answered Maxine. And to herself she trilled, "Oh do nyot laugh, Maxine, hold yourself ininin, Maxine, squish it down, laugh laugh go AWAY, come again another DAY."

She then bopped him some more with the muff, saying, "Warhoof, what you did. You said 'You'll laugh' and if somebody says 'You'll laugh' it gives me giggles on the wiggles and I get yuggies in the elbow. Elbow yuggies."

But Simon, calm and remote, strode slowly ahead; as Maxine tacked along he began to murmur, "Out of . . . outside . . . out of A night, out of THE night . . ."

He set his twisted, vexed face at the sky, saying, "Almost, almost," and "Nah . . ."

"My elbow yuggies are going nearly AWAY so now you should SAY what you wanted to SAY!"

"It was something sort of sort of about"—Simon held his lip an instant with his teeth—"life."

"You see? Warhoof. If you said to me before—if before when you were giving me TUMMY yuggies you said to me— 'I'm-mime thinking about life,' I would understand and I would not get yuggies because I could never get yuggies from a person when he is thinking about LIFE. You'd bebe surprised what I can understand, and when a person is thinking about LIFE that is something I can UNDERSTAND."

Maxine made testy noises with her tongue then abruptly said, "So what do you mean you were thinking about life?"

Simon pointed off toward Steeplechase, toward Sea Gate; and he sighed a sigh of ineffable melancholy; and he said finally, "My life and your life and all the different lives that are on Surf Avenue, they're on Surf Avenue all those lives, and it got me for a minute, for a second—depressed."

"Of corsica you got depressed. It's a DEPRESSION!"

"And the only way I could get out of it, my sadness and depression mood, was to touch, not to FEEL, only to TOUCH and reach a person, THE person"—Simon shrugged a shoulder —"who would help me feel better in my—soul."

"Jeepers."

Maxine blinked and blinked till her eyes grew moist.

"With me it has to do with soul, to make the soul strong. If you don't make the soul strong—unconquerable . . ."

"I would love a strong-iger soul," Maxine mused. "It doesn't have to be UN-conquerable, just stronger."

"You made my soul feel so unconquerably strong that what I did, and I was doing it when you thought, ACCUSED me of sex things"—Simon looked past her head and peered vaguely—"I made up a poem."

"Warhoof!" went Maxine. "Recite me, you have to do me a recite." She teased his nose with the muff. "If you don't do me a RECITE it will dee-dum not be POLITE."

"It's just just"—Simon's face was cynical, then hopeful— "a short little poem."

Maxine capered and clamored, "I love when a poem is short because in my English book-ee if a poem is long they put it in halfies on the page. Halfie is on one side, halfie is on the other side and I get so mixed up-pup it gives me head yuggies."

Whereupon Simon drew her into a doorway, saying, "The only only way I can remember the poem is . . ."

"You're being a PEST-y on my CHEST-y!"

". . . hafta get back, recapture my nice feeling."

To the tune of *Did You Ever See a Lassie* Maxine crooned, sweetly crooned:

> Every*body* on Surf Ave*nu*e
> Is loo*king*, is looking-guh . . .

"I'm recapturing the first line," Simon announced happily. "I got the first line recaptured . . ."

"Jeepers, you know who would enjoy-yoy this?" demanded Maxine.

"Wowee will this be a poem don't move for a second don'tdon't moveohwillyou hearapoem . . ."

"Mr. Lechender," said Maxine, relaxed and genial. "He's my English-ish teacher."

"What I do when I get inspiration I do this this I have to do I'll justjust dothis . . ."

"He would get such a kick if he knew I went out on a date-ee with a boy who makes up poems." And Maxine added glumly: "Mr. Lechender threw a hate on me."

"A littlelittle bit on the other one the other one now so I should remember the title . . ."

"When a teacher throws a hate on you," Maxine muttered miserably, "it means he'll never like you because he likes to hate you. That's why I said to him once, 'Mr. Lechender, jeepers, do you hate to like me or do you like to hate me?' "

"Why I'm doing both I'm doing both now now I'll do both is I'm getting a different title and to get a different title I haftahafta do both . . ."

"The reason I like my Biology-gy teacher," said Maxine warmly, "is conner he would like to like me."

Then she used the muff on Simon, saying, "Rotten terrible boy, I want a poem, where is my-yiy poem rotten terrible boy!"

Simon dug out his hands, shook himself like a wet dog and declared hoarsely, "To—Maxine."

"That's me, that's me-me-me!"

And Simon intoned:

> *Out of the night that covers me,*
> *Black as the pit from pole to pole,*
> To Maxine I'm grateful as I can be
> *For my unconquerable soul.*

"Deep deep boy," said Maxine, and she moved her lips on his lips in gentle nibbles. Then she gave him her goggle-

234

eyed look, pulled him into the street, and made him walk with one hand inside her muff.

"I am being nice nice conner you are a deep deep boy," she told him, "and you give me nice deep deep boy yuggies."

This was how they covered the last block to the Miramar. Where a lumpy boy with overgrown red hair swiveled from the front of the line and croaked, "Maxine, hi Maxine. You don't say hello Maxine?"

By the light of a Silly Symphony they mounted the balcony and scuttled to seats. "A cartoon, a cartoon," went Maxine, "little Maxine will get a balloon."

Then she helped Simon settle her coat and his mackinaw over their laps and legs, murmured "Maxine doesn't *like* cartoons, Maxine *loves* cartoons," bowed her head and gave herself altogether to the screen.

Then she nudged him with an elbow and pulled his sleeve and with her lips inside his ear whispered, "I am nyot going to doodoo any sex with you."

Then she sniffled, sighed moistly, sucked three fingers, and rolled herself away from Simon.

Then with a turmoil of springs she swam toward him, saying, "Si-yiy . . . ?"

He answered by separating his mackinaw from her coat.

"Make nice, Si? Si make a nice on Maxine?" She imprisoned his hand on the armrest. "Maxine won't do sex but she wants to be-be friend-erly."

But through the cartoon and the Coming Attractions Simon was silent. With the newsreel he levered himself up on the armrest and showed Maxine a face of dignity and desperate anger.

"Changing seats," he hissed.

"Do nyot go AWAY, I want you to STAY."

"All I'm interested in, my only only interest is to do sex. Sure. Tha-hat's *right!*"

"You can tell Maxine a dir-titty joke."

235

"I never did sex before. Nah. I needa do sex very very badly. Yeah yeah."

"Dir-titty but nyot disgusting. Not-tot where the person has a loose stomach."

"Sex is absolutely on my mind. Always and forever and continuously."

"That's why I threw a hate-ee on English. They were talking vowels and it reminded me of bow-ow-els."

"Sex is the only thing I care about. The only only thing. With every girl in the world I hafta do sex. I hafta. Every every girl."

And Simon struck his hands so resoundingly against his knees and worked up a groan of such dense melancholy that many heads turned and from as far as the loge voices reached for him:

"Easy-easy, gentle-gentle, you dirty moron dog!"

"Let a Jew watch!"

"On the radio do it!"

"Blow it outta your ass!"

"That's a bow-wow-el word," murmured Maxine. And to Simon, "Deep deep boy, make up with Maxine deep deep boy."

"I'll be honest with you," said Simon, grim, imperious, magisterial. "My feelings are honestly a little little too hurt."

But eight, nine seconds later Maxine with a wet smack tightly clamped her thighs and after a last stertorous breath whimpered, "Terrible pig boy."

"Heh?"

"Do nyot go NEAR Maxine-ee's REAR."

Unbelieving, Simon stared and stared at his left index finger. He said at last, "Isn't that something? That is something . . ."

But hisses and cheers diverted them.

"A boo-boo-boo," went Maxine, and "A yay-yay-yay."

In time to something slow, slumbrous, sinister, and Slavic she fluttered her tongue and swayed her head.

And though she drew a *"Shah!"* and a *"Shtill!"* Maxine read in a singsong voice from the screen:

> *One of the world's*-es
> *Most powerful rulers*-es
> *Shows himself to his*-is
> *Subjects in the U.S.S.R.*-rah-rah.

"I'll tell you something," Simon said softly. "One of these days, sometime"—every pound of his weight was engaged at Maxine's knees—"I would like to just just just go to the . . . Union of . . . Soviet . . . SovietSocialist . . ."

"Warhoof," answered Maxine, sinking down and backwards into the seat. "Jeepers. Can I-yiy go? Conner it's near Russia . . ."

"Definitely." Simon without missing a stroke shifted fingers. "Absolutely you can go."

"I MUST-go to MOSC-oh . . ."

"When I go you'll go. I want you to go. We'll go together. We'll go all the way around and around it. We'll go the two of us"—he slid in two fingers—"the two of us'll go if you wanna go and I would certainly certainly want you to go why not if you wanna go . . ."

"A good," Maxine said, parting and pressing, pressing and palpitating her thighs. "A good good good we're both going to-woo-woo Russia."

So they killed time till the Pete Smith specialty. When Maxine informed Simon, "I am not RUSSIAN to go to RUSSIA."

Three times, then three times again she cuffed him with the muff.

"Go yourself-ee," she told him. "You belong in Russia conner you're a VULGAR boatman."

"Sure. That's *right*," he said, while his fingers dried in the air. "Why *not*. Hurt and damage my mood some more . . ."

And softly, bitterly, he spoke through his teeth:

> . . . To Maxine I'm grateful as I can be
> *For my unconquerable soul.*

"I do not-nyot trust you in Russia, terrible communistical boy." And she gave out with "Si is a communistical boy-yoy, Si is a communistical boy-yoy . . ."

"Let me explain, clarify to you something. My philosophy belief is far far from communistic."

". . . Did a communistical thing-ging on my private proper-titty."

"If a person is a communist that person has to have, possess the belief in revolution. A revolutionary belief."

"Let go of my WRIST, you'll give it a TWIST."

"He wants by revolution, by means of utilizing force, to take and seize power, power and control."

"He's putting my HAND on a place that's not GRAND."

"Only I just just happen to be a Socialist, and a Socialist is one who doesn't want a revolution, a Socialist believes in a gradual and evolutionary way of getting the controlling power."

"Even for a present of GOLD Maxine will nyot grab AHOLD."

"His ideal wish and goal is that the factories, the means of production should really really be under the ownership and to the benefit of only only the workers."

By the time *The Jones Family in New York* was on Simon had covered the nature of capitalism, the class struggle, the origin of private property, and how the state was merely a tool, an organ, and worked with the ruling interests hand in hand.

Under the boardwalk, Maxine in a weak voice said, "I am still annoy-yoyed at you from the bench. Do you know-oh why I am annoy-yoyed at you from the bench?" Maxine let fly with the muff. "Conner on the BENCH you were not a MENSCH."

Simon set his face toward the water and silently scanned the far distance. A tremor seized him as he said, "Oh Maxine . . . Maxine . . . let's be . . . true . . . to one another."

"Jeepers," yelped Maxine, "that's how-wow my Spanish teacher talks. '*Me . . . llama . . . Señor . . . Gershberg.*' "

". . . Because in a world that's too much with us, you could say a world we never even made . . ."

He stole behind Maxine, unbuttoning his mackinaw and her coat.

"Warhoof, what I-yiy wish on Spanish," cried Maxine.

". . . When ignorant armies are clashing by night we should say, we *have* to say, farewell to arms."

He pulled backwards on her breasts till the whole dumb weight of her ass was pinning his crotch.

"I wish on SPANISH that it should VANISH!"

"Because I'll tell you the truth and I'll put it to you this way: For a while I was really really half in love with easeful death."

He commenced a bumping and a grinding, a grinding and a butting.

"I hate Spanish conner the verbs. Regular, irregular, warhoof. Those are bow-wow-el words."

"But when you have seen the future you realize the grave is definitely definitely not the goal."

He eased his pants and her bloomers down and around and sank with her slowly.

Maxine to the tune of *The William Tell Overture* sang, stridently sang:

> I am nyot going to dodo sex with you.
> I am nyot going to dodo sex with you.

With his last full breath Simon told her, "To Maxine I'm grateful as I can be . . ."
And he honestly honestly was.

They were at Maxine's door when Simon began wordlessly and with exceeding gentleness to stroke her thin, dry hair and the back of her neck and to gruffly growl and take nibbles and love bites along the length of her fingers.

Next he begged and begged her to say "Cheese," and when she answered "Swiss Knight-tight," he kissed her brow and the corners of her mouth and her eyelids.

While she whimpered "Bold bold boy-yoy," and shyly swished at him with the muff Simon set forth his plans.

He said, "How about that next week we do—this. This is what I have in mind as an idea, and it's only only an idea. My idea is—first I naturally call to make up and arrange— let's let's go next weekend instead of to the movies, I say, suggest we go on the ferry to Staten Island. In other words we could take the Staten Island ferry . . ."

"Let's be-be MERRY on the Staten Island FERRY!"

He said, "We take it for the whole whole day, not that we *take* it the whole day but we should plan and figure on coming back, returning late as there are places on Staten Island to have picnics. When I say 'late' I don't mean LATE, I mean after supper, so I would therefore propose the bringing along of sandwiches. Not only should we take and bring sandwiches, but for later, if, in case we feel hungry we should have a lot a lot of fruit . . ."

"With a TOOT on the FLUTE I eat my FRUIT!"

He said, "Also what I would love to do—and this you have to do on not just just one time, date—is for me to go into and examine with you, in other words the two of us would discuss significant and important issues of modern contemporary society. I could for example start by giving you a basic and fundamental familiarity about the Sacco-Vanzetti case, this would be an example, a milestone landmark of American injustice . . ."

"Knyock knock, who's there? Justice. Justice who? Justice syong at twi-li-light!"

The peephole shot up and they were under the beam of Mrs. Roseman's eye.

"Sing louder, bimbo," she advised. "Mayor Hague didn't hear you in Jersey City."

"Hello again," said Simon. And, "You know, you are

just just like my mother. Until I'm home she also doesn't . . ."

As Mrs. Roseman opened the door a seltzer bottle over-turned and rolled.

"Bimbo," she said, "roll with it."

"Ma. Ma? Break your GALL . . ."

"Have a blood vessel bust in that loud mouth. You should know about a blood vessel," Mrs. Roseman added, "from your biology, bimbo."

". . . In the HALL!"

A moment passed. And another.

Then Mrs. Roseman's arm swished up.

And she gestured at the muff, saying, "Ah, Maxine. Maxine. Maxine, Maxine, Maxine, Maxine."

"Ma. Ma?"

The door was softly closed in her face.

"You're being sill-illy dopey dumb dumbbell."

And Maxine asked Simon, "Isn't she a dumb dopey dumbbell? Warhoof, that tis a dumb dopey dumbbell."

"Maxine, nah. Nah," cried Simon.

For Maxine, hiccuping and tearful, was pounding the muff against the door and mumbling, "It's nyot from the beach. Ma. Ma . . .?"

Flecks, then clots, then lumps of sand hit the tiles.

"In the movies you can get-tet sand. Ma. Ma? I put-tut it in a sandy seat, the seat-eat had sand, dumb dopey dumb-bell!"

Before he got her through the door Simon had shed a few tears himself. "Staten Island—Sacco-Vanzetti," were his last chokey words as he waved and blew kisses off his palm; and all the way home he sniffled tragically, joyfully.

Even so this by no means stopped him the morning after from answering Boomie's cocked eyebrows with the slow, slow raising of one, then two, then three, then four fingers.

8

Then early in the evening of May 12, 1939, the very day
Yenta Gersh, angered by competition from Yankel the Refugee, affixed to her baby buggy the sign "BUY AMERICAN"; a
week since Dopey Duhvee's mother defended his chalkings
on the sidewalks and gutters of Brighton 3rd, saying, "By you
it's dirty, by me it's a trylon and perisphere"; not long after
Hymie's *bubbee* was taken by taxi to a certain Court Street
lawyer who so loved her signature that she came away from
his office with two packages of Mary Janes; around the time
Gelfman got rid of his Big Little Books at two for a nickel;
less than three weeks since Mrs. Aranow's Stanley first related how near a certain Swedish restaurant he had picked
up a bony, big-footed lady with a floppy hat and dark glasses;
how this lady, with a voice in the lower register and an out-
of-town accent, had praised his driving, his sense of humor,
his knowledge of current events, his build; how she had
hinted of great wealth and even greater sorrow; how she had
begged him finally to go to her hotel and to intercourse her;
how she would have been happy to let him even keep his
meter running; how Stanley, seeking not to hurt her feelings,
had improvised a sick wife and two sickly daughters who

waited for him to shop and straighten; how just before clumping off she had piteously announced, "I vill now half to be halone"; maybe three, four days after it was learned that Harry the Fish Man's daughter, Fat Rosalie, sold her junior high-school locket to an old-gold dealer and, with a good stock of The Original Hopjes and Louis Sherry thin mints, paid loge prices at the Capital for *Gone With the Wind;* just around the time Dr. Ringelman, surprised by Mrs. Binneberg as he reclined in his dental chair with an eight-by-ten glossy of a lewd nude, commented wonderingly, "I'm looking and I'm looking and I'm looking and still I don't see a thing wrong with her bridge"; right after the Workmen's Circle released its open letter to Gershon Feld, manager of the Syrup Makers Union, Local 16: "At a time when the Yiddish stage is beset and finds itself in urgently imperative need of sustaining support from each and every quarter we must regretfully deplore your late and recent decision to give your yearly annual theater benefit business to Hellzapoppin"; on the Wednesday that Willitz the Landlord tacked up signs near the 1881 dumbwaiters: "To honor the memory of our late and beloved super John Tovallito there will be no steam or hot water until Saturday"; the same week the Knishe Queen announced she would be adding to her establishment and premises a beautiful little dining alcove designed for afternoon affairs and to be designated the Belle Baker Room; somewhere around the time Old Man Danzig told his society optometrist, "Dr. Irving, do something for me with your prescription glasses, it's three months already I'm walking lopsided and vomiting blood," and was told, "Give yourself a little chance to get used to them"; not too long after Dora Schliefer submitted her World's Fair story to "Embarrassing Moments": "While waiting three hours on line at the General Motors building to see the Futurama I was afflicted by the need to visit the bathroom. Turning to a young man behind me, I excused myself and said to him, 'Would you do me the favor of holding my place while I go to the bathroom?' and he answered me, 'Well Miss, that depends on the place' "; when Madame Zenda once again entered the life of Bim Gump; when Steve the Tramp lost an arm dragging Dick Tracy from a warehouse fire; when Spud, duped and drugged, turned against Tim Tyler; when Louella Parsons mentioned temperament and trouble among the Ritz Brothers; exactly or very close to the time Chaim the Old Clothes Man let it be known that because of great demand he would henceforth and from now on be available by appointment only; a week, make it ten days since Marvin Ka!b's Uncle Nat sent him, in the name of the Family Circle, the following telegram: "Understand you were in Spain fighting Moors. Stop. Sending one Moor you won't fight. Stop. Dorothy la Moor"; Simon and Rita Lipsky and Adelee Sandberg tilted one end of the kitchen table and Joel Gertz and Morton Berliner worked at the other end till Mr. Sobler, faculty advisor of the *Lowell Lantern,* wedged in an extra leaf.

"*Bien, bien,*" rumbled Mr. Sobler, springing back, crouching and cuffing an imaginary handball. A small, dapper, fine-boned man who reviewed frequently for *Science and Society,* he could nevertheless hold his own with any gym teacher and worked out regularly on the parallel bars.

". . . A personal question," Adelee Sandberg began in her dusky Margaret Sullivan voice. "You have in the living room . . . a painting. Can you tell me what is the name? Because that painting is so—it has such—" She closed her eyes and slowly made a fist.

"Honey, that's 'Starry Night,' that's Van *Goff.* Van . . . *Goff.*"

Lips clamped on the last syllable, Mrs. Sobler peeped in, then flitted off on ballet slippers.

"You respond to him, don't you." Mr. Sobler crossed his arms. "Well, what you're responding to is his—the artist's— vision of a society in despair as the matrix, the basis, the essential fundament of bourgeois values decay."

"You feel that too," Adelee said softly.

"I wonder if you could say—could you say," Rita Lipsky

piped in, "that Thomas Wolfe shows also, that he reveals . . ."

"Ah, ah, but his ethos—" Mr. Sobler was nodding deeply, vigorously as his wife brushed by. "We use these as place mats," she said, clinking down one, two, three, four, five, six rose-tinted tiles. "They come from France."

"French tiles," Adelee murmured to Rita.

"*Alors,* I'm going, Moish," Mrs. Sobler pronounced gravely. "Now I am going, I will relax and read my Proust and *plus tard* I shall make the coffee."

Adelee said, "Proust has the long sentences."

Rita said, "Thomas Wolfe also has long sentences, but *his* long sentences . . ."

"It is going to be instant coffee," Mrs. Sobler told everybody.

"*Allez-vous-en,*" Mr. Sobler boomed dramatically, lovingly.

Giggling, Mrs. Sobler slid away from his back-handed swipe. "Moish, I want to say one more thing," she pleaded at the doorway. "One more thing? We—*prefer* instant!" And she charged off.

Then Mr. Sobler dealt out soft punches to the bicep of Simon's right arm. "Workers and writers," he said fiercely, "writers and workers"—suddenly he was waving his hands and using a Yiddish intonation—"so for what are we standing around, for what?"

All present plopped down. Mr. Sobler turned his chair around and mounted it like a saddle.

"*Eh voilà,*" he said, nodding and nodding, "isn't this better than the living room? We have a nice table, the table is circular, the circular invokes a sense of the—it's the communal, it's the *mir,* it's the *manes,* it's the *polis,* it's a dialectical unity. And the light is much better in the kitchen."

"When you say dialectical *unity,*" Adelee quavered, "the dialectic that you have in mind—you pertain to dialectical materialism?"

245

And Rita timed her nodding to Mr. Sobler's nodding, saying, "Marxist materialism, the Marxist dialectic."

"*Pardonez, excusez-moi,* I am interrupting . . ."

Springily squatting, Mrs. Sobler rested a hand and a cheek on her husband's thigh.

"Coffee ring, Moish?"

For a moment they shushed away. Then in a nice fluid movement Mrs. Sobler rose, announcing. "It's a Chez Boulanger coffee cake." She slipped away; in a second, though, she had her head inside the kitchen. "One last thing," she wheedled. "Moish, I will say one last thing, if I can say one last thing *je vous en prie,* because I am getting so steamed up . . ."

"Writers and workers, workers and writers," cried Mr. Sobler. "Engels, ah it was Engels in *The Origin of the Family* who predicted, prophesied, foretold how in modern industrial society woman, the woman and the wife was fated, destined to be *oy,* such a terrible *nudje!*"

A laugh went around the table; and Adelee gently chided: "*He* said that? He did *not* say that, Mr. Sobler."

"That Proust. That . . . *Proust!*" Mrs. Sobler wailed. "I know I should give it a chance, I am still only where he's eating that madeleine."

"That's a sort of cookie," said Adelee.

"A French cookie," said Rita.

"But he absolutely infuriates me. I would love to say to him, 'You silly, shallow, stupid person, why don't you go out into the real world of social conflict to reveal what ordinary daily life is like for the exploited French lower class!' "

"Ooh, are they exploited!" Adelee winced.

"Now *au voir,* really *au voir,* Moish."

Mr. Sobler smiled at her back. Still smiling he said, "*Literateurs et écrivants, écrivants et literateurs . . .*"

One, two, three large manila envelopes fell softly on the table; and one, two sets of loose-leaf rings were snapped.

"*Maintenant,*" he said, "the first victim . . ."

246

"Searcher."

Adelee worked something out of her throat.

"Searcher has a dedication."

She seemed to be swept by chills.

"Searcher I wish to dedicate to all those in mankind everywhere who look for and are seeking now the better social order. This quest, this *search* is not yet—not yet is it over. It will continue on . . . and on . . . and on as long as all people of the laboring folk seek . . . and strive . . . and quest."

". . . Goose pimples," said Rita, her eyes huge and pure.

"So . . ." said Adelee, filling her lungs.

She took up her papers, waited out all sounds around the table and even the running of water next door or downstairs. Then in a voice of dreadful solemnity:

"I sit upon the sands of Coney.

"Sands of grim and gray,

"Sands of body-burnished oppression.

"I see the bathers awash in the washing sea;

"I hear their cries, those memory-haunting cries that sound now through my being, even as they have always sounded.

"And upon those sands I think, I think, I think . . .

"I think of myself, myself, myself—the high-school girl, Adelee. Adelee of the common name. Adelee who sprang from the loins of Leo Sandberg, baker of the long and hard rolls called *pletzlach*. Adelee, the good student. Adelee of the *A* book report. Adelee of the wind-swept, grieving, night-haunted, nameless hungers. Adelee of Coney Island. Adelee who has read *The Soviet Power* and knows that it is good. Adelee, oh anger-laden Adelee who rose, tear-heavy and wrath-choked from the festive table of her Uncle Lester, that bitter-tongued soul-searing scorner of Negro maids. Adelee, foolish foolish Adelee who fled swift-footed to the kitchen, that food-clotted West

247

End Avenue kitchen, there to thrustingly press her tear-blotted dollar into that black and work-pitted palm. Adelee, who sat weary-souled and heart-bitter, pride-humbled yet anger-torn as that earth-rich voice came down, down from the Negro centuries, down, down from the slave ships, down, down from the lynchings, down, down from the chain gangs, down, down from the bull whips lashing blood from black skins to say, to say out of oppression-forged dignity: 'Ellie May thanks you . . .' "

On the "you" Adelee choked and silently signaled "Wait." Then, as if called back from a distance, she blinked, snapped down her head, and resumed.

"ELLIE MAY THANKS YOU. ELLIE MAY THANKS YOU. ELLIE MAY THANKS YOU. ELLIE MAY THANKS YOU.

"These simple-souled words clang, clang, clang bell-like in my dream-locked girl-young thoughts. ELLIE MAY THANKS YOU. Oh, they pursue me in the wind-borne sea foam. In the child screams. In the flap, flap, flap of gull wings. ELLIE MAY THANKS YOU.

"And so I walk the sands of Coney. I walk, I walk, I walk.

"By myself I must walk.

"I, myself.

"I, Adelee.

"Adelee, searcher.

"For what dost thou search, Adelee, oh Adelee?

"ELLIE MAY THANKS YOU ELLIE MAY THANKS YOU.

"But I know not for what I search. I know only that I must search, search, search.

"ELLIE MAY THANKS YOU ELLIE MAY THANKS YOU.

"And when shall thy search be ended, Adelee, oh Adelee?

"Then lightning-strong and soul-deep the answer rises. It rises, it rises.

"Oh when shall it end?

"Why, it shall be ended when worker stands with worker behind the bloodied barricades.

"ELLIE MAY THANKS YOU ELLIE MAY THANKS YOU.

"And it shall be ended when the factory whistle and the machine roar signal day-new birth.

"ELLIE MAY THANKS YOU ELLIE MAY THANKS YOU.

"I say end it, oh end it with babies belly-full, with the mob-shouting lyncher crying unheard as the tramp and tread of the mass militant rises, rises, rises.

"ELLIE MAY THANKS YOU ELLIE MAY THANKS YOU.

"And I know this

"This I know

"Ended it shall be, it shall be.

"For I have known this always, and always I have known this.

"I, Adelee, who sits upon the sands of Coney.

"I Adelee, a searcher."

Silence.

"So . . ." Adelee twitchily grinned as tears moved into her eyes. "Finished. . . . In a *sense* it is finished."

Lacing his hands behind his neck, Mr. Sobler called out, "Comments and criticism, criticism and—"

"Moish."

"—comments."

"Cher maître . . ."

Mrs. Sobler showed herself in a blue carpenter's apron and with the smallest of hammers pressed into her cheek.

"Moish, I must . . . may I say this? This I must absolutely . . . please let me say A LAST THING!"

Though his neck was being tickled and a fat braid was flicking against his face, Mr. Sobler remained impassive. "Hold back, ah, well, ah," he said softly, "hold back the stream of historical necessity. Hold back thesis as it links and locks, meets and merges with *anti*thesis to become, to become . . ."

His arm went back, his knuckles rapped an imaginary blackboard.

". . . it becomes what? What does it become!"

Rhythmically, righteously, all present chanted "Synthesis!"

"Before I go bang-bang upon the copper cufflinks *pour toi*" —she pretended to measure his head for the hammer— "I want *cette jeune fille-ci . . .*"

Adelee's lips shaped "Me?" then "I?"

". . . to have the spontaneous reaction of a Sociology-Major-Who-Only-Minored-In-English."

It was a good five seconds before Mrs. Sobler stopped applauding.

"As a former Sociology-Major-Who-Only-Minored-In-English," she said, "and who only heard part because she was preparing her copper *and* who responds on a personal level only and not on the critical it's-supposed-to-be-good, therefore if you don't like the thing-level there is something wrong with you *and* who only can give you a for-what-it-is-worth opinion, I will tell you what I think. I think from what I heard, the part I heard only because I was preparing the copper and *c'est la verité* and this is not *merde* and Moish can tell you what that means and this I can tell you with all my heart—"

Mrs. Sobler struck the hammer into her left breast.

"It reached me. I . . . was . . . reached."

To which Adelee earnestly replied, "That is my primary concern. First, in fact, I asked myself initially: Would it reach people? For my desire at the outset was to be not the creator of merely good writing."

"Oh, it is not good writing, no, oh no," cried Rita, blessing Adelee with her smile. "Oh, positively not and not at all at all!"

"I have to say," said Simon gallantly, generously, "it had very very good writing."

Then Joel Gertz drifted in, saying, "I . . . felt . . . about it a . . . positive reaction."

And Morton Berliner said, "My only negative criticism: I saw two typos."

"To me," Adelee was telling Mrs. Sobler, "my concern was if the message I had—my message—did it reach *the* people."

"He"—Mrs. Sobler pointed her hammer at the living

room—"Mr.-Decadent-Bourgeois-Aristocrat-*Rentier* should
have had a little of your willingness to step outside the rigidly
calcified limitations of an outworn social pattern. *Peut-être*
then, with his specialized talents, and notice I am trying to
stay objective because *malheureusement* he certainly had . . ."

She bounded into the air as Mr. Sobler's both index
fingers sneaked between her ribs.

"*Mon bête!*" she said with a pipe of pride. "Just because
you transformed my basically social-democratic orientation
. . ." And she zipped off.

Now Mr. Sobler slapped his belly.

Next he opened and closed, opened and closed his fingers
so that his wrists thickened with veins and sinews.

Also he folded back a trouser cuff, hiked up a sagging
sock, and with great pleasure watched the calf muscle coil
and uncoil.

He said then, "*Alors*, what shall I say? I know, I suppose,
I feel Adelee"—he nodded at her ruefully—"would wish
me to say, ah, well, ah, she would like me to say, 'Adelee,
you've written, produced, given us a fine piece of work.
Adelee, it's good stuff.' *Hélas*—"

Silence.

For a very long time.

"Adelee, it's not fine work." Mr. Sobler said at last.
"Adelee, it's . . . beautiful work."

". . . Knew you when," murmured Rita.

"It's beautiful, but why, ah well, ah, why is it beautiful?
Eh bien, it had, it had"—Mr. Sobler snapped the fingers of
his right hand once, twice—"it had what and what did it
have?"

"Emotion," said Rita.

"Im-pact," said Joel.

"Emotional impact," said Simon.

"Then it moved us, we were, then, moved. But to be
moved merely, only being moved . . . is that"—Mr. Sobler
flung out his arms—"*the* . . ."

"Oh no!" cried Rita.

I

"Not . . . only," Joel got out.

"Nah!" went Simon.

"*The Grapes of Wrath* moves us . . . Dos Passos, ah well, the *early* Dos Passos moves us . . . *Johnny Got His Gun* moves us. Once, ah, James T. Farrell . . ."

"Wolfe, Wolfe, Thomas Wolfe?" Rita wheedled.

"Wolfe? *Wolfe,*" conceded Mr. Sobler. "Now through them we are moved—how are we moved? We are moved in a special way. A special way which moves us, impels us, and this is the *key* word, impels and moves us to take—to take—"

He snapped the fingers of his left hand once, twice.

"What to take? To take what?"

Rita said, "Stand, a stand."

Joel said, "Po-sition."

Simon said, "Social stand."

"A position, a stand, a social stand. To stand, in other words, in a position. But is it a position that is *for* society or is it a position that is *against* society? In art, in social art, the position is, it has to be . . ."

And all present glowered and shouted: "Against!"

"Against society. Ultimately, inevitably, a stand, the stand, our stand is anti-society. And there's a reason for this. A reason that has its roots—rooted in, history. And what is the reason? Ah, well, ah, this reason we learn from the investigations, the explorations . . ."

"Moish."

"*Cheri, yoishe!*" cried Mr. Sobler, cupping an ear.

"*Seulement une, une moment!*"

"Wasn't it Marx? It was Engels and Marx . . ."

"Just please go to the refrigerator, *tu-même,* you go yourself so you will not be disturbed and have to move chairs. The refrigerator? Please. Just . . ." She slapped away his hand from his ear. "Nice, we'll go to the refrigerator, yes, he's a good good boy, isn't he a good widdle boy, and all by himself he'll findey the CHEZ BOULANGER COFFEE CAKE."

Mr. Sobler rose and went to the refrigerator, saying indistinctly, "Marx and Engels, Engels and Marx . . ."

"Because seriously, *mon âme,* seriously, a Chez Boulanger coffee cake really and seriously should not be ice cold, a French person would be revolted by ice-cold coffee cake, they believe in for cheese *and* for coffee cake a room temperature."

". . . making a point," said Mr. Sobler, peeping out from the refrigerator. "Where am I? *Écrivants et literateurs?* Physically I am at the refrigerator"—paper crackled, glass clinked —"but I was saying what? In making my point what was I saying and what was my last word?"

And all present joined in a "Marx!"

Presently, in the midst of a discussion, not an argument, between Mr. and Mrs. Sobler, he contending that she should finish at least *Swann's Way* in the hope of better understanding and grasping the French social structure as it cracked and then crumbled within the heartbreak house of European capitalism, she speculating that she might be better off and more productive matting and mounting a travel poster, the group was diverted by powerful coughs and deep, bass noises.

Whereupon Mr. Sobler got immediately to his feet and Mrs. Sobler ran wildly into the foyer, then radiantly reeled back into the kitchen hauling at and drawing slowly after her a small, red-eyed Negro lady who waddled forward on bent legs and began saying in a voice as rich and huge as the voice of Paul Robeson, "Morgan morgan droogan morgan morgan."

From this Mr. Sobler received great pleasure, and he chortled, though he hastened to point out that he could have easily waited, that she had enough on her rheumatism-ridden hands, that henceforth she should spare herself the folding and stacking of his handkerchiefs, as meanwhile Mrs. Sobler, starting with Rita, went clockwise round the table, five times repeating, "Lurinea Madison, our good friend, our co-worker," beaming and chuckling when Lurinea slowly waved her hand to include one and all in her cheery, "Droogan droogan droogan morgan."

Here Mrs. Sobler could be seen bending her knees and lowering her head, in this fashion managing to look fully into Lurinea's eyes and to hold both Lurinea's hands before bringing forth her question, her need to know, really know whether the Port Salut they had shared at luncheon, never mind its cost, showed distinction, ripeness, and maturity.

At once Lurinea grew reflective and doubtful and shuffled her feet many times till she replied apologetically, yet with great though simple dignity, "Morgan. Morgan morgan morgan droogan morgan," thus eliciting from Mrs. Sobler a kind of sorrowful realization, a look of wistfulness and bereavement when she declared that henceforth Charcuterie Française would not be fully trusted; and Lurinea sought to console her by a pleasant "Droogan droogan morgan," though unsuccessfully, for Mrs. Sobler now expressed fear that something had been altogether amiss at the luncheon, unto the flavor and savor of the lamb chops and the small Belgian carrots.

A good while passed before Lurinea spoke her mind, choosing her words carefully as she declared, "Morgan. Droogan. Droogan morgan, droogan droogan droogan. Droogan!" from which Mrs. Sobler drew great comfort, giving Lurinea to understand that henceforth she would forego garlic and *fines herbes* at luncheon, that Lurinea had enough troubles without an excess and a surfeit of spices.

Herewith Mr. Sobler pointed out that these sorrows, these burdens, the burden of these sorrows would one day surely pass, and he hoped that he had contributed in a fashion and in a small way to their easing with that pamphlet, now Lurinea's to keep, dramatizing, dealing with, dramatically dealing with the Scottsboro Boys.

Forthrightly, Lurinea made her views known, answering, "Morgan, droogan droogan, droogan droogan morgan, droogan," then with the kindest of smiles and a courteous and dignified, "Morgan," retired to the foyer.

Immediately, Mrs. Sobler followed, hastening to help with Lurinea's coat, responding to her "Droogan morgan" by a barely audible, "Yes, but Thursday isn't so good for *us*."

Slowly, slowly, Simon's chin sank toward his chest.

Simultaneously, Adelee and Rita caught sight of each other's faces and simpered.

And Morton worked and worked an invisible victrola crank.

Even so Joel did not raise his voice or alter its pitch.

With blood gorging his ears, with strained, earnest eyes and widened nostrils he persisted, saying, "This is—a poem. The title is *Lament. Lament.*"

"Lament Cranston," went Simon.

"The form it's in," Joel said hopelessly, "gave me trouble. I am citing it to the attention of all." He looked Mr. Sobler straight in the eye, "And the reason for my mentioning it is I thought the particular form would be easier to handle in the basic sense of coping . . ."

"Lam-ent Abner," went Simon.

". . . Because fundamentally one would be given to think that no difficulties should be incurred at all on the sole basis of what this form, the form I herein have employed to use for my poem, is known as and called: the free-verse form."

"How about the Count"—Adelee flapped her tongue at Simon—"The Count of Lament-ee Cristo."

"There is one more thing, a thing which has not to do with form but is concerning content," said Joel mildly. "About this content aspect and the using of certain words— may I hereby explain?"

Adelee instantly answered, "No."

"Certain words herein . . ."

Joel plucked his page from Morton who said despairingly, "It's not double-spaced!"

"These words are of Jewish vulgar idiom because I had the necessity of dealing herein, within the poem, with my grandfather. He was an elderly Jewish man. Finally, this is final . . ."

"Whee," whispered Adelee.

"Whoo," whispered Rita.

"Sincerely I would be quite appreciative to get whatever criticism and critique can be given of any aspect of the social values." He lowered, then lifted his eyes. "In the poem . . . social values . . . aspect."

No answer.

"*Lament.*"

And he began, just as his stomach growled:

" '*So, Zaideh Zach, so*' . . . *Zaideh Zach*," he said confidentially, "is herein meant as reference to the grandfather of my mother's maternal side. Customarily it was my early childhood habit to call him *Zaideh Zach* and to similarly call my other, of the paternal side—"

"*Zaideh Zee*," went Simon.

"—plain . . . *Zaideh.*"

Then with a commotion of feeling and gas:

"So, *Zaideh Zach*, so that's it.

What did I expect? You weren't God.

Though if as a child I had been asked,

'Draw a picture of God'

I would have drawn first your beard, then your

Big watch.

Because if there is a God, and if He has a watch

It must be a Waltham watch.

I called it—

Remember what I called it?

'*Zaideh* Zach's melon.'

"So, *Zaideh* Zach, so that's it.

What did I expect? That a hundred years would pass

And for a hundred years you'd sponge pants

For Malkin Brothers?

Or that you could keep your promise?

256

Remember what you promised?
'*Zaideh* Zach will go with you in a big car
To where you're married.
And when you get married
He'll bring your children also *Suchard* bars
And jujubes in the box.'

"So *Zaideh* Zach, so that's it.
What did I expect? That you could handle Death
The way you said you handled Polish farmers
In the old market at Robacki?
With a golden mouthpiece or an iron fist?
That you would be always big and tall?
Remember what you called yourself?
'*Zaideh* Zach the giant, the *hoicheh*.'

"So *Zaideh* Zach, so that's it.
What did I expect? That to bury you
They'd need the whole Mount Zion Cemetery?
Or a coffin big as the Loew's Delancey?
Remember what you would say
When you came back from a funeral?
'There's nobody left anymore in The Society.'
So *Zaideh* Zach, so?
So now The Society has one member less."

Joel had barely time to close his mouth when Adelee began, "I think . . ."

"To me . . ." Rita also began.

But Simon with a very soft "Personalism . . ." got the nod from Mr. Sobler.

He said, "Primarily, my first reaction was that the poem showed in it the definite personalist quality we once previously discussed in that it was too highly personalized and showed the reaction of the individual within the personal framework that fails to reveal and portray what it is that lies outside, beyond that which is of concern to the self only or only for the self. Aside from that primary criticism I felt, oh . . ."

He gave Joel a look of crisp, quizzical, detached amusement.

". . . The poem definitely definitely suffered from an excess and undue amount of racial- and ethnic-group material."

"Also," said Rita, making extravagant motions with her fingers, her hands, "it's too Jewish-y. For example, if he had put in instead of all the time 'Zaideh Zach'—if he changed that to Grandad Zach he would get and gain the more universal quality."

"It is not only too Jewish-y," Adelee cried, "but you see in it such—things. I mean, how would it seem to you, how would you feel if—let's say you were of Polish ancestry and extraction, and let's say you had returned to your home after a bitter and brutal day in—in the stockyards of Chicago, the Chicago stockyards—"

"A steel mill!" Rita burst out.

"All right. Fine! A steel mill is better yet because it is of even higher and greater advanced technology. So"—she made her sigh last the limit—"Picture yourself as being from Polish background, you are Polish . . ."

"A Pole," Rita said musically.

"You get home from a brutal and bitter day of rolling steel in the mill, that's what they have to do, they roll it, and you read how your forefather, the Polish farmer, he was dar-rad-dah-dah-dar-dah handled in the market!"

"Who was our best super?" demanded Rita. "A Pole . . ."

"And the thing is, this is the thing," said Adelee, lifting her upper lip. "Why is it of crucial necessity to do a Jewish mercantile-type portrait that portrays and pictures and shows people—the people—how Jews are so Jewish-y when one can draw upon for a source those from among an original Jewish faith who have anyway allied and linked and attached themselves into the forefront and vanguard struggle?"

"My cousin Harris," Rita cried gloriously, "when he was seventeen and he worked in the mountains sought in an unsung way to unionize the busboys."

"He had even gone, attended a"—Adelee unrolled her tongue—"a Jewish parochial school."

"Only a year," said Rita.

"To me," Joel began. "I would—"

He tried again.

"Basically, then, the general feeling is . . . in general . . . as I basically get a sense of what is felt in a general way the . . . my poem has . . . the fundamental feeling is basically. . . ."

Every last cell and secretion appeared involved in his one tremendous utterance.

"Buhlechchchchchch."

Adelee instantly replied, "Vlah."

Rita said, "Who said?"

Simon went, "Nah!"

And from Mr. Sobler a very soft "*Alors,*" was heard.

On his feet now he batted out flies, threw a block, a jab, saying, "Well, we've heard some shrewd, shrewd and perceptive comments, comments and criticism. Now, let's see now what it it is we've got, come up with, and developed and what is to be done. *What Is To Be Done?* is the name, the title of a pamphlet by, it's by . . ." His finger swung from Simon to Adelee to Rita, stopped at Morton, "By whom?"

"Lenin! Lenin?"

"We've got, well," Mr. Sobler declared, "a poem. By a poet of obvious, obvious and apparent talent . . ."

Joel sniggered, sniffled, shrugged.

"But a poet whose talent is imprisoned, imprisoned and encapsulated by, one, the problem of personalism, the personalist dilemma; two, a hesitancy and an unwillingness to move out and into the arena of a broadened social purpose. All right, fine, and *bien-entendu.* Then is there a way for him, Joel, the poet, to move out, out beyond personalism and on, forward to a broadened social purpose?"

He turned his back to the group.

I*

"I think . . . I see . . ."

He spun around, crossed his arms, and nodded his deep nod, saying, "I see, I think, the way out, the road ahead. What do I mean? I mean, well, this. One: Your, the grandfather's death could be made, converted into the symbolic."

"Sym-bolic," Joel droned, uncapping a fat fountain pen.

"Symbolic of what? Ah, well, ah, of modern man as he stands trembling and fixed, fixed and trembling in the midst of an ancient and outworn religious ethic, an ethic—"

"There's no—ink," Joel said helplessly.

Though Simon and Rita chose to see who would read first; though Simon, sticking with Odds, won three in a row; though Simon's clip was already off his pages and there was commotion in his breathing; though Rita had sworn to abide by the choosing she nevertheless made herself pitiful, whining "Please" and "Pretty-please" and "Pretty-please with marshmallow and whipped cream and sprinkles and cherry on top," clasping her hands and compelling the sympathy of all present in this fashion:

"I'll bust!"

Rita further pointed out that what she had was a play, that the group was altogether and absolutely familiar with this play and would need no explanations; that in fact this was not even a play but the last scene of a last act; that this was not only not the full and whole scene of the last act but merely and only and just three, not even three minutes of the concluding episode and portion; that she needed and required and could really use a reaction and response, a response and a feeling; that her reason for haste and rush was caused by, rose from, had its origins, basis, and primal roots in a contest and competition under the sponsored auspices of *New Destiny Magazine*.

Next Rita thrust her clasped hands close to Simon's face and Adelee whined, "Nice Simon, Simon be nice." And Mr.

Sobler praised *New Destiny Magazine* for its point of view, its viewpoint, progressive unto its crossword puzzle.

Therefore Simon showed himself capable of courteous capitulation, and in this fashion:

"So read."

"It will be remembered," said Rita, "that in what has gone before the mother of Cynthia Feldman, a type of person who seeks at any cost and price to assure the bourgeois security of her daughter, has by her nagging persuaded Cynthia into basically a loveless marriage with Sidney Zolt, a highly successful druggist who has a sweet but dull character."

"In that part," Adelee murmured, "I picture one person and one person only: Ralph Bellamy or Jeffrey Lynn."

Rita wrinkled her face and broke her "Well . . ." into three, then four syllables. "Be that as it may," she picked up, "Cynthia and the mother as I enter and go into this scene are discussing the different caterers for the loveless marriage when there is a ringing of the bell. It is a telegram that Lester who, whom the mother threw out of the house and who went down to the Deep South as an organizer of textile workers, has gotten very badly hospitalized from the result of the bullwhip lashing from the corrupt, southern textile-mill company security guards. And now Cynthia, as we pick up and proceed on the action, is starting in to denounce her mother."

"I wonder why," Adelee asked herself, "that in a denunciation part I envision and conceive only Jane Bryant?"

"This is not for her," said Rita, and in the same tone of voice began:

"It is you, Mother, you, not the bullwhips, who has done this to Lester.

"MOTHER: Why do you say it is I and not the bullwhips who has done this to Lester?

"CYNTHIA: Don't you remember what you said that night you found Lester and I singing songs of the people on the roof under the free and open sky?

"Mother. She sobs."

As Rita closed her eyes, as her voice faded out, Adelee was nodding. "That scene," she said, "that scene where they sing on the roof could be some great theater. If," she added, "you get a great director."

"A lot of and much of my nuance depends on who directs," Rita affirmed. She pointedly waited for Simon to stop scraping a fingernail underneath the table and went on.

"Cynthia rises."

Rita hurled herself out of her chair.

"Cynthia runs to window."

Rita ran in place.

"Cynthia looks out of window and down into the barren and bourgeois street of Flatbush Avenue and Newkirk."

"You changed that," said Adelee. "She changed that," she told the group. "Originally it was Avenue P and Ocean Parkway."

"Cynthia arrives at a decision. She turns from window, goes to closet, takes out a valise."

"When it comes to barren and bourgeois streets," insisted Adelee, "you can't beat Flatbush Avenue and Newkirk."

"CYNTHIA: I am going to him, Mother. To Lester.

"MOTHER: *Gedenk*, Cynthia. Think, realize, and consider carefully what you are doing.

"CYNTHIA: But I know, Mother, what it is I am doing, and what it is I must do.

"MOTHER: *Tuchter*, daughter, woe is me. *Vay iz mir*. You are embarking upon a foolish course by *shlepping*, traveling, and dragging down to the Deep South.

"CYNTHIA: Goes to door, opens door.: Goodbye, Mother. *Zei gezunt*. Be in good health, take care of yourself, and stay fit.

"MOTHER: Wait, oh wait, *maydeleh*. Little girl, tell me

what you will do once you have rejoined your Lester in the Deep South. How will you fare and *vos vet zien?*

"CYNTHIA: I no longer care. For the bullwhips which have beaten Lester have taken from me all desire and concern to sacrifice myself for a three-and-a-half room apartment.

"MOTHER: Seeks to pull and restrain Cynthia by the arm.: Three-and-a-half rooms and an elevator.

"CYNTHIA: I shall do without elevators, Mother. I shall accustom myself to—walking!"

A low long croon of assent came out of Adelee.

"MOTHER: She releases the arm of Cynthia.: *Lummir dir fraygen,* let me ask of you this question. When Lester is once more *gezunt,* well, and recovered and back upon his feet, what then will the two of you do and how will you both manage on the small stipend and salary he receives as a textile-workers trade-union organizer in the Deep South?

"CYNTHIA: To use, employ your phrase and terminology, Mother, *vos vet zien, vet zien.* Whatever happens, transpires, shall transpire and happen.

"MOTHER: But what will you do?

"CYNTHIA: What will I do? She lowers and puts down her valise. What . . . will . . . I . . . do? I do not yet know what I will do. I know only that I shall do . . . something.

"MOTHER: Cynthia, *oy,* oh, alas, Cynthia tell me, *zag mir,* let me know whereby I may write to you and where you will be.

"CYNTHIA: Where will I be? I will be, Mother, wherever hunger and oppression stalk and prey upon this land. I shall be in mining towns, speaking up and struggling for the rights of those who take coal and other minerals and resources from out the common earth. I shall be with those who pick cotton, with the harvesters of the golden, wheaten grain. I shall be in the automobile plants of Detroit and the steel mills of Pittsburgh. I shall be in the deserts and the dust bowls, in the northern industrial centers and in the southern agrarian villages. I shall be with workers, singing the songs of workers,

sharing the bread and the sorrows and the struggles of workers. There, Mother, I shall be.

"And slowly the curtain closes."

At once Adelee called "Author, author!" and Morton
rose and quite seriously bowed. But Rita, muted and morose,
only plodded back to her chair as though on some unspeak-
ably sorrowful road. And several seconds passed before she
said, "My primary worry, what is of chief concern is: Will
they be ready for this? The American Theater?"

"Be prepared for disappointment," Adelee counseled.
"Be prepared to hoe a very hard row."

Humbly, resolutely, Rita answered, "Believe me, you do
not have to worry. I am prepared that those of the American
Theater will tell me, 'Miss Lipsky, you have . . . you show
and reveal . . . buhrum-duhrum-duhrum . . . magnitude of
creatively talented ability . . . but and however . . . etzuh-
betzuh-shmetzuh."

"That's very funny," said Simon to Rita. "Not that it's
funny," he said to Mr. Sobler, "but it's sort of sort of a coincidence that in my story I also have something on what he
goes through and endures, the person of creative integrity."

He had nearly forced his papers out of the manila envelope when Mr. Sobler breathed a "*Dites-moi . . .*"

"It's an ongoing-continuation saga," murmured Simon
miserably, "on my worker-poet, Timberline Gibson.

". . . why am I reminded, why, wherefore am I compelled
to liken, compare Rita's scene to—Good Coffee?"

Joel said, "Why . . . coffee."

Morton said, "Coffee is beans, so she used her bean."

Adelee said, "You stir coffee, I was stirred."

Simon, struggling to smile, said, "For coffee it takes time,
she took her time."

"*Pour moi,*" began Mr. Sobler, "good coffee, and I said
good coffee, must be strong and bitter . . ."

All present groaned, but with pleasure.

". . . strong and bitter, bitter and strong. The strength
of bitterness, the bitterness of strength. This is what one

264

finds, encounters in a certain kind of drama. In the type and kind of drama called . . ."

He was on his feet, his arms soaring.

"Such drama has received the name and come to be called . . ."

As Joel went "So-cial" and Adelee went "Social social!" something glassy and metallic caught the light and appeared to levitate in the kitchen door.

"Moish?"

And Mrs. Sobler, yawning, hair unbraided, with pouches and faint half-moons of black under her eyes, pushed an alarm clock at his face.

"The guitar," she said.

"The guitar?" he answered.

"The guitar." Ominously: "The . . . guitar, Moish. Moish, THE . . . GUITAR."

And when all present had risen and had started to file out of the kitchen and had begun to sort and pass out coats and hats, she said, "Stay, stay. *Seulement* and just because I have to go early in the morning to have my guitar re-strung. . . ."

All the way from Shore Boulevard to Coney Island Avenue the five walked together, for they were restless and exhilarated and bursting with their impressions, and anyway they had only just missed a trolley.

Adelee and Rita started to do silly things, bawling together *"Viva la socialisme et la libertad!"* and "Everybody out for the Paris Commune!" and "Comes the revolution and we'll all eat strawberries and cream!"

Also they tore away to the corner and back and jumped off stoops and stripped leaves from hedges; and to an elderly man who was walking and smoking they yelled "Join us in the race!" and when he answered, *"Vos fahr* a race?" they cried, "The human race!"

Near Neptune Avenue they fell into step with the boys,

and very soon the five were talking of Mr. Sobler, of the feeling he gave them which was like no feeling any other teacher had ever given them.

What this feeling was none could exactly say, but all agreed that now, as always, they came away from him and his house with the belief that everything was possible and that there were possibilities in everything.

The five further agreed that what they felt was a joy, but also a sadness, and Adelee pointed out that this kind of joyful sadness was like, akin to the emotions and mood which had seized and consumed her when she heard her first song of social significance.

And in a strained but sweet voice she sang for them this song, which was *Kevin Barry,* and Rita joined her, and at Ocean Parkway the five took over a bench, linked arms, and for a good half-hour harmonized *Joe Hill* and *Union Maid* and *Which Side Are You On?* and other songs of the working people.

Simon's mother gagged.

His father lifted his *yarmalka* and unloosed a long, slow, ripping fart.

While Simon, once again at a kitchen table, made fast time on Cousin Phillie's old L.C. Smith.

Call me bum and bindle-stiff, rider of the rods.
You know me.
For you have seen me on your back porch, heard me say,
"I am hungry."

His father, doubled over and sliding slowly from his chair, said, "Ho-boy-oh-boy, a manager is a manager."

His mother answered, "That's it and that's it and that's how it is, what do you care, Shmuel, Shmuel forget it, let it be your worst worst trouble," and she ground her breasts, then her brow against the table.

266

While Simon hooded his eyes, shook his head, shushed at them, and typed:

Your limousines have passed me on the roads.
Your state troopers and your railway dicks
Have kicked and clubbed me behind closed doors.

His father, one hand against his truss, the other against a kidney, said, "The kid has to do work, let the kid work in good health, I neh-hever like to bother the kid when he has to do work."

His mother, through her wetted undershirt hem, answered, "Let him concentrate, he has to has to concentrate to do his work, he has plenty plenty time to learn what my momma used to tell me in her wonderful wisdom: 'A worker's lot is where they throw the garbage.' "

Here Simon stamped a foot, gurgled ferociously, and at his best speed typed:

You saw me at Flint, Michigan.
You saw me at Coaltown, Pa.
You saw me at Pittsburgh.
I'm the little fellow, the one you wouldn't look at twice,
Holding the sign that said ON STRIKE.

His father, bending to clean a toenail, fell to his knees, and from this position and with his eyes rolled back in his head croaked, "Malvena, ho-boy, I'll see, should I see what he says, this is a smart kid, maybe he'll say to me in a smart-kid way, 'Daddy, here Daddy dear is what to do.' "

His mother, raising up his father to slide a bunch of newssheets under his head, slumped slowly down beside him, and with her mouth on the linoleum said, "Shmuel, he's concentrating, he has to has to concentrate, leave him alone to concentrate, he doesn't need to know, what what does he have to know what you said to your manager and how your manager answered you that gave me such such a dropped stomach attack."

At which time Simon heaved himself up and to both of them, though mostly to his father, screamed, "Are you going to shut up and will you shut up and when are you going to shut up? Shut up, you dumb dumb stupid idiotic moron imbecile, you *schmuck*. SCHMUCK!"

And he was before long back typing:

> *Even if you didn't see me*
> *Buddy, pal, friend,*
> *I'll be around.*
> *I'll be around.*

9

Then on the morning of June 5, 1940, right after Teitlebaum finished grease-penciling his new window ("There will always be an England but there will not always be such a low low price on belly lox"); around the time Freilitz the Tailor started to charge a dime to sew on a button; four weeks to the day since the Knishe Queen got a letter on White House stationery ("We herewith acknowledge receipt of your parcel and its contents. Regrettably, neither the President nor members of his personal or official family can in any way whatsoever lend his/their endorsement to a specific product/item/foodstuff."); two, maybe two-and-a-half weeks after Dopey Duhvee went under Mrs. Heffler's skirt and rammed his head between her legs as his mother crooned, "That's how you make nice? Make for the Mommy a nice nice on Mrs. Heffler!"; around the time Bernie Kaiser raced up Ringelman's stairs with murder in his heart, then raced down all smiles to tell his Reba, "Honey, that's prophylaxIS, that's on the gums."; only a few days since Hymie's *bubbee* found out that power of attorney meant a strong lawyer; during the period Yankel the Refugee and Yenta Gersh continued to work the same street, their baby buggies colliding as he

269

yelled "We support lend-lease" and she yelled, "The Yanks are not coming!"; when Gelfman let it be known that he would this year take his annual Rockaway vacation during the July 4th week, from Monday night through Tuesday afternoon; after Willitz the landlord slipped under every door in 1895 a little notice: "Thanks to many numerous requests and popular demands your management announces the cancellation of exterminator service during this month which marks and celebrates the birth of Otto Bismarck, a good friend to our Jewish people"; pretty close to the time Harry the Fish Man's daughter, Fat Rosalie, depressed by Dr. Sontag's strict diet, finished off without help a jar of *Hellmann's Mayonnaise,* the industrial size; while Mrs. Malnick was drafting her postcard to the "Voice of the People": "This is for motorman, # 70387 on the Coney Island Avenue Trolley # C3420 who gave me such a nasty no when I asked him hold it hold it for my elderly mother who was right nearby Joe the vegetable man picking out a half a pound Freestone peaches and had a delay because she didn't desire Joe to put said peaches in a damp bag, I wish on you # 70387 what you most likely wish on our beloved president."; while people had not yet stopped talking of how Millie Bergholz, blowing hot and cold between Marvin the Designer and Moey the Piecegoods Salesman, brought them together finally at her father's *seder* and six weeks later got a gorgeous little card announcing the formation of Mo-Var Frocks; not too long after Charlie the Radio Man did such a botch job on Mrs. Kupferberg's Emerson that she had to defrost the refrigerator if she wanted to get W E V D; this following the recent action taken by the Workmen's Circle which, in a very close vote, passed a resolution calling upon all members to overlook all past and previous Socialist differences and throw full support and weight behind Winston Churchill; pretty close to the time people started taking notice of the billboard across the way from the solarium at Parkway Baths ("Brothers and Sisters, Friends and Neighbors ** Here is ONE PARTY willing to say in PUBLIC PRINT and FEARLESS SPIRIT

YES I AM A JEW, I AM PROUD I AM A JEW, and no DICTATOR
and no amount of MONEY in the WORLD could make ME give
up MY GREAT RACE and MY GREAT RELIGION ** This space was
paid for and donated as a public service by a Brighton Beach
community resident"); after Nehoc Clothes started to cut
uniforms; after Norman the Street Singer did so nicely with
God Bless America that he dropped *Eli, Eli!* from his program; after the injections helped Yeddi Kranzer get over her
hot-and-cold flashes and general nutsiness so beautifully that
she wrote to John Garfield: "I know from your *Four
Daughter* movies how I am dealing with a sympathetically
human person and a real *mensch* who will look away from
my past letters expressing a change of life passion and also
I noticed in one scene where you're standing between Ann
Sheridan and Claude Raines you're definitely too short for
me."; while Mrs. Aranow's Stanley went around telling the
tale of how at the 42nd Street Library he was hailed by a
bookish chap whose soft, white hair, going off in all directions, could have used a little trim; how this fellow had
puffed and puffed a big *shofar*-shaped pipe; how in nicely
accented speech he had asked Stanley for a snip of paper;
how Stanley, after profuse apology, had passed over part of
an old *Jewish National Fund* envelope; how with many a
muttered "*Ach!*" and "*Ja!*" this fellow had used up the en-
tire envelope and three match books besides; how he next
had asked Stanley to work out for him the sum of twentynine and forty-seven; how Stanley, modestly pooh-poohing a
pencil, had answered simply and swiftly, "Seventy-six."; how
this fellow had whistled in wonder and mentioned his own
weak head for figures; how Stanley told him it was merely a
knack, that this knack was common to both his folks, that
his mother, for instance, had only last week come out ahead
of a Chinese laundryman with an abacus; how this fellow
had speculated that the gift must run far, far back in the
family; how Stanley, winking and chuckling, had said, "You
mean it matters about my relatives?"; how this fellow, with
his own wink and chuckle, had replied, "Everything is a

271

relative matter."; when Mrs. Felder's Florence met on the bus up to Camp Tamiment a lovely boy who taught Business English at Boro Hall Academy; when Sea Scene Beauticians announced with pride that Mister Izzie, formerly of Williamsburg Woman, would be shortly available for scissor cuts by appointment only; while Smilin' Jack rotted away in Devil's Island; after the Dragon Lady admitted to Pat Ryan that she had been responsible for cutting off Big Stoop's tongue; after Walter Winchell dropped a hint about spats between Alice Faye and Tony Martin; when Luna Park had its pre-season fire; Simon, after his fifth fretful trip up the firetrap stairs, saw light at last in the Employment Shapers office and entered, setting off a little bell.

Immediately a toilet was flushed and a lovely vibrant tenor voice overflowed the boxy gloom as it sobbed out, "Adrian Levy here!"

Before long Simon heard, "In filling out requisal forms the client is reminded that calligraphy sloppiness is a frequent adversity factor in size-up of the first impression."

When Simon had sailed through EDUCATION, while he pondered PREVIOUS EMPLOYMENT, he was told, "Let the client consider well that his five personal references will be definitely and without fail contacted for confirmal of character fit."

After Simon had squeezed his signature into three places, a bellow of "Beware!" reached him, then a huge and beautiful trilling of "Take warning and give heedful care on the special italical authorizing *and* empowering Employment Shapers to collect not *only* all due money sums but through its legal appointed parts *or* represental the accruness *of* legal fee and such costs, charges, penalties as may portend."

And next, from behind a screen papered with N.R.A. blue eagles and peeling posters proclaiming the minimum wage, there stepped out a very short man or an exceedingly tall dwarf with a long, sallow, beaky face, blackish cockeyes, sharp teeth from which his underlip withdrew, and a few lifeless hairs combed straight back and hanging like fringes on a lamp shade. He had on a velvet jacket of royal blue, a snazzy silk cravat, and flaring corduroy pants belted high, almost to his chest, and he carried a wooden yardstick which he flicked like a riding crop against the built-up heels of his black and white shoes.

"Adrian Levy," he said, "shall see you presently."

Then, his step light, making surprisingly fast time on his doll's feet, he marched to a swivel chair, gripped both arms and after a wavering moment mounted in one light leap. From the enormous clutter of his desk he slid out a pair of foot-long shears, hefted them, and on his second try severed a dust fluff in mid-air.

Addressing the shears, he said, "Adrian Levy suggests that in the remaining interval time we compose on ourselves and do a personal appearance brush-up."

For a time he used the shears on his nails, emitting little gasps of pleasure as each paring flew from his fingertip. And meanwhile he was melodically murmuring at Simon, *"Have* we checked over the hang-right in our suit? Does our shoe-shine give off a *zetz* quality? Is our tie totally bereft of lack-luster *shmutz*? Will Mister Potential Employer look at us and say—will he say, 'Ha-ho, here's one more *nachshlepper* in the cosmic scene'?"

Following this, he opened a drawer and fished out a key.

With this key he unlocked another drawer.

From this drawer he removed a Swee-Touch-Nee Tea box.

From the Swee-Touch-Nee Tea box he shook out a white index card, and this card he cupped and held close to his sunken chest.

Ceremoniously he replaced the card and gripped his yard-stick in his fist like a scepter, saying, "You may have now Adrian Levy's full counsel attention."

Simon came with haste and sat by him on an embroidered mohair stool, one foot stepping on the other. Precise, over-articulating slightly, he said, "I should like to point out that my attraction to Employment Shapers, the reason for my presence here is because of and stemmed from the notice on my part of your recent Brooklyn College placement office ad."

Levy squinted like an optometrist into each of Simon's eyes before answering, "We are pleased."

"What especially especially attracted me," reflected Simon, "was the portion and part for creative summer work. Because something of a creative nature is what I would want and desire."

"We are impressed," said Levy. "But—but-but"—he extended a hand and waited until Simon had filled it with forms—"foremost and before the expressional of inner-motive desire we must give classification *and* coding to your personality type structures."

The little chap then riffled, read spottily, and after a few contemplative moments bent confidentially close to Simon. His mouth was jubilant, his eyes lighted strongly, and his voice built and built as he said, "Our preliminary tentative estimal of your achieving background reveals a nature, a type formed and forged, made and shaped by the *cocker* and *pisher* forces of heredity and environment."

He waited a second to let that sink in.

"But—but-but," he crooned, "to ourselves is also detectable yearnful tendencies bringing you into an oppositional course and contention state against aforementioned *cocker* and *pisher* forces, a pridefully *nudnik* voice who in its pride and *nudnikism* and while the whole universe world gives forth the herd-cry of 'Yeah-yeah' holds back its consenting to make the independent uttering, 'Maybe and maybe not, I'm in ambivalence.' "

Though his thoughts were fuzzy, though he only shrugged lop-sidedly and made slightly scoffing motions, there was a pleasurable heat in Simon's face.

"From yourself," mused Levy, "comes total recoil when we, we too got our share of writer awards—"

"Only only one reward," murmured Simon modestly.

In his songlike way Levy said, "We, we too with possessage of the material means might also, during our passional early

274

times have chosen for ourselves a Brooklyn College majoring in English plus—plus a History minoral."

"Also I might take a few Ed courses," said Simon chokily. "Just just in case . . ."

Whereupon Levy, moistening his lips and blotting an eye, his expression verging on pensive, rumbled out, "Recapturing from you our own former past, when hard times dealt on great expectationals a crusher blow, we are not preparing to render you placeage in a neutral nothing occupation by the humdrum orders of business enterprising. Take assurance that for your behalf the fully totalized resources of Employment Shapers will do a mobilized effort. So thusly, from our abundançe files—"

He flicked his yardstick at the Swee-Touch-Nee box.

"—we ask on you a considering of placement position as cinematic film critic to a certain respected but anonymal magazine of periodic weekly appearage. Could aforesaid position snatch your creating imaginal?"

"Sure." Simon had to work on his voice for a second, "Definitely definitely it interests me."

"From this pleasurable affirming," cried Levy, excited and keen, "let us put on you further guidance inquiry. Would something in the nature of foreign correspondal assisting give you a nice fulfillage?"

Simon was still nodding as Levy happily rumbled out, "Aforesaid postings are as of this momentary time in our filled files. But—but-but, and this is a highly significal but-but—"

His smile increased.

"—we got now a cognizing of your general interest scope."

Then he clasped Simon's hands between his hands, stroking and speaking emotionally. "Under these guidance lines we shall make seeking endeavor to embark you on a human adventure and in a placement wherefore your literature talents can get fruitful seasonage from significal experience. With this on view, Employment Shapers is readying you for positive reference to a personage of unusual depth quality. Aforesaid personage has needful use for a kinship spirit of phrase-making bookish ability and temperamental artist type—"

"Editorial . . . ?" Simon managed to begin.

"—such type could encounter, besides stipend salary open to a weekly eleven dollars, the opportunal range of independence learning effort—"

"Research . . . ?" tried Simon.

"—aforementioned effort getting enrichment from developmental closeness to an employing boss with utmost inner hope for partnering colleagueship and mutualized learning. With time's due passage we foreseeably predict how from a gainful job of summerized proportioning and with your application of strict self there could be arisal of not small possibility stuff solely but—but-but . . ."

"Real prospects," declared Rolnick.

"Not that salary is my only, sole concern," said Simon, forcing a half-smile. "I was just sort of wondering. Or wonderingly curious . . ."

Rolnick, hefty, ruddy, packed in the neck and shoulders, nearly blew him over with a "Naturally."

And he clamped Simon against his white-on-white shirt, and his froggy button-nosed face grew reflective and soft. "I'll put it to you this way," he said. "Rolnick's way. I am not looking to live forever."

"Dzoo," went Simon.

"What keeps me going *when* I keep going"—Rolnick pawed his left side—"is a dream. This dream, this vision—Rolnick's dream and vision—I would like to share on you."

And he suddenly had Simon under the arms and was walking him to the meager window. There he gently turned Simon, and together they stepped onto a wobbly platform of folded cartons to stare out through the old dirt.

"What is a gross?" he snapped.

276

"A dozen dozen," Simon answered pleasantly. "You could say—a hundred and forty-four."

"An old man, an aged man of Jewish ancestry"—Rolnick twice touched his face to indicate long beard, big beak—"walks into the premise and greets you a 'Sholem Aleichem!' You say on him immediately—immediately . . ."

"Aleichem Sholem," said Simon gaily.

"Fulfilled, fulfilled," murmured Rolnick.

One hand he held over Simon's head as though to anoint him; the other he stuck out the window.

"It is—fulfilled," he brokenly cried. "For in my dream destiny addresses me a special shipment. A one-of-a-kind. From out there, from"—he pointed toward the far distance —"among the pluralistic nationalities and race types that compose our five boroughs . . ."

He wagged his tongue at Simon.

"Name me all five!"

At "Richmond!" Rolnick smoothed down Simon's hair, saying, "From this hustle-bustle and from that bunch of huddled masses I vision up a special lad. The particular lad when he wends my way will stay with me at my side—Rolnick's side—and what David was by Saul he will be by me. This reference—the Rolnick reference—to David and Saul is . . ."

He snapped fingers under Simon's nose.

"To where pertaining?"

"Old Testament," was Simon's flashy reply.

"Also acceptable," said Rolnick, a shade coldly, "would be a plain '*The—Bible*.'" Nevertheless he laid his head on Simon's shoulder and played with each of Simon's ear lobes. "This special lad, this particular lad—Rolnick's lad—will reveal qualities, qualities and virtues in the following alphabetized sequence: A, he will be ambitious; B, he will be brilliant; C, he will be capable; D, he will be driving; E, he will be energetic; F, he will be friendly. This friendly quality . . ."

He waited till Simon sustained and sweetened his grin.

". . . will in time bring me forth from my loneliness and by me and the lad will start a relation of happiness not confined to the normal Rolnick working week of eight-thirty to six-fifteen Monday through Friday and half-a-day on Saturday. In the *shvitz* baths we will side by side drink mineralized water after tossing around the medicine ball each to each. He will join me in cat-house companionship when I get my natural need for pussy-wussy. As the *gesheft* little by little settles on his shoulders, as I lapse to a semiretirement, the lad will socially visit me at home in the Williamsburg area of Brooklyn which from here, from Canal Street—he should take—he must take . . ."

"The best way—the best best way," said Simon gleefully, "is definitely the Myrtle-Metropolitan Line."

A huge transit map appeared in Rolnick's hands, and as he shook it open he said, "From my house in the Williamsburg area of Brooklyn I will take the lad for a Roxy Theater or a Radio City first run movie. I will want to go by taxi, but he will take me his special way. And his special way—the way the lad will like to go . . ."

"Back to Canal, it's back to Canal and at Canal you change over. To change over you go down one flight, it's a long long flight, to where you get the express . . ."

"Express," purred Rolnick. "Which—which express?"

And Simon with a "Heh heh," answered "Any any any express!"

Whereupon Rolnick folded the map and stepped off the cartons.

"Welcome," he exclaimed caressingly, "to Rolnick Ball, Twine, Cord, Paper, Paper Products, Strictly Wholesale, Wholesale Only!"

While wolfing his little lunch (chocolate milk and buttered bialy) it seemed to Simon that he several times glimpsed Rolnick peeping from the middle of some crowd at the sandwich counter or the steam table. But he must have been mistaken, for when he got back his new boss was finishing up a head of lettuce and telling him how in such heat he could not enter the street or take heavy meals.

"It's very bad for the polyp condition," he said to Simon, "and it loads down the creativity—Rolnick's creativity."

"Talking, speaking of creativity," Simon slipped in cunningly, "I was thinking over lunch of some advertising slogan possibilities, they are some of the ideas that came and occurred to me during lunch hour . . ."

"Lunch *hour*"—Rolnick tapped his watch significantly— "is by me a very unhappy expression."

"These are just possible possibilities," burbled Simon. "And this is rough naturally and it's only a preliminary beginning, but on your letterhead you could have something something like A Rolnick . . . Paper Bundle . . . *Saves* you . . . A Bundle."

"Lovely," said Rolnick. "Lovely, lovely, lovely," he was muttering all the way to his stock room where he reverentially switched on the one bare bulb.

"The idea is, this this is the idea—paper wraps bundles, it's to wrap bundles in primarily. But your paper, the Rolnick paper . . ."

Simon tracked Rolnick's hypnotic finger into the stock room, around the sagging bins.

". . . because it is of better and superior quality, because it is *stronger*, so that means you need *less* on and around the bundle, and when you need less . . ."

He plunged into the butcher's apron which Rolnick was swishing like a matador's cape.

". . . therefore you *use* less. You save . . . bundle . . . money . . ."

After a last "Lovely . . ." Rolnick proceeded to instruct Simon in twine and tape winding.

"The way to do it—the Rolnick way—" he said, "is to go from big spool to medium spool, from medium spool to small spool with a pull, a little pull of delicacy and *finesse* like you would pull on your *putz*."

And some five, ten minutes later he plucked a ball of number eleven twine from Simon's nervous hands, silently switched off the bulb and smacked Simon lightly against the head, saying, *"Oy, tuchiss, tuchiss!"*

This was his last comment till both fell into a murderous rage over the fifteen cents he docked Simon for a long lunch hour.

Once again Levy was in his toilet.

"Our ablutions," he moaned, "shall be brought to speedy duration."

True to his word, the little chap soon danced out and was seated after a running start.

"Let all Employment Shapers clientele engage themselves with a reappraised assessment," he called out in good voice, "holding in fixed mind and careful forethought our recent ruling directive making requirement on all applications a notarizational sealing. Aforementioned notarizational sealing," he added, "is available from our parts for slight additionalized costage fee."

"Waha," said Simon sourly, immediately rising and moving upon the desk. "I just was here. Not just, but before. Recently. Brooklyn College . . . English . . . History . . ."

The little chap held him off with his yardstick and stared into his eyes, his soul. Then he pantomimed awe, wonder, and mounting delight.

"We are amazed," he said, "and we make happy notage of the rapid demeanoral change and maturity manner in your test situation handlement."

"Test situation? Look"—Simon's face expanded, his breathing ceased—"I am really somewhat somewhat"—he was ready to say "sore" but checked himself—"*sort* of . . . annoyed. Because what you sent and referred me to wasn't at all at all creative. That was creative?"

Serenely, formally, the little chap spoke. "Your respondal," he began, "gives us renewing confidence in Bernstein's First Law. From Bernstein, with his depthy probes and his exhaustion study of the literature personality, we get awaring perceptions how your talent type gives off beautiful emotional surge in its confrontation to the multiplicity quality of starked experience."

"Well . . ." began Simon in a baffled and bemused way. After a mild "Heh heh" he ventured something about it, that, the whole thing being certainly certainly an experience.

"Right—right-right," the little chap made haste to say, "and thusly fortified by graspy awareness of frail humankind and its lacking flaws in ethical morality your embarking readiness is set now for the next Employment Shapers ventural. In describing aforesaid ventural we would desire a wishful knowing if an evaluated reading of fictional story tales for a nameless and anonymal filmic genius is fixated in the conception of your limits."

"Artz," Simon solemnly replied.

"This is good," Levy came back, "for now—now-now we are able to fix on your limits!"

Thereupon he set forth to Simon a certain wondrous possibility which called for knowledge of all the language arts, a restless intellect capable of seeking out and exploring the connectives between character and culture, soul and society, mind and heart, life and action, between the state of nature and the state of man.

"Aforesaid restless intellect," he finished up, "should also not have handwriting like a Chink."

"You know . . ." Simon made a dumb sign of dissent.

And while Simon's breath gusted, Levy, engaging the full power of his voice got underway, saying, "To put the Adrian Levy story across the screen would give call for doubled feature plus selectage short subject. For the grand opening we would have commencal with a Cossack bayonet missing by an inch the Levy *pupik* . . ."

. . .

Barely, barely an hour later, Gribitz, droopy, paunchy, with trouser top turned down unto the union label, had this to say about his plaques, scrolls, and medallions.

"C-c-crapola."

He stamped a foot, thus dimming the amber-tinted lights lining the paneled wall.

"Crap-p-pini."

He worked a button on his desk till drapes of heavy, green silk slid across the wall with a kissing sound.

Then he walked around and around Simon, blinking and squinting his round Porky Pig eyes. "Wh-wherefore do I use on my assorted sectarian and nonsec-c-c—my *goyish* honors—common-mouth words?" he speculated. "Does it show me as a terrible per—per—a *paskudnyak* unmoved to the needs of varied ethnic people?"

He and Simon harmonized a "Nah!"

"What gives a Gribitz lasting sat—satis—*nochiss,* what counts for him here—"

He wet a finger and touched the top of Simon's head.

"—in his heart of hearts is to know he is looked down upon by those under his employ as truly a man with a neh—a neh—"

"*Neshomeh?*" ventured Simon.

"A knack of giving himself. Because what is the Torah all about? What does it teach us? Only this: If you can't give what have you got? And is this not the message of each and all religious teachers? Is not all and everything else merely and only comm—commen—*bubkes?*"

"The thing is," said Simon, "the figure you mentioned—not that it's the *the* thing . . ."

To himself, Gribitz said, "He w-won't let me give of myself."

To Simon, he said, "Let me give of myself. Let me reach you and teach you the m-m-meaning from our Judeo-Christian heritage!"

He loped to the door, crying out, "W-w-where, oh where is my favorite *shiksa?*"

282

An orange-headed baggy-chested lady in a polka-dot blouse came, pounding the floor with her wedgies.

"Mister G?"

Fingering the gold-mesh links of her crucifix, Gribitz said, "Cindy, C-Cindel*eh,* in short, sweet prose tell your future colleague here the meaning of our Judeo-Christian heritage."

"Be . . . a . . . *mensch,*" she answered, pushing an emery stick into a cuticle.

"Did you hear!" Gribitz exclaimed to Simon. "I wanted you to h-hear how I reach my labor force!"

And snuffling around her crucifix, he intoned, "Cindy, C-Cindel*eh, shtik dreck, oysgetrente shmatteh.*"

"When he talks his Jewish"—Cindy blew at a nail—"I can doy."

"*Koorveh,*" said Gribitz tenderly. "*Pirgeh.*"

"Your foynest chicken," Cindy told Simon, "is an all-kosher chicken."

"*N-nafkeh,*" Gribitz sang into her ear, "let me show you—something."

"Also what I go woyld for," she reflected amiably, "is those big, fat, red Jewish franks."

"Something veh-veh—*zehr* special!"

Legs spread and slightly bowed, his gaze dogged and dispirited, Gribitz was going for the bottom button of his fly.

"W-what you will now view—*azoy*—your next view," he said, "may be no world wonder, maybe you are accustomed to more spectaculars—*azoy, azoy,* goes down by the knees . . ."

"Is it before a Jewish holiday or something?" Cindy demanded of Simon.

"Not the f-fanciest—a little rough from wear and tear—by now, *azoy azoy*—not brand new—faded in the color . . ."

"Yarm Kippoor," Cindy reasoned, "was a long toyme ago. You know woy oy remember—?"

"Almost, almost—ut ut, ut ut . . ."

"On Yarm Kippoor we god orf at three."

And with utmost delicacy Gribitz drew forth and fingered

K

snip of shirttail, saying, "T-tell me Cindel*eh,* when in your life you saw a better shirt for seventy-nine cents?"

After she clopped out braying and neighing, Gribitz grew reflective and depressed. "This will be my downfall," he said. "Because I am entirely and altogether too ub—uber . . ."

"*Ubergayben?*"

"Paternalistic," cried Gribitz.

Early the next morning Gribitz, pumping Simon's hand, presented him with a skimpy towel and a sample-sized cake of Ivory Soap and turned him over to Randolph at the packing table.

To Simon, Gribitz said, "When it comes to the Judeo-Christian heritage you couldn't be in b-better hands."

To Randolph, he said, "T-treat him along the Ten Commandment lines as laid down by our great p-prophets."

Enthroned between cardboard boxes, Randolph, an elderly but muscular Negro wearing a baseball cap backwards and an immaculate T-shirt, removed his dead cigar, chuckled from deep in his throat, and told Gribitz, after a wink toward Simon, "Dat boy an Randy here gonna be reg'lar *chaverim.*"

"Without my Randolph and his g-grasp of our mutual moral code—"

Gribitz was silenced by the force of his emotion.

"Dat cause yo *reach* a colleague," insisted Randolph. "Yo reach him an yo put de Torah ethic into de heart ob de *gesheft.*"

Spitting into each palm he commenced to lift great pyramids of skirts, then a flat carton which he struck once and in such a dextrous way that it popped up rigid on all four sides.

"Again," Gribitz pleaded.

Randy obliged after a rich run of laughter. "Dat always fetch de *balabuss,*" he told Simon.

"Remember?" sighed Gribitz.

"Ah *gedenk,*" Randolph sighed back.

284

"You, me, and a few number-three cartons," moaned Gribitz. "In the s-s-springtime of our youth."

"Dat how it be," Randolph answered heavily, "an dat how she go, de *ganzer leyben*."

"T-twenty-two years . . ."

"Twen'-*three*," chided Randolph, "it be twen'-three come nex' *Slichus*."

"May He, the one Deity, the everlasting Ruler," Gribitz prayed softly, "oh may He continue to give my Randy in coming years and for our future brotherhood burdens s-s-strength and good health."

"Yo got de *gezund*," said Randolph emotionally, "den is yo twice blessed."

"Without him—" Gribitz said to Simon.

"Without you—" Gribitz said to Randolph.

And "Heads up!" were his next words as he went with two fingers for Randolph's crotch.

"He make *contac* wid his people," Randolph informed Simon. "He gib dem plenty *yichuss*."

"Can you help loving him?" demanded Gribitz. "Universal God, Et-t-ternal Father, how can you not love him with that eleven inches of sh-*shlong*?"

". . . Ob wut?"

"*Shlong!*" screamed Gribitz.

Chortling softly, Randolph said, "Lub dat word."

After they had peed at adjacent urinals, after they had swigged water from the same sawdust-flecked soda bottle, after they had traded Life Savers, Randolph lighted his cigar and gave himself utterly to meditation.

"Know wut we gawn do?" he eventually asked Simon.

He swayed clockwise, Simon counterclockwise.

"We do fust things fust . . ."

Simon uttered an exuberant "Blef!" and let expressions of eagerness, intelligence, and alertness slowly cross his face.

"An de fust thing be—de wrist. De—wrist," Randolph

repeated, adding, "Let us hol up—de wrist."

He held up both his own.

"Wid dis kine occupation it be ob par-moun potance dat we de-velop in de wrist de max-mum quality ob *shtark*ness."

Simon pantomimed awe, wonder, and mounting delight.

"Let's now fo-lex de wrist," commanded Randolph.

He crouched, peered, then made some small adjustment at Simon's elbows.

"Let's ob-serve dat once mo," he said, rising and bouncing on the balls of his feet.

Simon went into a frenzy of flexing.

"Unnh-huh," commented Randolph.

Then with a black grease pencil he put a dot on Simon's left wrist.

"She be wut Randy spected," was his diagnosis. "Fum de lef member we kain ticipate us a mite *tzures*. Deyfore . . ."

He took a long, appreciative whiff of cigar.

". . . dis wut we do: We gawn wuk on . . . de tenyons. De—tenyons. Les say dat word. De . . ."

". . . Tenyons," Simon obliged.

"Dat be T, E, N, D, O, N, S, tenyons. Now dese yere tenyons, dey be ob *su*-preme potance," he insisted. "Why dat so? Caws de tenyons render su-pport fo de lower limb or—de fo-arm. De—fo-arm."

With a blue grease pencil Randolph marked off the area on himself, then on Simon.

"We kin co-rrec de tenyon problem wid de-vices. Mong de de-vices is de wristband. Now as to de wristband Randy gawn make dis genrul statement . . ."

He chuckled, he winked, he took off his baseball cap and twirled it around a finger.

". . . unnh-huh."

With a red grease pencil he circled Simon's elbow.

"Use ob de wristband do cawse here fo reasons *un*known a skin mis'ry. Den wut do Randy puhscribe? Pears to me dat ob all de attorneys yo bes attorney be dis . . ."

And so it came to pass that Simon, using his right hand

as little as possible and with concentrated and continual flexing of his left wrist, spent all that afternoon squeezing skirts
off their clothespin hangers. For the first few hours he did
nicely, drawing from Randolph numerous chuckles and
cries of "Dat be a genwine *gedillah*." But then he developed
a cramp, and on top of this cramp a twitch and a sequence
of spasms which caused tears to roll from his eyes and skirts
to fall from his fingers.

Before the fifth skirt hit the floor Gribitz was springing
out from between two racks.

To Simon he said, "F-f-fin—*fartig!*"

To Randolph he said, "This is already the third one-
handed w-w-worker we got this month!"

"It do prove de merit ob yo message," observed Randolph, sadly contemplating his cigar. "Namely, de Judeo-
Christian e-thos jes ain't fo no *goyishe kopp.*"

Simon by morning was all steamed up and set to piss on
top of Levy and his desk.

But when he reached the Employment Shapers' door a
scant eight, ten steps behind Levy's unmistakable coattails
he found it locked and the whole place dark as Egypt.

"Hello!" he cried, then "Hey!" then "Heh?" his nose on
the frosted glass.

A shade descended sneakily, snagged mid-way, and sprang
back. It seemed to Simon he glimpsed Levy springing with it.

His anger rising, Simon set up a clamor of "Mr. Levy, I
wonder if I may come in I would like to come in don't
you think you should let me in I think you should let
me in you don't think I mean it I definitely definitely
mean it."

"Fongoo, pastafazool," he heard. "You-a craze or sum'tin?"

There followed a heart-stopping snatch of *Santa Lucia.*

"Take or give Mr. Levy a message," Simon demanded.

"You godda de mess, we take-a de mess. But—but-but-a,"
he was warned, "Levy no be back for longa time. He godda

go—how-a you say?—on a refreshmental course."

"Anyway, nevertheless, tell him—this. This is what you should tell him," Simon said cagily. "A client was here, a client was looking for him . . ."

"Clienza make-a on him da seekage . . ."

". . . with the sole sole intent . . ."

"De primal-a purpose . . ."

"This client who has already received a bill by mail, he has worked not even a day total and he's already already received a bill by mail, and never mind the distorted and complete and total misrepresenting of the jobs—a bill which is so ridiculous and preposterous and idiotic and so so—"

"Dis-a Mist' Lev'," he was informed, "he gotta de bigga overhedge."

"Not only am I not going to pay this bill, oh no," said Simon, "besides not paying almost and practically and nearly half of my earnings, forty percent is nearly nearly half . . ."

"Billament fee she includa small credenza charge."

". . . he is not handling or dealing with a lemon."

"Plus all-a da cit', da state-a and-a federated taxage where sheza applicational."

"And also I want the number of his license!"

Abruptly, Simon was admitted.

"Cheery-hi," said Levy, saluting with his yardstick. "We were doing a siftal on our professional journal backlogage."

"First of all, I am going to make a full full report to the Brooklyn College placement office," Simon declared. "That is first of all . . ."

"We render pish-posh on your emotion burst out," muttered Levy, "and give it ascribal to your creating artist type."

"Creating artist!" bawled Simon. "If I'm such such a creating artist what are you sending me out to garment houses?"

To which Levy replied simply, "For material."

"*Oy*," went Simon, and with such force that he was momentarily lamed. Then in grief and fury he made for the door.

288

But Levy blocked him with his body.

"Our lifetime saga," began the little fellow, using his yardstick on Simon like a shepherd's crook, "is the narrational account of a social history victim. Aforesaid lifetime saga had its commencal start during an upheaval midst . . ."

Himmelfarb, of Himmelfarb Hoover Aprons, pale, paunchy, with a swatch of Stalin moustache, came at Simon from the farthest end of the loft.

He right away embraced him, backed off, embraced him again and kneaded his lower back and kidney regions, saying, "I wonder if you're familiar with the expression, 'It was love at first sight!' "

Simon, on the snotty side, said, "I don't don't think so," and mumbled something about checking and looking through his English notes.

"There's another expression which in this case, in *your* case, is more—could I say it's *more* correct?"

"*You* could," answered Simon easily. "*I* would say 'more —accurate!' "

"What you *would* say is what I *will* say. More—accurate!" Himmelfarb scratched Simon's scalp. "So to employ toward you the more accurate terminology—terminology?"

"Sure," went Simon, coolly flicking dandruff off a shoulder. "That's—*right!*"

"I"—Himmelfarb raised his right hand—"employing toward you the present active tense, have . . . taken . . . to you!"

"In that case," Simon grumpily replied, "I really really should and must be truthful . . ."

"You are the type," Himmelfarb beamed, "who could not be otherwise. Otherwise?"

". . . because my interests lie in different areas and directions."

"I wouldn't want it different," answered Himmelfarb. "Different or differen*tly?*"

"I would be here only only temporarily."

"Only God is permanent," Himmelfarb brooded.

"By the time you break me in . . ."

"I break in only shoes," Himmelfarb sweetly scoffed.

"By the time I learn what has to has to be learned . . ."

"To quote—quote or cite?—Rudy Vallee," said Himmelfarb with great complacence, " 'My time is your time.' "

"Because I know, I can see, and I am aware by now, by now I am fully aware that when it comes to even even tying a bundle . . ."

Himmelfarb caught Simon by the wrist.

He said, "There is an expression derived—derived?—from carpentry. 'It goes—against—my grain.' And my grain is gone against when I hear from—an executive assistant—the prosaic word 'bundle.' By executive assistant," he proceeded to say, caressing his cheek with Simon's hand, "I mean seventeen dollars a week. By week I mean your convenience."

"The thing is, this is the thing," said Simon, groggy with delight, "I will be taking and carrying fifteen-and-a-half credits at Brooklyn College . . ."

"N.Y.U.," Himmelfarb countered huskily. "Or Columbia."

"Waha," went Simon.

"N.Y.U. or Columbia; Columbia or N.Y.U. It's optional. Optional?"

"Optional is the perfect perfect word," Simon said generously. "*Le mot juste.*"

"And yet, on the optional tuition check"—Himmelfarb scribbled in the air—"I picture putting only N.Y.U. N . . . Y . . . U . . ."

Three times he dotted the air.

". . . for the reason that N.Y.U. has a downtown . . . branch or division?"

"Optional," Simon chortled.

"By expense-paid taxi from downtown N.Y.U. it would be no time to the thair-ter or thee-yater, a mere stone's throw to Chinatown, assuming or *pre*suming you like Chinese food."

Simon whispered "Won Ton" and "Egg drop."

"At or by your side should be, as fits or befits an N.Y.U. executive, what I shall express in these terms: A member of—"

A tinted snapshot materialized in Himmelfarb's palm.

"—the fairer sex."

"She certainly certainly is!" exclaimed Simon, looking, almost leering.

" 'A father's pride, a mother's shame,' " mumbled Himmelfarb. "From the *Oxford Book of English Verse*, author not known or unknown."

"She looks like," Simon said dreamily, "you know who she sort of sort of looks like . . . ?"

"Hello, hello my Poopsie," Himmelfarb made love to the snapshot. "I call her Poopsie," he explained, "and she calls me Popsy."

". . . Francis Dee. Francis Dee in a way."

"Because it's written on or in her face," returned Himmelfarb. "Actress. Little, little actress," he moaned to the snapshot. "Chosen out of or from your whole school to play Elizabeth Barrett Browning, 1806–1861."

"I do, I used to do impersonations," offered Simon. "Not that that's *acting* . . ."

And he then and there gave himself up to a silent wooing, jealous of Himmelfarb for the loverlike way he was posed with her under a beach umbrella, for his copping of a privileged feel near tits and ass as he strained, all smiles, to lift her from where she was sitting in a—

"—In what is she sitting?" Simon suddenly yelped.

"Different surgical suppliers have various or varied names," replied Himmelfarb. "Poopsie calls it . . . her two-wheeler."

Conversationally, Simon said, "You know what I should, had better better do is take down her number." He uncapped slowly the last of his *bar-mitzvah* pens. "I can reach her at . . . her number is?"

"This model"—Himmelfarb squinted at the snapshot—"is the one that collapses for easy stowing or stowage. So in the trunk of your executive-assistant car . . ."

When next he spoke they were standing together by the elevator.

"Would a salary figure somewhat or somehow higher be . . . ?"

"I don't know what to say," Simon said. "I honestly honestly honestly . . ."

"There's a certain term," declared Himmelfarb, "which is always to me apt—apt?—for this occasion."

Even if the elevator had not sprung open seconds later Simon would still have suffered Himmelfarb's "Shit on or upon you" in silence.

In two days there came from Levy forms plus a personal note.

> As our news of you is bereft of communication
> we apply urgal that you stay abreasted
> for our current listage.

Simon never knew or even wanted to remotely know why he completed and mailed in the forms. Yet he continued to do so week after week throughout the summer, long past the time his Cousin Phillie made one little phone call and got him nicely settled in an office job with the Mercury Dental Supply Company.

10

He who steals my purse steals trash
But he who finds my notes gets cash
from
SIMON SLOAN
1653 Brighton 5th St.
B'klyn, N.Y.

History 1.1
Professor Chernowitz

CIVILIZATION:

Mod. Hist. begins approx. IVth millenary B.C. It developed. Best evidence in 3 basins of Nile: Euphrates, Tigris, Indus. Villages there. Agriculture, trade, writing in evidence. Houses, palaces, astronomy. Etc. Etc.

Egyptians origin   Couldn't hear, get later

Religion—idea of creator-god. But mostly nature worship. Osiris imptnt. A cult. God of life. Every spring reborn. With coming of grain. Resurrection idea. Read BREASTED for more on rlgn. Reserve book.

Water imptnt to all civs. ALL THINGS ARE WATER. THALES.

Code of Hammurabi. Idea of commercial responsibility. For first time. You could bring suit if businessmen. Prof. Chernowitz: "This would be known later as the code and suit." He fight in Spain? Supposed to. Find out if. Idea for poem/story. Hist. teacher back from Lincoln Brigade. As he teaches gets lapses of memory. He is saying ALL THINGS ARE WATER and thnks of how in Spn they crossed water to attack enemy

YOUR NOTES   COULD I SEE?

No

THANK YOU VERY VERY MUCH

Assnment: Finish up chptrs on fndtns modern era.

Call Mom Mrs. Plaut. 3 rings. She doesn't pick up, refrig. didn't come

Possible question for after class: Did Egyptian persecution of Jews have economic basis?

Sloan, Simon
Eng. 2.5 Professor Boynton Theme #1
A character sketch
Approximately 200 words
9/6/41

A writer?

Perhaps.

But must writers order and explore their worlds at kitchen tables, their spirits and their papers dampened by a mother's sloshing rag?

Never mind. For he is here. In Brooklyn. A Brooklyn boy, remembering that he must write of what he knows.

He knows. . . .

Of what does he know?

He knows of last night's egg cream, sipped and savored on the candy-store stool.

He knows of the penny-bought loose cigarette.

He knows he smoked it, as he has so many smoked over the long years, with friends, best friends, on a tenement stoop.

He knows he asked of Abraham, pet-named Boomie,

how it fared with him at C.C.N.Y., and that from his friend came discourse lengthy and phrases strange and alien: Business administration; office procedure; cost accounting.

He knows that Herman, in childhood Hymie, was filled with his new self as he treated all to ices of lemon and set forth his printing-jobber's destiny.

He knows he left, forsook, abandoned them at night's early hour for reflection solitary.

He knows that they called out to him of Saturday hence and a common movie afternoon.

He knows he gave them answer in a "Sure" derisive as he sped off to walk on wind-weathered sand.

And he knows, this perhaps writer, this Brooklyn boy, that he might as well join them at a theater named Surf, or Lyric, or Neptune.

He might as well—while he searches for another Spain.

Classical Civ. 05 Miss Gatcher

Warning—when we read OEDIPUS we should remember that while Oedipus as character is complex he doesn't have Oedipus Complex.

Review Ionic, Doric, Corinthian columns. Be able to draw on blackbrd Tsday.

To read; Platos's Cave

Platonic Idealism—that things exist when, if you think they do. In P's sense Bklyn College does not exist when we leave it.

Gods—Greeks took gds vry vry personally. Intimately. Much like ancnt Hbrws in this regard. Gods play favorites. Zeus gets angry, Jehovah gets angry. But Grk Gds don't have J's fearful powers. Less and less PROPITIATION as Grk civ. develops. Man increasingly equal to Gds. Why? Bcse Grks. too rational. MODERATION IN ALL THINGS. Scientific spirit. It awakens. Harmony—Apollo stands for it.

Ask later—Was this dvlpmnt due to growth of trade, bgngs of early capitalism?

Look up—hubris, dionysian

Call by Mrs. P. later abt refrig—2 rings, hang up, again 2 rings

Events Today
Grand Illusion **** 12:15, Ingersoll
Wrtng for Radio *** 12:30 255B
Amy Lowell, Rdngs* 1 PM, Eng Off.
Preparing yrself for Welfare dept, career 12, 301 B
Things to do—Student Discount Cards, Lewisohn Stad? For gym a combntn lock, 2nd hand ok. Buy *Atlantic Monthly* for Eng???

September 9, 1941

As I know you are interested to find out if the refrigerator is coming today and as I got a recent warning on my dropped stomach your mother is leaving you near your school books these few words to beg with all her failed strength please please forgive her if for once she doesn't get up from what would definitely definitely be by the next one a sick bed to make your nourishment breakfast

And as I know that in this hot weather an egg is the worst worst poison you will find in the ice box, don't don't knock over dad's mineral oil when you reach, a dish of sour cream and matzo broken up, save the wax paper

And as I know that when you call by Mrs. Plaut today Cousin Phillie will be in her house, I wish I didn't know him like I know him, how he will pick just just that time to bring me the paper plates he owes me from your bar mitzvah, its too too long a story for now, and how he will read my little note downstairs by the bell, Hitler I am recuperating from Hartford Connecticut and similar sufferings at your hands in the home of a good friend who knows my tragic story

And as I know how Cousin Phillie never even once hinted to me how fifteen years ago he was expecting the arrival of a beautiful set of Utica Cutlery Knives, you don't see knives like that any more, I had to find it out from Morris the Grinder, you wouldn't remember him it was a little before your time, he was a very spiteful person and someday I'll give you the whole story, how he yelled up to me from the street, Hey, Utica Cutlery Knives like your Cousin Phillie is expecting you don't see anymore

And as I know you will agree how if I didn't know Cousin Phillie's business he doesn't need to know my business and Mrs. Plaut has gotten strict strict instructions not to use the word refrigerator where Cousin Phillie could hear

And as I know you will be waiting for my news when you call your dad with his current-events head has set up the following following arrangements.

If you hear me say I'm upset France didn't fight a little harder it means the refrigerator came, it's a reconditioned model but I had no strength anymore to argue with the landlord.

If you hear me say Sad news from the Polish corridor it means they had trouble getting it through my door.

If you hear me say The lights are going out all over Europe it means I plugged it in and right away the fuse blew.

If you hear me say I'm very very sorry for what they did to Holland it means they got it so so filthy I had to go over the whole thing with Dutch Cleanser

> Yr. Mother who wishes you good
> luck, the very very best of luck
> in yr endeavors, and hopes you

make many many more new friends!

Tell Boomie, Hymie
Don't forget!! ******

The train, it's Newkirk Avenue—I'm figuring what I spent for books—I put down $2, $1.78, $2.19—six times I add it, six times it comes out different—all of a sudden woman leans over—$5.97 she writes on my notebook cover— she smiles and smiles—I smile back—who? Don't remember me Simon?—Don't don't think so miss—OK, you don't remember me—So who?—I'm someone who was always better than you in arithmetic—Ave H, I have to go—Finally!!— Who?—LILA EDELSTEIN—Only so fat!

When was she better in arithmetic?

OPEN LETTER   OPEN LETTER   OPEN LETTER   OPEN LETTER

President   September 19, 1941
Brooklyn College
Avenue H and Bedford Avenue

The members of the *Young Communist League* wish to express their thanks to you for helping to vilify Brooklyn College and to further debase the value of its degree.

By your whole-hearted support of the activities of the Rapp-Coudert Committee; by your summary dismissal of Associate Professor Salomon; by your obvious talent for red-baiting rhetoric—

You have distinguished yourself well and nobly and merit your rightful place in the front ranks of the forces of fascism.

Keep up the good work!

Bio 1   Prof Wishengrad
Bio Logy is from Greek   To some it will be all Greek.
Means Life, study of.

Not an easy course   If you want easy course he has DROP
CARDS If you want to just fulfill your science reqmnt DON'T
do it here.

How many here Protestant—5
How many Catholic—14
How many Jewish—91
Wherefore do I ask this of you? Because
There is no such thing as Protestant Biology!
There is no such thing as Catholic Biology!
There is no such thing as Jewish Biology!
Only BIOLOGY!

Our religions may differ, our political beliefs may differ. If I say to you Communism, Socialism, Roosevelt, write
down definitions of, these definitions would vary.

No such variance in biology.

When I say cell it will mean Nucleus and Protoplasm.

When I say tissue it will mean collection of cells engaged
in common purpose.

When I say organism I will mean a complex structure
with integrated parts and processes.

And when I say dismissed I mean GO.

Protestants, Catholics, and Jews are dismissed—Next
time a short-answer quiz on first 3 chaps of Mills & Wein-
stein.

Many of you, alas, will be unable to get text. Won't quiz
be unfair?

Yes, it WILL be unfair.

Psych. 5   Prof. Zachlauer

Get DIMENSIONS IN PSYCHOLOGY, Zachlauer & Hopkins,
2nd ed.

What is Personality?

A blend heredity and environment. Heredity beyond
control, environment partially controllable.

Which elements of environment controllable? Cultural
elements.

What is culture? Many different definitions. As used in course culture will mean—HOW man lives within given period after satisfaction of basic drives

What happens if man can't satisfy basic drives full? He suffers CONFLICT

Ask later—Can conflict in basic drive satisfaction be caused by economic factors?

What is man's tendency in conflict? He tends, seeks to RESOLVE it

Assignment—Chapter 1, 3

Sep. 9, 1941

Dear Mr. Sobler:

I write this to you in the Brooklyn College Library where I await the coming of my books.

Stay in touch and keep in contact you said, and though I have been somewhat remiss this is as good a time as any that will arise in my overcrowded schedule to tell you how impressed I was by your recent article or review—you managed, brilliantly, to encompass both—in *Science and Society*. To my mind it showed throughout a truly keen

The mother say I leave you by bell note

The mother say she no by mrs. Plaut she in her house

The mother say the cous Phil he in her house

The mother say she drink ice-cube water with the cous Phil in her house

The mother say be nice the cous Phil and no to open the big mouth

The mother say the cous Phil bring her the utic cut knife

SUPER   JOE

The mother show me knife you no see knife like that no more

301

Meeting Thursday, September 11, 1941
236 Boylan 1 PM
You're invited!

Call us old-fashioned. . . .

That's all right. . . .

For the Rosa Luxemburg Club would rather have an old-fashioned Marxist-Leninist discussion than waste precious proletarian time folk singing.

Because we're not like the Young Communist League.

We prefer ideas to guitars.

We know that all the corn Jimmy may crack won't drown out the screams of Stalin's suffering millions!

Dear Professor Boynton:

I have assumed the liberty of placing this note in your English Department mail drop only because I wished to further clarify some of the matters we discussed yesterday.

You asked me if I truly believed that a grade of C+ on my recent character-sketch assignment was "undeserved" in view or in light of what you felt were "serious stylistic errors."

You pointed out further that my treatment or handling of the character-sketch assignment did not represent precisely "what you had in mind."

You also stated, as we were walking in the hall, that I must or should remember that English 2.5 is a required, a "basic and fundamental" course, and that by the evidence of my "apparent attitude," especially my expressions of doubt regarding the use of the *Atlantic Monthly* as supplementary reading, I seem to be "reluctant" to accept what you consider "necessary" guidance.

Seated now at my typewriter and better able to order my thoughts, I should like to explain myself.

At the risk of immodesty, I truly believe that my background reveals some small and proven ability in the field of writing. Many of my former teachers at Lowell High School, where I was pleased to serve in the capacity of Associate Editor of the *Lowell Lantern,* showered a considerable amount of high praise upon my poems and stories. Their opinion of my work was climaxed at graduation by my receipt of one of Lowell's very highest awards: The Solomon Aarongleich Medal for distinguished achievement in creative arts.

Thus, from my formative high-school days, I have been trained to view an assignment as the basic starting point, the impetus from which to launch my own creative interpretation. The "serious stylistic errors" which you cited are part of a basic attempt to achieve and realize my own personal style, and it may prove of some interest to you to read more of my work, some of which has been rejected by *Story Magazine* with a personal note requesting me to "PLEASE TRY US AGAIN."

May I say that I immensely enjoyed our chance to chat, and I certainly hope your schedule will permit other such opportunities.

Cordially,
S. Sloan

P.S. In the course of rereading and reviewing my character sketch I did notice comma-rule errors. Though I cannot be certain, I believe these stemmed and arose from carelessness in typing

Classical Civ 05

Plato born approx. 427–347 BC—town of Elea, western Italy. Family very ancient, went back to early kings of Athens.

His real name—Aristocles. Which means? What? Anyone?

It's all Grk to me Dying to say
Said
She laughs also   Without teeth
Her question oh so silly. She realizes. But when she

ATTENDED Bryn Moor Grk and Ltn required of all. Had to, basic, for culture. Missing something, we all. Will see when we come to Homer. Her viewpnt extreme. But better no Homer than' Homer in trnsltn. If up to her.

Argument   Oy what I started!

Girl—Culture once belonged to, property of, it was province of mostly leisure-class aristocracy. Time for it, they had.

Leisure class just term   Not that much leisure   She from farm Wisconsin   Up for chores with rosy fingered dawn   Homer phrase that

Girl   Even so   So?   Why denied, we, should be kept from acqntnce with Homer etc. in trnsltn   Not our fault we blng to lower economic orders   At least can get smattering of ignorance   Oscar Levant phrase

Boy   Is not everything trnsltd? It is   Everything has to be   He math major and knows that without trnsltn he couldn't get even Euclid. Why shld he hve to lrn Grk for sake Euclid?

Miss G

Her uncle a Dr.   Learned Ltn   Not just for sake of wrtng prscrptns

Girl   May I offer example? Example is Hebrew faith It has bible, laws, dcmnts, other thngs   All in Hbrw lngage and tnge   But have been trnsltd. Therefore these things part now, blng to culture of world. Shld we of Hbrw fth not resent? Say that too much lost in trnsltn? Could make same argmnt on all trnsltn, it loses. She incidentally knows Hbrw, also once a leisure-class thng for priestly and clerical class study, but she has no resentment.

Miss G

Pointless, verging on. Back to work we

Plato as youth hesitated between poetry and politics   A good soldier   In 3 battles prize for Bravery   Left Athens when youth as political exile   Returned, founded academy. Intellectual center.

How did he teach   3 basic ways

Interesting

Bell she runs out Doesn't give us meaning of ARIS-
TOCLES name

Bio

Next time the test

Cells, cell structure, knowledge of comes with discovery
of microscope

Some cells big   But in course evolution cell size always
restricted Why?

Not 100% sure   Theories differ   Possibly because cells
need oxygen and nutrients. Which must be brought in then
brought out in form of waste   We call this waste never mind
what you bums in front call it   EXCRETION   Kind of an exchange system   Exchange has to be made   Bigger the cell
more difficult the exchange   Known as the WYSHLEPP theory
Cell Figures WHY should I have to Shlepp   Don't like my
jokes I still have a few drop cards   Limited cell size due
also to fact that parts can't be located too far from control
center NUCLEUS this

Structure of cell—Cell Membrane   Don't really know it
exists   From properties of cell we reason INDIRECTLY that
something like it exists   We call it membrane   Why membrane? Why not membrane? Don't like the name take
geology   But there even crazier names

Test maybe next time If in mood he

ARE YOU A PRE-MED?

ARE YOU NAMED SMITH OR JOHNSON?

KELLY OR BROWN?

IF YOU BEAR THESE OR SIMILAR NAMES

DON'T WORRY

YOU'LL GET INTO MEDICAL SCHOOL

BUT IF YOU'RE JEWISH

YOU'LL WANT TO HEAR

305

"Now that you are back from Spain." Al Katz's mother said to him across their kitchen table, "perhaps you can clarify to me why you had to had to go to fight."

"For a cause, Mother," answered Al. "For the plains and hills of Badajoz and Merida. For a shepherd drinking of his wine and eating of his cheese. . . ."

His mind drifted, drifted, and the green oilcloth of the kitchen table became for him the green jackets of the Moors, and he remembered the bucking, bucking of the machine gun, and he remembered how it had been when José had cried from his wound, José whispering sibilantly as his blood dampened and darkened the Spanish earth, "*Ay amigo mio,* but it turns dark for me!"

In the cafeteria the friendless youth sits.

He is not Stover at Yale, he is Sloan of Brooklyn College. Who, who knows him here?

The gym custodian knows him, for already he has lost a towel.

Two, two years have passed since a girl has known his urging loins.

Soon, soon now he will rise and go upon his sex-hungry rounds.

From cafeteria to library, from library to lounge.

Are there none, none now to whom he can say, "Look upon me, for I, I carry PM too, and I know that it is good."

Are there none, none to whom he can say, "Come, come with with me and somewhere we two together shall hear

306

Paul Robeson sing his *Ballad for Americans?*"

You, oh you dark girl, with your C.D. face, why dost thou turn thy Modern Library giant so I cannot see the title?

Thou knowest, surely, oh surely thou knowest, how at the milk bar I pressed and pressed against thee, for seconds I was pressed and in erection's state.

13 September, 1941

Dear Mr. Sloan:

We herewith reply to your recent letter which we have read with great interest.

Please be assured that we do not wish to question the judgments of your high-school teachers who have seen fit to praise your work. However, it has been our experience that many students who have distinguished themselves during their high-school days show a marked reluctance to apply themselves to the kind of rigorous grammatical and stylistic discipline which the English Department has seen fit to establish for this course.

During the last quarter of the present semester we shall be assigning themes of a somewhat more "creative" nature, and we shall be pleased to read any pertinent materials you might then wish to submit.

Very Sincerely,
Professor Lansing Boynton

Things To Do

Get rest of wds to Viva La Quince Brigada
Look for towel
? Call Maxine ?

OVERDUE NOTICE

Burns: A Handbook of Marxism
Due: Sep. 14, 1941
If material is not returned by 9/20 record must be automatically turned over to OFFICE OF DEAN as per Public Education Law G499901, City of New York.

History

In 313 Constantine proclaimed frdm worship for Chrstns. Called himself Protector of Church. Allowed Paganism to continue tho. Supremacy of Chrstnty comes in 324—Constantine triumphs. But not till 380 is it sole sole state rlgn.

No longer a god, the Emperor. But his authority divine, Starts divine right kings idea. Religions and civil separate tho. Diocletian merges church into empire struct. State officials appntd., bishops in cities elected. Soon become real rulers of city.

Ask if this was rooted in economic roots.

Church gave Emp. kind of legitimacy never had in past. Now Emp. could claim his power held from God. To say this had to have chrch suppt. To get suppt. had to accpt chrch discipline.

Emperors of West abandoned Rome. Most of time in Milan. 5th cent. they hand over Rome, ancient capitl to Pope. Prestige for Pope.

Now new cap. appears in Empire. Cap. of church. ROME Starts separating from auth. of Empire. Begins at this pnt to gather powers of

Tell Maxine this

This tell her

Why didn't call in 2 years

Hitch-hiked. All over USA. In every mine and mill. Rode rods. Heard birth of jazz in New Orlns. Wldnt write her till worthy. Till knew heartbeat & pulse of great land surge & swell of time and the river

Rdngs   Med Hist, Coulton, Chap 4, 5

Remember go Teitlebaum   Estimate on Swiss Knight

OUR RECORDS SHOW FOLLOWING EQUIPMENT OUTSTANDING IN YOUR NAME

Sloan, S.

Towel   1

Please see Mr. Brych BEFORE NOON 9/19/41

Dear Mr. Sobler:

I once again seek to obey your injunction to "Keep in touch."

As you predicted, I am continuing to collect rejection slips. My story, *Young Faust,* which you thought among my best—the one about the thresher of wheat who develops and builds a close friendship with the doomed Negro boxer—has been turned down by *Currents, Story, Esquire,* and *Here.* At *Currents* they put in a personal note, 'Let's see *more* of your work.'

I am right now considering and on the threshold of yet another story, and because it is apart from what has been my general trend and direction I would like to get your opinion and valuable comments.

Basically and fundamentally it is a conflict story. The time is the general present and the characters are three friends of Brooklyn-Jewish faith whose relationship is beginning to drift asunder. As the story opens, the central character, the protagonist, Joe, whose name will naturally be changed, picks his two friends up on Saturday morning. They discuss the different films currently showing in their Brooklyn neighborhood theaters. Joe's wish, his profound and yearning desire is to do something something different this Saturday morning. "Let us not go and once more view the foolish antics of the Hollywood glamour stars," he will say. For he wishes to go to the Stanley Theater and see an artistic and socially significant film. *Alexander Nevsky?*

The conflict comes about because Joe is laughed at and derided by his friends, whose interests and goals and social perspective are all of a sudden now in a *bourgeois,* middle-class light. In the story Joe takes the train to New York by himself, leaving behind his old friends. And as we see him last he is thinking to himself of the sadness and grief which always must be the inevitable handmaiden of one who seeks to fulfill a socially purposeful role. He might, in his thoughts and because he is on a train, have a reference to Lenin on the sealed Finland Station train, and of the thoughts Lenin would then have had.

This story, which has certain autobiographical elements and aspects, I see as a possible *New Yorker* story. What do you think?

May I now say that in my humble opinion your recent contribution to *Science and Society* was not only a truly keen

September 18, 1941

Dear Maxine:

I am the unknown caller and old friend who recently had an interesting and highly abrupt conversation with your mother.

Congratulations on your engagement and impending marriage. May I now say that in my humble opinion your future husband will be getting a very very good lay.

A Friend of Old

Sloan, Simon
Eng. 2.5 Professor Boynton
Assignment #2
Expository Theme
Subject: Mailing a manuscript to a magazine

Many neophyte writers of talent, no matter how gifted, are beset all too often by doubts when faced with the manifold problems of mailing that precious story or poem or essay to the professional magazine of their choice.

The failure to observe certain fundamental 'dos' and 'don'ts' oft spell the crucial difference betwixt acceptance and rejection, betwixt sympathetic and interested editorial perusal and cold disdain.

What basic rules are to be followed? What constitutes accepted procedure for the preparation and final mailing of the finished manuscript?

Jane Hodges, writing in the pages of *Penman Magazine*,

March *1940, Vol. 11,* has this to say about manuscript mailing and preparation: "As I look back upon my twenty-odd years of free-lance writing I realize now that many a manuscript consigned to the oblivion of a bottom drawer might have seen print and payment if I had summoned sufficient energy to retype a sloppy page or two."

And that noted fictioneer, Austin Chandler, reminded the erstwhile scribe in a truly keen article in the pages of *Author and Journalist, September, 1940,* that "editors are human beings whose judgments, regretful as this might be, can be influenced by manuscripts whose pages exert a basic 'eye appeal.'"

Thus, a manuscript must first and foremost be typed. Ribbons should be fresh, and white bond paper of high quality should be utilized. But once typed, what then? Here it would seem that writers are of two minds. Some advocate the use of the humble paper clip for the pages; others prefer a staple. Blanche Garvell, in *Writer's Guide, March, 1939,* recommends the paper clip, pointing out that most printers prefer this lowly device.

The most commonplace errors occur all too frequently in the mailing of a manuscript. A consensus of magazine editors taken by *Penman Magazine* on January 7th, 1938, reveals that only first-class mail is regarded as "acceptable." And once the manuscript is placed in its brown manila envelope, once the stamped self-addressed envelope is enclosed, once those precious three words "Do Not Fold" are inscribed thereon, little else is left for the writer. It is at this point that he will inevitably recall those wise and time-honored words: "Hope springs eternal in the human breast."

Psych.
Conditioned Reflex. A reflex that has been conditioned. By circumstance.
Example—Say a man is fond of chewing gum. Gum for some reason is withheld from him. (Poverty? Is there eco-

nomic basis for conditioned reflex? Later ask) He can be so conditioned that he moves jaws in chewing motions at sight of gum

But what if man hates gum. If he must chew gum as punishment? Then sight of gum or gum wrapper may cause him unplsnt sensations. Sweat, nausea, etc.

PAVLOV A Russian physiologist. The dog at proximity of food—his salivary glands begin to

Hello Simon Sloan
????
Are you still writing Simon Sloan?
I write sometimes ERNEST HEMINGWAY
Is that your treatment of an admirer?
Very very familiar. . . . .
An old fan
I am FLUTTERED
GOODBYE!

Conditioned-reflex theory smwht mechanistic in vw of man. Value, it has. But limited. Structure of brain far too complex. Brain analogous to telephone swtchbrd. It can

I, Simon Sloan, herewith promise to be SERIOUS! Please write your name in following space. My name is . . . .
What is in a name?
Comment vous appelez-vous? ·
Je m'appele HELENE GROSSBERG

Offers us way to penetrate minds of nonverbal animals. How different is man from them? Is he different in kind or degree? No easy answer. Yet we know this

You STILL do not REMEMBER me
From Lowell definitely
Lowell

Not from any class
Not

Capable of suffering pain. Man is. For sake of goal that is
distant. Defers pleasure he. Work can be unpleasant. But
wages at end of week joyful. Like college instructor

Once in the cafeteria I HELENE GROSSBERG
Different hair then? Same same hair, but the style—
man.
See! Now you're—
I wrote in yr Lantern
A++ for Simon Sloan
I, somethingsomething, my first autograph to Helen
Grossberg
HelenE

not only by cond reflex that we learn. Other method called
IMPRINTING   Orig desc by Konrad Lorentz 1935   Example
—ducklings. They follow mother. Why? Because they know
she is mother? Because she finds them food? Answer is NO.
Next time we find out why not.
Assnment: Not required but intrsting. To rd Caspar Hauser,
Wasserman. Reservd

.   .   .   .

May I, Simon Sloan, borrow your library card EILEEN
Grossberg?
Two conditions 1 you have to remember my name, 2 you
have to walk me to gym, I left it in locker
OK. Do you like writing of Hemingway?
Not an English major. Bio or math.

Read also ape and child experiments. Also give three ex-
amples each of cond rflx, imprinting

Things to do
****Babette Deutsch, What is Mod Poetry 354 Arts 12:15

Teitlebaum honey

As I am too too upset in my sick nerves from the news of your mrs. one breast removal I am sending through my kid these few expressions of sorrowing grief felt by an old old customer

And as I am crazy about your mrs. and under better and different conditions for brave brave little England I would pay her a visit in the hospital, I care a lot that they stopped giving you a free transfer to the Nostrand Avenue trolley

And as I know she has got by now the GET WELL postal I had my Shmuel send out from his society, I understand he himself wrote a few words because when he addressed it to the 14th floor he thought his mother was years and years ago on the 14th floor when the doctors begged the family turn over the body for science, she had a very very special kind of cancer, it has nothing nothing to do with your wife, don't be down in the dumps from my Shmuel who has no no common sense, anyway his mother was on the 9th floor

And as I know you have from the missus some terrible terrible expense and need all the business you can get it's my happy pleasure to ask you to put away for yours truly a can S and W tomato herring, Please Please don't think I forgot how last time I bought same from you I learned to my bitter sorrow there was a defection to the can and the key was on the inside, You said to me Don't don't worry, S and W uses only a highly intelligent tomato herring, Knock a couple time times on the can, ask for Herbie, he'll open it from the inside

> Yours truly
> Malvena the Orphan
> who has already got her full
> share of suffering and knows
> what you are going through,
> when the occasion is right I'll
> tell you how Cousin Phillie used
> to come over during my young

bridal days and fill up his hot
water bag with my hot water,
what could I do, I had no mother
to protect me

If You Have Some Spare Time
If you Can Use Some Spare Cash
PM
The Only New Concept in Journalism Since Journalism
Itself
Can Use YOU As a Campus Representative
It's Profitable—And It's Progressive

Helene Grossberg
2249 Shannon Lane
De 8-8116
Nr. Ave. U & Flatbush Ave.
Brighton local to Avenue U, Cross over
In front of Bakery get bus #11
Watch for Dunhill Place   Block after Avenue U   At
corner is an Ebingers Bakery   Two more blcks   Get off,
walk to RIGHT one block   Again go rt. This is Shannon   Big
big apt. hse with green canopy

Museum of Modern Art Admssn	25¢
Carfare her house, back	25¢
Carfare Museum, back	40¢
Chinks	$1.30–$1.50
Unexpected—*noshes*, etc,	25¢
	$2.45–$2.65

Upon presentation of this card and proof of college student status, the bearer (please print name clearly) ————
shall be entitled to purchase one (1) ticket at regular price
and receive one (1) ticket at half-price at the FIFTH AVENUE
PLAYHOUSE. This offer applicable only during week Sep.

L

315

17–24, before 5 PM for showing Blood of a Poet/Last
Will Dr. Mabuse.

  Author: Bessie, Alvah C.
  Title: Men in Battle
will be held in reserve until 1 PM, 22 Sept. Please present
this card at desk.

English 2.5
Prof. Boynton
Assignment #2
Expository theme
Subject: Mailing a manuscript to magazine
A—

  V. Good
  Well constructed—but check in *Mantland
  and Legget* on citation of refs.

Dear Mr. Simon Sloan,
We cannot be all writers who have your particular taste in
different things, though if we compare records of Lowell it
shows that my marks in English were as good as yours.
But in my capacity as a future accountant I want to say that
Hymie and I have talked of the matter you raised, that is
breaking up the Battle Aces. We both after discussion have
decided upon official consent to its ending, and this will
inform you of same. While dues payment has been poor over
the last few years there is even so a fairly large sum of money
in the treasury, this sum being the accumulated total from
those childhood years when I and Hymie and you and even
Marshey took seriously friendship. There is more I might
certainly say on this, but "we cannot be all writers."
Very Sincerely,
Abraham Liebert

P.S. I incidentally went to see your Alexander Nevsky which

I could not sit through to the end, it was such a boring stupid piece of shit.

The Young Communist League
in cooperation with
The Harriet Tubman Society
presents by popular demand
a repeat performance of
BALLAD FOR AMERICANS
1 PM Friday, Sept, 22

Lounge   Contribution 10¢

Sept. 24, 1941

Dear Simon;
    Yes
    & u r a
          Helene

Sept. 25, 1941

Dear Helene:

In Psych we shall see each other and by hungry gaze and word unspoken make yearning effort to utter the unutterable.

What can I, shall I, must I, Simon the erstwhile writer, set down, down upon this empty page?

How much simpler it might be if I had conceived, created all that had befallen us in some story! For then—then I might begin. . . .

"Soul-stirred still by that film of films, hearing yet the Mabuse voice in every voice, the two, hungry-hearted, saw only each other in the subway swarm.

"And as their train jolts and jounces them from the borough called Manhattan and over the mighty, many-cabled span, the steel and concrete-muscled bridge, the boy tells her this—this he tells her—

" 'The film was for me great.' "

" 'For me too,' " she answers him.

"In gladness he shares with her his Marxist views, his manifold insights into Mabuse, symbol of agonized capitalism as it turns to fascism's madness. He shows off for her—for her he shows off—in mind and wit quicker, swifter, more deadly than he has ever been.

"Into vast-hearted Brooklyn they meanwhile ride, eating of the Black Crows which she in her gentle-fingered way puts one by one into his waiting mouth. . . ."

So, then so might I begin, launch this story.

But all, all I want to say is this, and this is what I want to say: Helene, I like you very much.

I like you very much, Helene.

Because even though it was late and you had to get up early to go pick out a dinette set with your folks you went, willingly you went with me to the Riis Beach boardwalk.

Because you forced, tenderly forced me to dance in the dark, saying I would teach you Marxism and you would teach me dancing.

Because the stimulation of your proximity brought on my instinctive masculine reaction.

Because you did not verbally rebuke my self-control loss but only said, this you said, that we should perhaps sit down and I should explain why I see the dictatorship of the proletariat as so necessary.

Because on the steps you found in your pocketbook more Black Crows.

Because when I then said to you I have a desire to make with you a physical contact which is not impelled by merely and solely sexual desire and drive, although there is probably a sexual motive also in my emotion, I am striving for open honesty with you, the reply on your part was Oh he is such an explainer.

Because you positioned yourself in the fashion that your body's upper half rested its lovely weight partially on my chest and partially on my lap, making it thusly easy for me to inhale the fragrance of your hair and to taste of your lips.

Because when I said something about whether I would find success in my writing ambition you took my hand and you stroked each finger and you said I am not worried about you, about you I am not worried.

Because while you thusly held my hand I started and commenced a teasing thing, I said You put your palm into my palm, we'll both push and see who is stronger.

Because you let your hand be pushed back by my hand and said Oh he is so strong, even though you are definitely able to put up a greater resistance.

Because when I then kissed you I was immediately relaxed by your words, Oh he is such a kisser.

Because as the intensity of my ardor increased and I definitely could not restrain and hold back myself from the overwhelming, surging desire to seek contact with your breasts and was initially unsuccessful, you facilitated my efforts by a guidance of my ineptly clumsy hands to the necessary undergarment part which thanks then to your sweet unmoving stillness I was able to sufficiently loosen.

Because while I placed my touch upon the loveliness of each of your breasts in turn you did not act in the fashion, the foolish fashion of many girls in similar circumstances, as though they are doing on the boy's behalf a huge and great favor.

Because when I lowered my lips gently, gently onto each of your breasts you reciprocated with the patting of my hair and said Now I will absolutely have to read Marx.

Because when I in ensuing excitation utilized my hands in an outside and external stroking of what we agreed to call later The Essential or Infinity and you said Oh what he is doing and Oh he is hurting me, expressing the highly understandable fear of an irritation or a rash from my manual actions, you nonetheless placed trustful confidence in my subsequent explanation that if you could permit yourself a relaxed attitude there would occur for you a natural lubricosity designed to facilitate and ease such matters.

Because on our homeward journey you asked me How does he happen to know of such matters and when I made frank and honest reply, in that I could not be to you otherwise, saying I suppose because I have found these matters out firsthand, you answered Oh he is so funny, in the belief that I had made deliberately a pun.

Because as I at last left you to begin my lonely return I heard knocking on a window which was your window, even though you took the risk of awakening and arousing your parents, and then you you threw down a little note. Sleep well.

Because I then as quietly as I could asked Do you like me?

Because there was something going on in your apartment and you only could nod.

Because you probably then felt the answer to my question was not full, full and complete, therefore going to the thoughtful and considerate trouble of mailing me the note you mailed. . . .

So for these and many other reasons and motives I like thee very much, Helene

Thy Simon

SECOND NOTICE!!

OUR RECORDS SHOW FOLLOWING EQUIPMENT OUTSTANDING IN YOUR NAME

SLOAN, S.

Towel, (1)

PLEASE SEE MR. BRYCH BEFORE NOON 10/3

FAILURE TO COMPLY WILL RESULT IN REFERRAL TO OFFICE OF DEAN FOR DISCIPLINARY ACTION AS PER PUBLIC EDUCATION LAW

G499901A, City of New York

Dear Mr. Abraham Liebert:

I first of all wish to say at the outset that your phrase regarding Alexander Nevsky ("a piece of shit") shows all too well the regretful difference between us in political and intellectual viewpoints.

Be that as it may, I

Never mind, though

Withal, I can say only

Things to do

Get wds. Viva La Quince Brigada

See Blockade 266A 3:15

Buy Trojans

Draft for Eng. A physical desc. Give sense of PERSON. Movements, significant details. CATCH him. 200–300 words. Prof. Boynton's favorite—from Swift, the King in Gulliver— He is taller by the breadth of my nail than anyone in his court—keep simple—thin better than acquiline, fat better than obese.

Hist. 1.1

Time now to pay some attention soc-eco conditions. What in silent films wld be intrcd by phrase Meanwhile back at the farm.

Tndcy is to thnk of pre-med hist in HUGE categories. ROME CHURCH CONSTANTINE JULIAN DIOCLETIAN ETC. But daily life much less drmtc. Alwys struck by smthng in Mach's Hist. of Florence. Desc. there of imptnt battle there for brdge. Clshing of 2 grt armies. One is dftd. Dynasty in one city is ended. New Pope, other signfcnt thngs arise frm this battle. At end Mach tells us kind & size of battle.

GUESS!

2 mercenaries wounded.

Hist more like that thn anything else. To US a dffrnce

who won, who lost, name of pope and king, this sect, that schism. OUR prspctive. Some future histrn—suppose he gives us evdnce tht all grt evnts tied to intrdctn of bathing? Or dvlpmnt of prsnal hygiene? Did u no how sldm grt mnrchs bathed? A whiff of Qn Eliz. prbly. preprd way for Spain's defeat. No wndr she The Vrgn Queen.

Sea lanes opened, trade, bgng of capitlsm, midd class emerges   Can be this time seen, all

But

Mnwhile back at the farm

Nothing

Hard, fast, tied to, and locked to soil is landowner, serf, freeman, slave.

Men-soil enter prptual bond. He who owns land cannot sell it. He who works on land cannot leave to marry, work for others. Mobility and fluidity of soc-eco relations of comparatively mdrn status. Till rcntly NOTHING much happened back at the farm. Repeat, nothing. No wonder some peasants supposed to have welcomed BLACK DEATH. No wonder we attch neg. meanings to such words as serf, churl. SURLY, CHURLISH.

Arises then state of mind for psnts described best prhps in lit, not hist—in Chaucer, Cervantes, Dost., Balzac.

Ask him now—

Does Marx not speak of, refer to this. Phrase. Idiocy of Rural Life?

Now—

Yes. Exactly. Marx lacked charity, but more accurate than Steinbecks and Caldwells who rmntcize. Joads too good to be true. More truth in JUKES than in Joads.

Hands, a bunch.

Don't you think it is highly possible Stnbck who did lot rsch on Okey life knew his sbjct better than Marx, Marx after all urban type, also don't you think, don't you feel for exmple Ma Joad stands for can't hear

Yes. And mnwhile back at the farm. Read Feudalism, sctn on, Enc. of Soc. Science.

Psych.

Is lrning only the accmltn of cndtnd reflexes? No dog, once it lrns to dstngsh betwn circle and square will fail to do so no matter how large or small these objcts. This knwn as

Hi, Helene Grossberg
Hi, Simon Sloan
So, Helene Grossberg?
So, Simon Sloan?

anml has performed ACT OF ABSTRACTION. Lrns CONCEPT of crcle and square. This rprsnts INTELLIGENCE. It can be

Did u get my letter?
Did u get my card?

Various mns to msre intlgnce. Test. STANFORD-BINET. Msrs INTELLIGENCE QUOTIENT IQ

My friend Sharon likes you. I think.
???
Because you did impersonation for her. She says you are a person of many parts.
I like to concentrate on only ONE part.
See? I do not like that. That is the sort of tendency I notice is in your character. I will say it now once and I hope once is enough for me to say it because I hope very sincerely you will understand and it can be my LAST word on the subject. Of what I notice is in your character.
Apologize   Forgive
No   Maybe and perhaps

But we measure intllgnce in lmtd fshn. Intellgnce itslf not a clrly dfnd cncpt. Real life can cnfrnt indvdl with mny prblm situations which

Because a person of your sensitive type should not have to go in for coarse humor to embarrass the other person. I want this as my LAST word on the subject.

High IQ indvdl cld be wrse driver than low IQ. Or gifted in some drctn, not another. Prhps dffrnt kinds intllgnce. Yet we

If that is humor you learned from Marx then I will not read him.

Intllgnce as trm must be used cautiously. In smlr way we might say STRENGTH. But strng where? Strong how? A term. Useful but debatable

So, Helene Grossberg?
So, Simon Sloan?
Mea Culpa, Helene Grossberg.
???Simon Sloan.
Latin. My fault, my sin.
You see? That's how you can be intelligent. That's why what you said is not becoming to YOU, it only is a demeaning of your intelligence.

Begin 2 chaps. on condtnd. neuroses. 15–20 min. quiz Thursday

Teitlebaum honey,
    As our personal relation is for me a very very dear thing I am having my Shimmy deliver this by hand
    And as there is enough sorrow in the world, you ought to read what Shmuel's Cousin Beshe wrote us from Liverpool, England, although who could read it, the German schools teach them to write so small, I asked her please please send me a small jar of a certain English candy, toffee, I'm still waiting, that's it and that's what it is with family
    And as I under different conditions would never fall on

you like I fell on you yesterday just because I found pits in 2 out of 6 black olives, you charged me for the pitted

And as anyway you must have figured Something something is probably bothering this party who has already had her rightful tragic share

And as you will anyway hear the whole whole story from Mrs. Harlib, How last night in the middle of Mr. Keene tracer of lost persons my Shmuel had to run down and beg her to pinch my cheeks on an emergency basis

And as it was only her pinches and GODS HANDS that brought me back to myself from what gave me such a terrible terrible grab, that last night was my MOTHERS birthday, she would have been 94, if she could see her Malvena doing the windows with a dropped stomach she would jump out from the grave to give me a help, not that I would let her, I'm just just the the right type to take advantage, a woman of 94 shouldn't do windows, Let her only sit and talk to my orphan loneliness it's enough, all right I know her how she likes to be useful, I would let her take my mattress on the roof to air out, in a dream I told her what the schvartzers charge for their few hours she couldn't get over it

> Yours truly Malvena the Orphan who will be seeing you very very soon with a coupon from Sweet Maid farmer cheese, it entitles the bearer to five cents off on the 6 ounce size and the grocer gets 2¢ for the handling, what kind of handling, we have time to talk about that

Still, still he is friendless, the youth.

In the cafeteria's eleven o'clock exile he smokes and waits, waits and smokes.

Between the milk bar and the salad counter he sits and offers himself.

"Take me, take me," is his silent plea to each table,

To each group which expropriates its own table.

With the YCL he sings along and happily signs their petitions.

Yet none, none amongst them know or care to know his name.

And there are the athletes
From whose mouths the nicest word that passes is
"Fuck!"
"I was in duh fuckin locker and I took a fuckin shower
And you know what dat fuckin Mutzi did?
He takes duh fuckin soap and he ties it in
Duh fuckin towel
An he gimme a fuckin smack on duh fuckin ass."
No, he is not of them—
Even as he is not of the newspaper bunch,
By Marx called 'Prostitutes of the pen,'
Smiling servants of the social order
Talking leads and captions, heads and subheads. . . .
Then where, where and with whom?
Well, one table there is
And toward this table he turns begging glance.
On pretext false he has squeezed past its chairs
And filled his eye with colors dazzling—
The colors of magazine covers,
Magazines called PARTISAN and POETRY and VANGUARD—
Here none seem to go to classes,
But sit long, long after bells and warning buzzers
Talking of Marx and Freud,
Contending, contesting.

Over the silver clatter the friendless youth hears "Kronstadt!"

Then "Kerensky!"

With cries of "Stalinist putz" and "Trotskyite renegade!" do they seek to wound each other.

A girl, inky-fingered, unwashed of neck and brassiere,

Gives the figures for cow and wheat production during the N.E.P.

And she is answered this, oh this she is answered:
"You are full of shit. . . ."
Then one, one there is,
Who in slowness studied
Folds, smooths and tickles out with finger tender
Each last pinch and crease and imperfection in his New
York Times
To say this, oh this is what he says:
"SCHMUCK!"
Of that one, of him,
Simon, friendless youth, must speak again. . . .

LOUIS UNTERMEYER
reads from
Selected American and British Poets
Friday, Oct. 1, 1941, Noon
1330 Science

Author: Bessie, Alvah C.   843.8
Title: Men in Battle   B 91
was due on 9/27. Failure to return this book by 10/7 will be
reported to office of Dean for disciplinary action as per PUB-
LIC EDUCATION LAW G499901A, City of New York.

Things to do
Jaffee Surgical Supply cor. Church & Flatbush   Bring in
Dad's truss.
Find out how much La Fouchette or Cantonese Joy
Buy Trojans

I, ———, a student of ———, am entitled upon presentation of this card to CARUSO RESTAURANT between Mons.
& Fris. to full course dinner at regular price and one (1) full
course dinner at half-price, dessert and beverage not in-
cluded. Management reserves the right to change or discontinue above offer WITHOUT PRIOR NOTICE.

327

October 2, 1941

Dear Mr. Sloan,

I want you to know you are a lucky young chap and that luck was with you I answered the phone and that it was not my husband (Mr.) Barney Grossberg. For without a doubt he would have let you have it and from him you would have heard words in your language type.

Heres what I dont understand, why such a chap as you, my understanding is of high intelligence and that you come from a home of Jewish people, has it in him that he would tell a young girl of my Helene's type what my husband would not dare to tell to me and I am a married woman, such was the joke type. My Helene's good friend Sharon who heard it, thank God she has a friend who tells me things, she started to write it down and I flushed it where it belongs.

Please come around no more and call again.

Please also do not think I wasn't informed that you were forcing my Helene to puff on your cigarette and be littled her that she doesn't want to turn into a smoker.

I remain yours etc etc
(Mrs.) Pearl O. Grossberg

Oct. 3, 1941

Dear Simon;

The occurence of my mother's letter is known to me. I in fact sought reaching of you for discussion at the candy store number you wrote down. A lady came to the phone and refused absolutely to take a message because she was an orphan. What to do now? *I* know that in the telling of the "joke" to me you had in mind a political reason and were attempting the further training of my political knowledge. *I* however am not so smart in the political field and when *I* tried to explain the inner meaning of the "joke" as you explained to to *me* I got lost. As you know I cannot tell "jokes," this joke especially which forced upon me the necessity of finding synonyms for "certain" words and expressions. My father wished to know where Russia came in and my mother, may I say her feeling regarding you hitherto was favorable, saw nothing humorous in the "joke." This is because she herself has been to doctors for reasons similar to the woman in the "joke."

Oh what a SIMON he is!

Oh will he learn his lesson ever and halt his propensity for coarse humor?

Thy Helene

Oct. 4, 1941

Dear Helene:

These lines I pen for thine and thy parents eyes.

Who, who can say what sorrowed grief was mine? Or how in lonely and long beach-walk I sought words of explication—and explanation. . . .

This, Mr. and Mrs. Grossberg, this I shall write as I have never written before. What little power of expression, what small talents I possess—may they be used to their fullest! For nothing I have ever written has carried with it such great stakes, such great hopes. Truly, truly I pray that when I have herein set down the last word you, Helene, will realize how far from my mind was any idea of prurience, and that your parents will show what a former and beloved rabbi of mine spoke of once as "justice tempered with mercy."

Had I known, known and foreseen the consequences of what was to follow from that moment when I took my customary cafeteria seat how happily would I have foregone my lunch! But I *did* take my seat, I *did* overhear what passed at the next table. . . .

Idly at first, then with greater interest, I commenced to observe one, one student whose eccentric appearance and manner had already come to my attention. His formidable powers of argumentation, his apparent ease in the area of politics, politics and literature would make him, I thought, a

329

fit subject for the few brief descriptive paragraphs requested by my English professor.

And thus, as an erstwhile writer, as a student of writing, I watched him, I listened to him. To me he was a challenge, a project, an assignment to be met and mastered even as I have sought to meet and master all of my assignments.

Thus, it was only clinical detachment that held me to my seat as in a manner loud, loud and coarse and vile—a manner, Mr. and Mrs. Grossberg, foreign and alien to my own nature—he fell upon one who saw the Moscow Trials and the destruction of the Trotskyite Conspirators as necessary, necessary and vital to the Soviet Union's security.

And he said this. This is what he did say. . . .

(Bear with me, Mr. and Mrs. Grossberg, as with reporter's candor and for record's sake I set down what must be set down.)

"Your position is to me fantastic. It is a fantastic position. It is so absolutely fantastic that to understand it, to grasp it, to break through your disordered and lunatic ravings I would need . . . I'll tell you what I would need. A whole course in the Russian novel and an attack of what they used to call in the 19th century BRAIN FEVER. Facts, logic—on you that would be absolutely an encumbrance. So let me therefore seek to reach the inner *yolt* with what I will call . . . you know what I will call it? . . . a left-handed Talmudic parable."

(Here, Helene and Mr. and Mrs. Grossberg, followed a definition of Talmudic parable so distasteful and offensive to my early Judaistic religious training that I shall expunge it.)

"There's this Mrs. Cohen, and Mrs. Cohen gives her husband trouble. From one thing she gives him trouble. She goes to doctors for SPECIAL INTERIOR HYGIENE TREATMENTS. From doctor to doctor she goes, from day to day, from treatment to treatment—and there isn't one, not one doctor for who she has a good word. Until. . . .

"Until one day she comes in happy, she's glowing, and

she tells her husband, 'Oy oy Izzie, I got such a doctor, he's giving me such wonderful treatment, oy I feel hundred percent an improving.' 'This,' her Izzie answers, 'I got see by myself on a looky-looky basis.'

"The doctor is called, the doctor gives them right away an appointment, they go. 'Come right in, Mr. and Mrs. Cohen,' says the doctor, who got on him a build like Johnny Weismuller, a face like Robert Taylor, a dimple like Clark Gable.

"The next minute Mr. Cohen watches while his wife gets behind one screen, the doctor gets behind another, and they both come out absolutely naked. Mrs. Cohen makes herself comfortable on the examination table while the doctor. . . .

(Here, Helene and Mr. and Mrs. Grossberg, followed a description of the principals, especially the doctor, in a highly stimulated state.)

"Mr. Cohen is watching, Mr. Cohen sees the doctor take a dab of medicine and apply it to his . . ."

(Ibid.)

"Next he sees the doctor blithely start in . . ."

(Op cit.)

"Mr. Cohen is quiet, he's absolutely quiet, he's speechless while Mrs. Cohen gets herself dressed. He pays the doctor, he shakes the doctor's hand, he goes with Mrs. Cohen into a taxi, and still he's quiet, he's absolutely speechless.

"They get home, Mrs. Cohen is happy, Mrs. Cohen is humming, Mrs. Cohen is giving him chicken soup, he eats the soup, he turns on the radio and still he's quiet, he's absolutely speechless.

"He turns off the radio, he puts on his pajamas, he gets into bed, he sets the alarm, he goes to sleep, and still he's quiet, he's absolutely speechless.

"He gets up in the morning, he takes a bath, he has a nice breakfast, he's ready to go to work.

"When all of a sudden he looks up, he looks down, he shakes his head and he says finally, 'I'll tell you something,

Beckie—if I didn't see him put on the medicine I'd never believe it!' "

And here, Helene and Mr. and Mrs. Grossberg, the narrator of the above, using many of the crudest Anglo-Saxon and Jewish words upon his hapless victim, drew a lengthy, exhaustive comparison between Mr. Cohen and all those who held and maintained their belief in the Moscow Trials.

I turn to you now, to you I turn, Mr. and Mrs. Grossberg, as honestly and sincerely and openly as I have turned and shall continue always turning to my own parents to ask these —these questions. . . .

Was I wrong to pass on to Helene this bawdy story—a story meant, intended to serve a political purpose?

Was I wrong to tell Helene—with whom I do not fear to share my deepest and most profound inner thoughts—that the issues and matters raised by the narrator were worthy of her consideration?

Was I wrong to use and employ this story, for all its vile vulgarity, as a means toward stimulating in Helene a desire to learn and read more concerning the Moscow Trials?

If your answer, Mr. and Mrs. Grossberg, is YES! to any of the foregoing questions then—then truly shall I know that I have erred and done wrong!

Sincerely,
Simon Sloan

P.S. May I say—nay, I shall say!—that no matter how you shall render your verdict I very, very much enjoyed that piece of *lokshen kugel.* If, if only you can find it in your heart to forgive me I know that my mother would love to share the secrets of your culinary art.

S.

Hunter Gals Rap Rapp-Coudert
Four Hunter College students yesterday costumed themselves as witches and broke up a college-wide chapel meeting when they swept down the aisle on brooms and shouted in-

sults at the Rapp-Coudert Committee which is currently investigating communist activity in the city's public colleges.

"A witch hunt is a witch hunt!" the four were heard to shout before being forcibly evicted from the chapel premises by a hastily summoned force of matrons. One matron, Candida Toscano, 48, is reported to have suffered a bruised ankle in her efforts to collar the girls as they shielded themselves behind a small group of sympathetic fellow students.

A spokesman for the college told the *News* that "the matter is under close study and will certainly result in proper disciplinary action up to and including expulsion and criminal prosecution of the four students." The four: Judith Langbitzer, 18; Marion Halevy, 18; Clare Dushler, 18; and Sheila Baron, 19.

Oct. 6, 1941

Dear Fine Writer and Sincere Person For Who I Will Have Waiting A Piece of *Lokshen Kugel* Any Time,

We in the Grossberg Family are pleased to say a simple WELCOME BACK to you.

The words to describe your letter I saw on the cover of a book that if you haven't read you should read, its Hatters Castle by AJ Cronin. The words are A HUMAN DOCUMENT.

Your letter I put in a special draw of treasure possessions. In this treasure possession draw I have my answers from famous authors, my hobby is to write them letters and you'd be very surprised that I get answers back from each author. I believe in coming years you will also be famous and be the author of books that they will put cover words A HUMAN DOCUMENT.

I remain yours etc etc
(Mrs.) Pearl O. Grossberg

P.S. I talked over with my husband (Mr.) Barney Grossberg and he agrees. Give my Helene stimulation in Russia as much as you want. But do not encourage her in puffing on

333

your cigarettes. This is a girl who when she was a kid was so sickly I had to make her milk and egg drinks.

Dear Professor Boynton:

Much thought have I given to the enclosed physical description which, I fear, is being turned in some three days late. May I ask—for the first time during my academic life—your indulgence?

Explanations, as you said at the term's outset, should be implicit in the work itself. Yet I feel compelled to explain that the enclosed theme represents the fruit—"bitter fruit," I am tempted to add—of many hours of work and of many drafts. And in the writing I fear that I may once again, alas, have overstepped the boundaries of the assignment, seeking to encompass within the confines of a few hundred words a character and a personality who merits treatment in some larger future work. I am troubled, too, by my definite inability to follow the stricture you so well set forth to Miss Rubin when you bade her "Universalize." For once again have I herein placed heavy, perhaps too-heavy reliance, upon my Judaistic background.

Now—now shall I be guided by your grade, your comments.

Cordially,
S.Sloan

I imagine him to be taller by the length of a Modern Library Giant than anyone else about his, his table. But I cannot be certain for not once have I seen him rise. And who, who can say what it would take to bring him to his feet? The collision of planets, the toppling of a social order, the voice of the Lord booming, thundering out of the Pepsi bottle from which he eternally swigs. . . .

All right, I make him out to be somewhat over six feet. Crumb flecks abound in his moustache, and there is in his hair natural oil in surfeit and abundance, as much, surely, as might be found in a large piece of lox.* (*Lox is a somewhat spicy delicacy enjoyed by Russians and other national groups, but especially by members of the Hebrew faith. Generically, it is referred to as smoked salmon.) Long, long are his hands, and these hover lovingly about a sweater whose greenish hue can be likened only to the greenish hue under his fingernails. "When, when will you clean those nails?" a fellow student was heard to ask. His reply? "I am waiting until I know definitely whether the monarchy will be restored in Russia. . . ."

For this, this is his verbal style. None there are who have yet bested him, though from day to day he is pitted against those who stand for all causes, all viewpoints. One by one and day by day they are destroyed, demolished—to a chorus of laughter loud and ribald.

And his cafeteria table is his court. Over it he presides like a king, like a rabbi, a wise and wonder-working rabbi of old. For who, who can withstand him when he puts aside his *Times,* when he takes his fortifying swig of Pepsi, when his eyes begin to glitter, his voice to rise in a powerful, a piercing "Schmuck!"*

*(This word, used generally as a noun, is derived from Judaistic language sources. Much of its meaning depends upon the tone and volume of the voice when uttered; in terms of my above usage a definition of *fool* or *stupid* is acceptable.)

Tell to Helene this
This
The closeness of our relationship grows   In mind spirit intellect attuned
Innermost thoughts & deepest desires shared
With above a physical attraction
It has grown, this phys attrctn aspect   First one breast five minutes   Now both brsts 15 mins. and with brassiere

hooks open   Limits I have not overstepped, exceeded, gone beyond

Have I disobeyed injunction and stricture?

Never

You have given stricture and injunction to not remove panties, not removed

Restraint and self-control utmost

When upon insertion of digit into aperture did I move manipulate wiggle digit?

Always a rigid digit

Her stand position logic of, ridiculous

That her parents would know

But of above they do not know?

They know

Give them high high praise

People of intllgnce, undstnding, dpth, boobooboo. Careful   On this work

Try "Helene, did they not, oh how could they not have suspected and surmised! When you acceded submitted consented to my digital request. . . ." HE WANTS TO SHUT THE LIGHT OFF, MOTHER I AM GOING TO LET HIM SHUT THE LIGHT OFF HE SHOULD LISTEN TO THE MUSIC BETTER

Try "Helene, nay Helene, I render to thy mother greater insight and depth. . . ."

Try from Marx concept of stagnant society   Lenin? Analogy   Human rltnshps must advance even as must society   Or slip back   And where WHEREFORE has ours advanced   As it was on first date so now   Basically

My physical sufferings (Euphemism for blue balls)

Try with art   My art has suffered   Knock off a poem on this

Sweet sweet Mrs. Grossberg

Believe me that tears are in my eyes and slight slight cramps in my dropped stomach from a condition which my Simon will tell you about when he brings you this, the reason he's bringing you this is not that I'm cheap for the 3¢

336

stamp, It's a very long story and not for now as to how come I have not same in the house, I used to go and buy them in bunches, Only we have a new super in our building with a little boy that is terribly sick from a nervous condition, And as I am the type who knows what it is to have a nervous condition my broken heart went out to the family, So the first first thing I did was I made an investigation and in my investigation I found out that the nervous little boy loves to save stamps, I ran right away downstairs with my whole bunch of stamps that he should save them for me for the next few weeks, I figured God would bless me for my action and he could save them better for me in his cellar as I am very very crowded in my draw space,

Anyway to tell you my feeling over the piece of lokshen kugel you sent this orphan is not for now, It will have to wait for what our president used to call Better Times, when I am back on my feet again and can reveal the truth of my many many sufferings in Hartford Connecticut, These sufferings gave me such an emotional crippling that even right now $26\frac{1}{2}$ years later I can't go near the oven to light it, Otherwise rest assured I would bake for you the farmer cheese cookies I used to bake for my whole whole family until I was done in and taken advantage of by a certain Cousin,

So let me say finally that I and mine who have in our time eaten many a lokshen kugel never never tasted anything like yours, I go down to our local merchant the Knishe Queen for her lokshen kugel, the midget size, I end up bringing back something I can describe to you in one word, the word is vicious, That is how dry her lokshen kugel is, What causes the vicious quality is that it comes from her takeout section very very badly wrapped and gets dry, For me to eat dry lokshen kugel is the worst worst poison on my dropped stomach, When I saw the way you wrapped up your lokshen kugel I was right away not worried and knew I was in the hands of an artist, Where you got yourself such wax paper I won't even ask, I had a wise wise mother, She would

337

say to me If you want to get along in life there are two two things you should never discuss, god and Wax Paper

Yours truly,
Malvena Sloan who was all set to invite you to her house this Sunday for a lovely lovely radio hour with Seymour Rechzeit if she had the extra chair back from a certain already mentioned Cousin, He borrowed it that his mother should have something to sit on for his boy Marty's briss, The boy is now a big shot doctor, He came to the house once and I was wearing a certain dress and on that certain dress the hem is always opening behind, He tells me Malvena you know your hem is open behind, The next day I got a bill $2 for diagnosis of a back condition, I shouldn't complain, that's it and that's how it is with family

Oct. 15, 1941

Dear Clare Dushler:
    How strange it is that
My Dear Clare:
    It may well seem strange
Dear Clare:
    Strangely, I had

We herewith return your <u>money order</u> in the amount of <u>one</u> (<u>1</u>) dollars.

Regretfully we are unable to fill your request for <u>two</u> (<u>2</u>) ticket(s) due to unprecedented demand at this time.

338

All of us in the PEOPLES CHORAL GROUP join in extending our sincerest regrets.

Be assured that we will attempt to bring MR. PAUL ROBESON back for another recital in the very near future.

Sloan, Simon
English 2.5
Professor Boynton
Theme # 3 Physical Description
    B++
    Let us observe rules for annotation. See
    my chap. V, *Turning in the Scholarly Paper.*
    Remember all foreignisms shld be at foot
    of page. Refs. must be numbered.
    (i.e. 2). *Schmuck,* a foreignism, der. Yiddish,
    pejorative, as
        "It is the feeling of many a scholar that
        Shakespeare's Polonius was in the main
        a *schmuck. . . .*"

Psych
Nervous system   All animal grps above level of sponges have nrvs systms   Some form of   In dffrnt ways they rspnd to STIMULI   By IRRITABILITY   This a unvrsl chrstic   A manifestation of irritblty is univ charactc of protoplasm   Proto detects change in envrnmnt   It will

Is he sorry?
No, he is Simon.
See, he is sorry. See, Helene is starting to know him and that when he kids he is showing he is sorry

Diffrnt organisms behave dffrnt ways to same stim   In fct the same stim may well effect higher organisms in diff ways   At diff times same stim may cause diff reaction in same orgnsm Depnds upon prcptn of

Oh was he a grumpy Simon. He didn't want to talk his Marx and he didn't want to talk his writing. Why was he in such a GRUMP mood?
You want to know why? I will TELL you why. . . .
NEVER MIND

Reflex arc is simple neural pathwy linking RECEPTOR and EFFECTOR Smple rspnses to stim   Example   Knee jerk   This invlves only

He thinks Helene is a dopey   But Helene is not a

dopey

She knows if she lets him do CERTAIN things he would want to do OTHER things
ONE ONE ONE 1 THING
His ONE thing was a pig thing

By chmcal mns rflxes frqntly altered   Example is what happens to frog leg when salt is

Did you ever see a pig do it? I never
AGAIN he is starting. His PROPENSITY for coarse humor

German scntst   Bernstein   In 1902 he dvlpd modern thry of nerve actn   Membrane theory   But little exprmntn to prove or disprve   Till 1933 when J Z Young found that squids wld

Oh is he depressed! Again he is depressed and is a grumpy Simon! Oh see how he looks! He looks like

Has ylded us mny sgnfcnt fndngs   Going back to cndtnd rflx we find it can be cndtnd and UNcndtnd   Dog who hrd bell saw food   But if bell rngs and NO food and NO reward dog stps

salivating   Bring food back later thn dg slvtes   To UNcndtn
we use sme process as to cndtn   Who knws if

Oh, see how he still looks grumpy! He is making Helene
look like

Helene can't stand that he is such a grumpy Simon. If he will
be nice I will read the Power Struggle and

&

And then Helene will do SOMETHING for her Simon.

Swear?

Not SWEAR! I do not like to swear. In these things a girl does
not swear. I promise a MAYBE. A WILL TRY.

Arises this spcultation   Cld we cndtion or uncndtion the

That I will CONSIDER it. That I will SEE
You don't don't have to SEE!
As a favor I have asked him stay away from such comments.
As a favor. He does not do me that favor why should I do
him a favor?

To reestblsh cndtng tks mch less tme thn to estblsh it   There
is sme conjctre that man is

And now he is angry. What is HE angry?
Because. FAVOR. Is it? Why is it?
AGAIN he starts. He wants to get me angry AGAIN.
Because. Your idea, your concept of favor. If I asked you to
render me complete total physical satisfaction it would be a
FAVOR.
It CERTAINLY would!
Or a favor would be to render me satisfaction by fellatio
means which I will show you STATISTICS how many girls
I will show HIM statistics how many girls jump off roof!

341

But what is such such a favor to render me satisfaction by manual manipulation means?

To ME that is a favor. To me if I handle something that makes me nauseous that is a BIG favor.

Freud's thrys on memry while of inrst lacks clncl tstng   We mst rmbr that if psych ever to be science it mst meet tests appld to other scncs   Objectve criteria whch

I explained and went into how to handle it. The object. Not even SEE it. On the outside with a handkerchief.
PLEASE

While Frd has contrbtd much we mst rmbr he is rprstve of one of svrl schls of psych   Each of these has mrts and poss fctrs of grt intrst

Do not make me THINK about it. If the opportunity arises MAYBE.

What will arise is not called an OPPORTUNITY.
He starts again. And again he starts!

Read: WOLF BOY
Turn in rslts of Equilibrium Tests   No Faking

Dear <u>Simon</u>
Café au lait, gateaux divers et légumes en vinagrette await you *chez nous*

November 3, 1941

8 PM

For that's the day and the hour we'd like you to join us in an evening of musings and memories *á la recherche du temps perdu.* Lets hear about your days and ways in <u>Brooklyn College</u> as we break out those old issues of the *Lantern.*

Do send along the enclosed card to tell us we can expect you for some Good Talk at

Les Soblers
Moish *et* Norma
Norma *et* Moish

342

Read

READ

READ!! !

Trotsky   The Revolution Betrayed

Lyons   Assignment in Utopia

Gide   Return from the USSR

Sidney Hook   anything

Oct. 23, 1941

Dear Helene:

Why, oh why art thou angry?

And must thy Simon suffer for the sins of others?

I know, oh well I know the crudeness, the common coarseness, the loose, foul, vile, and vulgar tongue of Irv Bernardick.

In fact, what was his first word to me?

"Schmuck!"

And his next words?

"It is the privilege of youth to be callow but you—you abuse the privilege!"

A moment later I, who had signed a YCL petition, was bade, called, summoned to his table.

There, seeking to marshal, marshal and muster all my knowledge, my resources, I nevertheless fell silent before his onslaught.

As he showed me how the Bolsheviks have obscured with the carbuncles of history the true nature of the Russian Revolution.

As he showed me how Lenin overthrew a democratic, democratic and truly Socialist government.

As he showed me how the Bolsheviks never permitted free, free and open elections, how at bayonet point they forced out a government which had received 75% of the popular vote.

And though it has been barely, barely two weeks since that day I have learned this. This have I learned. . . .

That Irv's is, essentially and in the main, a tender spirit. That in his way he suffers, suffers deeply over the follies and

M

foolishness of mankind. That he will hurl insult, insult and vituperation only upon those whom he likes. . . .

And it is because he likes, likes you and cares for you, because he was hurt by your defense of PM's definitely pro-Soviet position and stand that he called you "Nitwit pussy." Also he made clear to me his high regard for the manner of your reply and retort when he said to you, "Go eat a mallomar" and you gave him swift and speedy answer "Right away!"

Thy Simon

Irv's joke
Tell Grossbergs

News send reporter to interview Schwartz, oldest living man in Brownsville. 105. "Mr. Schwartz, as the oldest living man in Brownsville we want to get the story of your life." "Gledly, gledly. Came to America 1900, worked as hah pretsser pretssing pents. For hahtempted unionizing mine boss got me such hah beating I was in hospital 14 months on the calendar. I come out, I send for mine vife and mine 6 children. With mine family we open up dry goods store. Burns in two weeks the store with 6 children plus wife. Next 12 years I put together a few dollars as waitner until I spill soup on a gengster who gives me such hah beating I'm a crippled hunchback until year 1920. 1920, I go back hah pretsser pretssing pents, slips on me the iron, brings terrible terrible inflection. For recuveration I make a Western oil field trek, thank God I discover a pinch oil, comes again a fire burns me out with second wife plus second set 6 children. And again I'm hah pretsser pretssing pents. 1929, depretsson, I sell coal from hah coal wagon, trolley runs into wagon, wagon runs into truck, truck runs into restaurant, kills 12 people, they sue from all 12 sides. I come out from hospital, again I'm crippled up, got not even a pot to piss in, I'm on relief now.it's 9 years."

Reporter writes it down, photographer takes picture, they thank him, they start to go. Schwartz stops them.

344

"Dunt forget in your story you should write vun important thing—America has been to me a vunderful country!"

Trip
The Trip
RETURN TRIP

Two old revolutionaries talking. What they suffered under Czar. How they got exiled to Siberia. Cold and hunger, hunger and cold. For sake revolution. For sake democratic socialism. What sustained them through cold and hunger, hunger and cold? Chess games they used to play. Both great players. Final game they were supposed to play. For championship. Came revolution. Both freed.

"Perhaps now—now we shall play that final game," said Petrovich.

"Ample will be our opportunity," retorted Sharkinov, with a long, long and strident laugh.

Ending—that again they're going to Siberia.

Try short short story markets.

Sloan, S.

It has been reported to our office that you are delinquent in the return of following supplies:

One (1) towel 404661 A

Please arrange for an appointment with Dean Sullivan before 10/28/41

BRING THIS NOTICE WITH YOU!

Dr. J.N. Connersy
Dean of Men

sr/jnc
ref.404661A

Things to do
Dad's truss   MOE Kaufman, the brother   For HIM ask
Grossbergs to Night of Stars   WHEN find out
Buy Trojans
Remind H—5 minutes on both tits   By HER watch

345

J'attenderai . . . .

Je regrette . .^x. . . .

Getting In
What Irv says

To get into *shikse* easier. But *shikse* has to be crtn type.
LIBERAL SHIKSE To get into libshik use (a) Guilt ("After what
YOUR people did to MY people. . . !) (b) Eroticism, Jewish
skill in ("It's all in the wrists. Jewish knack. From 5000 years
of grating *latkes*.")

For Jewish girl (a) Praise *shikses* ("With Jewish girls I
never secured, enjoyed sexl flfllment.") (b) Work on their
mothers ("Go, go ahead Mrs. Cohen, hurt my feelings, you
want to hurt my feelings! My flngs will get hurt if you don't
let me take out garbage.") (c) Wash her hair—Scalp of J.
girls very big erogenous zone (d) Carry around applctn to
med school ("Years and yrs of hard work. How can I ask you
wait, withhold ntrl blgcl appetites.") (e) Talk about wall to
wall carpeting ("You like ww crptng I like ww crptng we
both like ww crptng you'll see how I'll get you ww carpeting. . . .")

Oct. 24, 1941

Dear Simon;

Oh will he get angry at this!

Oh will he be a grumpy Simon!

But thy Helene can not help it.

She knows how much he was looking forward to IT.

To show him how her intentions were she is enclosing a
pink facial tissue from the box she had bought; in fact, her
mother who is far from a dope and saw this box wanted to
know why it is needed if we have an uncle in the ladies
handkerchief line who gives us a dozen boxes at a time.

This tissue is highly absorbent and thy Helene will say no more about what it was going to absorb.

Also thy Helene had a rubber glove put away in a galosh.

What is more important is that she was Conditioning her Reflexes and was on the verge of overcoming her natural prejudices to the manual performance.

Now try to understand and bear with thy Helene in thy intelligent and sensitive and well read personality.

Last night when thy Helene had her reflex perfectly conditioned her mother had to be rushed in a house dress to the hospital. She held thy Helene's hand in the taxi and used it to stroke upon her cheek; it was her belief that this stroking took away her severe pain. In fact she even kept saying and saying to me, "Tartehlaw, your stroking makes me feel better, Tartehlaw, stroke a little more." And thy Helene was thinking only Oh, it is the same hand!

That Un-conditioned the reflex.

More important to thy Helene who loves her mother very much was the diagnosis of a kidney stone; though we are not highly religious people thy Helene sees this as what she once learned when she took Commercial Law, AN ACT OF GOD.

In the hope that thou willst see and view it in the same warning light and not "chipper" me too much I am

Thy Helene

P.S. If he will not look like 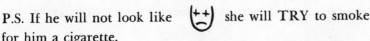 she will TRY to smoke for him a cigarette.

Oct. 25, 1941

Dear Mr. Simon Sloan,

The accumulated total of twenty-seven (27) dollars is your rightful share from our childhood Battle Aces S.A.C. years and will be shortly mailed to you by postal money order.

Be informed that I am holding in escrow the sum of two (2) dollars for the reason that my friend Herman Foner will be the honored guest at a forthcoming surprise party occasioned by his pending enlistment two weeks from now into the Coast Guard. Should the contribution of same be to you unsatisfactory please inform. This two (2) dollar sum will go toward the cost of a cake and gift which we are not as yet decided on. You are of course naturally invited to this and I hope you will see your way toward attendance on behalf of a fellow who I recall got into a fight many years ago with Sal Puzello* when you were picked upon.

Very Truly Yours,
Abraham Liebert

*P.S. He and two ginzos grabbed your hat, they were playing sallugee with it.

Sweet sweet Mrs. Grossberg

I am having my Simon give to your Helene this jar of the Lofts sour balls as he will get it to you in good condition, I was warned by a man who used to work in the post office not to not to put it through the mail as they took in lately a certain worker that he's partly paralyzed, let him handle somebody else's sour balls,

So pass your stone very very soon, if you wait too long it can rip out the whole kidney lining, Also don't worry if the jar has a slightly slightly empty look, you'll notice on the label bottom in small print it says DUE TO HANDLING AND PROCESSING THE CONTENTS OF THIS JAR WILL SOMETIMES SETTLE

Yours truly
Malvena the Orphan
who begs you that if you can
please please remember try to
save the rubber band around the
jar cover, it happens to be something
very very precious to me
as it is all I have left from the
set my mother in law gave me
for my engagement

Hist. 1.1

Black Death   A terminal point   Histns divided   Will prbbly never agree whether was high pnt of Drk Ages or low pnt of Rennsnce   But this we know   Black Death actlly was Bubonic Plague   So called from BUBOES or underarm swellings   like knobs

Tell her Irv was paying her highest compliment   By not not handling her with kid gloves

From East it came   Rched 1st Sicily in 1347   3 yrs later killed nearly hlf popltn Europe

By treating her as equal   By talking to her not as a TYPICAL BROOKLYN BOURGEOIS JEWISH GIRL

Disaster so total no msrng   No records as are now   Can only gss   A fmly wped out, a vllge   Crpses piled up in stacks and burned   There is a desc of how Pope Clem. VI

What he said prhps wrng   In WAY he said or phrased it But you wrng too   Because u dont dont start bopping guy with paper   Could take eye out   Left him with v bad red mark

BD defly wkned athrty of Chrch   Bcse people saw GOD'S hand   Could not understand how they sinned   Or why priests also died   For first time prhps sensed an equality in justice   Or injstce   But these only guesses   They

Definitely Irv was good natured   Not many many people would be so   You bop him, he just just sits   Being bopped didnt bother him—But you bopped him with PM

BD prbably hastened demise of feudal systm   Pple no longer fixed to land   Labor scarce   Could no longer

What did he anyway say so so terrible Do YOU HAVE
TZOORIS WITH YR CLITORIS A scientific trm In every dict
Show her
In Cmbrdge Mdvl Hist two chaps on BD By ZIEGODORN,
best for mass of detail

27 Oct. 1941

Comrade Si,

A certain actor of the jewish stage that must be dead
twenty years well and long before your time used to have
a line in his each show

Favor me a favor

So I now ask you as friend to friend

Favor me a favor

This favor will be easy to you, it will not be I WANT you
to do something for me, it is I do NOT want you to do
something for me

In general I do not butte in and I never butte in! When
do and did I butte in? I dont prove all your ideas and what
you have against FDR I am not smart to figure, if you remembered where there was no hope he put hope in you
would feel like me more and want to kiss his dirty soks.
Probably I was worse then you in my time, nothing he did
Woodrow Wilson pleased me.

The thing I want you to NOT do, the favor I want you to
favor me is

Dont go yourself and dont take Helene to that church
which is my understanding of your mutuel plans.

Fourbid is not in my diktionary but here I would like to
fourbid because what little jewish religion I posess now is
sickening me at the thought that my child pays them that
respect, to listen to there holy music. She tells me you say
its wonderful music. Fine, its wonderful music. Let them
drop dead with there wonderful music. On our high holy
days we also have wonderful music, I will put our kol nidre
beauty as sung by a 1st class cantor to anything they got, do
you see them coming into a synagogue?

350

Your friend Leo Trotsky, I notice all of a suden hes your friend lately, is a case of what happens when you go forget your little jewish religion, For a while this guy was at the hiest hites, where is he now? He forgot who he was and what he was, they told him.

Take the closed $3 my pleasure and go with Helene to the best picture show of your choyce. Road to bali is in the paramount, go. Youll get a good laugh.

Best personal regards
(Mr.) Barney Grossberg

Directions rent party
70 Perry St get off with IND Sheridan Sq. From 14th 1 local stop Last car take Ask for NICK'S From Nick's only 2–3 blocks No # on bldng Red brick, the only one Apt 19 FARBSTEIN don't ring downstairs, broken
Bring something!!
Have to!!
Bottle wine best thing CHIANTI
69¢ half gall VENTURA or DE ROSELLI
Tell Helene this
This tell her

NO HI HEELS!!

29 Oct. 1941

Dear bad influence,
Do we in the Grossberg house hold treat you so bad you should bring a girl home so late and in such bad condition? One heel is broke off altogether, this is from an eleven $ I. Miller Shoe, and my velveteen evening bag where the tissue paper still was in the change purse is going to the super's wife.
Let me hear why a chap of high intelligence takes a girl up six flights into a cold water flat to give her a good time? I can tell you plenty about cold water flats, I was brought up in one, all you have to do is write my story of those days for

351

A HUMAN DOCUMENT. The same early life was led by my husband (Mr.) Barney Grossberg who has lingering chronic rheumatism from when he had to bathe in the hall and who swore his children would have better. That is why we stay in Flatbush, the best air in the world is right here, that is why we took an expensive apt. in one of the first elevator buildings they put up around here. Don't think you have to live like a slob to be a fine writer, I have a letter from KATHLEEN NORRIS, it came on stationary my husband swore had to cost nine $ a hundred and maybe even more.
Now I will close to let my husband put in a few words.

I remain yours etc. etc.
(Mrs.) Pearl O. Grossberg

PS I dont butte in and I never butte in! What I wanted to tell you only is youll walk up 6 flites or youll walk up 106 flites, the Esquire is not taking your storys one day sooner.
Best personal regards
(Mr.) Barney Grossberg

〜〜〜〜〜 lecture from the bench Judge Frowley told the four Hunter students they had "behaved themselves shamelessly and without the slightest regard for their parents, for their city which was providing them with this free education, or the country whose way of life they seemed to despise."

He sentenced the four to write a 5000 word essay on the American way of life and on how the Constitution "fostered and protected it."

Upon pronouncement of the sentence one of the four, Clare Dushler, 18, was heard making a long sustained noise. When asked by Judge Frowley if this noise was meant to be a Bronx cheer she answered, "Yes, it is known by that name."

Judge Frowley thanked her for the information and promptly sentenced her to write another 5000 words essay on the history of the Bronx.

Dear Clare
    How long, long and far back seem
Dear Clare:
    Far back and long, long ago we two
Dear Clare Dushler:
    From the distant and long gone past, from the time when
we two

Things to do
Dad's truss
Helene's birthday toilet water (?) or T.S. Eliot (?)
Irv's house for Bessie Smith records   Work with him on my
bsc anti-Stlnst argmnt
    Stlnst will say YOU CAN'T MAKE AN OMELETTE WITHOUT
BRKNG EGGS
    I answr SCHMUCK, SO DON'T EAT OMELETTES

                                              Nov. 1, 1941
Dear Irving Bernardick;
    You are such a terrible tease that though I am beginning
to grow used to it and to take it in stride (Notice that I am
past the stage of being upset by your continuous raising of
my dress and offering to buy me an egg cream) I have asked
Simon to kirdly give you this INVITATION to my BIRTHDAY
PARTY. In this way there is lesser risk that you might utter a
joking witticism to hurt my feelings.
    The party will be at my home this FRIDAY night. I men-
tion FRIDAY night for the good reason that our family is a
somewhat ORTHODOX family where we do not on this night
and until Saturday sun down use the electric lights. Though
I am not in agreement with my parents on this I RESPECT
them and give them this little bit they ask of me. I know you
will do the same WITHOUT remarks. Aside from not using the
electric lights my parents do not mind about anything else
and we will be able to play the radio and put the phonograph on.

O this birthday girl nearly forgot!

You will be seeing my best friend, Sharon Einfargel, who has heard about you only the GOOD things. Sharon has a wonderful sense of humor, which does not mean to right away become vulgar with her, and she is a music major who can talk about ANY band as much as you like. She plays the accordion and has done so last summer in the mountains. Take my word that Sharon does not need on her behalf my efforts to meet a person, and has many boys. While not a RAVING BEAUTY, which very few of us are, she is highly attractive. If there are any problems on her part they have to do with a height complex because she is five feet nine inches. You will tower way over her and the two of you can have a most pleasant evening. That is provided you do not attack her as a PM LIBERAL, you will find her even stronger than I am for PM.

O finally a last favor, a favor I know you will enjoy performing.

Absolutely do NOT eat a supper before you come! Hold out! If you get hungry before you shall arrive have a small little "Narsh" to hold you! I can not begin an adequate description of all the awaiting food, including a whole ton of Isaac Gellis cold cuts

Affectionately (I think)
(Miss) Helene Grossberg

P.S. PLEASE do not utilize to Sharon your favorite word. I happen to be already used to it from you, she is not and would "Karlish" away.

P.P.S. Also do not say anything against Y.C.L.; she is a nonactive member mostly because it helps her in learning the guitar.

For Helene
Of whom a poet has written
Let us go then you and I
While the evening is spread out against the sky. . . .

May the scent of these toilet waters
Sweeten her path through life!

Thy Simon

Teitlebaum honey

What do you say and what do you think?

What is going to be with the brave norwegian people, I get very very sick when I think of whats going to happen to them, GOD should only only spare them and the person who loves' freedom should never forget their tragedy

Thats why in their name and for their memory Im requesting in a very very nice way you should take back this can of King Oscar Sardines on the ground that I have 21 cans already of same, I will always always bless Mrs. Harlib, she came in to ask maybe I have an empty matzo box, otherwise Id never never go open the linen closet

Yours truly
Malvena the Orphan
who doesn't know yet how an
a & p deposit bottle got mixed
in with your deposit bottles, its
definitely the dirty work of
somebody from my building that
if I whispered her name you
would immediately remember
what I did for her when she
moved downstairs to 3AA, but
thats how it is and thats what it
is with neighbors.

Irv's joke   Work into basic anti-Stlnst argmnt

Who has biggest prick in the Kremlin?

Who?

Russian people.

Give Irv directions H's house

Remember bring EASY MONEY & PICK UP STICKS

TYPE instructs. for GHOST

M*

Dear bad company keeper,
Please educate this party.
Keep me up in the world
Who is this PHYLLIS STEIN?
I know Sharon Einfargels mother for many years, she is in my mah jong group, also she is an associate national vice chairman in the Jewish Womans Council. This is a modern person, she held her own once with Rabbi Stephen S Wise and got our group to see TOBACCO ROAD, this was our first non musical since OF THEE I SING where we got misled by the name. What I bring out is here is a clever woman of some vocabulary who knows every name in cross words but in all her life never heard of a Phyllis Stein.

I can think of only that she has something to do with AJ Cronin because I was praising to your friend HATTERS CASTLE and he said to me how in years he hasnt met such a PHYLLIS STEIN.

From a normal chap I wouldn't see umbridge. But your friend showed right away he belonged to the nut class by what he did, he takes in both hands half a pound corn beef, this was the fatty end, and then he wipes the hands on my drapes. I said to him do you know that just to clean those drapes cost me $33.95. He answers I dont like to hurt your feelings but they ruined the pleats.

More on him and his birthday party actions is forth coming from my husband (Mr.) Barney Grossberg.

I remain yours etc. etc.
(Mrs.) Pearl O. Grossberg

Comerade Si,
Its not your fault and still I hold you responsible.
I do not butte in and I never butte in except your palzy walzy comes over to me a deprived person.
Because only a deprived person asks in a strange kitchen

do you have some chulent, where an American Boy hears about chulent I dont know because it goes back well and long before your time. When Pearl (Mrs Grossberg) answered him in a sarkastik way is there any thing else you want he says make me hard eggs, she had to make him in the middle of a party hard eggs. Also he was annoyed that he wanted coffee and she told him we use in our house POSTUM only.

Maybe you can tell me what hapened after the POSTUM, we dont know and its like we went down under ether. Only 2 words I remember, I remember fantastik and 1913 1913 and fantastik. You left and Sharon left and every body left and I set the alarm and I helped clean away and I folded the bridge chairs and its still 1913 and fantastik and fantastik and 1913. We (Mrs Pearl O. Grossberg and me) excuse ourselves and we get in bed he gets in bed with us and again 1913 and fantastik fantastik and 1913. What I did to him I never before did, I bums rush him out of the Grossberg house hold, next time your here youll take back his sweter it was so filthy we had to tip the super to do us a favor wrap it.

Best personal regards
(Mr.) Barney Grossberg

PS Pearl (Mrs) Grossberg wants to tell you that to make chulent is an all day job and you have to take meat and carrot and potater and they have to tsimmer, its not for an active woman of modern intrests.

November 6, 1941
Dear Mr. and Mrs. Grossberg:
Simon says he'll be seeing you tonight, so I'm giving him this book which he can put directly into your hands.

You will note herein how Meshnikoff makes, in essence, the very same points I made—namely that it is absolutely fantastic how in the Stalinist revision of history the figures for steel and coal production, to say nothing of the total of

357

new acreage put under cultivation during 1913, have been completely and deliberately and absolutely distorted.

Where Meshnikoff goes wrong, and this is to me an absolutely fantastic fallacy, is in his utter refusal to project even further the 1913 figures he so accurately cites for meat and potato production.

I mention these last two items in the hope that you will be making chulent on my next visit.

Cordially,
Irving Bernardick

Things to do
New story idea   A german Communist   JWSH finally fnally escpes Htlr, escps conc camp, gets to Svt Union   Jst Jst in time for PACT
Note to Boomie vry vry polite all gd luck to Hymie I wish grt time in Cst Grd boobooboo alas pressure of studies and wrtng prvnt me frm

Nov. 9, 1941

Dear Simon;

Dost thou miss thy Helene as verily much as she misses thee? And didst thou find out yet what she got in Psych since she still feels she did not do so well on the last part?

Well the way it definitely looks we will all stay on, except Daddy, a few days more in Baltimore because my Aunt Pearlie has not come yet to herself. As Mommy says, and here I agree with her, "these things have to take time." What I would like to do is to have Aunt Pearlie come back with us after her "shiver" is over even though I know for the next eleven months it is against the religion to go to things like shows or movies. But even if we took her merely to A & S it would be the biggest of "mitz voors."

And talking of "mitz voors" perform one for me please by eliminating from your vocabulary the word FRIGID. I have known you for not even a three month period while my Uncle Heshie I have known all my life. In the consideration of my forthcoming seven hour train ride what you should have said out of RESPECT for me was, "Helene, I want you to forget about it; Helene it is too much bother; Helene you have to do packing; Helene you have enough on your hands; Helene there will be another time; Helene it is not running away, it will be there next week."

Instead you went away from the house in a terrible grump mood looking like ☹ and leaving me with such cramps that I could not rest until I had looked the word up. I did so, and this is what I found, that FRIGID pertains in usage to person or persons who toward a sexual stimulus does not make ADEQUATE RESPONSE. Well I think you will recall a CERTAIN night where you stretched out of shape my good bra. Do you recall that you said to me is it nice, Helene, is it good, Helene, and I said its all RIGHT. That was my truthful RESPONSE and to me it was ADEQUATE. You should have dealings with such as my friend Sharon, the girl could be in a movie or she could be in a subway, she will think nothing of giving a boy who starts up a real "Frosk" in the face with her silver fox collar.

Anyway I forgive you and if you write me a long letter I will MAYBE once again feel "Let us go then you and I

> While the evening is spread out
> against the sky!"

Thy Helene

P.S. Mommy says that because you are such a good writer you could send a little note of condolence to my Aunt Pearlie. YOU it will take a minute!

November 10, 1941

Schmuck!

You don't deserve it.

It is absolutely not coming to you.

For your fantastic inability to grasp the implications of the fate of the Fisheries Section in Solvetzki I should show you the same *rachmones* Trotsky showed the Kronstadt sailors.

I offer you instead the greatest pair of tits ever produced in Thomas Jefferson, a lover of big cocks and little magazines, a real intellectual twat who goes through phases like the moon. When I honored her with a Bernardick bang or two she was at the time hot to translate Sholem Aleichem. She stopped putting out because I said to her in a nice way, "You crazy cunt, how can you translate *Sholem Aleichem* if you don't even know Yiddish!" Then I heard she became a Marxist. Then I heard she became a Freudian. Then I heard she became absolutely stark raving *meshugeh;* what happened was she tried to do a synthesis of Marx and Freud and she found out she would have to first read Marx and Freud. She is now IN analysis. Which I will repeat because I am dealing with a *shmuck*. She is IN analysis. She is not *going* for analysis, she is not *taking* analysis, she is not *having* analysis, she is not *under* analysis. She is IN analysis.

From here we shall move on to the vertical pronoun. You will say now, and with absolutely fantastic conviction, "*I* am in analysis, I've *been* in analysis, I shall *continue* in analysis." Who, *shmuck,* is your doctor? My doctor? Why, my doctor is Dr. Norton Feigenbaum. I am in analysis *with* Dr. Feigenbaum. He is my analyst, I am his ANALYSAND.

Thus are you built up to Tashka Dorfman. I have further fed her hints of a nine inch dong and a lifetime subscription to *Southern Review*. She awaits you with such a passion of pure reason that she has already uncapped her tube of vaginal cream. Naturally, you will need a few nice symptoms, dreams, significant details—couch or chair, leather or cloth, towel or tissue for the head. Which I will provide tomorrow night. *If* you return my copy of *Their Morals and Ours*. That is no kidding around; I WANT it.

Yours,
I. Bernardick, P.N.S.P.
(Predictor of the Nazi-Soviet Pact)

Nov. 13, 1941

Dear Simon;

So?

Art thou still (⁺⁺☹) ? I have a feeling thou art.

Mommy says if and when you write a condolence to Aunt Pearlie you should try to mention how Uncle Heshie was so active for Benny Brith.

Thy Helene

P.S. Most likely it is ending up that we will not take Aunt Pearlie back with us. It would not work out because when it comes to meat she buys from only STRICTLY KOSHER and we are frankly not that particular.

november 16, 1941

dear simon sloan—

    I write your name and feel o so much

    S

     O

       M

      U

       C

      H

as e.e. cummings might put it.

O Christ, Christ, the thought of your body upon my body exploring what d.h. lawrence has called 'those dark secret passional places!'

Myself, tashka dorfman saying, as molly bloom has said, 'o yes yes yes yes'

      conjugating like verbs
      coupling like trains
             (mine, t.d.)

    But I-WE can't
    For I told doctor loebler about you
        your anal/oral/ego/id

Look, without bullshit he said with those symptoms I shouldn't screw around with you.

Liked-liked what you you read to me of your writing. Can I still send a batch of poems when you get that mag going?

tashka

Nov. 17, 1941

My Dear Mrs. Lefkowitz:

Words seem hardly adequate to describe my emotions when I heard the sad news about your husband's passing.

Though I did not have the good fortune to know him personally, the love and the high esteem in which he was held by Helene and Mr. and Mrs. Grossberg could scarcely help but prove contagious.

Your loss is shared by your family, your many friends— and by B'nai Brith and the many many other great civic and humanitarian causes to which he so very very generously gave of himself.

Compassionately,
Simon Sloan

A DATE TO REMEMBER
November 19, 1941
when the
HILLEL CLUB OF BROOKLYN COLLEGE
presents
Rabbi Arthur K. Belker
author, *Why the Jewish Center?*
speaking on
NEW DIRECTIONS IN AMERICAN-JEWISH
COMMUNITY ORGANIZATION
REFRESHMENTS ONEG SHABAT SERVICES

Basic anti-Stlnst argmnt

Stlnst will say Red Army's heroic boobooboo resistnce agnst Hitler shows wisdom Stalin policies

I will say Absolutely definitely right right right. And

what happened with Npln in 1812 shows wisdow of CZAR policies.

Teitlebaum honey

Your ears must be burning because last night I was talking about you, Cousin Phillie came over and he threw up to me how right right after my mother died he told me my house is your house, I didn't tell him Sure, why not, you had there all my mother's furniture, what I said was Phillie Phillie life is too too short for such concerns, Ill tell you what Teitlebaum tells me, Forgive forget ignore dont worry over every every little nonsense, realize and understand youre not alone in the world, if you cant say something nice bite your tongue, youll never never go wrong looking away, instead of getting all steamed up you should always always look away, thats why yesterday I just just looked away a second to see on what scale your wife was weighing my chicken carp so you slipped me in a sickly jersey jumbo, this is something even Hitler wouldn't have the heart to do, he would show more appreciation for the kind of customer who gives him such an order, the order came to 97¢ first after you took off for the deposit bottle

Malvena the Orphan who wants to remind you of whats going on and whats happening in the world, Ill say the way Irving Berlin says, America mustnt mustnt be next, Which reminds me that where is it your business and how is it your business to butt in if Im having a little spat, it wasnt even an argument, with Mrs. Wachtels daughter, She says shes next and I say Im next

Psych

Spoke 1st time abt bhvr pttrns   They occur in rspnse to
stim detected by the STIMULI RECEPTORS   But lets exam role
of stimulus that triggers bhvr pttrn   Why do orgnsms rspnd
to some stim but not others   Why do they DISCRIMINATE
Take case of hen whn she hrs distress calls of her chick

So Simon Sloan?

if her chick is in trble hen is oblivious unless hen hears its
call   Chick might be in full vw of hen   Struggling and
endngrd   Even so hen wnt react until

So Simon Sloan?

or driving an auto man will see mny objects   tlphone poles,
hses, grass, trees   He does not rspnd to all   To whch ones
does he rspnd? To RELEASING MECHANISMS which initiate his
bhvr   Still not enough knwn abt these to

Simon, do you want me to say I enjoyed it? I will in that case
say I enjoyed it. I ENJOYED it!!!

delay statistical analy thgh attmpts made to

I enjoyed it in a WAY. If you ask me in WHAT way I would
say I could not say.

much actn oftn seems irrlvnt   During process of mkng
dcsns people crack knuckles drum fngrs on desks doodle
Called DISPLACEMENT ACTIVITY   I.e., an actn prfrmed in
wrong context   Smthng which had to be done cld nt be
done at prper tme   The actn is thn DISPLACED   In hmn
bhvr this rvls a great

You know why I didn't really enjoy it?

if an animal to survive & fnctn cant pssbly rspnd to all stim
it rcvs   If it did there

Because it is hard work. Because it is not AT ALL like what
you said and the motion is ALTOGETHER different.

all of the anmls energy wld be wasted in random and fruit-
less actns & it cld not pssbly fnctn or adapt itself to speclzed
needs & envrnmntl chnges

Where does it come to rinsing stockings? That is what took
so long. I kept thinking RINSE A STOCKING RINSE A STOCKING
and it is more CHOP AN ONION CHOP AN ONION.

in this way the species is cntnd   Stability insured   Psychic
enrgy gets chnnled twrd basic drives

THEN first he is not satisfied. THEN first he gets an arousing.

othrwse species because of inablty to differentiate would
suffer frm ACUTE ANXIETY

So Simon Sloan?
So Helene Grossberg?

and be rendered incpble

I am curious if you have ANYTHING ELSE to say to me.
What what should I say?

smtmes PSYCHOTIC

Never MIND! ! ! ! !

Nov. 21, 1941

Helene:
    I miss thee.

365

Why dost thou flee me down the labyrinthine ways?

Why dost thou behave to me like ignorant armies that clash by night?

Hast thou forgotten and dost thou no more wish to see together *Mrs. Miniver?* Then. . . .

Let us go then you and I
While the evening is spread out against the sky. . . .

Thy Simon

nov 23

Simon
   sigh man
I know what it is to resolve an oedipal

(edible)

conflict

and under different circumstance I'd say o come and let's have a good screw on it. but that's the nite I start recorder lessons.

tashka d

Nov. 25, 1941

Dear Mr. Sloan,

Sharon Einfargel has been gracious enough to pass on to me her report of the fact that you lately are "Chapping" her with inquiries pertaining to my welfare.

In answer I might say that while I of late have been suffering a depression over my disappointment in individual persons and their failure to surmise and figure out what is behind a girl's mood change, I have "snapped out of it." Due to the forcing of Sharon, who has during this period proved herself a loyal and true blue person, I managed even to go to the movies. As usual she was quite right, for *Mrs. Miniver* got my mind to some extent off "things."

I do not know what to say and reply in answer to Sharon's report of what I consider an accusation, namely that I am acting in a "Bourgeois" way. If that is the case the best answer I can make is to repeat the words of Sharon. "That is just too bad." Maybe you would be happier if I went out to overthrow a few governments.

I remain yours etc. etc.
(Miss) Helene Grossberg

Basic anti-Stlnst arg
Stlnst will say if Stln went in for minor excesses it was for good reason, to get USSR prepared.
I will say if I'm a dentist and I squeeze yr nuts it's also for good reason, to get you to open yr mouth

November 26, 1941
Dear Simon,
Though my mother somehow mistook your name for Cohen I remembered you immediately.
Alas, what can I say? The exigencies of history, I fear, oft require of us a certain ruthlessness. I therefore see no point in renewing "old acquaintances."

Best,
Clare

Nov. 29, 1941
Dear Simon,
As per my promise I spoke to Helene on your behalf.
She was furiously angry at first that I showed toward you any sympathy and maintained that irregardless of the fact that you were "hocking and hocking" at me I should simply let you "plots."
But thanks to my prevalance and that Helene is basically a "zoosir" person she agreed to let me give you this hint.
The hint is that her recent actions toward you are because she was awaiting a "certain" suggestion on your part. I pointed out to her that you might well take this in the wrong light, as from what I know you have been already too suggestive. I have therefore her permission to tell you that the

N*

367

suggestion can be stated in three words and that the three words are AFTER the word "Let's" and begin with these three initials, G S M, with a stress on the S.

You can do me this favor. Tell your friend that if I am a Stalin-oid he is an aden-oid.

Optimistically and Hopefully
Sharon Einfargel

P.S. Tell your friend that as a future psychology minor I am genuinely sorry for him and definitely do not hold him entirely responsible for his remarks about Max Lerner.

Nov. 30, 1941

Dear Sir,

I think it is only fair to tell you that the suggestion which Sharon Einfargel passed on to you as having the word "Let's" and then afterwards the initials G S M could occur to you in the form of "Let's Go See Miniver." Because that is definitely NOT the suggestion I am authorizing a slight change of the initials from G S M to G M S.

I remain yours etc. etc.
(Miss) Helene Grossberg

WRITE IT DOWN LEST U FORGET
COURTESY OF FOX'S U-bet
Is it time to reorder our fine syrups?
From: Mrs. Pearl O. Grossberg
For: Sloan kid
Time message taken: right while I'm talking
price to a new fire inspector
Message
Helene got her Sarah call or her caracul

Psych
Disappntd in rslts of test   Carelessness   Now review once mre and gt right def of Teleological

So Simon Sloan?
So Helene Grossberg?

to layman a tlgcl answer is prfctly stsfctry   If you ask why
do the wheels of car turn a tlgcl answr wld be they turn so
car will move

You know I am very proud of my mommy. She was very cute
    last night.

answer wld not stsfy scntst for whn scntst asks Why his why is

You know what she said to me before you came?
That I should only only have a good orgasm.
Do you notice now something? How I am not becoming in-
    sulted?
I am starting to realize that what you say is true. With you
I should start getting used to such words and terms.
Especially after we

> Get
> Married
> Secretly

most common mstke in class was tlgcl one   When asked why
rat goes thrgh maze it is not engh to answr

Anyway what mommy said to me before you ARRIVED

as in old joke why does chicken crss the rd

Poor Daddy is giving me "Parches" to stop my shaking and he
is crying because he had to do it, he has many times threat-
ened to do it but never in my life do I think he gave me a
"Parch."

not merely to get to the other side

And because Daddy is crying he makes MY crying worse, so that is when Mommy comes over and she says

action is brght abt by MECHANISM, not goal

SOMEDAY TARTARLAW YOU WILL BE LAUGHING AT THIS

also it is not AUTOMATIC nrvs system it is

By the way, she didn't SAY anything but if next time she should mention she has for us Wear-Ever pots

AUTONOMIC

You don't have to look like

26 November, 1941

Dear Hotblood,

My friend Little Fat Dora, you shall shortly be meeting her with our mah jong group, uses a wonderful Jewish expression. The expression is "bar shirt" or in other words God's handy work is in everything, He is still the best caterer so let HIM make all the arrangements.

If it was "bar shirt" you should meet my Helene and if it was "bar shirt" you should like each other it is also "bar shirt" that things will be nice and it will work out.

So believe me that I want you to do what you want to do and only what is "bar shirt." If you feel it is the RIGHT thing to keep your marrying a deep dark secret, not to have even a little bit of an affair, I don't say a big and fancy hall or under a "kipper," I and (Mr.) Barney Grossberg will go along. Helene's grandpa who still holds her on his lap, he is 78 and almost blind, we can keep it from. Likewise we can try and keep it from her Aunt Sheila, Helene can tell you of their closeness, how this aunt took her to eat her first chinks.

But all I would appreciate is your open mind and that you and Helene have an enjoyable experience talking to Rabbi Melvin Goodship in his chamber. What I want is you should SEE why we in our mah jong group love him and listen to him and use him on everything, likewise why he is THE rabbi that they call up from the mayors office when they need dedications by a priest and a minister and a rabbi. Rest assured that even if you and Helene decided that you WANTED him there is no guarantee to get him, that is how he is booked up.

As far as where you should live is concerned, remember that YOU have to live there and that it is up to a daughter if she wants to go where it is too far from a mother. I am as you know an active woman of modern interest, if my Helene is willing to go with you an HOUR away, it comes to more if you figure door to door, that hour I can use in charity work for my Jewish crippled. My only fears are on your benefit, you will be both doing part time work and for my Helene to keep a house hold on her two pronated ankles will be good news for the cock roaches. I admit to you I take all the blame in this, I should have trained her different, she doesn't know what it is to cut her own Velveeta. Naturally you should do what you want to do. If you feel for moving near the bumhemians to get far from a future motherinlaw who most likely would turn out to be a terrible pest if you lived close, twice a week she might come with chicken already boiled and cooked and on Wednesday she would take back with her your dirty things, inclusive of shirts and pillow cases, so I would pay my Louella for another hour, I don't blame you.

For more on this subject I turn the letter over to my husband (Mr.) Barney Grossberg.

I remain yours etc. etc.
(Mrs.) Pearl O. Grossberg

I do not butte in and I never butte in. If I can eat and talk and laugh and make jokes yet after reesent events in

371

this house hold I can manage not hearing ever from a child down in Green Itch village. My fervid hope is you shall make future sales of your storys to the Esquire from the inspiring given you by the people there, the fairy nice boys.

Best personal regards
(Mr.) Barney Grossberg

Please inquire from your nutsy fagin friend who is inspiring you in the above if he will know what I know when you have to pick out bedding.

(Mrs.) P.O.G.

You have an appointment with Rabbi Melvin Goodship on 12/11/41 at 8:10 PM in his home, 1871 E. 5th St. Transportation to his residence is offered by the Kings Highway Bus.
Please remember to bring with you all or any records of your religious training, as well as a skull cap.

November 30, 1941

Dear Shaynee Birdchick,

This is what I will from now on call you henceforth because my Aunt Sheila kept calling and calling you it. She honestly could not get over how good looking you are and has almost haha convinced me. Also she thought you were highly intelligent and kept excusing you when I on your behalf apologized. You perhaps did not realize how it sounded somewhat FRESH that if she is showing an interest in the apartment and about the floors you tell her not to worry about the floors, you are worried more about where you would do your writing.

Any old how, I do not think you are being objectively fair to the apartment. It is quite a good kitchen and I do not see what we need more than two rooms. You have to picture the place in your imagination when it is all fixed up, it would look not only cute but adorable with mommy's love seat and my big mirror and some nice modernistic prints. I admit the bathroom is small, but if you look carefully it is bigger than you think. And it at least is INSIDE the apartment.

As far as the proximity to my mother is concerned, I somewhat agree with you. Do not think I also want to live on top of her, and do not think also I am not aware of her weaknesses. But we would not be THAT much on top of her. Remember, close as it may SEEM, it still is a local stop away, and for my mother to just get on the subway is a major production. She would maybe come to us twice a week at most and we would go to her ONLY Friday night for dinner, which we don't even always have to do. I in fact gave her fair warning that if we WANT to come we will come, but not to EXPECT it from us.

Meanwhile you should know that thy Helene practices her touch typing and is at the stage of 20 words a minute.

Meanwhile I type out MRS. HELENE SLOAN!

What more shall I say to my Simon? Only

Let us go then you and I
While the evening is spread out against the sky. . . .

Thy Helene

P.S. Never mind how my mother teases, I intend being a real "ball booster!"

Dec. 2, 1941

Shmuck!

Hold off if you can!

Pull off if you must!

For what you're getting it doesn't pay to sell out!

I am telling you I have absolutely fantastic plans for us.

Together we were going to fuck the 11.5 *shiksehs* in Brooklyn College.

Like they do the cathedrals we would do the Marx Brothers.

We'd look to rent a nice little shop in the Village and I'd teach you how to insult the customers.

In time I was going to explain to you why Trotsky didn't come back for Lenin's funeral from Sukhum in the Caucasus and how a whole generation of Soviet experts has displayed such fantastic ignorance of the fact that the funeral was on a Saturday and in a million years and for all the Russias Trotsky would not ride on *Shabbes*.

Meanwhile, where is my *Their Morals and Ours?* That one I *paid* for.

Yours,

I. Bernardick, Wʙꜱɪʟʜ

(Who Believes Stalin IS Lenin's Heir)

December 1

Dear Shimmy

I don't know why but I had to send you this postal. We are on our way for a training cruise in the Chesapeake. That is near Baltimore and there is a story we will go to Sheepshead Bay after for a few weeks radio school. A bunch of Jewish guys are here, we have a little group. You ought to see me make the Kiddish. So far I like the Coast Guard. King Kong was playing last night in Baltimore, I thought of you.

Hymie

December 2, 1941

Dear Flamingyouth,

It is perfectly fine and dandy with me and you should continue to do what you want to do. If you with your talent do not feel like writing a few little lines for a future announcement card it must be you have put aside a big cash bundle, what is called a "car nipple" and can not utilize the nice presents you would get. My head naturally is not able to go on your shoulders, but I hope you shop around soon with Helene to see what it can cost to set up a house hold, and I am not talking FURNITURE. I am talking BEDDING, I am talking basic STARTER dish ware, I am talking POTS AND PANS which you want to your own tastes because my brand

374

new Wear-Ever, steel wool has not yet touched it, doesn't meet your liking.

However please tell me where in your Marxism it says not to even CONSIDER having made up a lovely album of wedding pictures to have the rest of your life. Show me the ruling against a few photographed human documents of a 78 year old grandpa who is almost blind and who you can rest assured will not be around in years to come to pose for another "simca."

My friend Little Fat Dora got a kick out of it when I mentioned your idea to paint your floors black and red. She wants me to let her know when so she can come over to play checkers.

I remain yours etc. etc.
(Mrs.) Pearl O. Grossberg

December 3, 1941

Dear Simon,

It is a quarter to ten, Sharon has just this minute left because she has an early gym, and I wish you were here to drink with me Ovaltine and to talk about THINGS and to tell me "Let us go then you and I while the evening is spread out against the sky." This was the night I was going to catch up on all my old *Posts* or at least Samuel Grafton, but I am in such a good mood that I for once do not feel like being depressed by him. So do me something if I write to my Simon to put him also in a good mood. As Sharon says, and you always underestimate her sensitivity, this is the time when the fellows start feeling neglected and have no way to vent out their tensions like girls. That is why she and I can go into a bathroom for two hours and she will comb my hair and I will comb her hair.

Any old how, I want you not to be nervous and not to look like ⌣ .

I have confidence and I am not worried about you.

I will tell you the same thing I tell my mother when she

starts in "harking" and "harking" me in the "cup."

I do not expect and I do not want you to kill yourself so we should go to the mountains in the summer and I am just as happy to share a locker in Manhattan Beach.

You will earn a very good living, and if it is not by your writing it will be by something else. There are getting to be plenty of civil service jobs where you have all the time in the world to write on the side.

We do not have to continually go to concerts, especially since I am not really from the GREAT music lovers, and if our pleasures have to be a movie every two weeks that also is good enough.

GOD FORBID and we should have a baby I can quit my college and live a million years without my Ed courses. I would anyway work and work until the very last minute to help put YOU through, that is why I am keeping up with my touch typing. And if it "treffs" us it "treffs" us. So what? You would then be not only happy, you would be in seventh heaven to live close to even the world's worst mother-in-law.

The important thing is we are starting a life as young people who have time and do not have to have everything at once. In fact, because we are young we can look forward and look ahead to having even more pleasure when we finally GET a nice kitchen and we GET enough closet space.

Now I am going to mail this and then I am going to take my bath and think of my Simon who has made such a hit with my Aunt Sheila that I have instructions to give you her fondest "grease."

Thy Helene

L. Marvin Bardash, M.D.

Residence: 11 Brighton Towers

Off: 3002 Coney Island Ave.

Hrs: Mon, Wed, Thur   10–1

Tues, Fri, Sat   4–9

& by appnt.

376

Dec. 4, 1941

TO WHOM IT MAY CONCERN

Simon Sloan is under receipt of my medical attention for diarrhea and fever. As several days bed rest is here indicated he should get no penalty for any cutting of his Brooklyn College classes.

L. M. B.

Monday, December 8, 1941

In the men's room near the lounge of Brooklyn College. Whence this writer, unable to force through the maddening cafeteria crowd, has found himself a booth and seeks to set down, set down and compose these lines after President Roosevelt's speech.

O I thank you Hirohito, Hitler, Tojo, Mussolini.
For now—now the sty is burst, the poison gone,
The splinter drawn from the skin.
I go forth to my enormous room, my retreat at Caparetto.
I, Simon Sloan of Brighton Beach,
I, Brooklyn boy.
O take me, send me,
I am ready!
I think I have always been ready.

Things to do
Dad's truss
Teitlebaum—Octagon coupons for safekeeping, ask
Tell Helene this
This tell her

377

11

Then on the first Tuesday of April, 1942, when Teitlebaum in his best hand and using a fresh box of Crayolas prepared a mock-up of his new sign ("To speed up the Second Front we will from now on be forced to sell our farmer cheese in quantities of no less than half a pound"); not long after Harry the Fish Man's daughter, Fat Rosalie, was taken to the Hotel Dixie by three soldiers who fed her on pecan pie and abused her most barbarously; the week Hymie's *bubbee* signed away her last two-family house in the East Bronx so that the Big Three would have a place to meet; right after Freilitz the Tailor found out which naval hospital Mrs. Heffler's Buddy was in and sent him a postcard, "We cannot be held responsible for articles of clothing left with us for more than thirty (30) days"; after Willitz the Landlord circulated a petition wherein the tenants of 1894 pledged themselves, out of respect for their former beloved super, Gustav Gromajinski, felled in battle while serving with the Free Polish forces, to do without hot water during the month of May; two weeks after Norman the Street Singer sold his route to become musical director at Zilber's Twin Pines; at most a week since the Knishe Queen sent her follow-up letter to Mahatma Ghandi:

We want to once again wish you good luck in your free-
ing of India. Our biggest hope of the Brighton Beach
Jewish community is that you don't overdo it with your
fasting because your country is not going to appreciate
if you come out of prison a nervous wreck. May we
therefore suggest that you think of yourself and do what
is good for you by breaking your fast on one of our
blackberry or gooseberry currant knishes which are so
lightly fried in the finest quality peanut oil that the
word fried *doesn't even apply. As made in our modern*
kitchens these knishes are strictly parveh, *meat doesn't*
go anywhere near them. If you should get a chance we
would give interested attention to your comments and
suggestions on the enclosed form;

not too long after Mrs. Malnick used up three postcards to
the "Voice of the People" ("Hitler would be glad if he saw
that serviceman with campaign ribbons, one definitely was
a purple heart, who fell down and stayed down on the Sea
Beach, the car was jammed with people, nobody went over
and everybody looked away, they didn't lift him and they
didn't move him, where he was is where he stayed, this is
what he gets from a grateful America, I could barely step
over his feet to get off at my station, FED UP"; even as the
Workmen's Circle, though expressing itself as "deploring"
the condition of their brothers and sisters in the needle trades
in her country, nevertheless urged Secretary of State Cordell
Hull to "show every possible courtesy" during Madame
Chiang's impending visit; this being the same week Mrs.
Wachtel somehow fought off two healthy M.P.s till her Moey,
twelve days A.W.O.L., washed down his delicatessen lunch
with a little tea; during the time Mrs. Wasserberg, having
learned that her Ruben had been seen going down in flames
somewhere in the South Pacific, went around telling people
that even as a kid he had been the same way, that he never
cared how he would hurt his mother; not too long after
Belle Baker finished off her farewell performance at the

Brighton Theater by asking everyone in the audience to clasp his neighbor's hands and join, without fear or shame, in the refrain of

> Come eat your nuts and drink your wine,
> For soon we'll get our Palestine

most likely the very same week Mrs. Aranow's Stanley wrote the boys in his garage about how in London, England, on a night of fog and drizzle, he had hailed a cab: How this cab had broken down; how a long limousine had pulled up alongside; how he had heard a "Hop in, Yank" from a huge voice; how he had immediately plopped himself and his duffel bag next to a fellow with an Edward G. Robinson build and a Baby Leroy face; how he had declined this fellow's offer of a long cigar and a short brandy; how he had begun to bemoan his *mazel* to the fellow, insisting that the army, knowing the condition of his sinuses, should have shipped him better to Hawaii; how this fellow had pointed out that HaVaii was spelled with a W; how he had pleasantly answered that while it was spelled with a W it was nevertheless pronounced with a V; how he further pointed out that this snip of information he had gotten years ago from a Filipino busboy; how this fellow had persisted in his W; how he had countered with his V; how after much contention he insisted on being let out; how as he stalked off from the limousine this fellow raised a fist at him and blared out a last "W!"; how he had raised his own fist and, with added spite, shot out two fingers and spread them slowly in a mocking V; when Skeezix, home for his first furlough, walked to his old clubhouse and wept for a dead friend; when Tillie the Toiler's Mac made corporal; when Ella Cinders and Dixie Dugan went with their old bosses into government work;

Then Simon and his parents, a little bit apart from the small mob by the basement office of Local Board # 201, stood like three enemies.

Till his father, after a hoarse and croaky "Ho-boy!" said, "My manager claims, listen what he claims, this is interesting. He cla-haims that when we have a Lash LaRue picture we do better then when we have a Gene Autry picture."

"Try try another topic," said his mother, grinding her teeth.

"You kno-how, when you were a kid . . ." his father began, and flinched.

"When he was a ·kid—go go ahead Shmuel, go from there."

"When you were a kid—*and* as a youthful child"—his father's face swelled, his eyes sank deep in black—"I can't do it," he said, arms dangling at his sides, "the *goyisher* stuff with the small talk."

But Simon's mother flew at his back, pinching and punching, saying "Give him a common interest thing and a mutual memory."

Pause.

Then,

> *Zupkee dubkee dopkee doo*
> *Rahtzee tahtzee poo poo.*

sang his father desperately, and he banged his fists with sudden and terrible violence, and said, "Ho-boy, you remember Malvena, I would all-hall-ways have to do it for him, that was his only song and his big favorite song and without the Daddy singing him his special Daddy song he didn't eat."

"What I used to go through he should eat," said his mother. "The dopey dopey Malvena. The Malvena fool. The Malvena dumbbell. On her dropped stomach she would take bread and she would make it into just just so snips and she would cut away the crust and then—then first she would dip it for him into sour cream . . ."

"Listen what else I remember"—in the excitement his father's cheeks were shining, his nose was leaking—"how he was four and I was lining caps yet for Kelbish and Klein;

this is when if you were a cap mechanic, a *good* cap me-chanic, the hah-whole world was your easy street . . ."

"We lived and we laughed," mourned his mother.

"And on every Friday night the Daddy that was so *meshugeh* for his kid would bring him home a little some-thing, like a Daddy present: one Friday I'd surprise him with a marker's chalk, the next Friday maybe a shipping label . . ."

"We laughed and we lived," said his mother, a tear cours-ing down a cheek. "Three, four sheets at a time to the Chink!"

And nothing.

For a nice few seconds.

Then in a languishing voice Simon's father sang his "Zupkee dubkee dopkee doo."

And when he was done with this and also with "Potchee potchee kichalach" he peered in panic at Simon's mother.

"Try with him a little little philosophy," she cued.

At which he began a subdued and melodious humming, grabbed Simon's head, brought it low and fussed with the hair. He said, "We'll do the philosophy in our old way, our palship Pop way, with the tousles."

"Heh heh," went Simon, and he battled their bodies to-gether into something like an embrace.

Excited, keen, filled with turbulence, his father said, "For a first of all, *boieleh*, you should realize in eh-hevery human heart is a killer instinct. Any minute—any minute can be the minute you get murdered for a nothing."

"Wowee, that is so so true!" cried Simon wonderingly, delightedly. "You could say—the irrational—you could say Eros and Thanatos . . ."

Squeezing Simon's hands tighter and tighter, his father spoke out strongly.

He said, "I'll give an instance. In a dairy cafeteria once the Pop goes on line. And I'm wondering and I'm wonder-ing—wha-hat should I have? Right in front there's a man that he says, 'You know, you look like you're wondering wha-hat you should have.' I ask him 'Let me ask you this: Wha-hat would you have?' He says, 'The protose steak is good and the vegetable cutlet is good and the *kasheh varnish-kes* is good and the *pirogen* is good. But—buh-hut for me there is only the *matzobrei*.' 'Ho-kay,' I tell him, 'I'm sold, let it be for me the *matzobrah*.' He shakes my hand and he gives the lady the order: 'For myself let's have the *matzobrEI* and my friend here—he will try—the *matzobrAH*.' Then I wished on him something and he wished on me something and the next—the neh-hext thing we're *zetzing* trays . . ."

With a terrible tearing sound he cleared all the passages in his head. As Simon's mother whimpered, "Good for you. Next time, moron dope, order only only the *kasheh varnish-kes*."

Then after Simon and his father had traded gruff, teasing, manly whacks, after they had gone through motions of scrubbing and soaping and vigorous toweling, his father went on.

"Learn—learn also from the Pop." His long face tightened with concentration, "Listen to me *boieleh,* pal, Jackie Cooper kid: The person doesn't understand, he doesn't understand and he doesn't want to know how he is not in charge of himself, how by history is possible everything and that this—thi-his everything can happen on him."

"Everything. Everything, everything," cried Simon, roused and working to sort out his feelings. "You figure it, you *think* you figure it, you start to and you can't. Absolutely absolutely not. The—*ironies.* Like Hymie is in the Coast Guard so—so he doesn't *drown*. Nah! From a truck . . ."

"That? Ho-boy!" his father returned gleefully, bitterly. "The Pop can tell you better. Years—years ago he had an idea. *He* noticed how people are going in bih-hig for paper plates. Hokay, *if*—ih-hif people are going in big for paper plates how about . . . paper *yarmalkas?*"

"Shmuel the Dreamer," murmured his mother.

"The rest"—his father poked in a pocket—"belongs already to the ages."

"This," said his mother, "definitely definitely began him on his downfall."

"To the secretaries and purchasing agents of burial and fraternal societies," his father read out from the ancient postcard. "We are highly pleased to announce that to our fall 1935 season of sacred and religious articles there will be added a new and original line of paper *yarmalkas* designed and fashioned by expert craftsmen to our own strict standards. These will be offered in all colors as well as in basic black and white, rah-bah-boi, cordially, Mogolescu Brothers."

"You hear who he wanted to compete with?" demanded his mother. "Only only Mogolescu Brothers!"

A silent interval.

"What it is," resumed his father, "and the whole thing, *boieleh* and the biggest thing and with this thing you could forget every other thing . . ."

But a whistle was blown.

And again the whistle.

People stirred and lurched forward, dragging feet as though through the traffic of dreams.

Someone sounded a *"Mamenyu . . ."*

There started also a long deep sleepy *"Mar*-vin—*Marr*-vin Mar-*vinnnn"* like the lowing of cattle.

"It's a thing," his father was saying, "that I hear all the time from my manager . . ."

"I give you a number? You get a number?" a bony, big-eared soldier was asking Simon.

"Three, Three, Five, movie-actor face," chirped Simon's mother. Then she ground an elbow into an old woman alongside, winking and whispering, "What what do you tip them?"

"Mine," murmured the woman, "I gave a few hopjes."

"Goes like this . . ."

His father stepped back, stood at attention, and held up the middle finger of his right hand.

" 'Birds don't shit on a chicken plucker's head!' "

Bumping bellies, he and Simon embraced.

"Always—ho-boy—always be from the chicken pluckers."

Now Yenta Gersh parted the crowd with her baby buggy, in zingy cadence going

> Urine the army now
> Urine the army now . . .

Behind her Dopey Duhvee pedaled his tricycle and punished his mother with his stocking hat.

In his bloody apron Harry the Fish Man came out to shake hands with the sons of his customers.

From across the street Charlie the Radio Man fiddled with his phonograph and got the Red Army Chorus going nicely.

Where he could, Yankel the Refugee passed out little cards designating him official collector of *shmaltz* and other fats for B'nai Brith.

And a brawny, hay-headed soldier with a splotch of discolored cheek and a chipped tooth cleared a way to the gutter where he strode powerfully back and forth, clapping his hands flamenco-like. "Cain wave sum odor?" he called.

"Should I tell you something about him?" said Simon's father, gazing mistrustfully. "He—ho-boy!—he definitely is not from New York!"

Then in a monotonous uninflected voice the soldier went on to say that that the enlisted men were now under army supervision; that within the next minute or so he would be blowing his whistle; that once it blew each man was expected to pair off with another man; that maintaining silence and order they would file up the stairs of the Brooklyn Manhattan Transit System or "Bayamtay"; that they would be passed through the gates free of charge; that they would entrain to 42nd Street; that from 42nd Street they would proceed to Grand Central Palace; that at Grand Central Palace they would be turned over to other hands for processing and induction.

"Bar the way," he said, starting a smile, "stew laid to chain yaw mine . . ."

There were shrieks of laughter about this.

"... no more puttees," Simon's father was telling people. "And when I was in the army I loved—ho-boy!—did I love puttees!"

The whistle.

"I would lecture buddies: 'Wear—puttees. They support the feet, they support the worker.'"

"Hah-left, left," chanted Yenta Gersh. "Hah-left mine wife and twenty-two kids, half was *goyim* and half was *yids.*"

"Say—leh-hets say you had a million soldiers"—Simon's father wet a finger—"makes it—ho-boy!—two million legs, and on every leg a puttee. Gives you an inkle of what they lost out in the clothing trade. Woolens alone ..."

And Simon took a place on line.

And his mother took a place with him.

"Nah!" he said, shaking his hands, his head.

"You'll see how you'll use them," she whispered, pushing into one of his pockets. "Rubberbands," she kept on whispering, "you can always always use."

The line moved. Two by two and foot by foot.

"Put back the shoulders," Simon's father crooned after him. "Back. Bah-hack. Don't be a posturepedic."

"I left my carp at the stage-door canteen—"

But Yenta Gersh froze.

Along with everybody else.

While Dopey Duhvee, a little ahead of the line, pounded in a pig-trot up, up the elevated to the last step, dug both hands into one banister, hung by an ankle from the other, and blocked the way nicely.

"Who has maybe a jelly apple?" his mother asked around.

There were no jelly apples.

"I'll do it even *without* a jelly apple."

She went without hurrying to the stairs.

"In a second," she said over her shoulders, "you'll see something cute, it's worth a million dollars."

And she yelled up, "Hitler is coming; Hitler is on Coney Island Avenue; Hitler is coming from Coney Island Avenue;

Hitler is going to *potch* Duhvee; oh, oh, oh, he'll give the Duhvee boy such terrible *potches* . . ."

All the way down the stairs Duhvee cried and cried.

"Ho-boy!" said Simon's father as the line disappeared.

"That's it," said his mother. "That's it and that's it and that's it."

And they walked off to have dealings with Teitlebaum.